THE ENEMY WE KNOW

A Letty Whittaker
Whittaker
12 STEP
Mystery

Donna White Glaser

White Stone Press
Chetek, WI

D0324556

This book is a work of fiction. The characters, incidents, and dialogue are drawn from the author's imagination and are not to be construed as real. Any resemblance to actual events of persons, living or dead, is entirely accidental.

Credits:
Cover design by Cormar Covers

ISBN-13: 978-1461098379
ISBN-10: 1461098378

ALSO BY DONNA WHITE GLASER

THE LETTY WHITTAKER 12 STEP MYSTERIES:

THE ENEMY WE KNOW

THE ONE WE LOVE

THE SECRETS WE KEEP

THE BLOOD WE SPILL

COMING SOON:
THE LIES WE TELL

THE BLOOD VISIONS PARANORMAL| MYSTERIES:

A SCRYING SHAME

For Ma,

It was hard, but not too hard.

STEP ONE

*We admitted we were powerless over alcohol—
that our lives had become unmanageable.*

CHAPTER ONE

I heard him coming. The hall funneled the sound of his rage, racing just ahead of the man. Our clinic's manager screamed, "Letty! Watch out!" but he already filled the doorway. Despite training, I leapt to my feet. Waves of booze and the clamor of civilized people fumbling in the throes of chaos seeped around his mass. In the distance, the thud of running feet, objects careening into each other, and panicked versions of "what's going on?" littered the air.

After the first instinctive reaction, my training reasserted itself, and I recognized the intruder as a client I'd just begun seeing. Now he stood swaying on the threshold, jean jacket straining at the shoulders, barely covering a ratty t-shirt which offered sexual favors to my sister. His bleary, pig-mean eyes stared straight through me. So different from the shy, hurting man I'd met with a week ago.

We'd met together twice for counseling. Despite an initial complaint of marital conflict, Randy had kept the focus squarely on a seemingly trivial dispute with his boss. At the time, I'd thought he was avoiding the real issue, but we were still getting to know each other. Any attempt on my part to bring the subject back to his troubled marriage was charmingly, but firmly, deflected. Maybe he was ready to talk.

He slammed the office door so hard I flinched and bit my tongue. Maybe not.

"Where is she?" The dead monotone scared me more than if he'd yelled.

"Who?"

"You *bitch*." His teeth chewed at the word, turning his face into a lupine grimace. "You think this is a joke?" He pulled a hunting knife out from under his jacket, moving deeper into the room, still blocking the door.

"No, Randy," I said, eyes locked on the weapon. My voice sounded high and thin, squeaking past my closed throat, a far cry from the professional calm I wished for. "I don't think this is a joke. I can see how upset you are, but I don't know what you want."

"I want Carrie to stop this bullshit. Get that? Real simple. And I want *you* out of our lives. *Where is she?*"

It was hard to think. All the oxygen pumping from my thudding heart seemed directed to my extremities. My legs tingled in helplessness; flight was impossible.

My mind scrambled to mesh together the bits of information from our sessions with what he was saying now. "I thought your wife's name is Debbie?"

"What?"

"Debbie?"

"Don't play stupid with me. You knew the whole time, didn't you? You knew why I was here, and you played me for a fool. You think I don't know? The whole time you're yapping about trust, and you and that bitch are setting me up behind my back."

"Randy—"

"My name ain't Randy!" he exploded. "Quit pretending."

It finally sunk in that "Randy" had given me a fake name. So much for trust. I jettisoned any information gleaned from our previous sessions and pretended he was just an irrational stranger—which he was—leaving very little to go on. Just a name, really. The name of the woman I was supposedly conspiring with: Carrie.

It clicked.

Carrie, the client usually scheduled in this time slot, had canceled at the last minute. She and I had been working for the last four months on self-esteem issues, gathering her courage to deal with her relationship with her abusive boyfriend. She'd recently decided to get out and had begun making practical plans for her escape.

Guess who showed up?

His eyes darted around the room, hyper-alert, as if he thought I had her stashed in the file cabinet. My office held an old metal desk, an ergonomically challenged chair, a tattered love seat, and a waist-high, two-drawer file cabinet sans escaping girlfriend.

Ethically, I couldn't even acknowledge that Carrie was a client. Stacked up against the stark reality of the buck knife, however, confidentiality seemed like a vague, misty concept. Problem was, I liked Carrie, and I refused to draw a map for her asshole boyfriend. And there was the added issue of not having a freakin' clue where she might be.

"Where is she?" he repeated.

Drunk, dangerous, and impatient. The unholy trinity.

What the hell was his name, anyway? She must have said his name a half-million times, at least. She'd even divulged having it tattooed in the shape of a crescent moon on her left breast. Why should her boob tattoo flash into memory and not his name?

"Look, I know you're upset. I want to help." I worked to keep my voice calm, dropping it low and soft in direct contrast to his anger.

"Don't you try that psych crap on me, you bitch! You've been trying to break me and Carrie up ever since she started seeing you."

Well, not exactly, but I doubted what's-his-name could distinguish the fine line between encouraging Carrie to make her own decisions and telling her to leave the jerk who kept throwing her against the wall whenever she disagreed with him.

"It's not crap to tell you that the police are coming. You know that, right? You can make this so much better for yourself if you just give me the knife." My eyes were glued to the weapon—it looked like something that could gut a deer with one flick of the wrist. My stomach rolled, stomach acids sloshing loosely from side to side.

"Give *you* the knife? Why? So you can stab me in the back with it? You bitches are all alike. First chance you get, you kick a guy in the teeth." The blade whispered evilly as he sliced it through the air. I hated that knife.

"I wouldn't hurt you," I said. Sweat rolled down my face, tickling.

"Bullshit! You're taking Carrie away!" His face flooded with incredulity, and the next few seconds blurred as he charged forward. Flipping the desk chair aside like it was made of Styrofoam, he pinned me against the back wall, the knife a silver glint below my chin. Its tip nicked my skin, not cold as I anticipated, but burning a slender line across the thin layer of flesh guarding my throat.

"You just don't get it, do you? I love her. And you got no right coming between a man and his woman. That's a sacred thing and you can't just—"

"I'm not taking Carrie away. She's—"

"Liar!" Rage twisted his face into a grotesque mask, barely human. "You think I don't know? You think I'm stupid because I don't have a stinkin' diploma stuck up on my wall?"

He smashed the knife into the glass frame above my head, shards splintering like frozen rain on my hair and the floor below. He'd just killed a cheap Monet print, but now didn't seem like the time to point out the error.

"You think you're so special, don't you? Got your college education, and your tight, little ass that you like to shake in front of all the men. Bet you make them crazy, huh? Make them come back for more, just 'cause they got the hots for you. Do you wear that long, black hair up just so's we wonder what you look like at night, when it's down?

"And then you act all concerned about me, like you care. Just like *her*. I'm not stupid," his voice dropped again to that frightening, raspy whisper. "I know what she's planning. She's been checking into those shelters like she thinks that's gonna keep her safe. I bet you been workin' on her, trying to get her to go to one of them places."

The knife skimmed my throat again; I couldn't even shake my head to answer without slicing it off. Tears of frustration pooled in my eyes, ready to fall. Carrie and I had talked about the possibilities of domestic abuse shelters, but that was weeks ago. At the time, she wouldn't even take the brochure that I'd tried giving her for fear that her boyfriend would find it. *Was her cancellation today part of an escape plan that she hadn't trusted me with?*

"Did you try her at work?" The question popped out of its own volition.

"Huh?"

"Well… she canceled her appointment. Maybe she just got called in to work."

Stopped him cold. Suddenly, as we stood there in a grotesque parody of an embrace, the wail of police sirens filtered through the strip-mall thin walls of the office. No soundproofing, another cheap aspect of our working arrangement, but I loved it now. His eyes locked on mine, briefly, and a disturbing emotion rippled between us. He stood there only a few moments more, but it felt like hours; his breath fanned my cheeks while his body held mine hostage. Rearing his head back, he spit full in my face, then bolted for the door. Turning right, away from the front lobby, he ran toward the back fire exit. I heard shouts, and a thunk as something heavy

5

tipped over. Seconds later, several police officers flew past the office door in pursuit.

Now that the time for panic was officially over, it took possession of my body, unhinging my knees, crashing me down to the floor. I cowered there, heart pounding, adrenaline turning my mouth tinny, shaking so hard my joints ached.

The sound of more running feet jolted me to my knees, but it was just my supervisor Marshall sprinting down the hall. The back door slammed, and then Marshall was at my side.

He guided me into the chair. I watched disinterestedly as his mouth made noises over me. My brain tuned him out until a shout of astonishment from him pulled me back to focus. Marshall knelt beside my chair, holding my right hand. For a brief spasm of time, I imagined he was going to propose. That is until I saw the bright red blood pooled in the cup of my upturned palm, seeping over the side and into his beneath like a water fountain in a particularly grisly park. My first instinct was that I'd been stabbed, but then I spied the glass shard sticking straight up, cleaving the pad of skin between my thumb and forefinger. I couldn't stand the sight of the alien object stuck inside me. So I pulled it out. More blood.

Marshall's noises grew more agitated, but this time a wave of dizziness blocked him out. A uniformed policeman pushed into my tiny office, crowding us, using up more air. My ears started ringing, and the cop pushed my head between my knees. I closed my eyes, concentrating on not throwing up while someone squeezed the cut on my hand real hard.

"Wayne," I said to my knees.

Someone's head orbited into my vision. "What?" the someone said.

"His name is Wayne."

CHAPTER TWO

I may have been powerless over the precipitating events, but the drama that came after was my own fault. Between the dizzy spell and the gash in my palm, the consensus was to haul me off to the hospital. I hate hospitals.

I argued, but Marshall dug in, overriding my objections. He was my boss, after all, and in today's litigious society, I guessed I understood his point. Concerned about lawsuits, he'd want the record to show that I'd been provided services immediately after. Besides, Marshall Tannor was fairly new to the clinic, and he was a sweetheart. And cute.

I caved on the hospital but refused an ambulance, which meant someone needed to drive me. A clinic full of helping professionals in the middle of a crisis turned the simple favor into a battle of the co-dependents. Our intern Mary Kate won, and I found myself praying she wouldn't wrap my car around a telephone pole as we caromed across town to Sacred Heart.

After all the hoopla, I ended up waiting more than two hours behind a guy with chest pains, a cow-kicked farmer, and a lady who held an ice pack to her head and moaned every forty-seven seconds as if wired to an alarm. While I sat there dripping blood, an officer showed up to take my statement.

Two minutes into the interview, a nurse signaled us back. In order to stay out of the way of the medical staff, the officer took up a position slightly behind the cot I was sitting on. The interview took on a surreal quality as the physician stabbed and tugged at my palm while the officer droned on just out of sight, over my shoulder.

Descriptions of the knife became the main focus, and I couldn't figure out why. I kept tilting my head back, frustrated at not being able to see the cop's face, his expressions. I answered every question, but we circled back again and again to the buck knife—how big was it? what brand? did I see a sheath? where was he standing when he pulled it out? Over and over again. Even the doctor looked up from stitching to eye the cop questioningly.

Marshall came in at the tail end of the interview, Mary Kate slipping in behind. After the officer left, my boss informed me that in addition to the back lot and the roof, the police had spent quite a bit of time searching my office for the missing weapon.

"No, he had it when he took off," I said. By now, I'd repeated the facts so many times the words felt blurry, insubstantial. "He ran off with it. He must've ditched it somewhere." "He only made it a couple hundred feet from the clinic before the cops nailed him. The options are pretty limited."

"Maybe the roof?" Mary Kate ventured. She handed me my keys.

"First place they looked," Marshall said.

"The dumpster? No," I shot down my own suggestion. "That was emptied yesterday; the back-up beeping almost drove Mr. Nilson nuts."

Marshall raised his eyebrows.

"Um, I mean he was irritated at the interruption. Anyway, all the police would have to do is look inside and maybe shift a few bags around. They would have found it.

"I don't know what he did with it," I continued, suddenly tired. "Maybe he flung it away. All I know is he had it pointed at my neck one minute, then took off when he heard the sirens."

"He's denying it all." Marshall looked more uncomfortable than I'd ever seen him. Either hospitals gave him the willies or there was something going on I was unaware of.

"That's crazy. Why would I lie?"

"I believe you, Letty. But after all, the police don't take anyone at face value, and they can't seem to find it. They've been interviewing clients and staff at the clinic. You were the only one who saw the knife."

"How do they think I got this?" I pointed to the cut on my neck, shivering. "Nobody else saw it because he had it tucked under his shirt. Behind him. Great, big, honkin' buck knife."

"I'm sure they'll find it. After all, they're professionals. For now, they have enough to charge him with Drunk and Disorderly, at the very least."

"We can press charges for trespassing or breaking in or something, can't we?"

"You mean the clinic?" Marshall suddenly looked embarrassed. "There is that option, but administration would prefer to keep the clinic out of it as much as possible."

"What? How is that possible?"

Marshall's discomfort grew more obvious. Turning to Mary Kate, he asked her to step outside. Still an intern, she wasn't experienced enough to control her expressions; her face registered a burning curiosity. She'd have her ear plastered to the door, sure enough.

"Letty, I'm sure when things have calmed down and you've had a chance to think about it, you'll see their point. I'm not saying I agree with them. But the fear is that the public might assume you—and by extension the clinic—are responsible for this guy's acting out, some kind of misconduct or something." Marshall licked his lips, his eyes on the floor. "Or they'll be afraid to come in for services. We're already going to have an issue with the clients who were present during this incident. I'm sure we'll have to make some arrangements for trauma counseling."

"Wait a minute. Wait a minute," I interrupted his to-do list. "Are you saying admin thinks *I'm* to blame here?"

"Of course not, but that wouldn't stop some lawyer from making that claim, would it? They just want to keep a low profile, if at all possible."

"And that means what? Not pressing charges after I've been attacked by a complete stranger?"

There was a pause, an uncomfortable one.

"A complete stranger, Letty?" Marshall's voice grew soft, gentle. He finally made eye contact.

My face flushed red, my heart pounding in protest. This felt accusatory, but I wasn't sure where to go with it.

"Okay, not exactly a complete stranger," I conceded. "We met together twice, but he lied about everything. I didn't even know his real name."

"Why? Why would someone do that? Why would someone pay over a hundred bucks a session out-of-pocket and waste it by telling lies?

The realization that Marshall had already been digging into Wayne's file shouldn't have surprised me as much as it did. Wayne had paid cash, which *was* a little unusual. At the time, he'd claimed he didn't have insurance. Not an unlikely situation these days.

"I don't know why he did it. He was probably spying on his girlfriend. I don't know." My eyes filled with tears and I turned away, ashamed of my weakness.

"Look, this isn't the time to worry about all this. It will work out, I promise. And besides, that's not why I came."

"Why did you come?" I sounded prissy and sullen.

"To see you," he said. "To make sure you were okay. And, well, I know it sounds lame, but to tell you how amazing I think you are."

10

I rolled my eyes, making him laugh. "That *is* lame."

"I'm serious. Not everyone could have made it through all that in one piece." My mind flashed again on the hunting knife—not Marshall's intention, I knew—but my stomach rolled at the thought of "pieces."

"Your courage is impressive. And," he smiled again, "somebody's got to take you home."

Home sounded heavenly; I smiled in return. Marshall was right. There was enough time to worry about the fall-out tomorrow and nothing I could do about it tonight. One day at a time, after all.

I turned down Marshall's offer of a ride and Mary Kate's offer of continued chauffeur services, and drove myself home. Probably a mistake since I sailed through a red light without so much as tapping the brakes. By the time I made it home, I felt too jittery to stay there, so I called a friend to give me a ride over to the club. It was either that or drink.

Tuesday wasn't my usual night for a meeting, but even though I'd only been sober a handful of months, it was long enough to know I needed to be in a safe place. Ugly, but safe.

The HP & Me Club is a testament to the fact that sobriety doesn't guarantee good taste. By virtue of living in denial and manufacturing a steady stream of excuses, drunks are some of the most creative folk I know. In recovery, however, our energy goes into day-to-day survival while most of our money goes for coffee and cigarettes. There was never enough left over of either commodity for beautification. The décor at HP & Me was a queasy mélange of church rummage sale items, leftovers, and "found" items. The find usually materialized on the side of the road on trash day and was generally considered upholstered manna from our collective Higher Power. If HP thinks threadbare, velveteen, orange love seats are good enough for the club, who could argue?

First thing I did when I got there was head behind the counter to the rows of members' coffee mugs hanging from pegs on the wall. Like everything else, the cups were a weird assortment; the wall displayed equal amounts of basic brought-from-home cups, those decaled with local business ads, and mildly obscene joke mugs.

As I poured coffee into my *Alice in Wonderland* mug, I sensed the presence of a warm body, way too close, behind me. I jolted, splashing coffee over the counter and down the front of my shirt.

"Whoa! Cut her off." Ben, an auto mechanic who four years ago had passed out and set his house on fire with a dropped cigarette, slid behind the counter, grabbing paper towels to help mop up.

Ignoring Ben's helpfulness, I spun, anger flaring. Scared the hell out of the new guy lurking behind me. Sober only a week, Paul was already a trial. Tall and skinny with a tuft of blond hair sprouting from the top of his head, the only thing differentiating him from a corn stalk was the black framed glasses that repeatedly slipped down his narrow nose. My fear-induced anger drained away.

"Wow! Hi." Paul seemed surprised by the reaction he'd caused. Most people just yawned when he spoke to them.

"Hi, Paul. How are you doing?"

"I'm sober another twenty-four, right? One day at a time."

"That's great, Paul."

"Yeah, well, I'm doing ninety in ninety so I've only got eighty-one more to go. But this is where I'll learn to walk the walk, right? Not just talk the talk."

Hopefully when he'd completed the suggested ninety meetings in ninety days he'd have found his own voice instead of parroting AA slogans. Still, he was sober and working the program—huge accomplishments, both.

One of my friends from the Wednesday night women's group eased up on us. Stacie and I had stumbled into AA on the same night nearly five months ago. Sobriety twins—we got a lot of Mutt and Jeff remarks. Stacie stood 5'2" in her three-inch heels, but her abundance of body art, piercings, and orange-dyed hair kept her in the limelight. Tonight she was wearing a red plaid skirt along and a bright purple T-shirt with the legend *Love Goddess* scrawled across her boobs. This was her demure look.

"Hey, girl. How's it going?"

A ghost memory of the knife slashed through my mind at her question, setting off chain-reaction shivers.

"It's been better."

Stacie looked a question, but I didn't want to get into it in front of Paul. Not having an insightful bone in his body, he had no clue we wanted him gone. Stacie was going to have to wait. Normally, neither of us would have had any difficulty shoving past a guy to have a girl-chat, but Paul was equal parts vulnerability and annoyance, and he was just too new to sobriety to risk hurting his feelings. Instead of rescuing me, Stacie had likewise been ensnared.

"Yeah, I'm not doing so good either. I asked some of the guys to be my sponsor, but they all said no. Too busy, you know?" His eyes skittered sideways, not wanting our looks of disbelief to confirm the lie he told himself.

The rejections he'd received in his sponsor hunt pissed me off. Although working the AA program did wonders for teaching guys empathy and compassion, there were plenty of sub-Neanderthals around, fighting extinction. I'd seen several actively avoid Paul's company, and the few who let him join the conversation spent their time making sly comments that, fortunately, went over Paul's head. Finding a man willing to put up with Paul's eccentricities would be difficult. I made a note to talk to a few of the more evolved men. I wasn't optimistic.

As the time for the meeting approached, Stacie and I, with Paul trailing along, went to claim seats around the tables in the side room. I zoned out during the usual readings of *How It*

13

Works, The Promises, and *The Traditions,* tuning in just in time to stick a dollar in the donation bowl when it passed. When it finally got to the point where the group was asked if anyone had a "burning desire to speak," I was ready.

I passed.

The old-timers eyeballed me pretty heavy, wheels turning as they mentally put a check mark next to my name under the "to be watched closely" column. I abandoned my recent quit-smoking vow, bummed a cigarette from Stacie, and hid behind the smoke. Nobody calls you on your crap as skillfully—or with as little hesitation—as a group of recovering drunks. Tough love was invented around the tables.

After the meeting, a bunch of folks decided to head out for coffee and pie, but I declined that, too, and headed for home. Stood in the parking lot for five minutes before remembering I didn't have my car. I ended up having to bum a ride from Paul, which really put the icing on the cake. One of us was pleased.

A pile of messages awaited me on my voice mail when I got home. Robert, my boyfriend of three months, was the first. He knew nothing of my day, and I was too exhausted to catch him up to speed. I'd call him tomorrow. Marshall had called to tell me to take the next few days off, and Mary Kate had checked in on me. The next four messages each recorded a few seconds of silence before clicking off. I checked Caller ID, but it'd been blocked.

Frowning, I deleted the whole mess, then crawled into bed.

CHAPTER THREE

"Letty, what are you doing here? I thought Marshall gave you the day off." Lisa, our office manager, looked peeved at the glitch in her seamless schedule.

I'd always envied Lisa's crisp, put-together style, although whenever I tried to copy it I ended up looking more icy-dominatrix than was advisable for a therapist. She favored chilly blues and wintery whites and wore spike heels that could drill a hole in concrete. Her hair was clipped short with frosty, blond spikes that—rain, shine, or tornado—did as they were told and looked like they could hurt you. We liked to keep Lisa happy.

Unfortunately, I discovered that Marshall had also given word for Lisa to cancel my clients' appointments. It upset me that the decision had been made without my input, but I tried convincing myself he had meant well.

"Lisa, can you try to reach my people and tell them there was a slight misunderstanding?" Her efficient eyebrows gave me silent attitude. I sighed. "A misunderstanding on *my* part, and see if any would still like to come in."

"I can try, but I'll tell you now, your morning is shot. I'll work on the afternoon folks and see what I can do. The Thursday and Friday client list should be a lot easier.

"Thursday and Friday! Everyone got canceled?" Now I understood her irritation. She'd probably spent the better part of the morning making phone calls and would have to repeat the process all over again with suitable apologies.

"Just do your best. I'm sorry about the inconvenience. If you see Mary Kate, could you ask her to set up a meeting with me? We were supposed to have her supervision yesterday, but..."

"No problem," Lisa breezed over my explanation. "She comes in at ten; I'll catch her then."

As I escaped down the hall, Marshall stuck his head out of his office. From this angle, he looked decapitated.

"What are you doing here?" he asked.

"I work here. Why did you cancel my clients?"

A frown creased his face as he stepped into the hall. "I'd think that was obvious."

"I just wish you'd asked me first. That's all." I sounded petulant, which only increased my agitation. Although he didn't see clients in therapy, I could feel him scanning my words and actions, sorting them out, searching for clues and nuances to my state of mind.

Skip this. I turned away, heading for the sanctuary of my office.

"Letty?"

I turned back.

"I'm afraid I have to insist. I'm sure if you take some time to think it over, you'll agree. Besides, it'll give you a chance to catch up on your paperwork. I'd like us to meet today, later on."

Irritation bubbled up but I kept it from leaking out through my face or voice. "You'll need to catch Lisa before she calls everyone back." I'd be damned if I was going to face her moody eyebrows again.

Uncharacteristically, I shut the office door, closing myself off from the bustle of the clinic. Closing myself *in*. Also uncharacteristically, I toyed with the idea of rearranging my furniture. Like into one big pile barricading the door.

My office was no longer a sanctuary.

Pissed me off so bad I opened the door, then flung myself down in the chair. Three seconds later, I slammed it shut again and sat back down, holding my face tucked behind my hands. Not good. Not good, not good, not good.

I buried myself in the backlog of paperwork, telling myself it was a good thing I had something to keep me busy. It wasn't. First of all, it wasn't nearly intense enough to keep at bay the images of Wayne's rage. I'd think I was making progress, then realize my muscles were twitching with edginess, nerve synapses miscuing and sending me into unnecessary panic-mode. My fight-or-flight button was stuck in the ON position.

For another thing, writing was almost impossible with my throbbing hand.

When Mary Kate tapped on my door, I nearly exploded from my skin. She came in like an irresistibly bouncy puppy, gushing equal parts solicitude and nosiness. Despite the fact I'd asked for the meeting, I was irritated at her energy.

Also, like a puppy, she'd attached herself to me from the beginning of our acquaintance. At some point, she'd gotten the impression that I'd specifically requested to mentor her internship, when in fact it was Marshall who was in charge of the assignments. Although older than most interns—in fact more than seven years older than me—Mary Kate exuded an eager vulnerability, making her seem much younger.

Completely devoid of fashion sense, she was constantly twitching her too-large skirts back from their meandering circuit around her hips, constantly retucking blouses into the front of her slacks while forgetting about the back, and—although she'd never to my knowledge had toilet paper stuck to her shoe— something made me anxiously check her foot for offenders every time she exited the bathroom.

Supervision with Mary Kate was always interesting. She possessed an innate understanding of people, and her insatiable curiosity to *know* her clients, inside and out, stood her in good stead. That same desire could be a pitfall, however. In supervision, we were working on her need to recognize the danger signs of over-involvement and how to establish boundaries. We hadn't gotten very far.

Trying to redirect the conversation away from yesterday's ordeal and back to her internship was like trying to thread a hysterical chicken through a needle. Not gonna happen.

"Oh my gosh, I couldn't believe it when I heard some psycho had you trapped in here! I thought my heart was going to stop. I'm just so glad nothing happened to you."

"Mary Kate..." We needed to talk about her choice of words. "Psycho" wasn't a favored label in the clinic.

"I mean, nothing *really* bad. Of course, just being held hostage is bad enough, don't get me wrong. If the police hadn't shown up when they did, who knows what could have happened. But I bet you probably could have talked him down if you had more time." She smiled, her confidence in me as humbling as it was alarming.

"I doubt that, Mary Kate. I didn't have a lot of history with this guy. I wasn't having much success before the police got here and, besides, it's important to realize that we can *never* be certain of containing a situation like that."

"No, but you did know some of his history, though, right? Through Carrie?"

I was too startled to reply. Our client list is confidential. Despite the uproar yesterday, and even though Wayne's relationship with me was sure to be disclosed, there was no reason why Mary Kate should have known of Carrie or of Wayne's connection to her.

"I snuck back," she said.

"You did *what?*"

"When Marshall cleared everyone out yesterday, I snuck back to Regina's office." Mary Kate pointed to the wall separating my office from my co-worker.

"Why would you do that, Mary Kate? That was so dangerous! Who's to say the guy wouldn't have killed me and then gone on a killing spree? That happens all the time these days."

"I would have heard that and could have run away before he got out. But, I don't know... I know it sounds stupid, but I didn't want you to be alone with him. I knew I couldn't do anything, really, but if it turned into one of those murder-suicides, we'd at least know *why*."

I'm trained to hear the most awful things and stay impassive, but listening to Mary Kate blithely discourse on my hypothetical murder nearly did me in. The fact that she'd hunkered down, ear pressed to the wall as Wayne toyed with my life, upset me so much I couldn't figure out how to respond.

I finally just sent her away, and slipped out back behind the dumpster for an illicit cigarette. Although one or two of my colleagues smoked, too, we were all ashamed of it, treating the subject as taboo. Marshall, a health nut, was known to slip the 800-number to the Tobacco Quit Line on our desks when we weren't looking. He'd even initiated an incentive program for those trying to meet health-related goals. He was weird that way.

By the time I met with Marshall, I had a raging headache and serious chinks in the wall of denial I'd erected about coming in today. Marshall was either too nice or too smart to say "I told you so," but the glint of it twinkled behind his eyes.

"How are you holding up?" he asked.

I debated my answer. If I denied any repercussions, he'd know I was lying and might very well push for an extended leave of absence. If I admitted that my office felt more like a crime scene than a safe haven, same thing. Luckily, I hadn't been sober long enough to lose my tell-just-enough-truth-to-make-the-lie-seem-plausible skills.

"I have a pounding headache, and I wanted to throttle Mary Kate just now in supervision."

Marshall's grin sparkled. "Just *wanting* to throttle interns isn't cause for alarm. You didn't act on it, I take it?"

"No, I restrained myself." I considered filling him in on Mary Kate's voyeuristic grand adventure, but decided not to yet. For one thing, her revelations upset me too much to evaluate her behaviors from a supervisory perspective. Objectivity is critical in performing both supervision and therapy, and I didn't want Marshall doubting mine. More importantly, I didn't want to rake up all the nitty-gritty details of my ordeal. I'd gone over it with the police, but only because I'd had to.

"Have you heard from the police?"

I jumped as if he'd read my mind. "No, not yet."

Marshall looked at me curiously. My passivity in not contacting the police was an admission of sorts, and we both knew it.

Time to go on the offensive. "Has administration decided whether to support me or not?"

"I hope you know you will always be supported here, Letty." Marshall's hurt and sincerity shown in his eyes. I almost felt guilty—until he went on. "Even if they disagree with you on an issue that doesn't mean they don't want what's best for everyone."

"But you can't please everyone, Marshall. And in this case, it sounds like the clinic will take care of itself, first and foremost."

"Wouldn't any entity? It's survival. If administration doesn't make the clinic its number-one priority, then we're all out of a job. What good is that to us or to the community? And it has the board to answer to as well. There are all sorts of complications in a situation like this and, frankly, no easy answers."

"Explain to me how letting a dangerous man go scot-free is a service to the community."

Marshall ran his fingers through his dark hair. I'd seen him do that before in meetings when he was about to announce an unpopular policy change.

"What am I missing here, Marshall?"

20

"He's denying ever having stabbed you. He says you cut yourself, that you broke the glass and slashed at your own neck."

I stared blankly. Dread rose in my chest as a horrible suspicion bloomed. "Why would I do that?"

"He says..." Marshall cleared his throat. "He told the police the two of you were having an affair. That you wanted him to leave his girlfriend."

"That's crazy!"

"We know that. Unfortunately, the police haven't found the knife. There are a lot of ways for this story to get twisted. It's obvious that he needs treatment."

"He can get therapy in prison."

"I know how you feel, but the clinic itself is not in the business of punishment; we're more concerned with him receiving treatment. If the clinic gets the reputation for prosecuting clients, how many do you think will trust us to provide services?"

White-hot rage washed through me. "What do you mean? Are you saying the clinic will be offering him services? Am I going to have to worry about running into him in the halls here?"

In the face of my anger, Marshall ditched the party line. "I'm against that. I really am." I waited for the worst. "It probably won't go anywhere because of the conflict of interest, but there is some talk about offering... uh, Wayne... anger management therapy as a sort of image clean up. I really don't think anything will come of it."

I literally could not speak.

"Letty?"

"*Don't.*" I put up a shaky hand; my right hand, the white bandage a visible symbol of the betrayal, hung in the air between us. Struggling to stay in control, brain sizzling and popping like water dripped in hot grease, I rose unsteadily from the chair. Marshall rose, too, distress etching lines into his face, dark brown eyes never leaving mine.

Before I'd taken two steps, he was around the desk. His hands like two bands of heat, circled my shoulders, holding me fast.

"I promise. I promise I won't let them. You won't have to deal with him. I *promise*."

His eyes—so dark they were almost black—pouring into my own, held me tighter than his hands. I didn't pull away. I don't know where the moment would have led if Lisa hadn't knocked at the door.

CHAPTER FOUR

The dramatic gave way to the ludicrous. At Lisa's knock, we fell apart like guilty teenagers when her parents walk through the door. I scrambled for the chair, and Marshall's giant steps got him as far as the corner of the desk when Lisa popped her head in. He tried leaning James Dean-casual against the desk edge but knocked a potted plant over with his ass.

Lisa, trained in the nuances of office life, kept her face frozen in efficiency, but her eyes were backlit with astonishment and curiosity. "I'm sorry for interrupting, but I wanted to let Letty know that she has a client asking to see her today."

"What's the problem? Is it an emergency?" I struggled for normalcy, but giggles rose like frothy bubbles.

"It's Carrie."

I sobered up. Lisa went on, "I tried to ask her to come in tomorrow since your schedule's been cleared. Anyway, she said she's leaving, and this is the only time she has. She really wants to see you."

"Leaving? As in, leaving town?" Lisa's shrug was eloquent. She'd given me all the information she had. "Have her come in, please. Whenever she's available. If necessary, I'll have someone sit in with me." I looked helplessly at Lisa. Given the ethical complications, it would be smart to have a third-party present, but I hated imposing on my co-workers.

"I'll check to see who's available. Mary Kate, probably. Carrie said three o'clock would work for her. I'll let her know to come ahead."

"Great," I said, not meaning it. "Put her down for three." I rose, using Lisa's presence to prevent an awkward moment with Marshall. *What just happened?* When I looked back at him, he nodded once, a wry smile twitching at his lips.

Walking next to me, Lisa exuded a wickedly silent mirthfulness. I fled to my office, the non-sanctuary.

Once there, I decided to call Robert. No reason, really. None.

As a real estate agent, he was usually pretty busy, and we had a tacit understanding that I wouldn't bother him at work. We'd been dating for a little more than three months, which was a source of contention between myself and my sponsor, Sue. AA dissuades newcomers from making any major decisions in our first year of sobriety, and that certainly includes relationships. I'd been sober just over a month on our first date. Sue didn't like that Robert had ignored that, and she didn't like that he lived in the Twin Cities, an hour and a half west. We saw each other on weekends when he'd come in to Chippewa Falls for his AA meeting.

I expected his voice mail to pick up. It wasn't until he'd said hello twice that I finally squeaked a greeting.

"Hi! Have you got a few minutes?"

"Just barely." His voice sounded pressured. "What's going on?"

I hated feeling rushed. "Oh, nothing. We just hadn't talked in a while so—"

"Listen, hon. How about I give you a buzz tonight? I have someone coming for a showing in about twenty minutes."

"Um… No, that won't work. I have my meeting tonight. Something happened yesterday—"

"Ok, how about Thursday? Will that work? Listen, hon, I gotta scoot. I need to make a run through the house and make sure it's all set."

Robert was a perfectionist. He liked having at least a half hour alone before a house showing to tweak curtains and flick dust. I'm pretty sure he rehearsed his spiel, mumbling to himself and practicing his jokes, but I could never get him to 'fess up to that. We said good-bye, and I hung up feeling guilty for bothering him and pissed at myself for feeling guilty.

Lisa was right, as usual. Mary Kate was the only one available to sit in with Carrie and me. For several reasons, however, she wasn't the best choice. I wished now that I had talked to Marshall about her snooping, but it was too late now. She was already knee-deep involved anyway. Under strict orders to be seen and not heard, Mary Kate was nevertheless thrilled to be my sidekick. Carrie signed the HIPAA release form, and I had my witness.

When I'd first met Carrie I'd been astonished at the perfection of her doll-like appearance. Blonde and blue-eyed like so many of northern Wisconsin's population, her features were delicate rather than hardy. Despite her situation and appearance, however, she was tough in the gritty, persevering style of her ancestors.

She wore a navy blue windbreaker to ward off the spring chill, jeans, and tiny white sneakers. She'd scraped her hair back in a no-nonsense ponytail and wore less makeup than usual. Dressed for flight.

As we took our usual spots, wedging Mary Kate into the corner, Carrie offered up a wan smile. "I feel like I should apologize, but I know what you'll say."

I waited, smiling gently.

"You'll say I'm not responsible for him, for his actions." Sighing, she leaned back in her chair, casting her eyes to the floor. Not counting Mary Kate's fidgeting, we sat in silence for a few heartbeats. It was the calmest I'd felt since Wayne stormed the citadel.

"But the whole thing is embarrassing, you know?" Carrie continued. "I never expected to be one of those women caught up in this kind of crap. You always hear stories and you think you know how you would react. Like, 'I'll never let any man pull that crap on me!'" Her voice took on a pseudo-tough tone as she mimicked the imaginary response. "But you just don't know until it happens."

"What don't you know?" I asked, keeping my voice a soft murmur.

"You don't know about the love, for one thing. I loved him. I still do. And he loves me. It wasn't always like this, you know. I think it started when his dad died. And, even now, it's only…" Her voice trailed off.

"Only what, Carrie?"

"Only when he drinks. When he's not drinking, he can be so sweet. And before his dad died, he could drink and, you know, no problem. But now…"

"Hasn't it been getting worse? His drinking, I mean?" A rhetorical question: we'd been covering this same ground for weeks—months—now. Carrie's need to defend the worthiness of her love for the before-dad-died Wayne kept her mired in both the past and the relationship. This kind of ambivalence was the most frustrating part of dealing with abused women, professionally or personally, but as part of the grief process, it didn't go away just because people got irritated with it. Carrie's biggest weakness wasn't fear or denial; her own compassion trapped her.

"I can't believe he was seeing you the whole time. He told me he was seeing a counselor, but I couldn't find any record of it so I didn't believe him. Do you think it was one of those silent pleas for help?"

The image of the knife broke my concentration and I shut my eyes to keep Carrie from seeing my anger. At thirty-two, I was too young for menopause, but I got a preview as my body flashed heat. I heard a puff of air—not quite a snort—from Mary Kate's direction. We'd talk about that, too, but at least the distraction helped me rein in my temper.

"Anyway, I never expected him to come after you, that's for sure," Carrie continued. "Are you really okay?"

"I'm okay. I'm glad you weren't here. I think it would have been worse, in that case. A *lot* worse."

She didn't answer right away. Lately, we'd gotten to the point where she didn't automatically offer up excuses for Wayne, but his eruption into the office raised more than just safety concerns. Carrie's worlds—her life with Wayne and our work here—had collided, and we had passed from a theoretical examination of Wayne to a very real one. It shifted things for both of us.

"I think you're right." Carrie said. "I know you are. Anyway, that's why I'm taking off now. Coming here in disguise, spying on me, *attacking* you. I don't know what he thought it would accomplish. It's all so creepy. He's getting worse, not better."

I debated telling her about the accusations Wayne had made and decided to go ahead. Better she hear it from me.

"Are you aware that Wayne told the police that he and I were sexually involved?"

Mary Kate stirred uneasily, but held her silence. Carrie's eyes teared up. She looked away.

"He also told them I cut myself." I pointed to the livid, red line on my neck. "That I was angry that he wouldn't leave you."

Carrie sat in silence, still refusing to look at me. I couldn't tell what she was thinking. Despite the circumstances, it was possible that Wayne's hold on her extended clear from his jail cell. After several tense moments, she said, "At least if I leave now, while he's in jail, I've got a head start."

Not exactly a response, but at least she wasn't heading home to slip a nail file into Wayne's favorite chocolate cake. "Do you have a safe place?"

"Yeah, but I'm not telling you. It's not that I don't trust you, it's just that… Well, you need to be careful now, you know? He'll come after me. It's like a game to him, only worse. And he'll be after the people who might know where I went. I already told my mom, but she's mean enough to hold him off. I'm not worried about her."

"But you are worried about me?" Shit. So was I.

"Yes. Just, you know, be careful." She rose, even though our time wasn't up. "I need to get going. I still have some packing to do and some last-minute stuff. You know?"

"I know." I stood, too, not quite ready to see her leave but knowing it was for the best. "You be careful, too. Don't assume anything. From what we've seen, he's no dummy."

"There's one more thing." Misery etched lines into her face, aging her. I stood awkwardly, waiting. "He wants me to bail him out. I won't. I promise. But he might get someone else to.

I studied her eyes carefully, wanting to believe her.

Despite the doubts raised, we hugged goodbye. Tight. Fear of the same thing, the same man, bound us together more surely than even the mystical nature of a counseling relationship had.

CHAPTER FIVE

By the time the clock swung around to announce the start of my Wednesday night women's meeting, I was limp with exhaustion and sick from headache. I went anyway. Nowhere else on earth did a group of people exist who knew the real me the way these women did. If there was any dirty secret they didn't know about me, it was because I hadn't thought to tell them yet. Or I'd been in a blackout and didn't remember it myself. With any other set of women, my recent attack would have shocked—maybe even repulsed—people. Not this group. AA's women are not strangers to the violence men can dish out. And some have dished out a little of their own.

Our Wednesday group was a traveling meeting. Members volunteered to host the meetings at their home for a month at a time. Like any long-running meeting, individuals drifted in and out over the years, but a core group of eight or nine were there for the long haul. Any one of this core group knew me well enough to call me out whenever I tried to take the easy way out of a problem, whether it was lying, denial, avoidance, or whatever. Of course, they didn't call it those things; they called it "bullshit." And then they'd laugh.

This month we met at Charlie's house. Charlie, a retired librarian, had been sober eight years. Her kids had grown and moved out, but she'd raised them as a single mom and had spent much of her sobriety learning to accept their forgiveness

29

for nights she drank herself to sleep long before story time. I liked it when she hosted the meeting because her house had aged like its mistress: relaxed, sprawling, comfortable. Safe.

In the weeks following my last drunk, I'd considered asking Charlie to be my sponsor. Since she already sponsored two women, I'd asked Sue instead. I didn't regret it, either. Charlie's easy-going nature was soothing, but even though I loved to wallow in it, I needed someone more willing to kick me in the butt every so often. Sue had seven years, nearly as long as Charlie, and was considered in AA parlance to be an "old-timer, hard-liner." Now retired, she'd taught ninth grade, scaring the crap out of otherwise belligerent teenagers. She scared me, too. Underneath her gruffness, however, she was as soft as Charlie, and they were good friends.

Charlie's house smelled like lasagna and raspberry-scented candles. Although most meetings at the club still allowed smoking, it was up to the hostess of the month whether or not to allow smoking in her home. Charlie didn't. She'd quit smoking years ago, and it was one of the few things she refused to bend on.

Those of us who still smoked understood why Charlie didn't want to stink up her house, though only on a theoretical level. I tried to hide the slightly whiny emotions created by the constraints.

Recognizing my childishness didn't stop me from feeling deprived, however, so I sublimated my nicotine craving into a sugar rush by grabbing a brownie the size of a paving brick. I almost made it to the best seat in the house—an oversized armchair—but Stacie scooted in, snagging it out from under me. I almost landed in her lap, which would have served the wench right. Laughing, she scrunched down, snuggling her butt into the puffy softness. Sitting in that chair was like being hugged by a cloud.

As I settled into the rocking chair next to her, I couldn't help but notice it was all hardwood and motion. I coveted the puffy chair.

By six o'clock, the women ringed the perimeter of the family room, and Charlie got the meeting rolling. This time I volunteered to go first. Leaving out names and other identifiers, I described the happenings of the day before. As I spoke, their faces turned toward me in the soft light, heads nodding in sympathy, eyes mirroring the fear I described. No one in that room was a stranger to the powerlessness evoked from the brutality of a drunk, angry man. We'd all been there.

An unusual hush filled the room after I finished speaking. Stacie, my sobriety twin, went next. A fifth-generation drunk, Stacie had chosen to break the chain before it broke her. "Dead or insane" wasn't an AA catch phrase for her; it was her family's legacy.

"Hey, girls. I'm Stacie and I'm a grateful alcoholic. And I'm even more grateful that you're okay," she started. "When I hear something like this, it's a good reminder of how dangerous alcohol is. At least, for me. I used to think a drink would help me relax, you know? It did at first, too. But after a while, all it did was make everything ugly inside me come out bigger, badder, and uglier. I couldn't stand to be with other people for fear they'd see the real me, and I couldn't stand to be alone either. I hated myself so bad! It just got too ugly to take.

"Today, at least, I can look in the mirror and like what I see. Well, not in a swimsuit, but other than that. . ."

Amidst the laughter and mock groans filling the room, Stacie signaled to my sponsor Sue, next in line. While I would never call Sue frumpy (to her face), most of her clothes were at least a decade old and shrieked "school teacher." She hated makeup but refused to go without, settling the impasse by wearing badly applied, clumpy mascara and lipstick in various shades of brown.

After rattling off the ritualized, "My name is . . ." AA greeting, Sue wasted no time. "Get a restraining order." The room hushed. "Don't screw around with this guy, no matter what your dingbat boss says. They don't have a right to tell you to back off. That's crazy. We let too many people off with slaps on the wrist, and look where that's gotten us. If he wants treatment, he can get it in jail.

"And you watch yourself," she continued, spearing me with a no-nonsense gaze. "That girl may say she won't bail him out, but don't count on it. Besides, if she actually whips up the courage and takes off, it won't be pretty. First thing a guy like that will do is head for the nearest bar and the coldest beer. You make sure you're not his next stop.

"Anyway, my day was good. That's all I got." She sat back with an abrupt jerk, tossing the conversational baton to her couch mate, Charlie.

"Geez, Sue, tell us what you really think, huh?" Charlie laughed. "But I agree with you. Mostly, anyway. I'm not sure a restraining order is much use." Charlie raised her hand traffic-cop style when Sue surged forward. "My turn now, you can tell everyone I'm wrong after the meeting."

"Won't be the first time," Sue said.

"Oh, shut up. My point is that a restraining order will only leave a paper trail. It's not a safeguard. Get it or don't get it. Either way, what's important is to be careful and stay alert. I know you have special training and all, but words won't stop a knife. And no matter what, stay sober."

"Well, I don't like the idea of involving the authorities," Betty said next. Deeply religious and prone to anxiety attacks, her still-drinking husband had made the eighteen months of her sobriety a living hell. "I can't see how a piece of paper will do you any good, and it will probably just make the guy even madder."

Rhonda, the group's official man-hater, burst out, "The authorities are already involved! What, she's supposed to roll over and let this asshole walk all over her? You let these jerks get away with an inch and they'll beat you over the head with it. All of 'em! Now just—"

"Rhonda, that's enough. You know you're not supposed to interrupt. You'll get your turn. Go ahead, Betty." Using her decades-old teacher's tone, Sue deftly re-established order.

"I'm just speaking my opinion. Take it or leave it." Betty shrugged indifferently. In contradiction, her voice, tight and clipped, prickled with hurt at Rhonda's tactlessness. Betty passed abruptly.

Unfortunately, it was a rare night that Rhonda didn't manage to piss off someone, and lately she'd seemed especially focused on Betty. Lots of drinkers claim that alcohol loosens the tongue so that people say what they *really* feel. True or not, Rhonda carried the unfettered freedom of openness and honesty into her nondrinking life, much to the dismay of everyone else. Apparently, the "Truth According to Rhonda" had proven more addictive and twice as destructive as whiskey ever had, but she never seemed to hit bottom with it. We did, though. Frequently.

In any case, there wasn't much we could do about it. Talking with her had proven fruitless and we couldn't kick her out for being a bitch unless she turned into a drunken bitch. We tried to interest her in other meetings, but she clung to our Wednesday group, blissfully unaware that she, alone, thought candor her best feature.

Unlike most of the other women, Rhonda spent only a few moments on my issues, which was fine with me. In fact, it was rare for the meeting to focus so exclusively on one person's topic. That it had was evidence of both how unusual the event was and how deeply it resonated with most of the women.

Indeed, once Rhonda finished her usual I-hate-men monologue, the topic veered back. My headache crept another notch higher as most of the comments divided evenly between for- and against- advice about restraining orders. I grew more confused than ever.

After the meeting, the women milled around the kitchen table chitchatting and ditching their diets in favor of a late-day brownie. Stacie and Sue made their way to my side.

"What did Robert say about all this?" Stacie asked.

"We haven't really had a chance to talk about it," I said.

Two pairs of eyes narrowed in disbelief, and Sue's nostrils crinkled as if scenting the lie.

"Huh. Awful busy guy, ain't he?" Stacie remarked.

"Stacie—"

"Oh, yeah, he's so busy he doesn't have time to pick up the phone and give his girl a call." I practically heard Sue's tongue sizzle from the acid in her voice. "But wait?"

"What's wrong?" Stacie played straight man.

"What's that black thing stuck to his ear at every meeting?"

"Gosh, I don't know? Whatever could it be?"

"Maybe we got him all wrong! Maybe that's, like, a tumor?"

"You know, studies show that cell phones cause cancer. I've heard that," Stacie went on.

"I think we owe him an apology," Sue said. "All this time, I've been thinking he's an arrogant, selfish jerk and he's actually a cancer victim?"

"No wonder he doesn't like you."

"Who said he doesn't like me?" Sue asked, all astonished.

"Anybody who's ever seen him sit next to you. Believe me. He looks like he swallowed a lemon whenever you come near."

"He looks like that all the time."

I walked away, their giggles trailing like litter behind me.

CHAPTER SIX

The media found out. While I was at my meeting, the local news—as Mary Kate breathlessly informed my voice mail late Wednesday night—ran a two-minute segment on the incident. Mary Kate had tried taping the piece, but it was over before she could figure out how to work her ancient VCR. Nevertheless, she'd been able to take notes. Apparently, they'd gotten shots of the exterior of the clinic and posted a mug shot of Wayne. Not only was he scheduled for a court appearance Thursday morning, but she'd learned that his criminal history included domestic violence. No big surprise there.

Marshall met me in a lather at the clinic door first thing Thursday morning. The Powers-That-Be wanted to be very clear that under *no* circumstances was I allowed to speak to any reporters. To be honest, I didn't expect anyone to contact me, but I didn't appreciate the cover-our-ass approach that administration was choosing. And I *really* hated being told what to do. Besides, if anything would alert the media, it would be the hospital's own paranoia. Left alone, the story would blow over, I was sure.

I'd forgotten the extent of a small town's curiosity, however. When a particularly obnoxious reporter discovered my hiding spot behind the dumpster—and took pictures of me puffing guiltily on a cigarette—I conceded defeat and fled back to my office and the dwindling piles of reports on my desk.

35

Unfortunately Mary Kate wasn't the only one who'd caught the drama on the nightly news. My office line buzzed and I—all unsuspecting and brain-numb from paperwork—picked up.

"What on *earth* is going on there? Looks like they had a whole SWAT team busting in there. Did one of your crazies palm their Prozac?"

"Ma—"

"Geez, if I'da known my daughter was going to need a bulletproof vest to go to work I wouldn't have sent her to a big, fancy college."

"You didn't send me to college. I had a scholarship and paid my own way."

"It's the principle of the thing."

"Oh, that."

"Yeah. So why didn't you call me? I gotta hear about the cops raiding my daughter's workplace from Wanda Skolnik at the bank?"

"The police didn't *raid* us, Ma. A man got upset and—"

"Listen, honey," she interrupted, "if that's upset, I'd hate to see pissed off. Is that what college does? Teaches you to use big words to pretty up something ugly?"

No, Ma, I learned that from you. Do not say it. Do not.

"Ma, I didn't call because I know how you feel about dealing with the police. I didn't want to…" I scrambled to find a synonym for "upset," but it was pointless. Ma had the bit between her teeth and was off on her favorite tirade.

"Listen, honey," she said. "If you got cops running around there, just keep your head down and let someone else deal with them. They was bad enough before, but now with this Homeland Security stuff, there's no tellin' what they'll try to get away with. They hounded your father 'til the day he died, and look what happened! They feed off a man 'til he snaps, and then use that as an excuse to gun him down.

"Just wait and see what happens. This guy they caught at your place? Next thing you know we'll be hearing he tried to

36

escape and they shot him or something. I'll have to tell Wanda to keep her eye on the news. *If* they even bother to report it. You'd be surprised how much stuff they keep from us."

"Listen, Ma, I've got a client waiting. I'll give you a call this weekend." Yes, I lie to my mother. But if we both know it's a lie, does it really count?

"This weekend? Listen, honey, why don't you just come over? I haven't seen you in weeks. We could play cards or something."

I felt bad. It was more like months since I'd been out, not weeks, but my mother was the Queen Mistress of Gloss. She lived in a small town less than twenty miles away where her life consisted of her job at the turkey factory, her crappy apartment, and the re-construction of her version of the past. Just when guilt nearly pushed me into a promise I'd surely regret, she said, "We'll call Krissie, get a case a beer and catch up. Just us girls. It's been ages."

"Ma, you know I quit drinking." My mother persisted in the belief that my sobriety was a health fad like Tai-bo that I would soon get bored with. My sister, Kris, on the other hand, saw it as a judgment of her behavior. The whole thing gave me a headache.

Ma finally relinquished me to my nonexistent client, and I dry-swallowed three Tylenol for my all-too-real headache.

Later, when I finally dragged myself up the stairs to my second floor apartment, I was beyond ready for jammies and a drink. Sighing, I settled for jammies and a chocolate shake. Freudians call it sublimation—the transference of a negative impulse to a more acceptable one. Given the skin indents my size eight jeans left on my hips these days, I wasn't so sure that "acceptable" was necessarily the right term.

I hoped Robert hadn't noticed. Despite my friends' opinions, Robert wasn't a bad guy. He had his issues; who didn't? And he *was* gorgeous. At one end, a nice, round tush while at the other, honey-blond hair so thick my fingers got stuck. Heads *and* tails: a win-win situation.

Best of all, he had a decent job, his own car and a valid driver's license—all commodities that sent his desirability rating soaring in AA. Truth was, with as many women thronging around him, I was amazed that he'd gravitated to me. Not that I'm a complete schlump, but he was the kind of guy who'd had a cheerleader on each arm in high school.

Except that he hadn't. According to him, he'd been the misfit in school and still resented the popular group, most of whom had gone on to college. Lacking funds, he'd poured himself into the family business, a realty agency, managing to expand it several times over the next few years. I respected that about him.

Stacie and Sue didn't understand his ambitious nature and thought his drive to succeed was just another form of arrogance. It was true that Robert didn't always do well with some of the more outspoken men and women—which was most of AA, as far as that went—but he did have a group of guys he hung out with regularly. And besides, even though we'd been dating a few months, we really only saw each other on weekends. We still had a lot of getting-to-know-you to do.

When he called Thursday night, we finally were able to talk. His concern for my ordeal soothed my jangled nerves like a cold beer in August. Not the best analogy for an alcoholic, but there you go.

"So, what's going to happen with this jerk? Will you have to go to court?"

"I'm not really sure. Probably. There's a lot I don't know yet. Mostly I've kept my head buried under the paperwork on my desk."

"That's understandable, I guess, but Letty, you can't afford to be passive on this. I'm not saying that to hurt your feelings, honey."

"I know, Robert. You're right. I'll call the police tomorrow, I promise."

"All right. Hey, listen, you haven't … uh …"

"No, Robert. I haven't gotten drunk over it."

"Good! Although, knowing you, you'd have said that straight out already." Pitching his voice into a lousy falsetto, he shrilled, "*Robert, I was attacked by a deranged client and I went out and got trashed over it!*"

I laughed at his theatrics and in delight at his faith in my truthfulness. While honesty isn't automatically rebooted with sobriety, it's an essential part of AA's program.

"Thanks," I said, meaning it. "But I got myself to a meeting right away. I won't say I wasn't tempted, but everything went so fast I was in a meeting before it took hold."

"Good girl. But how come you didn't call me?"

"I did call you." My answer came a little too quick, a little too strident.

"Not 'til Wednesday, and you never said anything then, either."

"I was too wiped out after the meeting the first night. And I tried talking to you Wednesday, but you were in too big of a hurry. "

"Letty, you know it's difficult for me to concentrate on anything else when I'm at work. Look, let's just leave it at this: I hope someday that I'm the person you turn to when you're hurting."

A part of me wanted to continue to defend myself, but Robert's last sentence took my breath away. Normally, he was tantalizingly aloof. And had I *really* tried to discuss the incident with him or had my people-pleasing instinct to not bother him shut me down before giving him the chance to be there for me? Self-doubt of my own motives as well as pleasure over Robert's overture combined to quiet my ire. Besides, I didn't have the energy to fight. After making plans for the weekend, we hung up and I tucked in for the night.

Since Marshall had okayed seeing clients again, Friday was hectic with a mandatory staff meeting to evaluate how we were all coping and back-to-back sessions with the clients I'd rescheduled. The next day looked just as busy, too. I usually tried to keep my weekends free for Robert, but I decided to schedule some hours Saturday morning to pick up the overflow. With his work ethic, I figured Robert would understand, although I wished I'd remembered to tell him last night.

I felt even worse when I walked my client Sarah up to the reception area and discovered that a beautiful bouquet had been delivered. Three plump roses—one a deep red, one white, the last a blushing pink—nestled in a froth of greenery and white and purple blossoms. Upon closer inspection I identified lily of the valley, violets, and baby's breath. The whole arrangement was bordered by ferns and leafy stalks with tiny bunches of white flowers, whose scent hinted of an herb. Centered on Lisa's desk and surrounded by precariously high stacks of manila client files, the lovely blossoms looked as out of place as a peacock in the desert.

I thought it was someone's birthday until I noticed the amused grins directed my way. Lisa, Mary Kate, and Carol, our addictions therapist, crowded into the tiny front office, giggling. Sarah, catching the mood, circled around to lean over the half-wall dividing the office from the lobby. All eyes were on me.

"Looks like someone's been a very good girl."

"What are you talking about? Are these for me?" A goofy grin bubbled up from my heart, spreading across my face irrepressibly.

I crossed to the desk and stood looking down in amazement. A stiff, white envelope addressed to "Violet Whittaker" perched in the greenery. As I pulled the card out, the girls crowded in, shamelessly peeking over my shoulder at the inscription: *"To my 'forward Violet'—Thou hast all the all of me."*

Whoa.

"So, who's the Romeo?" Lisa kidded.

I turned the card over, searching. No name anywhere.

"Um ..." I said.

"Letty! You're kidding, right? You're seeing someone, aren't you?" Carol said.

"Well, I'm dating a guy, but we're not to this stage yet. We've only been going out since January."

"*You* might not be at 'this stage,' but he sure is!"

"Maybe with all the craziness on Tuesday, he's realized how much he cares," Lisa piped up.

"That's so romantic! I never knew your name was 'Violet.'" Sarah was leaning so far over the partition she nearly tipped over.

Displaying slightly better manners, Mary Kate, who had been hanging back, moved forward, touching a rose petal gently with her fingertip. "They're beautiful," she said, smiling.

"They sure are. You know something? I've never gotten flowers before."

"Really? Not even for prom or something?"

"No, I—"

In an instant, the atmosphere changed. Lisa snapped to attention, bustling up to Sarah at the partition. Carol scooped a stack of files into her arms and vanished into the filing room. I turned around. Marshall stood, arms crossed, leaning against the door jamb.

His eyes rested thoughtfully on the vase of flowers, then moved to mine. I blushed and looked away. Reaching blindly, I picked up the vase, accidentally splashing water down my front. Feeling ridiculous, I crossed the room to the door.

Instead of moving aside, he hesitated a bit too long for comfort, then stood back abruptly, letting me pass. I scurried up the hall like a runaway bride fleeing the chapel; his scrutiny and the half-formed suspicion flitting through my mind warming me uncomfortably.

41

CHAPTER SEVEN

I usually tried to get to the club at least twenty minutes early so Robert and I could share a cup of coffee and chat with friends before the six o'clock meeting. Tonight, even though I could have left them in the car, I ended up running the flowers home instead. Made me late, but I couldn't quite convince myself that Robert had penned that passionate declaration. On the other hand, who else could it be? At least I had a chance to grab a quick cigarette before meeting Robert. He didn't smoke.

Chewing gum and newly spritzed with perfume, I pushed through the double doors of the HP & Me. It was ten after six and the meeting had started. A few stragglers hung around the bar drinking coffee and catching up. I grabbed my mug, filled it, and headed for the big hall in the back where the larger meetings were held. Robert volunteered as this particular meeting's treasurer, which was why he hadn't waited for me. Plus, waiting made him crazy.

His clear blue eyes lighted on me as I crossed the hall and found a seat. Whatever issues he'd had as a teenager had been transformed into a prototype for a Norse god in later years. A dark blond with highlights women were forced to pay serious money for and a physique kept tight from daily workouts at his Minneapolis gym, he was a stunner. He even had those crinkles at the corners of his eyes that came from smiling—or in his case, squinting to read the fine print of contracts at house

42

closings. Either way, very attractive as evidenced by the dramatic increase in female attendance at the Friday night meetings when he'd appeared on the scene a year and a half ago. I wasn't there, but Sue was happy to fill me in on the competition—and all the attendant rumors—when Robert started talking to me early on.

Which also explained the second pair of eyes tracking my progress. Sandra, a blonde by bottle only, flipped her fake hair over one half-naked shoulder and rolled her eyes at my late arrival. Even though it was only mid-March she wore a sleeveless top, showcasing buff arms. Like Robert, she worked out, and some of the rumors about him included not only Sandra but the "special" exercises they'd practiced on her home gym equipment as well. Made me want to dip him in a vat of Lysol just thinking about it.

I spent most of the meeting demonstrating a ladylike disregard of Sandra's squinting eyes and contemptuous lip curls by directing a demure "you may have had him once but I have him now" smile in her general direction. The facial calisthenics cost me; distracted, I had to pass on speaking once again and was surprised when the meeting ended sooner than I expected.

As the crowd let out, I tried catching up to Robert but got trapped in the bottleneck caused by the narrow hallway. Few, including myself, were patient enough to simply wait for the crowd to clear.

Stuck behind Anna in her wheelchair, I wasn't surprised when an eager voice behind me said, "Hi, Letty! What a group, huh? There's a lot of good sobriety here tonight, huh?"

"Hi, Paul."

"Yeah, this is great. I didn't think you were coming tonight, but then you did. Did you have another emergency at work?"

"No, I just had something to take care of."

"Oh, that's good. I heard about that guy busting in on you. That must have been horrible."

We'd cleared the hall. People stood in casual clumps throughout the lobby, chatting. A curious few turned in response to Paul's overly loud remarks.

"It was." My answer shot out more abruptly than intended. Knowing he meant well, I took a deep breath. "Listen, Paul, I'll talk to you later. I need to catch up with Robert."

"Oh sure, I understand. Tell Robert I said hi. You take care now, okay?"

Robert stood with a group of friends watching ESPN on the TV bolted high on the wall. I made my way over, tucking my arm into his. He leaned down, kissed my forehead, then turned back to the conversation. Sports bored me. I tuned them out, content to people watch.

After a few minutes, Robert's sponsor Chad turned to me with a smile.

"Sorry, Letty, we seem to be leaving you out."

I'd always liked Chad. Second-generation Norwegian genes supplied blonder-than-blond hair and a propensity to communicate mostly with his Delft-blue eyes, saving words for really important occasions like when the Packers won. As a typical northern Wisconsin farm boy, he'd been raised on homegrown beef, outdoor chores, and beer. The beer didn't take. Making a sudden decision, I brought up Paul's search for a sponsor.

"He's asked a couple of guys and they all turned him down. He's not the most socially gifted, but his heart's in the right place. Any suggestions?"

A game of social freeze tag ensued—one of those awkward moments where nobody moves out of fear of drawing attention to himself. I waited them out. Therapists can wait forever. Someone would break.

Not surprisingly, it was Chad, although I'd secretly hoped Robert would offer.

"I guess I could," Chad said, looking over the crowd at Paul.

Across the room, Paul stood against the wall as people streamed past. He caught our stares and waved happily, glad to be noticed. I was the only one who waggled my fingers back.

Robert grabbed my hand, pulling it down. "Don't encourage him! Oh great, here he comes. Chad," he continued, "I'm sorry. You don't have to do this."

"It's no problem," Chad said. "Besides, AA isn't a popularity contest. Remember?" Significant eye contact and a raised eyebrow underscored his message, signaling some secret sponsor issue.

Nevertheless, just before Paul bounded into our midst, Chad leaned over and whispered, "But you owe me."

I giggled for the first time in days.

Robert wasn't so light-hearted. Throughout the evening, I'd failed to see any indication that he'd sent the flowers, and if he had, the gesture had made him cranky. After meetings we usually went out for a late supper with friends. His, mostly, since he didn't see them during the week. Tonight I just wanted for the two of us to spend some time alone.

Didn't happen. My suggestion, admittedly offered a tad late since we were already in Robert's car heading to the restaurant, just caused more irritation.

"Letty, we always go out with the gang. If you wanted to change the routine, you should have said so earlier."

"I didn't have time earlier. We get so little time together; I just thought it would be nice."

"I don't get much time with my friends either. Sometimes I feel stretched too thin as it is. I just hope Chad doesn't drag Paul along. What were you thinking of, roping him into being that geek's sponsor? He's so busy now I hardly get a chance to see him."

Stung, I replied more harshly than I wanted. "I didn't rope anyone into anything! Chad's a big boy. If he didn't want to sponsor Paul, he would have said so."

"You don't think it put him on the spot? My girlfriend asking him for a favor? He probably thought I put you up to it."

"Why on earth would he think that? That's ridiculous. And I wasn't just asking him; I asked the whole group. Why didn't you volunteer if you think Chad's too busy?"

"Because I'm twice as busy as Chad, and I live too far away. I can't be available in emergencies."

I'd heard this before, but it didn't explain why Robert didn't sponsor someone in the Cities or why he chose a long-distance sponsor for himself. I'd always been charitable, figuring that he'd subconsciously arranged his closest relationships with built-in barriers. Long-distance relationships have a nice buffer zone for people with trust issues, me included.

We shelved the discussion when he pulled into the restaurant lot. Chad had, indeed, brought Paul, who was nearly delirious with joy at the invitation. Robert and I sat at the opposite end of the pushed-together tables.

Screw it. I ordered a chocolate shake for supper.

CHAPTER EIGHT

The rest of the evening churned out more of the same. An on-going source of tension between Robert and me included the fact that we had not yet been intimate. Tension was building in more ways than one. Truth was, I'd never been with a man without being liquored up, and with Robert living in the Cities, we hadn't had any real time together. Trust issues, indeed.

So far Robert had acquiesced, but with visions of Sandra's "workout" sessions hovering in the back of my mind, I'd been stressing enough on my own. That evening, while dropping me off before heading to a rental property where he stayed on weekends, Robert didn't even *try* to put the moves on. That pissed me off, too. As he pulled up next to my little Focus, I realized I still didn't know if he'd sent the damn flowers or not.

"Did you send me flowers today?"

"What?" The confusion wrinkling his face was answer enough.

"Never mind," I said, shoving the car door open.

He grabbed my arm. *Again.* "What flowers?"

"Someone sent me a bouquet at work." I yanked my arm away. "I thought maybe it was you. They didn't sign it so—"

"Who's sending you flowers?"

"Apparently not you. Look, just forget about it; it's no big deal."

"Maybe it was a client?"

"Maybe." Not with that inscription, but why borrow trouble?

"Listen, Letty, I'm sorry about tonight." Proving he was capable of learning, he laid his hand lightly on mine. "I know I wasn't very patient. Things have been really rough at work and I may have let that carry over to tonight. I'm sorry."

I thought about my last few days at work and decided I wasn't very impressed with his apology. Besides, I found the timing of it a bit suspect. Guy finds out his girlfriend gets a bunch of flowers and suddenly he's Mr. Sensitive. Big surprise.

On the other hand, I didn't want a big fight, and I knew I'd been on edge, too. Capitulating for the moment, I leaned across, and we kissed good night.

When I got home, I was greeted by a vase full of anonymous flowers and a voice mail filled beyond its capacity with blank messages. Deleting the latter, I briefly debated throwing the stupid bouquet away. They were too pretty. The passionate card, however, I ended up stuffing between the pages of my AA Big Book.

I was glad when the next day kept me busy. I focused on the clients passing through my office and, for the first time in many days, felt confident and sure of myself.

I finished before both Carol and Mary Kate, the only other counselors working, and headed out as quickly as I could. Patches of snow still covered the ground, the day promising a teasing hint of spring. My car was parked on the far side of the lot, its nose butting up against the massive berm of plowed snow piled along the edge. Compacted and ice hard, that stuff wouldn't melt until at least May. If we were lucky.

As I went to unlock my car, a sudden movement at my back made me jump and drop my keys. Feeling foolish, I turned to share a laugh at my clumsiness with the in-going client.

Wayne smiled, too, but he wasn't exactly oozing friendliness. He stood about three feet away, leaning up against the rusted side of a van, arms crossed in a manner recognized by bouncers and therapists as belligerent.

A quick scan of the parking lot told me two things: we were alone, and I was trapped in the canyon made by the vehicles. If I decided to make a break for it, I'd be forced to scale the pile of ice at my back like a mountain goat on steroids. In high heels. Right.

I'd have been so impressed with myself if I could have managed a calm response. My voice didn't cooperate, however; the trembling squeak betrayed my fear. "What do you want?"

Wayne shook his head in disgust. "You're gonna keep playing these games, aren't you? You know what I want, bitch."

His voice worked.

I scanned the lot again. *Where the hell was everyone?*

"You're looking for Carrie," I said, not bothering with pretense.

He clapped his hands together, mocking my effort. "Oh, very good. Very good. You've decided to cooperate."

"Cooperation has nothing to do with it. I don't know where Carrie is. I can't help you."

I'd expected rage, and it was there but buried under a sly smirk. A fission of shock swept through my body as I realized he'd expected my response. Planned on it. "Games," Carrie had said. Still smiling that awful smile, he pushed off the van, drawing closer. Time slowed, my heart measuring out staccato thuds.

I don't know what he would have done if Mary Kate hadn't exited the clinic yodeling my name just then. We froze in place.

I took one step backward, closer to the pile of ice but farther into Mary Kate's view. Wayne, sneering at my retreat, slid the van's side door open with a rusty screech. He climbed in, carefully keeping his face turned away from Mary Kate. He paused once, looking deep into my eyes. Again, just like in the office, a strange current passed between us. Primitive. Hunter and prey.

Then he slid into the driver's seat, cranked the engine and pulled out, tires spitting bits of gravel and ice chunks as sharp as broken glass. Dropping to my knees, I scrambled on the still-frozen asphalt, skinning knees and knuckles until I closed my hand around the hard metal of my keys. Moans escaped my lips, and as I yanked my car door open, I cracked my shin. Stoked on adrenaline, it registered as a dull thump—sound more than pain.

I suppose I could have cried, but shaking and screaming and pounding the steering wheel came more naturally.

Mary Kate tapped on the glass, face looming up next to mine, scaring the crap out of me all over again. I'd forgotten about her, but at least I quit screaming. I clicked the locks open and pointed to the passenger seat, still gasping from my outburst.

She was babbling before her butt hit the seat. "Oh, my gosh! What's going on? Are you okay?"

"Didn't you see him?"

"See who? The guy in the van? Was that him? That Wayne guy? That was him, wasn't it?"

"Yeah. That was him."

"Did he hurt you? What did he want?"

The questions made me want to scream again, but I forced myself to answer. "He wanted to know where Carrie is."

"Do you know?"

"No, I don't know. I have absolutely no *freaking* idea. She didn't tell me, remember?" The hysteria started to build again, alive and out-of-control. Dangerous.

"Good thinking. On her part, I mean. But not exactly helpful for you, is it?" Mary Kate said.

"If I knew, I couldn't tell him anyway."

"Right," she said, face scrunched skeptically.

I didn't bother arguing. Closing my eyes, I leaned my head back against the head rest. "I'm so sick of this," I whispered.

"Are you going to call the cops?"

Good question. I thought about Robert waiting for me and weighed the likelihood of the police accomplishing anything with this episode. Doubtful.

On the other hand, if I were counseling someone I would advise her to at least make a report. Document the incident. Whatever. Now that I was sober I realized how much being responsible sucked. In the past, I would just get drunk over it. Nice and simple.

"Letty, if I hadn't come out, who knows what would have happened? I mean, gosh!"

I didn't want to play What If. As if on cue, my brain released its emergency response hold and alerted my shin to its recent abuse. With a gasp, I opened my eyes. "What did you want anyway?" I asked Mary Kate, aiming for distraction. Hers, not mine.

A contemplative look washed over her face as she debated letting me get away with the obvious tangent. Staring at the frantic, make-the-pain-go-away massage technique I was using on my leg, she finally answered my question.

"We're planning a surprise birthday party for Marshall," she said. "I wanted to talk to you about it. Obviously, this isn't a good time."

"His birthday?" I persevered.

"Yeah, well, it's not for a while, so there's time. I just figured I'd start collecting ideas. I had no idea what was going on out here." She twisted around, watching the lot for Wayne's return.

"Why are we planning a party in the first place? We don't usually do that." "I know, but you aren't looking to get hired after graduation. A little butt-kissing never hurt. Anyway," she continued, "don't worry about it now. Do you want me to wait while you call the police?"

I pondered that for a minute. *Was I going to call the police?* I didn't want to. What I wanted more than anything was a drink. Distracted, I said, "No, you don't have to wait. I'll be okay."

I stuck my keys in the ignition and started the car. Mary Kate looked disturbed. "Letty, I don't want to leave you alone right now. Let me help."

"You did help, Mary Kate. You're my hero!" I said it lightly, hoping to ease the tension, but she flushed anyway. "I just need to get going. I'll be careful, I promise."

She didn't like it, but she climbed out. Before shutting the door, she leaned down, "Call me, okay?"

"I will," I lied. I shifted into reverse, leaving her no choice but to shut the door and back away. When I pulled out of the lot, she was still standing on the sidewalk watching.

I refused to think. I cranked the radio, but didn't listen. My body hummed, a subliminal vibration. Nerves, dormant for four months, woke hungry, restless.

Thirsty.

Autopilot deposited me outside The Bear Cub, my old stomping ground. I sat there, sweating, car running. I smoked a cigarette, then dialed Sue. No answer. More sweat and another cigarette.

Dialed another number. Charlie picked up.

CHAPTER NINE

She was real clear. If I was still outside when she got to the bar, she'd pick me up. If I was inside, she'd keep driving. That's love, AA style.

I stayed outside. When we got back to her house, she let me curl up on the puffy chair and fed me chocolate chip cookies and ice-cold milk. That's love, too.

"So, this guy jumps you in the parking lot and you decide to head for the bar."

"It sounds kind of stupid when you put it like that," I said.

She snorted and pulled the plate of cookies closer to herself. "OK, let's break this down. Besides scared, which makes sense, what were you feeling standing there in the parking lot?"

"Alone." The word popped out of its own volition. She nodded, biting into a gooey cookie. With her non-cookie hand she waggled a circle in the air in front of us, signaling "*and?*"

"And ... little."

"Little?"

"Helpless. Alone. *Little.*"

"Right. Before you were attacked, when was the last time you felt alone and little?"

I sighed. "The night before I got sober. The night before I came to AA. But, Charlie, you said yourself it made sense that I was scared of Wayne today. I don't see how the two tie in."

"Doesn't it make sense to be afraid of drinking? Isn't it just as dangerous? For us, I mean."

Damn, she was good.

"But Sue has me working the steps and I've already done Step One. In fact, I'm almost done with Step Two." Step One said, "We admitted we were powerless over alcohol and our lives had become unmanageable."

"Good for you. And good for Sue. But sometimes life has a way of bringing us back around again."

"I don't want to start over!" I sounded like a child being told she had to go to bed an hour early.

Charlie snorted again, a lovely sound conveying amusement, sympathy, and "tough luck" in one economical exhalation.

"Life on life's terms, babe," she said, quoting an AA cliché at me.

"Well, crap."

"Look at the bright side," she said, pushing the plate over. "At least we have chocolate."

This time, *I* snorted.

In the end, I stayed more than three hours. It felt like home, or at least how I imagined home should be. When I finally called Robert, I expected him to be pissed, but he surprised me. We made arrangements for Charlie to drop me off at my apartment, where Robert had been waiting since just after noon.

"He has a key?" Charlie asked.

"Don't start. It's just for those nights when he gets into town before I get off work. Actually, he's never used it before today. It's just for emergencies."

"Uh-huh," she said, leaving no doubt that we'd be revisiting this subject on a less stressful day. Couldn't wait.

54

Fortunately, Robert went out of his way to prove my friends wrong. After retrieving my car, we went on to the Open Speaker meeting at the club. I always liked the Saturday night gatherings when one person told his or her story to the assembled crowd. Poignant and often hilarious, Open Speakers took the place of the bar scene for me and were a lot more laid back than their closed-to-anyone-but-AA-members counterpart.

Usually Robert preferred skipping them in favor of dinner and a movie—what he called a "real" date. Although I loved the time alone with Robert, I sometimes missed hanging out with my girlfriends, too, and it was one more thing that Sue held against Robert.

Tonight, however, Robert was tender, supportive, and attentive—everything I needed him to be. He hardly even made a face when I lit a cigarette during intermission and, wonder of wonders, came close to charming Sue. At least, she smiled at him—once—after he agreed with her that, although coming to the Open Speaker was good, after such a close call I needed to get to a real meeting. Defenseless against the united front, I agreed to go the next morning.

"Good," Sue said, "and we'll meet tomorrow night. My house. Five o'clock." Not waiting for an answer, she spun around and headed back to her seat to catch the last half of the speaker's message.

"Glad I won't be there for that one," Robert said.

"Oh, she's not that bad. And she's right. We have work to do. Today was too close."

"Close, but you reached out. You called someone. You got help."

Neither of us brought up that he wasn't who I'd reached out to. I was too distracted to figure it out. Besides, Sue would be more than willing to examine that little factoid tomorrow night.

At the end of the night, Robert walked me to my door without making a big deal about coming in. I was grateful for both gestures. It's not like I thought Wayne knew where I lived, but when the bushes lining the sidewalk rustled, I dove behind Robert with a shriek, using him as a body shield while simultaneously propelling him forward into battle. After all, what are boyfriends for? He must not have agreed, because my brave knight did a little shrieking of his own, heels digging in against my driving push. He twisted out of my grasp and caught me around the shoulders. What finally calmed me down was the realization that if it *was* Wayne, he had to be lying flat on his back and wiggling the two-foot high bushes with one hand. Not likely.

Robert parted the bushes carefully, reaching in with an exasperated sigh. As he turned toward me, I saw a cream-colored bundle mewing querulously in his arms.

"Here's the culprit," Robert said. He waved the kitty's paw at me, either not hearing or not heeding the ominous hum vibrating from the cat's throat.

Kitty didn't like waving.

"Uh, Robert—"

Too late. With a frenzied yowl, the cat twisted out of Robert's grasp, scratching and clawing its way loose.

"Damn it!" Robert dropped the cat, which scurried back into the bushes. "Ugh! Damn thing bit me!"

"Let me see."

"It *bit* me! I'll have to get a rabies shot or something. Did you see that little bastard?"

"Robert, let me see." I led him into the brightly lit lobby and examined his wrist. He did have a pretty nasty scratch. "That's not a bite; it's a scratch. But you'll have to wash it really good with soap and antiseptic. Come on up."

"No, I'll clean up back at the rental. Maybe you should call an exterminator or something. You don't want that little bastard running around out there where people are walking."

"Exterminators do bugs, not cats. And you really need to use an antibiotic on that. You've heard of cat scratch fever, right?"

"Ted Nugent?"

"Not the song, the disease. It's a real thing. Wash up."

He left, muttering, and I went upstairs to my apartment. Exhausted, I washed my face and crawled in bed expecting to conk out as soon as my head hit the pillow.

The day had been bad enough, but it was the kitty that kept me from relaxing. It looked skinny. Maybe it was hiding in the bushes because it didn't have a home. Such a little waif. Kind of ornery though, but maybe it was just scared.

Sighing, I got up and rifled through my fridge. Not a lot going on here for a kitty. Or a woman. I didn't bother sniffing the milk; the chunky thumps bumping around inside the container were clue enough. Would a cat eat leftover Chinese? I refused to sacrifice my chocolate-chocolate chip ice cream. I finally grabbed a red and white can of whip cream, shook the hell out of it and shot an experimental squirt in my mouth. That and the last slice of bologna would have to do.

Padding quietly downstairs in socks and sweats, it occurred to me too late that I should have worn shoes. And a coat. March in northern Wisconsin is just plain cold. Warm nights don't happen for another four months. I made the added mistake of stepping off the concrete, thus soaking my socks. Ignoring the discomfort, I squirted a puffy cloud of whip cream onto a flat rock near the bushes where the kitty had disappeared. Then I sat on the stoop, watching the darkness under the foliage.

Fifteen shivery minutes later, the pale triangle of a head peeked out from the leaves before disappearing again. Another peek, and a tentative paw reached out, tapping the air as if testing it. Another retreat. A good five-minute wait this time, and then a shape flowed like milk, settling next to the now-dripping rock.

I watched in silence, while my backside froze, as he licked the rock clean. Every few seconds he'd raise his head, stare at me. A little strip of dark fur under his nose, on three paws, and the tip of his tail gave the impression of having been dipped in chocolate.

I held still under his gaze, despite my shivering, and channeled pleasant thoughts. When he was done eating, he lifted his head once more. I held the slice of bologna by my finger tips, wafting it gently through the air.

"Still hungry?" I whispered.

His ears twitched, and he blinked. Was that kitty code? I rose stiffly, gently tossing the slice toward the rock. He bolted for the bushes.

Not the response I was hoping for. With a sigh, I sat back down and waited. After another ten minutes, I gave up. My feet ached and I'd achieved maximum butt-chill from the cold concrete. He'd be back out for the meat, but this was going to be a longer process than I'd bargained for. At least now I could sleep, knowing he was fed.

He didn't show himself the next morning, and I couldn't hang around without making myself late for the Sunday AA meeting that I'd promised to attend. I didn't really know many of the people at the meeting—different crowd from mine—but it didn't matter.

Admitting I almost drank was embarrassing, but it quickly turned into an atta-girl session when everyone heard that I'd phoned an AA member at the last minute. As far as the group was concerned, I was a poster child of success. I left the meeting feeling better than I did when I went in.

Robert showed up soon after, and we went for a late breakfast before he hit the road for home. He had four Band-Aids strapped across his wrist, so he'd apparently taken my advice seriously. I considered telling him about my attempts to tame his wild beast, but decided not to. He didn't really seem like a cat person. Besides, I've never held fast to the open-and-honest philosophy of relationships. Why start now?

CHAPTER TEN

Life was quiet for several days. I met with Marshall for the good of my job and with Sue for the good of my soul. Every evening after work, I'd dutifully trudge to an AA meeting, then head home to sit on the stoop to watch Siggy eat.

After the second day of watching the delicate hunt-and-peck approach to eating, I'd noticed the dab of "chocolate" beneath his nose extended under his mouth in a mini-goatee. I named him Sigmund, in honor of the Father of Psychology. After all, the nightly vigils were as therapeutic as anything I had to offer my clients. Maybe I should prescribe cats.

The third night, after finishing the morsels in his dish, Siggy strolled a few inches away from the bowl and sat down to stare at me. I waited. His ears twitched back and forth like radar, testing the air for safety vibes. I concentrated on exuding an aura of trustfulness. Apparently I sucked at aura emissions, because Siggy bolted for the bushes. Maybe next time.

I decided to stock up on cat supplies.

Thursday was my late day at the clinic, but my last client canceled, so I ended up leaving at 6:30. Marshall had just finished up whatever administrative types like him do and walked me to the parking lot. I felt bad that I hadn't told him about Wayne's reappearance the other day. I didn't want to have to explain why I hadn't reported it to the police. He'd logically ask why not, and, since he didn't know I was in recovery, I couldn't explain that I'd had a near relapse. Again, honesty ditched in favor of what-*you*-don't-know-won't-hurt-*me*. I'd been worried that Mary Kate might tell, but so far she hadn't. At least as far as I knew.

Still, I was grateful for his company. Even though the last few days had been Wayne-less, I was jittery and on-edge all the time. As we walked, I kept an eye out for decrepit vans and smiling assholes.

Marshall continued past my Focus toward his own Saab parked farther down. "Whoa, you've got a flat."

I walked around to the passenger side and gazed at the puddle of rubber my formerly round tire had turned into. "Huh." I looked at Marshall, deadpan.

"You don't know how to change a tire, do you?"

"I could figure it out," I said. "If I had to."

With a good-natured sigh, he set his briefcase down and waved his hand in an "open this" gesture at the trunk. My brief fling at feminism extinguished, I popped the trunk and commenced supervising the boss. Mary Kate joined me about five minutes later, and we had a fine time watching Marshall work. I could get used to this.

After wrestling the tire off, Marshall pointed out a nail embedded in the tread. I supposed it was possible that I'd picked it up on the road, but the image of Wayne pounding it into my tire fit better. I looked at Mary Kate, who waggled her eyebrows at me, making significant eye contact. This was Mary Kate being subtle.

Meanwhile, Marshall had rolled a teeny tire the size of a Cheerio from my trunk to the empty socket.

"Is that thing big enough?"

"Don't drive far and don't go too fast. This is only to get you to the service station. Do you have someplace that you usually go?"

"Yeah. An old family friend runs an auto repair shop in town. It's closed for the night, but I can get there first thing in the morning."

"I suppose you're telling me you'll be late." Marshall frowned in mock severity.

"I've got a real understanding boss," I said, smiling.

I got another sigh in answer and, for a moment, just a flash, I thought I saw Marshall's eyes travel the length of my body. Mistake. Had to be.

Since my imagination seemed stuck in overdrive, I decided it was better to not assume that Wayne was responsible for the flat until I had more evidence.

Keeping an open mind lasted twenty-four hours until the next flat tire. This one was on the driver's side, and I was alone when I discovered it. I briefly debated asking Marshall for help, but I'd had enough of the damsel in distress crap. How hard could it be? Copying what I'd seen yesterday, I wrestled the tire off and stood panting, hands on hips. Yay, me!

The sound of clapping made me whip around. Thankfully, instead of Wayne, Marshall leaned against his car, shirt sleeves rolled up, briefcase on the ground, watching my progress.

"You couldn't lend a hand?" I said, heart still thumping with residual fear.

"What? And interfere with such a fine example of feminine independence? Not on your life. Besides, I have faith in you."

"Thanks," I grunted, rolling the lopsided tire toward my trunk. Dragging it across the blacktop uncovered the source of the flat. Another nail. No surprise there. Marshall let me bumble along as I hauled the Cheerio out and prepared to stick it back on. It was weird having an audience, and, karma-senses tingling, I got the distinct impression that Marshall was staring at my butt. I tried catching him at it, but every time I'd turn around his eyes would be innocently fixed on my face. The sneak.

I felt marginally more comfortable when Mary Kate joined us, although she about killed me trying to help. In her eagerness, she tripped over the jack while I was twisting the lug nuts tight, knocking me on my butt. The specter of my car falling off the jack and landing on top of me almost made me hope that Wayne got me first.

With a muffled chuckle, Marshall took possession of the iron, twisting the lug nuts an extra couple wrenches. In spite of my assertion of independence, I appreciated the added security. No sense winning the battle for feminism and losing the car in a roll-over. Priorities, after all.

And, anyway, I'd already done all the hard stuff.

When I left, the two of them stood in the parking lot as Mary Kate lay her plot to lure Marshall to his surprise birthday party.

I didn't have time to get to Al's Auto Body before closing and was already late for the Friday night meeting. Again. I decided to go straight to the club and deal with the tire in the morning.

After I parked, I spent several minutes hunting around the junk in the backseat, looking for my AA Big Book. I usually tucked it under the mini-landfill of paperwork and books in my backseat, hidden from anyone passing by. Finally found it wedged under the seat.

As I made my way across the dark parking lot, my stomach knotted with anxiety. I hated being late, I hated dealing with smug Sandra as she draped herself over my boyfriend, and I hated the stares I knew I'd get from the old-timers for being late. Again. The feeble lighting added to my nerves.

As I neared the corner of the building to the front entrance, I felt the hairs on the back of my neck prickle. I stopped. For a moment, I stood frozen in an eerie sensation. *Someone was watching me.*

Instinctively, I moved closer to the brick wall, putting it at my back. I scanned the parking lot, searching the shadows between each of the cars and trucks. After several seconds, I felt stupid. Then a car door slammed, and a man emerged from a dark-colored sedan. A Buick, I thought, like Dad always drove. My heart pumped wildly, sweat erupting like liquid popcorn from my forehead. He moved through the lot, keeping to the shadows.

My brain screamed *run*, but my body added a new "F" for Frozen to Fight or Flight. If it were up to my genes, the human race would be extinct.

Unexpectedly, he moved into a weak pool of light grudgingly provided by one of the few working overheads. It was Paul.

Well, shit.

With a burst of hysteria that I tried to pawn off as laughter, I waved at him. A smile cranked over his homely face, and he waved furiously. And kept waving. He seemed to be experiencing a waving spasm. Waved all the way up to me.

"Hey, Letty! Hi! You running behind, too? I got stuck at work. Don't you hate that?"

Paul's chatter covered my embarrassment at overreacting. We turned to head into the club. My eyes, though, still hopped up on adrenalin, continued scanning. Then found something. Giddy with relief and slower to catch up, my brain hiccupped at processing the new information. A leftover giggle morphed into a gasp of fear.

Across the street, Wayne stood leaning against the wall of my favorite bakery. Staring. Smiling. He waved, too.

CHAPTER ELEVEN

No question now about talking to the police. Or Marshall, for that matter. I couldn't keep denying that Wayne was a problem. Enough already.

Al from the garage wasn't very encouraging about the situation, either. When I pulled into the station early Saturday morning with the second flat tire in as many days, he came out of the bay wiping his hands on a greasy rag. My dad's best friend, Al had always been good about taking care of me. Better than my dad, actually.

"Looks like you got another flat."

"Yep."

"Gonna make a habit of this?"

"I hope not. But . . . maybe."

A man of few words, he nodded, letting his eyes ask the questions.

"Some jerk is harassing me. I'm going to the cops on Monday."

Over his shoulder, he called to one of his workers. "Rick! Come take care of my girl here." Crooking a finger, he motioned me to follow him into his office.

As we passed through the five-by-seven foot "lobby" lined with metal chairs, he pulled a key out of his pocket, opened the pop machine and grabbed two cans of generic cola before continuing on to the small office behind.

Like Al, the office was geared for hard work and efficiency and smelled like grease. The only bright spot came from a calendar featuring a red Corvette and a buxom blonde, both high maintenance and artificially engineered. Seeing me glance at the babe made Al clear his throat uncomfortably, casting his eyes in the opposite direction. Al didn't like to think about boobs with his best friend's baby girl in the same room.

He handed me one of the pops, taking a long slug of his own. I took a sip and waited. For as long as I'd known Al, I couldn't remember a single time where we'd had a conversation that involved anything more personal than the weather, but I could tell he was gearing up for something big.

"You know who this guy is?" he asked.

"Yeah, but I can't prove it. Not yet, anyway. He's making it pretty obvious, though."

"You scared?"

I almost couldn't answer. My throat closed up, and I was afraid the sip of pop I'd just taken wouldn't go down. A memory from when I was twelve flashed into my mind.

Al brings Dad home after the VFW picnic, hauling him up the back steps into the kitchen. Mom takes over, guiding Dad into the bathroom and dumping him on the floor. Dad misses the toilet, of course, puke splattering noisily on our tile floor. I hate him then, knowing I'd have to clean up the mess, scrubbing the vomit from the grout lines with an old toothbrush. We stand there—my brother, sister, and I—in the kitchen with my father's silent, steady friend, listening to the retching. I wish Al was my father.

Sitting in his office nearly twenty years later, once again wrestling with the shame of alcohol-flavored secrets, I found myself wishing the same thing.

"Yeah," I finally answered. "A little scared."

He nodded, looking away again. "Smart girl. If the worst thing he does is go after your tires, that's a good thing. Not for the tires, o' course. Still, you could run through a lot of money even if that's all he does. Especially if he gets tired of sticking nails in and starts slashing the side walls.

"I had a guy in here a couple years ago. His daughter's boyfriend started up the same kind of trouble. Went on almost a year. I finally put him on a budget plan. He's still paying us off, although the boyfriend eventually moved on."

"I hope it doesn't come to that," I said. "I'm going to the cops, tomorrow and I'm going to talk to my boss too. I'm not sure there's anything they can do, but—"

"There's cameras, nowadays. Those hunting ones, you can pick one up, but they ain't cheap. Don't wait for your boss or the cops to start taking care of you. And here." He yanked on the top drawer of his metal desk and pulled out a gun.

"Oh shit, Al!" I jumped in my seat.

"Don't be a sissy," he chuckled. "It's not like you ain't seen a gun before." His chair squeaked as he leaned back, hands folded across his belly. The gun sat on a stack of old invoices like a particularly lethal paperweight.

"I know, but I wasn't expecting you to haul one out of your desk. I appreciate it, Al. Really. But I think I'll pass on the gun for now."

Reluctantly, he put it away. "It's an open-ended offer, Letty. You may not think you need it now, but if you change your mind, you call me at home. Any time, and I mean that."

"I know you do. Thanks, Al. Actually, there is something you can do for me. I would appreciate it if you didn't mention this to Ma. I'm not telling her that I'm involving the police. She'd freak." More than anyone, Al knew my family history so I didn't have to spell out Ma's hatred of the authorities or of the circumstances that caused it.

"Been a while since I seen your Ma. But if we cross paths, I'll keep this between us. It'd just upset her anyway."

67

We waited in a not uncomfortable silence until Rick stuck his head in the office, telling us my car was ready.

Every day, I expected to run into Wayne. Every day, the relentless dread felt like I'd swallowed broken glass. Every shadow, every crunch of gravel, every shift of movement caught out of the corner of my hyper-alert eyes added to the strain. Wayne wasn't interested in being predictable, however, and his absence, instead of easing my tension, raised it.

Siggy seemed tuned in to my anxiety, coming every night to lap up the food I set out, but keeping his distance. We had narrowed the gap to about three feet, but any nearer and he'd slink away, casting an apologetic look over his shoulder. I gave him food and space; if he wanted more, I was ready for that, too.

Early Monday morning, I made out a police report to an Officer Hanson. It only took a few minutes to recognize that, in addition to gray eyes, we shared the ability to hide a multitude of emotions behind pleasant features. We smiled a lot.

For my part, I was hiding an inexplicable sense of guilt coupled with embarrassment. I'd walked into the building under the influence of both feelings, and neither made any sense. Despite my best efforts, both emotions resisted attempts to exorcise them, which only increased my irritation. I'm a therapist, after all; I'm supposed to be good at this crap.

Instead, my mind picked at the lies Wayne had accused me of—having an affair with him, cutting myself, violating ethical standards. Hideous to think someone might believe any of that. Nobody had questioned me about them, and I'd convinced myself that it was because they couldn't possibly take Wayne seriously. On the other hand, Marshall knew about it, so *some* attention had been given to it. Of course, I had no way of knowing if Hanson had even heard the story in the first place. Or cared, in the second.

My decision to omit mentioning Wayne's appearance outside the HP & Me club raised my anxiety an extra notch, too. *Why should I have to reveal my most shameful secret just because some asshole was throwing a tantrum over the disappearance of his favorite punching bag?* But explaining why it had taken more than a week to report the incident could be a problem.

So I lied. Sue me.

Which, of course, increased my guilt. Certain that Hanson *knew* I was lying, I fell back on the therapist's trick of staring at the center of his nose bridge. It gave the impression of staring deep into his eyes, but in reality I was counting the number of hairs that trickled across the broad plain between his brows. Twenty-four. And a blackhead.

Felt pretty confident until I realized he was staring deep into *my* eyes, making me wonder when I'd last tweezed.

In the end, he took the report and filed it. If I decided to go forward with a restraining order, at least the incident was documented.

When I met with Marshall later, he was considerably more sympathetic, but equally short on action. I brought up Al's idea of installing a camera in the parking lot.

"I know money is always an issue," I said, "but safety should take priority. If none of us had seen Wayne before or if he hadn't stuck around long enough for the police to catch him..." Unexpectedly, my throat closed, cutting off the rest of the sentence: Wayne could have killed me and gotten away easily.

"If it had been a blitz attack, you mean." Marshall filled in the blank.

I cleared my throat. "Exactly. And that's not impossible. We've just seen that."

Frowning, he ran his hand through his dark hair. I braced myself. "I see your point, Letty. I do. But I don't see how a camera would help as a preventative measure. I agree wholeheartedly that we need to be more security conscious, but

I'm more concerned about finding ways of keeping you safe and out of harm's way in the first place.

"I'm also doubtful that the board would ever go for the idea of a camera in the parking lot. There would be issues of vandalism or theft. And inside the clinic? Then you get into all kinds of problems with client confidentiality and so on. I just don't think they'll go for it." Although his words and tone conveyed professionalism, his eyes spoke volumes about how sorry he was to be the bearer of bad news.

"It's too late to 'prevent' anything. I'm already in harm's way," I pointed out. "Right now it's just a nuisance, but what if he escalates? I can't just ignore him."

"I know we can't. We have a board meeting coming up, and I've already put security first on the agenda. This won't be brushed aside. And, no matter what, we're not going to risk any more run-ins in the parking lot. If I'm not available to walk you out, then ask Lisa or somebody. You are *not* to go out alone under any circumstances. And that includes when you get here. You have a cell phone; just buzz the office when you pull in and we can watch out the door."

I sighed. I hated the idea of being babysat. Marshall leaned back in his chair, watching me, a gentle smile on his face. He knew I was struggling with the thought of asking for help every time I walked outside. But I was spooked enough at this point to give in. At least until this blew over.

"Letty?"

I met his eyes. He was holding a slip of paper between us.

"Call me first. Here's my cell phone number."

I reached out to take the paper. He didn't let go. It hung suspended tautly between us, connecting us. Again, the eyes, dark and limitless.

"You don't have to wait until you need an escort to give me a call, you know. If you need to talk or something. Feel free."

Face hot, I tugged the paper from his grasp, nodding.

Walking down the hall toward my office moments later, my breath whooshed out. Hadn't realized I'd been holding it. *Wow.*

Later, when my two o'clock appointment hadn't shown up, I wandered up to the front. Checking the schedule, I saw that it was a new client. Or, at least, it was supposed to be. Unfortunately, it's not unusual for a new client to ditch the session at the last minute. I always wondered if the crisis that initiated the call had resolved itself or if the brief flicker of courage that reached out for help had dwindled before they could get to the building. And I had to admit, it felt a little like being stood up for a blind date. Even though I didn't take it personally, it was a nuisance. By the time I realize they aren't coming, it's too late to start a different activity, and, of course, there's no charge for an initial session skip.

As I stared at the schedule, I discovered an unusual amount of new clients had been scheduled with me this week. Counting this afternoon, five in all—today's, two on Tuesday afternoon, one on Wednesday, and another on Friday. I enjoy the freshness of starting work with a new client. Keeps my mind off myself... and off other distractions as well.

Lisa was entering data into the computer but looked up with a grimace as I studied the calendar.

"No-show, huh?"

"I hope not, but it's not looking good. Can I see his file?"

She handed me the manila file. A lot can be learned from the basic information given in the first contact. Gender, age, initial complaint and so on. Of course, the information was scant, the vast majority of the forms still blank. Something about the name, though ...

"Lawrence Harmon?" I asked.

"Huh?" Her brief episode of empathy over, Lisa's eyes stayed glued to the screen, fingers dancing across the keyboard as she funneled data into the system.

"Doesn't that name sound familiar?"

"Nope," she answered.

"Bozo," said a voice from the lobby.

I leaned over the half-wall. A tiny lady in turquoise sweats, presumably waiting for a family member, sat reading a two-month-old news magazine.

"Did you say something?" I asked, not sure if she was talking to herself or commenting on an article.

She lowered the magazine. "Larry Harmon."

"Yeah?"

"He's Bozo the Clown. You know? Big red nose, blue jumpsuit? *Bozo!*"

Straightening back up, I met Lisa's eyes. *Now* she was paying attention.

"Uh-oh," she said. "You don't suppose …?"

Not answering, I picked up the phone and jabbed in the numbers listed on Harmon's intake form. A shrill atonal squeal pierced my brain as a fax machine attempted to interface with my ear.

"Damn!" I slammed the receiver down.

"Heard that," Turquoise muttered from the lobby.

"Lisa, what's the name of the other new client?"

"Umm, let's see." Normally unflappable, she clicked to the scheduling screen, overshot into calendars and had to click back. "Robert Keeshan?"

I leaned through the window. Turquoise raised her eyes from the magazine. "Clarabell. From *Howdy Doody.*"

I plopped into a chair, fuming, while Lisa pulled up the remaining names.

"John Favreau, Bill Irwin, and Carl George."

The names weren't familiar to any of us, including Turquoise, which gave me a moment of hope. Unfortunately, when we Googled them, we discovered Favreau was an actor who'd appeared on *Seinfeld* as Eric the Clown, while Irwin portrayed Mr. Noodle on *Elmo's World.* Carl George gave us some trouble, but when we switched first and last names we found a ton of references for an "American clown who received the coveted Golden Clown award." From Princess Grace, no less.

Clowns. All of them.

Trudging back to my office, I spent the hour needlessly filing my nails down to slivers

.

CHAPTER TWELVE

I may have been angry over the prank, but Mary Kate was absolutely livid. We went to Culver's for lunch on Wednesday, and she was still spittin' mad. Unfortunate, since I was sitting across from her at the time.

"Mary Kate, relax. It was just a prank. I'd rather he did that than flatten my tires again."

"Why doesn't he just leave you alone? You already told him you don't know where Carrie went. What's the point of harassing you?"

"My guess is partly revenge and partly to stay connected to Carrie. I'm a surrogate."

"A surrogate?"

"Sure, it's a form of transference. He's taking his feelings for Carrie and dumping them on me. Just like they teach us in school."

"Does that mean he's in *love* with you?" Mary Kate's face was taut with emotion.

"I don't know," I said. "I'd have to think about it some more. I'm just talking it through, myself. I guess I've mostly been focusing on the revenge aspect. Was what he felt for Carrie love? Carrie had mentioned he was into games, remember?"

Mary Kate nodded. I noticed we'd both avoided mentioning his name.

"Anyway, it might be smart to consider his motivations. I've been so busy reacting, it would be good to take a step back, examine the big picture."

Looking at Mary Kate, I smiled. A blob of ketchup dotted the side of her mouth, her face bright with excitement at using our professional skills to address the problem. If she'd had a tail, it would be wagging. Impulsively, I reached across the table and grabbed her hand.

"Thanks, Mary Kate. It's been good to talk this out. I feel better."

She flushed with pleasure, dropping her eyes, and I realized how important such a small thing as a compliment could be to her.

"Hey, how's the big party coming along?" I asked.

"Oh!" She sat up straight, excited again. "It's this Friday after work. It's so great! Everyone's coming." She must have seen the brief look of consternation flitter across my face. "You can come, can't you? You have to!"

I hated missing yet another AA meeting, but I could probably meet up with Robert at the restaurant later. Besides, I knew how important this was to Mary Kate.

"I'll be there," I said. I even kept the sigh out of my voice. "Wherever 'there' is. Where are we meeting up?"

"Didn't I tell you? Sherm's."

"*Sherm's?* The bowling alley?"

"Yeah, on Columbia. It'll be great. Everyone loves bowling … right?"

Warring emotion flickered across her face like an old-time movie reel: happy confidence in the allure of renting used shoes and heaving a weighted ball down a slick pathway at a bunch of skinny pins, exhilaration at being in charge of the festivities, and deep down—surfacing in the dilation of her pupils and the slight quivering of her lip—fear that she'd screwed up, that people would laugh, that she'd been a fool.

"Hell, yes, everyone loves bowling!" I couldn't have been more enthusiastic if I'd had pom-poms and a butt-skimming miniskirt. "How are you getting him there?"

"I need your help with that. With all this stuff going on with you, I figured we could use it to our advantage. How about if your car 'broke down?'" Her fingers and eyebrows waggled imaginary quote marks. "You could tell Marshall you need a ride and then ask him in."

"To bowl a couple of frames?" With a straight face yet.

"For a beer, whatever. Do you think it would work?"

I thought about the subtle glances and smiles passing between Marshall and me in recent days. My mouth went dry. Took a sip of watered-down Diet Coke.

"I think so."

Needless to say, I didn't mention to my women's group later that night that I was taking my boss out for a beer. Why borrow trouble? Besides, Stacie had brought in a new girl, Trinnie. Even though she'd had a First Step meeting at the club, we decided to do another. When it was my turn, I took a deep breath and told the story of my slide into misery.

"My last drunk was on November 17. Hard to believe that was only a few months ago. There was a conference in Madison that a few of us from work went to. It was like a college road trip, and we stayed over at the conference hotel for the weekend. It was nice, you know? We didn't have to worry about driving because there was a bar in the hotel and several within walking distance.

"I'd always been careful the few times I went out with co-workers. Mostly, I just avoided drinking around them altogether. I'd leave early and let them think I was going home, when really I was heading across town to drink with my buddies. I kept those two worlds separate."

Several women nodded in understanding.

"I started the night out thinking I'd just have a few drinks," I continued. "But that didn't go quite as planned. Don't know why I thought it would. I have no idea how much I drank, but you know the saying: One is too many and a hundred not enough?" Soft laughter around the group was answer enough.

"Anyway, I ended up blacking out. Not for the first time, either. I have no idea what I said or did. Somehow, I made it back to the hotel room I was sharing with the other two girls, but they ended up sleeping somewhere else because I puked all over myself and the bathroom floor. Then I passed out in one of the beds, still covered in my own vomit.

"I was so hung-over the next day that I had to leave the seminar three times to throw up. Nobody spoke to me on the way home. Which was okay because it gave me time to really think. To see myself through their eyes.

"It scared me. I have a family history of alcoholism, but that's not why I drank that night. My dad wasn't in that hotel bar that night. Neither were my sister or my aunts and uncles. It was just me. Just me and the booze.

"So I went to an AA meeting the next night. I was lucky; I knew where to go for help. And the thing is, all the things I drank over—loneliness, trying to fit in, trying to fill the empty place inside—I'm finding all those things taken care of in sobriety.

"So I hope you find it, too, whatever you're looking for. It's there for you if you just take it one day at a time."

The group's focus turned to Rhonda as she began the account of her decision to come to AA. Not big on taking accountability for her own actions, she droned on about drinking because of the rotten men in her life. I'd heard it before so I tuned out and thought about that last night of drinking. Thankfully, both of the women I'd attended the conference with had moved on: one returned to college and the other on maternity leave with no desire to return. It was nice not having to face them every day. The rest of my co-workers, not having been there, had laughed and teased me for a while and then forgotten about it as new items of gossip turned up. But I hadn't forgotten.

The humiliation burned deep, but that could be a good thing. It powered my resolve. What stood out for me tonight was the part about keeping my worlds separate. I hadn't thought about it that way before, but I'd *always* been careful about keeping parts of my life categorized and boxed up. Learned that from my mama's knee, you might say.

Friends from school stayed at school because if they came to my home, they'd find Daddy drunk or Mama crazy. College years were spent achieving during the day and partying at night; I told myself that's what college kids did, purposely ignoring those who didn't. Even now, the most defining aspect of my personality—alcoholism—was concealed from the people I spent the most time and energy on, my clients and colleagues. Even from Marshall.

What was I thinking? Especially Marshall.

CHAPTER THIRTEEN

Friday morning I stopped off at Al's and sought advice on how to disable my own car. He showed me which doo-dad to unscrew and which hose to jiggle loose. That afternoon after work, I had Mary Kate walk me out to my car, where I followed Al's directions. Soon after, Mary Kate, Lisa and Carol—all giggling and shrieking like demented geese—piled into Carol's Suburban and pulled away. Not so very subtle.

Forty-five minutes later, when Marshall strolled out of the clinic carrying his jacket slung over his shoulder, looking end-of-a-long-week corporate-cute, I had the hood up and my head stuck under it, poking around. As he approached, I realized he had a cameo-shot of my butt, so I scooted behind the steering wheel and cranked the key to add credible sound effects to the scene. The motor made a lovely ratchety, grinding sound, then stopped.

Marshall came up and stood with an arm propped on the open car door. Raising help-me eyebrows to him, I heaved a theatrical sigh.

"Why are you out here alone?" he asked.

"Technically, I'm not alone," I pointed out. "You're here."

His lips twitched into a smile before he mastered them, turning his expression into a head-shaking scowl. Stepping back, he held the door open and spread his free arm in an "after you" gesture.

I locked up and jumped into the Saab. Sinking into the buttery smooth seats, I momentarily closed my eyes, inhaling the pungent mixture of spicy aftershave and leather. Very manly.

When I opened my eyes, I found him smiling at my obvious pleasure. I sat up straight, folding my hands good-girl fashion in my lap.

"Where are we going, Letty?" he asked softly.

Good question. And he used "we" again.

Trying not to stutter, I gave the address of the bowling alley, without naming it. Even Marshall might have heard of Sherm's, although he seemed more of a hiker-type to me. Despite all the elaborate planning, I hadn't gone beyond getting him to the bowling alley. *In* was another matter.

When we arrived, he parked in front of the building, leaning forward to peer quizzically at the dancing bowling pin billboard over the entrance. He looked back at me. Here's where I needed to come up with a clever ploy to lure him, all unsuspecting, into Mary Kate's clutches. Unfortunately, I was too conscious of sitting alone with him, too aware of his bemused flirtatious smile to develop a coherent plan.

I reached over and confiscated the car keys.

"I need you to follow me, no questions asked, and act surprised when we get inside."

He stared blankly for a moment, then his forehead crinkled.

"Is this going to be painful?" he asked.

"Probably."

"Is Mary Kate involved?"

"Absolutely."

He sighed and got out of the car.

Cigarette smoke, the explosive clatter of pins falling, and more than a dozen people screaming "Happy Birthday!" greeted us as we entered. It looked like Mary Kate had been able to coerce everyone—part-timers, interns, and all—to show up. She'd even managed to pry Bob, the office curmudgeon, and

Regina, a PhD in attitude, out of the office. How she got them into the bowling alley was scary to contemplate. Mary Kate had unknown powers.

She'd gone full out on the decorations. Balloons, streamers, and a banner blazoned with *Hoppy Birthday* and dancing green frogs in pastel party hats stretched across the back wall.

With dismay, I noted a side table piled high with gaily wrapped presents. We'd all agreed that presents were unnecessary, but judging by the size of the stack, I was the only one who'd bypassed the opportunity to kiss butt. Well, crap.

Giddy with joy, Mary Kate bounced up, flinging her arms around me. As cute as Marshall was, she was probably too shy to approach him so I ended up with the birthday bear hug. Marshall, for his part, did a very credible job of acting surprised.

"Whose idea was this anyway?" he finally asked.

Next to me, Mary Kate fairly vibrated with delight as all hands pointed out the guilty party.

"I should have guessed," he said, walking over and tossing his arm around her shoulder. "Who's going to buy me a beer?"

Big stampede up to the bar to get the boss a beer. *Big.* I snagged a seat and immediately regretted it, since it landed me next to Regina, sitting like the debutante she formerly was, and across from boring Bob.

I'd tried to like Regina since, in addition to a full client roster, she volunteered several hours a week at a local domestic abuse center. Very commendable. Problem was, she insisted that we pronounce her name like the female body part, which both grossed me out and made me want to giggle. I was forced to avoid her name altogether. At the clinic, Regina was our resident expert on Attention Deficit Disorder in children. Unfortunately (for us, not the children) she didn't like kids and refused to work with them, instead concentrating on what she called "feminist psychology." Mainly she worked with divorcées, disgruntled housewives and wild-eyed women prone once a month to homicidal rages—a group with legitimate needs, but one that kept Regina perpetually angry, eternally hostile.

Despite his theoretical maleness, she'd established an uneasy alliance with Bob when Marshall was hired on. Bob, nearing retirement, was tired of dealing with needy people and called it a "bonus hour" when clients blew off their appointments. He played a lot of Solitaire on the computer and alternated between bitching about his bleak future of staying home with the missus—I couldn't imagine she was thrilled about the prospect either—and complaining about Marshall, whom he resented in an apathetic kind of way. Bob hadn't bothered to apply for the position when it was posted, didn't want the headaches that went with it, but he enjoyed complaining about the changes that accompanied the new administration. He constantly referred to Marshall as "that young guy," while patting down the thinning strands of his own deserting hair.

So far I'd managed to maintain a decent working relationship with each of them by the combined tactics of distant cordiality and active avoidance. When forced to interact, I smiled pleasantly and listened a lot. Come to think of it, I should have charged for therapy.

It would have been awkward to leap up as soon as I'd recognized my error in sitting next to the pair, so I resigned myself to the situation. For the first five minutes, I fretted over what we could possibly talk about. I needn't have worried. They both ignored me, but not in the hostile way that they reserved for many of my co-workers. I was free to people-watch.

With the notable exception of Regina and her merry band of Bob, it looked like folks were trying to have a good time in that stilted, beginning-of-the-party, don't-know-the-rules-for-this kind of way. The laughter was a little bit too loud, the tone a little too forced as people groped for conversational topics that didn't revolve around work so they could prove A.) they really *were* interested in each other as people and not just co-workers and B.) they really *did* know how to relax. Knowing how to relax is important to us mental health types; it demonstrates good coping skills. No one wanted to admit that we occasionally burrowed under a quilt and wished the world would go away. Or that we might drink ourselves into oblivion as a way of numbing our pain.

However, when Marshall popped on a garish pair of blue and red rental shoes, cuffed up his shirt sleeves, and started rolling strikes, the ice officially shattered. Yet another colleague with undiscovered talents. *I wonder what other. . . ?*

"Letty, your face is all red. Are you hot?" Mary Kate said as she plunked down next to me. I patted my cheeks, but luckily one of Lisa's gutter balls—and the pungent vocabulary that followed—distracted her. Mary Kate hooted her condolences across the entire bowling alley, causing Regina to squinch her eyes shut in grim forbearance. Across from us, Bob rolled his eyes, tipping a "can you believe this?" smirk that included me. I ignored them both. The only thing worse than Mary Kate bellowing in my ear would be inclusion into their mini-clique.

"Aren't you drinking anything?" Either Mary Kate had had a few drinks already or she'd forgotten I was sitting next to her, because she was still bellowing. Judging from the hops-scented breath, I'd go with the former. Still, it was a good excuse to get away.

Mary Kate followed me up to the bar where I ordered a diet pop. A huge cheer broke out behind us as Lisa's ball finally managed to navigate the lanes, connecting bowling ball to pins. A closer look showed she had knocked over a grand total of two pins. An even *closer* examination revealed someone had raised the kiddy bumper rails as an assist. I grinned as she wiggled her butt and waved victory fists in the air.

The game ended soon after, Marshall winning by a large margin. As they began to choose new teams, squabbling over who got to use the fluorescent pink ball, he made his way to the bar next to me.

"Whew!" Marshall fanned his shirt collar while I forced my mind onto images completely unrelated to droplets of sweat rolling silkily down his torso. Mary Kate waved at the bartender.

"Nice game," I said.

"Well, I had an advantage in that I wasn't part of the advance decorating team." He pointed at the banners and balloons. "Apparently, they'd already gone through a pitcher before we even got here."

"Two!" Mary Kate clarified cheerfully. And then, "Shots!"

Behind us, the bartender lined up shot glasses, tipping a bottle of Cuervo over each. Oh shit.

"Uh…"

"Da don da dada dada da… *Tequila!*" Mary Kate sang an aborted attempt at The Champs classic. She shoved a glass in my hand and one in Marshall's. Oh shit, oh *shit*. Saliva pooled in my mouth. Marshall reached over, clicked his glass against Mary Kate's, and downed his. She laughed and chugged hers while I sat stupidly. Sweat beaded down the center of my back, an irritation that heightened my anxiety. Tickled, too.

"Come on, Letty!" Mary Kate said. "Your turn! Go, go, g—"

Marshall reached over, casually took the glass out of my hand, and tossed it back.

"*Mar*-shall!" Mary Kate broke Marshall's name up into two whiny syllables, a weirdly combined version of petulant adolescent and prissy maiden aunt. Eyes watering, he smiled charmingly and dug his keys out of his pants pocket. Handing them over to me, he said, "Letty's my designated driver. You don't want your boss getting pulled over for a DUI, do you?"

Hard to argue, but Mary Kate looked just drunk enough to consider it. She had a closed, obstinate look on her face.

"Hey, you're in charge here. When do I get my presents?" Marshall tried distracting her. It worked. Squealing and grabbing us each by the hand, she pulled us over to the table piled high with brightly wrapped gifts, then flitted back and forth trying to herd everyone over to the table. After about ten minutes, she gave up on "everyone" and settled for "most." I sat a couple of chairs down from Marshall, holding his keys in my hand. They were still warm from his pocket.

I tried hard not to let my imagination wander to his warm-pocket regions.

The gifts helped distract me, too. In addition to several gift certificates to area shops and restaurants and a stack of instant lottery game cards, Marshall also became the proud new owner of a pile of latex vomit and a Pull-My-Finger fart machine. But it wasn't until he unwrapped a package of Raspberry Sorbet edible underwear—female, size 4—that the crowd really went wild.

He turned bright red, but whether it was from laughter or embarrassment, I couldn't say. Carol and Sarah, our other intern, dove under the table for the discarded wrapping paper, searching for the giver's name.

"It's only got Marshall's initials, MT."

"Let me see," Lisa confiscated the tag. She frowned, then turned the tag upside down. "It doesn't say MT. It says LW."

Silence descended on the group, then they turned as one to face me.

I blushed so hard my brain almost ignited. "*Me?*" And then, stupidly, "It's not *my* birthday."

Everyone burst out laughing, and someone passed the panties over to me. I flung them at the garbage can fifteen feet away, making a basket. The group cheered wildly.

After the wrapping was pulled off the final present, people started sorting themselves into two groups. Led by Regina and Bob, about two-thirds grabbed their jackets and started making good-bye noises. The others—made of sterner stuff and tougher livers—headed for the bar.

Lisa walked up, a slip of paper pinched between her fingers. The gift tag. "I thought you might want to have this," she said.

My initials in sloppy block letters were written on one side, a used piece of tape with shreds of gift wrap running along the top edge. I flipped it over to examine the back. Nothing.

"I already looked there," Lisa said.

"I don't suppose you saw who carried it in earlier?" That was stupid. If she had seen someone she would have said so already.

"That won't help. I brought it in."

"You did?"

"Yep," she said, nodding. "When I came out of the file room I found it on my desk. I was afraid Marshall would see it, so I shoved it in my purse without looking. When I got here, I remembered it and stuck it on the table. But if you're wondering if I got you raspberry flavored undies…" She gave me an I-don't-think-so look. "Anyway, the whole thing seems kind of creepy, so I figured you'd want to know."

"Creepy is right. Thanks, Lisa."

CHAPTER FOURTEEN

I found it strange to sit with my hand wrapped around a sweating glass of generic pop while all around me people laughed and drank. Not strange in a bad way though. Strange in a *Gorillas In The Mist* kind of way. I felt like an anthropologist watching the mating rituals of an obscure race.

Almost everyone I watched managed to party without forgetting the essential point that we would all have to face each other on Monday, but there were a few who got a little blurry around the edges as the night wore on. Several offered to buy me a drink, but nobody seemed to mind when I refused, especially when I jangled Marshall's keys and used the code words: designated driver. I couldn't help trying to figure out what made these folks different from me. Where was the line between social drinker and raving drunk? When had I crossed it? *Was there really no going back?*

I was so absorbed in the scene I almost forgot to call Robert. He'd been less than thrilled when he'd heard I was canceling our Friday date night, especially to go to a bar. But eventually, grudgingly, he acknowledged the importance of attending the boss's birthday party. Originally I'd planned to leave and meet up with Robert once the party got rolling, but since Marshall had entrusted me with his keys, I was stuck. It was past 9:00, which meant the AA meeting would be over, so I called to let him know the change in plans. He wasn't as irritated as I expected, which perversely annoyed me almost as much as the mini-interrogation that he put me through.

"You're not drinking, are you?"

"Of course not."

"No urges or cravings?" Robert asked.

"No; it's weird watching people drink, though."

"Weird how? 'I feel left out' weird?"

"No, more like wondering what makes me ... what I am ... and not them."

Speaking of weird, I discovered I was twisted into that strange body posture that people on cell phones in noisy places assume: hunched over, one finger stuck in my ear, head turned from the room like I could find a cone of silence if I put my nose two inches from the countertop. On top of turning myself into a pretzel, I was striving for a voice range that would allow Robert to hear me over the bar noises but not inform the entire bowling alley that I was, indeed, an alcoholic.

"What do you mean 'what you are'?" Robert misinterpreted my attempt at subtlety. "Why are you avoiding?"

"I'm not *avoiding*, but I'm in a public bar and I don't want—"

Somebody was tapping on my shoulder. I held my ear finger up: one minute.

"Yeah, well, you already know how I feel about the whole bar thing," Robert continued. The tapping grew more insistent, and I swatted backwards, waving the tapper off. "You're not getting hit on, are you?"

More tapping. Giving up, I swung around abruptly. Marshall held a bowling ball, pointing at me, then him, then the ball. Trying not to giggle, I shook my head and turned my attention to the phone again.

"Letty? Hello?"

"I'm here, Robert. I just got distracted." Marshall grabbed my foot, and I slapped at his back. "Stop it!" I hissed.

"Stop what?"

"Nothing, Robert. Things are getting a little goofy here." Marshall stuck his tongue out at me, which I ignored, turning my back on him. Seconds later, something tugged at my foot again, sliding my shoe off. I decided I was dealing with a shoe fetishist—not something one normally learns about one's boss. Or ever wants to.

I tried to pick up the trail of Robert's conversation, but I'd missed a chunk. He was talking about a new guy who'd had his First Step meeting earlier that night. Apparently, Robert had asked him out with the gang for coffee, which explained why he didn't make a fuss at my no-show. Robert liked meeting newcomers and showing them the ropes. My foot was getting cold and I needed to track down the shoe-napper, so I didn't mind when Robert signaled he was ready to go.

After hobbling up and down the lobby area, I finally located Marshall at the shoe counter. He'd convinced the clerk to hide my shoe, and he triumphantly held up a pair of petite bi-colored rentals.

"You can't just steal my shoes and expect me to join you bowling."

"I only stole *one* shoe. So you can play *one* game."

I didn't need a degree in Alcohol to know it was useless to argue. Sighing, I took the shoes and shuffled over to the chairs.

Bowling can be fun. Bowling with a crowd of inebriated therapists—not so much. Nobody paid the least bit of attention to when their turn came up, leaving huge blocks of time open for important stuff like doing shots and falling off the molded plastic chairs. Hannah, a brilliant social worker who wore granny skirts and spoke in whispers, kept insisting that we should play strip bowling, which lent a whole new meaning to gutter ball. Mary Kate kept getting on her hands and knees, crawling to the line, and rolling her ball by shoving it two-handed from the prone position. Apparently, the lane was being "wiggly."

Being the only sober one in the batch, I should have been able to wipe the floor with all of them. However, Marshall was just drunk enough to be relaxed and not drunk enough to see double. He kicked butt. He also shook butt—his own—every time he got a strike. Absolutely made losing worth it.

When he finally let me pour him into his car, it was nearly midnight. Thankfully, Carol's husband, Steve, showed up to chauffeur the more "relaxed" co-workers to their various homes. He'd come prepared, shoving empty plastic ice cream tubs in everyone's laps as they giggled and crawled over each other and wrestled with seat belts. Some, I suspected, were not quite as drunk as they portrayed, but were simply reveling in the freedom from their normally staid professional lives. Mary Kate, on the other hand, sat in the front passenger seat with her nose smooshed flat against the window, gazing blearily out the window. I waved. She blinked, which I interpreted as "good-bye." Close enough.

I got in the car and started the heater. Marshall sat with his head canted back on the seat, eyes closed, a slight smile on his face. Soft jazz played on the radio, but I turned it off, preferring the silence. Carol's husband tapped on the window while I struggled to adjust the seat forward.

When I lowered the window, he asked, "You sure you're okay to drive?"

I smiled. "I haven't had a single drink all night, but thanks for checking."

"Letty's a good girl," Marshall murmured. "A very, very good girl."

"I got an extra bucket," Steve said, waving it at me. I looked over at Marshall.

"Are you going to need a bucket?"

"No way. I'm smooth."

"*Smooth?*"

"Smooooth," he said. "Like velvet."

I looked at Steve. "He says he's smooth."

"Take the bucket." Steve shoved it through the window, and I placed it on the floor between Marshall's feet. I expected an argument, but the only sound of life from the passenger seat was soft, rhythmic breathing. Well, great. Velvet Boy was asleep.

Luckily, Marshall's fancy car was equipped with a user-friendly navigation system. I hit "Favorites" and "Home" and let a robotic female direct me through the dark night.

I hadn't been out driving this late in a long time. Toward the end of my drinking days, I had taken to drinking at home, alone. Such a cliché, but at the time I thought I was cleverly avoiding all the drunks out there on the roads. Silly me. The only drunk I had to fear was locked up in my apartment with a bottle of booze.

Outside of town, the darkness became more than just the absence of light. The black night had texture, a thickness that pressed impatiently against the bright swath the headlights cut into the inkiness. Marshall's quiet exhalations and the vulnerability induced by sleeping in another's company created a cocoon of intimacy.

Marshall lived on the outskirts of town where the land reverted to farms. The car sped by quiet barnyards and empty fields, the frozen stubs of corn stalks waiting out the long spring.

After a few miles of deserted country, the GPS chick steered me up a long, dark, twisting road. Gravel crunched under the tires, and I almost woke Marshall to make sure I hadn't taken a wrong turn when we came around a bend. The drive opened to a clearing with a small house perched near the ice-edged river. Frost gilded the wild grasses and trees, outlining the scenery in pale silver.

"Wow," I said.

Marshall came awake, rubbing his eyes like a toddler. He peered sleepily out of the window.

"Hi, honey. I'm home."

"You live in an enchanted cottage?" I asked.

"Wanna come find out?" He tried to waggle his eyebrows, but ended up blinking and twitching his nose like a manic bunny.

"Out," I ordered, pointing at the house.

"You can't kick me out. This is my car."

"Nope. You made me designated driver, so it's *my* car tonight. And it's beddy-bye time for you. Out you go."

"Aren't you going to walk me home? What if I can't make it?"

"It's fifty feet."

"I could fall. There's bear out here, you know. I've seen them."

"Have you really?" I looked around the clearing.

"Well, no, but I have lots of squirrels. Big ones." I looked at him blankly. "Great, big, mutant, hairy squirrels. They scare me."

"Get out."

He started wrestling with his seat belt. After five minutes, I reached over and sprung the catch, releasing him.

"I could make coffee," he offered.

"No, thanks."

"Wanna see my etchings?" He smiled wickedly.

I reached over him, opening his door. "Don't make me push you."

"How come gorgeous women are so cold-hearted?" He scrambled from the car, losing his footing twice. Righting himself, he began a slow, meandering walk up to the front porch. Halfway up the porch stairs, he paused, digging in his pockets. Turning back to the car, he spread his arms wide.

I rolled the window down and leaned my head out. "What now?"

"Neemkees."

"*What?*"

"I NEED MY KEYS!"

Sighing, I turned the car off, pulling the keys from the ignition. Wary of a ploy, I checked the key ring. Sure enough, along with the car keys and a silver master key to the office dangled two brass keys that probably opened the house. I got out and trudged up the path.

"Don't you try anything!" I warned as I climbed the stairs beside him. In an act of surrender, he laced his hands behind his head and nearly lurched off the porch into the bushes. I grabbed the front of his shirt, slipped on the frosty wood deck, and we both went down.

Luckily, I landed on top.

CHAPTER FIFTEEN

I lay full length on top of him, heart thumping wildly, my hands splayed across his chest. And a very firm chest it was, I might add.

"Help. I've fallen and I can't get up," he said, smiling up into my eyes.

"You can't get up because you're grabbing my butt."

"I thought it might be cold. I have very warm hands."

It's true. He did. And my butt *was* kind of cold. Shaking naughty thoughts from my head and warm hands from my butt, I scrambled up, leaving him stretched out on the cold planks. He groaned, then rolled to his feet.

"Oh, great! Where're the keys?" I asked. "I must have dropped them when you fell."

"I didn't fall. You pulled me down and jumped on me. I thought it was my present."

"I *rescued* you from falling off the porch," I clarified.

"That's not how I remember it."

"Well, you're drunk." I searched the ground for glints of metal, but even with the moon, it was too dark.

"I am not drunk," he said with great dignity. "I am relaxed. Besides, I'm not the one who lost the keys."

Then he walked over to the front door and opened it. Reaching around the door jamb, he flicked the exterior lights on, shut the door and began weaving around, searching for his car keys.

"Your door was unlocked the whole time?"

"Of course it was. This is northern Wisconsin. Who locks doors?"

I slapped a hand over my mouth in an effort not to scream. Didn't want to scare all those freakishly hairy squirrels. On the other hand, with luck, one might attack Marshall and bite him on his cute ass. Stomping past him, I pushed into his house.

I flicked the lights on, illuminating the open space of a living room to the left and kitchen to the right. It must have been converted from a three-season cabin. Realtors would use words like "cozy" and "rustic" and "charming," and all of them would fit. There wasn't any entryway to speak of, just a tiled rectangle where you could pull your shoes off and hang a coat on the wooden pegs jutting from the wall. An insulated, red flannel jacket with bits of wood shavings caught in the worn fabric drooped from one peg. Against the far wall of the living area, a half-log staircase rose to a loft, which spanned the back half of the tiny house. Windows ran the length of the wall facing the river, the leather couch angled to catch the view. Everything was done in rich browns and dark greens with bits of cobalt blue glassware accents scattered throughout.

I found it easy to picture Marshall living here. However, as much as I wanted to poke around, this wasn't what I'd come inside for. I slipped out of my shoes, padded to the kitchen, and began opening cabinet drawers. Behind me, the door opened and closed.

"Did you find the keys?" I asked without turning.

"Nope. Looks like you might be staying." He rummaged through the refrigerator. "You should have kept the panties. I need something sweet."

I kept my back to him so he wouldn't see me blush. Or smile. Instead, I continued pulling drawers open, eventually finding the one I was looking for. I pawed through it.

"Looking for something?" Marshall asked.

"Found it." I held up a set of keys, jangling them. A piece of cardboard attached to the ring by a thin twisted wire identified them as belonging to a 2007 Saab.

"How did you find those?"

"This is northern Wisconsin. Everybody keeps their extra set of keys in their kitchen junk drawer. Good-night."

Scooting by him and out into the night, I heard him laughing, presumably at himself, since the keys worked and I was soon tooling down the road. I grinned all the way home, more relaxed and happy than I could remember in a long, long time. Part of me knew I should examine what was going on, but I really didn't want to. Most of the time I was good at fretting myself out of contentedness, but tonight I just wanted to *feel* it.

Walking up the sidewalk in front of my apartment, a pale patch of moonbeam flitted under the shadow of the bushes.

"Siggy? Here, kitty, kitty." I didn't expect much. He'd avoided direct contact ever since Robert had hauled him out of the bushes, but I hadn't given up. I'd even stocked up on kitty supplies, just in case. "Bet you're hungry, huh, little guy?"

To my amazement, he left the shadows and twined figure eights around my feet, purring and rubbing against my slacks. "Siggy?" I reached down slowly and ran my hand across his silky back. He arched and circled back for more. I picked him up and smiled when he tucked his head under my chin. His whiskers tickled my neck and I could feel the mini-vibrations of his purring.

"Want to come inside?" I made my way up to the entrance, ready to let him go if he showed signs of tensing, but he lay limp and warm in my arms, letting me carry him through to my apartment.

Delighted with Siggy's company, I didn't realize anything was wrong until I flicked the lights on. Or tried to. At the sudden return of tension, Siggy leapt down and scampered off into the dark. I don't usually leave lights on, but I had that morning knowing it would be late before I got in. Even if I hadn't specifically left some on, there should still have been some illumination from the stove or microwave clocks. The apartment was too dark, too cold.

Arms out in front of me a la Frankenstein's monster, I shuffled across the tile to the cupboard where I kept my flashlight. Finding it, I fumbled with the switch, shaking, suddenly convinced that I wasn't alone. I grabbed up a steak knife and made my way to the phone. It was dead. *What the hell was going on?*

I fled back to the front door, grabbing my purse on the fly, and plunged out into the brightly lit hallway. Obviously, the power outage only affected my apartment. I didn't want to wake my neighbors, and there was no way I was about to explore my apartment in the pitch dark with only a flashlight and a cheap knife.

Ma would kill me, but it was time to call in the good guys.

Forty-five minutes later, two patrolmen walked me through my apartment in a very non-CSI manner. No drawn guns, no crouches, no ducking around doors—very unimpressive. As far as I could tell, nothing had been disturbed. We discovered Siggy lounging in the center of my bed, eyes glowing like flat green disks as the flashlight swept over him. Moments later when we reconvened in the hallway, the younger cop held Siggy, purring, against his chest. The little traitor.

"It doesn't look like anyone's been in there. Did you pay your bill?"

"Yes, I paid my bill," I said, affronted. "And it's not just the electricity. The heat and the phone are out, too."

They exchanged a glance. "Well, we can't see that anything has been bothered and nothing's been cut on the outside. So it must be a glitch in the system."

"How can it be a glitch if it's several utilities?"

"Look, Ms. Whittaker. It's not a break-in. You'll have to call the power company tomorrow and figure it out."

Handing Siggy over, they clomped down the stairs and out the door. Although the dark apartment wasn't very appealing, I couldn't sit out in the hallway all night. I slammed the door, immediately wishing I hadn't. Siggy kamikaze-dove from my arms, fleeing into the blackness. With a sigh, I went about setting up the cat box and put out food and water. It was surprisingly awkward trying to pour litter with the flashlight clamped under my armpit. It dropped twice; at least it landed in the clean litter each time. Once I had Siggy settled in, I groped my way through the living room to the couch.

I had choices. I just needed to figure out what they were.

Despite their lack of excitement—or maybe because of it— I didn't believe the cops were wrong about whether anyone had broken in. I'd watched them checking window latches and I knew for myself that the door had been locked. But I didn't agree that some glitch had coincidentally shut off the electricity, the heat, and the phone—I knew that I'd paid my bills. That was something I could verify, however.

Flashlight back on, I detoured into the kitchen for matches, extra batteries, and every candle I owned. Tonight they would offer something other than romance. I also grabbed my checkbook on the swing through. My coffee table ended up looking like an altar with flickering bits of fire and perfumed scents mingling in a heady aroma like incense. A quick search through the check register told me that although the gas bill wasn't due, I was about eight days past due on the power and twelve on the phone. Not long enough for either to have been shut off, but very unlike my usual habits of paying on time. Back to the desk for my little stack of to-be-paid bills. Flipping through the pile took mere moments and didn't uncover either bill. I sat back, thinking.

If nobody had physically cut the power, then the services were turned off at the source. If the utility companies didn't do it of their own accord, and if I certainly didn't, then who did? I knew the answer, of course. How was more difficult, and worth investigating.

Gathering a small screwdriver, an expired Sears credit card, and a jumbo paperclip, I tramped down the stairs back to the lobby and stood in front of my mailbox. Tiny scratches marred the brass, but it was impossible to tell when they had occurred or if they were the result of daily wear-and-tear. A cursory look at my neighbors' showed similar markings. I tried the credit card first, mainly because that's how they did it in movies, but I couldn't pop the lock. One look told me the screwdriver would probably work, but it would leave more damage than could now be seen. The paper clip, however, worked just fine, popping the mail box door open with ridiculous ease. Shutting it took longer, but it could be done, too. All of which explained how that rat bastard Wayne had gotten hold of my mail and tampered with my utilities

.

CHAPTER SIXTEEN

I pretended it was frustration, not fear, that kept me awake all night. Wayne had cleverly chosen late Friday to play his prank, thus ensuring I'd be without power and phone until Monday at the earliest. To make matters worse, my cell phone died and my car charger was nestled in my glove box of my car. My car, of course, had been parked at the clinic all night and probably sported four freshly flat tires.

In my heart I knew I should try to make the Saturday morning AA meeting, but I skipped it. Instead, I spent the morning participating in cat-therapy, sitting on the floor, back against the cabinets, watching Siggy pad around exploring his new domicile. After my butt finally went numb, I loaded dirty laundry into Marshall's pristine car and set out for the laundromat. Although my building had a couple of washers and dryers, it would have meant heading down to the basement with its spiders, weird, moaning building noises, and one-way-in one-way-out cinderblock hallway. No way in hell.

Truth was, Wayne's invasion into the very heart of my life creeped me out way too much to chance it. He knew how I spent my work hours, he knew my darkest secret. And now he knew where I lived. But, true daughter of Denial, I chose to sit with the laundry zoning out to the music of sudsy water and the low hum of industrial dryers. Cheap hydrotherapy. Smelled good, too.

After lunch, I headed out to Marshall's to switch cars. If I could have figured out a way to extend my designated driver duties 'til Monday or, say, the year 2020, I would have. At the very least that would have meant stranding my boss at the enchanted cottage for several days without a ride. Probably not the best career move, although the anonymity of driving someone else's car made it very tempting.

A wrong turn cost me twenty minutes, but I wasn't on a schedule. By 1:30 I was standing on the porch, knocking. When no one answered, I thumped harder. Even with the hangover he must be suffering, I found it hard to believe he didn't hear me. Hands on hips, I slowly pivoted, scanning the clearing. A distant cracking sound, followed by a thud, drifted through the trees lining the river. I knew that sound.

Growing up, we'd had a wood burner, and I used to go with Dad to cut wood. My job was to stack it; I hated the inevitable slivers but loved the time with my father. He'd be sober—Ma would make sure of that before turning him loose with an axe and her first born—and he'd be feeling good about providing for the family. The smell of split oak would fill my nose, an earthy mixture of sap and crisp, fresh air, promising warmth through the long winter. My dad laughed a lot on wood-cutting days. I did, too.

I hung back from going into the woods, although I spotted a wide path next to a huge pile of logs stacked near the edge of the clearing. I couldn't be sure it was Marshall out there and didn't want to walk up on a stranger in the middle of the woods. As I debated waiting in the car or making myself at home in the sure-to-be-unlocked house, I spied a big, old-fashioned dinner bell at the corner of the porch. A frayed bit of rope dangled from the crown invitingly.

Quite loud, that bell.

I soon heard the rumble of an ATV starting, and minutes later, Marshall drove up the path wearing the flannel jacket over a denim shirt and faded jeans, looking particularly scrumptious.

101

He exuded a sexy lumberjack aura, and, if not for his bloodshot eyes, I might not have guessed that he'd tied one on last night.

"I was hoping you'd show up," he said, smiling.

A clean, woodsy smell drifted to me, and I wondered if he'd think I was coming on to him if I jumped in his lap and buried my nose in his jacket. Pulling myself together, I said, "I almost didn't. That car is nicer than my apartment. But I figured you'd run out of food eventually and I didn't want to be responsible for starving you to death."

"You should have let me keep the panties."

"Yeah, 'cause that's what all the survival manuals tell you to pack. Edible underwear." I tried to not blush, but failed. Miserably. "You know, I was hoping you'd forgotten about that."

"Not a chance," he said. "And I don't plan on letting you forget it, either. Who do you think sent them?"

That squashed my laughter. I leaned against the porch railing, looking out across the river.

"Letty? You don't think it was him, do you?"

"Who else? Somebody had my electricity and stuff turned off, too."

"Your phone? I tried calling this morning. It said it was disconnected."

"Well, not by me. In fact, I'm afraid to see what my car looks like after sitting there all night."

Marshall frowned. "I didn't think of that. Maybe we should head out and see if everything's okay."

"Did you find your keys?" I asked, tossing him the set of spares. Grinning, he pulled another set out of his jacket pocket.

"Good thing, too," he said. "I'd have to pay to have all the locks changed if I lost the office keys. Might be hard to explain."

A half hour later, we pulled up to the clinic. Marshall parked next to my car and we got out. I was stunned to find nicely rounded tires and intact windows. Marshall stood back a bit, arms crossed, while I circled looking for damage.

"Looks good," I said, shrugging.

He got down on his knees, examining the undercarriage.

"Are you looking for bombs?"

"No, but I wouldn't be surprised if the brake line was cut. Everything looks good, though."

Unlocking the driver's side, I got in. As I turned the ignition, the car made a not-so-lovely ratchety sound, and I remembered sabotaging myself on behalf of Mary Kate's surprise party. I popped the hood and reversed the damage, managing to look like I knew what I was doing.

The car started up nicely and I sat, half in and half out, feeling the deflating aftermath of adrenaline and suspicion. Marshall leaned casually against the door.

"Everything looks good, huh?"

"I guess."

"Geez, don't get all excited or anything. That's good news, isn't it?"

"I just can't help feeling like I'm missing something. I mean, why would he miss a chance to hit my car? It was practically wrapped up with a bow for him."

"Maybe he had a hot date. Even stalkers have to have a night off, don't they?"

I sighed, and we said good-bye. Our car doors slammed simultaneously, but I waited for him to back out first while I sat pondering. Heaving another sigh, I decided he was right, I was being ridiculous. Before shifting into reverse, I checked the mirror and froze.

The next thing I knew I was out of the car, staring at it from the middle of the parking lot. Marshall jumped out of his idling car and ran to me.

"What's wrong?"

I pointed at my little Focus, hating that my hand shook. "Somebody's been in my car. Somebody's been *inside* it."

"What? In your car? How do you know?"

"The mirror is off. It's pointed sideways."

He walked over and sat in the driver's seat. Screwing up my courage, I joined him on the passenger side, but I couldn't force myself to sit. I hovered in the open door, looking for anything else that felt wrong. The jumbled mess in the back seat looked like it always did. Meanwhile, Marshall leaned over and popped the glove box.

A stiff lump covered in matted gray fur dropped out onto the passenger seat with a soft thump. Screaming, I slammed the door, clearing the distance to the curb in one wild leap. Once there, I stood with a hand clamped to my mouth, little squealy noises slipping out between my fingers, and the other arm wrapped around my middle. Marshall didn't exactly scream, but he grunted a man-version of "ugh" and moved pretty quickly to put distance between himself and the car. We stood on the sidewalk together, a his-and-her portrait of shock and disgust.

"That was a rat," he said, his voice flat but overly loud.

I almost threw up. "No. No-no-no-no-no. There is no dead rat lying on my seat."

"Did you see the *teeth* on that thing?"

I sat on the curb and put my head between my knees. Just a little dizzy. My knees shook so hard I almost gave myself a concussion, but I was in the correct position to see if I did, indeed, wet my pants as feared. Marshall nattered on and on listing the creature's various attributes—big as his neighbor's Chihuahua, stiff enough to use in batting practice, fangs as long and yellow as. . .

A little humming was in order.

"What is that sound?" he broke off the litany to ask. "Are you moaning?"

"You can't leave that thing there." Lifting my head, I came eye level with the car's front end. An amazing amount of dead bugs and ragged feathers were embedded across the metal grillwork. My car was a rolling morgue. Put my head back down.

"Aren't you going to call the police?"

I groaned. "What good would that do? I can't prove anything."

Marshall sat on the curb beside me. "I know, but I think it's important to document everything."

I chanced raising my head. "Isn't that what they tell people to do when there's nothing useful to do?"

Instead of answering, he rose and dug his cell phone off his belt clip. I thought he was overriding my objections, but he walked to the car and used the camera feature to snap a couple pictures of the thing on my seat. Then he reached in, picked the vile thing up by the tail and carried it to the dumpster at the end of the lot. I shuddered at his bravery. A loaded gun to my head couldn't induce me to touch that thing.

"I sent copies to my email and yours. I still think you should report it and get a file going on this."

He reached down to pull me up, considerately using his non-tail-touching hand—frankly, I wouldn't have touched the rat hand—but instead of letting go, he held on. We stood there for a moment in silence holding hands. His quiet tenderness did me in, tears sliding down my face. He pulled me close, and I finally got to bury my face in that warm jacket.

CHAPTER SEVENTEEN

First thing I did after leaving Marshall was head to the nearest store to pick up some Lysol. My car now reeked of disinfectant, but at least I could bear sitting in it without hyperventilating from images of plague-ridden fleas biting my ankles. I sat inhaling pine-laced fumes, fervently hoping they weren't flammable since I smoked cigarette after cigarette. My life was as out-of-control and as chaotic as it ever had been— one client in hiding, another stalking me, a crush on my boss, and dead rodents falling out of the glove box. I quit drinking to *stop* this kind of insanity.

And as long as I was facing hard truths, I had to admit that I didn't like how I was behaving with Marshall. Okay, part of me liked it. But still, it was bad enough that Robert and I lived so far apart, I now had to wonder if *I* was the one sabotaging our relationship. Early on, he had said he wanted to be the one I turned to. Had I even given him the chance? Instead I seemed to be letting Marshall's attentions distract and titillate me.

With the power out at my place, maybe this would be a good time to take up Robert's offer to stay at his weekend rental. It might be good to have the time alone and really let him know what's been going on. Well, most of it anyway. Maybe not the panties.

By the time I got to the AA club, I was eager to see Robert. That is until I walked in and found sleazy Sandra practically in his lap. Technically, they were sitting across the table from each other, but her smirk when I came in said *lap*. I took the seat next to him and, as I hung my purse on the chair back, noticed her foot sliding down his leg. She and I locked eyes.

"Do you *mind*?" I hated the high school-ish quiver in my voice and, even though she broke eye contact first, felt no victory.

She rose, smiling, and sashayed over to join the gang at the coffee bar. I caught a couple of raised eyebrows from the gossipmongers watching the silent drama before they turned away, knowingly.

"What's going on, Robert?" I asked, tight-lipped.

"Maybe you should tell me," he said.

"What are you talking about?"

"I've been trying to reach you all day. You're out all night with god knows who, you blow off our dinner and ignore your messages, and then you sail in here and are rude to my friends."

"Do your friends normally run their feet up your crotch?"

He had the grace to blush. "Why don't we go outside?"

I followed him silently. This wasn't the best way to start a conversation; we were both defensive and on-edge. It only got worse when we climbed in Robert's pristine Tahoe, and he frowned at the muddy parking lot slush my shoe trailed in. He reached into his briefcase on the backseat, tearing out two sheets of notebook paper.

"Here," he said, handing them to me.

"What? You want me to take notes?"

"No. Stick your feet on these. I don't want the mats all dirty."

Not even years of training could keep my mouth from falling open. "They're floor mats! That's what they're *for*."

"Does everything have to be an argument with you? I have to drive clients around in this truck. I don't come to your office and sling mud around, do I?"

My brain stalled trying to decide whether to defend against "everything an argument" or the mud-slinging crap. I settled for rolling my eyes so hard I almost gave myself a brain aneurism before slamming my feet on the papers.

"Fine. There. Now, do you want to quit with the bullshit and tell me what the hell was going on in there with Sandra?"

"Nothing's going on with Sandra. She's just a friend."

"Yeah. You said that already. So tell me: do you let Chad run his foot up your leg?" Screw diplomacy—he wasn't a client.

Robert's jaw clenched.

"What's going on, Letty? Are you *trying* to piss me off? First, you ditch me, and then you come strolling in to the club later having a hissy fit and embarrassing me in front of my friends."

"I did *not* ditch you." I took a deep breath trying to calm down. Didn't work. "I joined my co-workers for my boss's birthday party at a bowling alley, which I told you about several days ahead of time.

"Secondly, I was not ignoring your calls. My utilities were shut off, including my phone, and my cell was charging. I didn't even get your messages. And for your information, I'm not required to check in with you!

"Third," I was ticking the various points off on my fingers, so angry they shook, "you can expect a 'hissy' fit any time I walk in to some bimbo playing footsie with Mr. Happy!"

"You know what?" Robert's face flushed an ugly burgundy. "You know why I wanted to talk to you? I wanted to tell you I agreed to sponsor the new guy. I wanted to share that with you. Instead, I have to deal with all this drama." Not averse to his own drama, he punctuated the word by waving his hands in the air.

"*Drama?*" My voice rose precipitously. "If you paid any attention to what was going on in my life, you wouldn't talk about drama. Just this morning—"

"You know what?" he interrupted. "Maybe you need to take a look at the common denominator here."

"What are you talking about?"

"*Letty* has problems with a guy at work. *Letty* has problems with a girl at the club. *Letty* has problems with her boyfriend. How many meetings have you missed lately? When was the last time you met with your sponsor? Maybe you need to take a long, hard look at your part in all this. Even Sue, your own sponsor, is asking me what's going on with you. And, I have to tell you, I'm starting to wonder myself." Shaking his head, he exited, slamming the truck door.

I knew he was full of shit, but the part about Sue bugged me.

I sat for about ten minutes trying to calm down. Instead, I found myself replaying the scene, coming up with all the things I *should* have said. Sighing, I got out of the truck. The notepaper stuck to the bottom of my shoes like a trail of cheap toilet paper. I peeled them off, wadded them up and threw them back on his immaculate floor. Let Mr. Neat Freak clean them up.

Sue showed up a short time later. I was tempted to sit out the meeting and talk with her privately, but Robert's comments rankled. I settled for asking her out for coffee after the meeting.

We went to The Brew Ha-ha which, although ridiculously expensive, was close to the AA club. Instead of the traditional, northern Wisconsin rustic décor, it tended toward funky eclectic and attracted a young crowd. Sue looked vaguely cranky and out of place as she perched in a modernistic, orange scoop chair.

"Why are we here?" she asked, her gaze settling like a sleepy lioness on a group of teen girls two tables over. One girl with a hunk of metal skewering her lower lip tried a little alpha-female posturing, tossing her hair back and rolling her eyes, but the other three shifted nervously under Sue's teacher-aura.

"Because I haven't talked to you lately and Robert said you were asking about me. He made it sound like you were worried." That got her attention.

"He did?"

"Were you?"

"Well, I might have said something like 'How's Letty doing?' but if I was worried about you I wouldn't waste my time asking *him*. I'd come straight to you." Her eyes bore into mine. "Is there something I should be worried about?"

I filled her in on the hell Wayne continued to put me through all the way up to the rat-in-the-box incident, finishing with the argument with Robert.

"I think he was just trying to put me on the defensive," I concluded.

"Sounds like it worked. But if it got you to come talk to me, I guess it could be worse. I bet you picked this place because it's not likely that Robert and Chad and the rest are going to pop in here for a nonfat, soy latte."

"Exactly."

"You don't have to tell me what the fight was about—unless you want to, that is. But I need to know if it's something you might drink over."

I smiled. "I can't see myself drinking over this. I'm upset, but I'm not... I don't know... I'm not *distraught*, you know?" Sue nodded. "And anyway, it seemed like we were fighting about two different things. I was pissed about Sandra, and he was angry that I hadn't called him."

"Why hadn't you called him?"

"My phone was out."

Sue crooked an I-don't-buy-it eyebrow at me.

"It was! Well, I suppose I could have used Marshall's cell phone but—"

"Whoa, whoa, whoa." Sue put up a traffic cop hand. "Marshall?"

"My boss. I've talked about him. It was his birthday last night, and I was his designated driver. My intern Mary Kate set up a surprise party at the bowling alley. So, yes, there was drinking there, but I didn't drink. I was careful. I wouldn't have

110

gone if I didn't think I could handle it, but it really didn't bother me. At least, not in the sense that I thought I might drink."

"In what sense did it bother you, then?"

I thought for a moment. "For one thing, I didn't like seeing what people look like when they're drunk. I mean, most of them were just happy and a little silly. But one or two kind of slid over the line, if you know what I mean."

"Oh, I know what you mean all right. So, it was a reminder?"

"Yeah. Of what I *don't* want."

"Okay then. That's good. What else bothered you?"

"What do you mean?"

"You said, 'for one thing.' That implies there were other things. What are they?"

"You'd make a good therapist, you know that?" I shifted my eyes away. "I'm kind of attracted to Marshall."

"Mm-*hmm*?"

"Not that I would act on it, of course."

"Oh no. Of course not."

"You're mocking me, aren't you?"

She sighed and shook her head. "Look, kiddo. You know how I feel about relationships in the first year of sobriety— you're too vulnerable to make good decisions—and now you're asking for a double helping? Let's look at the big picture here, okay? What is it you like about Robert?"

"He's got a nice butt."

"Yes. I'll grant you Robert's nice butt."

"Marshall's butt is nice, too."

"I'm happy for him. But we're not talking about Marshall now. Keep to the point."

"All right. I guess… I liked how he picked me out of all the other girls." I blushed at the admission. "He could have asked anybody out. Instead he asked me."

"We're going to have to do something about your self-esteem. Why wouldn't he ask you? As far as him asking anyone out, I guess he could have. But, believe it or not, there are actually some women who think Robert's an egotistical pinhead." She raised her hands defensively. "I'm not saying me, mind you. Just in general."

"You don't think he's an egotistical pinhead?" I teased.

"Of course I do. But I also think he thirteen-stepped you, and that's what pisses me off."

Thirteen-stepping is a serious offense. Technically there is no real Step Thirteen, but the term is used around AA to describe what happens when someone—usually a man, but not always—preys on a newcomer, exploiting her sexually and sometimes financially. The implication is that the newcomer is being victimized, which didn't fit with my view of either myself or Robert, and I said so.

"Maybe not in any extreme sense," Sue said. "But you turned your whole world upside down when you got sober— your way of thinking, your coping skills, your social network, and, most importantly, your way of thinking about yourself— everything changed. You can't have that kind of upheaval and not, to some extent, be vulnerable. You're a shrink. You know better."

"I'm a therapist, not a psychiatrist," I nitpicked. I hated that she might be right.

"Whatever. Being a therapist probably makes it harder for you to accept that you can be taken advantage of. I call it 'Terminal Uniqueness.' It's that voice that tells you that you're different from other drunks, that you can handle it yourself. Whatever 'it' is for you. Maybe it's dating when you're still trying to figure out the program, maybe it's hanging out with your old drinking buddies at the bar, maybe it's telling yourself you can drink just one, just a little.

"But the bottom line is, Letty, that you are in a relationship with an arrogant jerk, you're flirting with your boss, and Willard the Rat Boy is stalking you!"

I shuddered. I'd always hated the movie *Willard*.

"Look, kiddo. You need to make your own decisions here, but don't pretend all this isn't getting to you. That's when you'll get yourself in real trouble and try to find the answers in a bottle. Go back to the First Step and the Serenity Prayer. Figure out what you *can* control and what you *can't*. Change what you can; let go of the rest."

I smiled at Sue, reaching across the table to grip her hand. Blunt and ornery, but she had the gift of distilled wisdom.

Shortly after, I made my way across town to my apartment and my hungry cat. Sue had given me plenty to think about. I whispered the Serenity Prayer over and over in my cold car, across the parking lot and up the stairs to my place.

"God, grant me the serenity to accept the things I cannot change,
The courage to change the things I can,
And the wisdom to know the difference."

Straightforward, a bit of a cliché, but packed with good common sense—a lot like Sue herself.

Things I couldn't change: that was easy to figure out. Wayne spread over that list like a malignant tumor. My stomach coiled into a knot just thinking about him. I anticipated lots of nightmares about rats. But I couldn't change that, at least not tonight.

I could, however, change how I'd been reacting to his harassment. I'd been sticking my head in the sand, pretending that Wayne wasn't getting to me, ignoring his escalating behavior. Sue was right. Although what she didn't know was that it wasn't just because I was a therapist that led me to cling to the illusion of control. At some point, I would have to look at how my childhood played into all this.

But that would have to wait. If I didn't come to terms with the present, I might not have the chance to work on the past. Wayne had already shown his capacity for violence, for thwarting the law, and for invading the very heart of my life.

If I were advising a client in this situation, I would have insisted that she document every encounter and develop a safety plan. More significantly, we would have involved the police long ago.

Just the thought of bringing in the police made me sweat. Against my will, memories bubbled up like blisters on a burn.

The doorbell is broken, so they knock. Always a light sleeper, I wake in time to hear Ma's robe whisper against the wall as she hurries to the door. Then the low murmur of a man. Ma's voice in response, quavering, lilts a question. Her scream cuts through the quiet dawn.

I wet myself even before Ma rages into our bedroom, hands fisted in her hair, face naked without the coke-bottle glasses she always wore. She never even spoke on the phone without her glasses. Her pale blue eyes had shrunk without them.

"They did it! Yes, they did! They finally went and did it. What will we do? What will we do now?" Her voice clamped down on the last word, stretching it into an elongated howl of pain.

"Ma'am?" The door swings open gently, a uniformed policeman fills the entrance. Behind him, shadows and movement indicate the presence of another.

Oblivious to everything but her private hell, Ma stumbles back and forth in the narrow aisle between my sister's twin bed and my own, tripping erratically over the litter of our childhood: dirty clothes, naked Barbies, my overdue library books. Kris and I huddle under the blankets, shivering beneath the thin, cotton barrier between us and the craziness loosed in our soft dawn.

"Ma'am? Please. Why don't you come out here with me? Please."

Ma moans, low and deep, and bends over at the waist. One hand clutches her stomach, the other remains clenched in the tangles of her hair. When Kris starts wailing, the shadow behind the policeman finally moves.

A woman. No makeup, plain hair pulled back in a ponytail, jeans and a grey sweatshirt. "Mrs. Whittaker? I'm Pastor Sue, the jail chaplain. You're scaring the children. Come on now."

Ma allows herself to be pulled out, the sound of her moans dopplering back from the living room. The policeman stands awkwardly, looking down at Kris and me.

"Get out," I say.

CHAPTER EIGHTEEN

Siggy jumped feather-light onto the bed, gliding through the slanting moonlight, settling at the end of the bed between my feet. Trapped, unable to shift around, I lay still, sharing the night with my new friend. Desperate for distraction—from the past and from the malignant craving it awoke—I did the next best thing. I focused on someone else's problems. Story of my life.

If my whole life had been upended, the same could be said for Siggy. For both of us, a change for the better. A life-saving change, in fact, but certainly something that took getting used to. A rich sound of contentment—Siggy purring—rose in the dark. I guess he dealt with change better. I fell asleep.

Typical male, Siggy was gone from my side when I woke early Sunday morning, but he joined me in the kitchen as I ate an English muffin.

"So, what do you think I should do about Robert?" I asked.

He looked at me and slowly blinked.

"I don't understand," I confessed. "Let's do one blink for yes and two blinks for no. How does that sound?"

Siggy turned away to look out the window.

"There's nothing out there but a brick wall. Stop being inscrutable. Just answer this: should I break up with him?"

Siggy jumped down from the counter top and padded across the floor to the litter box for some private time.

That couldn't be good.

The breakup went about as well as Siggy predicted. Which is to say that Robert rapid-cycled from stark incredulity to petulance and, finally, hissing anger. He didn't buy my explanation about needing to focus on the program, either. He summed his opinion up in one word: *shit*. Maybe he and Siggy had more in common than we realized.

I'd wanted to keep it amicable, especially since we would continue to see each other regularly at the club. But that wasn't to be.

I spent the rest of Sunday in a mood as dark as my apartment, leaving barely enough energy to wrestle with utility companies on Monday. Luckily, after being routed through various departments and false connections, I was transferred to a very nice lady at the telephone company. She even gave me some security tips. In addition to considering an unlisted number, Tammy reminded me to contact my credit card companies, in case Wayne had nabbed those bills, too. She also suggested adding a password—we settled on "1asshole"—before allowing changes to my account statuses.

In gratitude, I told her about the rat and grossed her out. Didn't seem like a fair trade really.

I was surprised at how simple making the change to an unlisted phone number was; it could even be put into effect the same day. Unfortunately, I also learned that every time I called someone I'd have to punch in *67 so my number didn't pop up on their Caller ID. Not sure I wanted to deal with that hassle, I decided to wait.

By the time I got to work, I was feeling overwhelmed at the energy I'd have to generate and maintain in order to protect myself. Usually I only needed that level of paranoia with my family.

Lisa was at her desk when I trudged in. My heart sank further when I saw the expression on her face.

117

"What now?" I asked.

"Good morning to you, too, sunshine. Starting a new reading program, are we?" She waved a magazine lazily back and forth.

I snatched it out of her hands. Wearing only buccaneer boots and a *seriously* misplaced eye patch, a chiseled, tan-from-a-can hunk stretched supine on the golden sands of a tropical beach. A three-masted ship topped by a skull-and-cross bones flag rode at anchor in the sparkling waters beyond. From the rigging, a crew of laughing, butt-naked sailors dangled. Literally. To the hunk's left, a battered treasure chest overflowed with scary-looking sex gizmos that, while not exactly in keeping with the theme, were at least of an adventurous nature.

I dropped the magazine onto Lisa's desk before my blush could spontaneously combust it. "That's not mine!" I said.

"Is too."

"Is *not*. Why would you even say that?"

She flipped the mag over, pointing to the white mailing label addressed with my name. Violet Whittaker, it said. Well, damn.

"You're kidding me."

"Hey, look at this one." Lisa pointed a pearly pink nail at the pirate standing aloft in the crow's nest. "Doesn't he look like Marshall?"

Drawn like a perverted magnet, I peered closer. "I should *be* so lucky," I thought.

"What?" Lisa asked.

"What? Nothing. I didn't say anything."

She looked at me with a funny grin, then slid the magazine into her top drawer as Marshall walked in. I fled down the hall, not able to meet his eyes, but unable to keep from hearing Lisa's "Ahoy, matey!" greeting.

I was still fluctuating between guilty embarrassment and hilarity that afternoon when Marshall called an unscheduled

118

staff meeting. We tromped into the group therapy room, and I grabbed a seat in the back. A tripod with poster paper had been set up in the front. Marshall stood next to it, a mini-frown creasing his forehead. Lisa leaned over to whisper, "The poop is about to become airborne."

"What?" I whispered back.

"Wait for it."

Marshall started the meeting by asking if there had been any additional fall out with our clients from the "incident" two weeks ago. A few patients had canceled and—except for my clowns—there was a drop in first-time appointments, but it was difficult to say if there was a direct connection to Wayne's blitz attack. For the most part, people were proving unexpectedly resilient or completely oblivious to the situation.

After a pause in the discussion, Marshall cleared his throat and ran his hand through his hair. Signal for a controversial topic.

"OK, folks. One of the things I've been talking to corporate about is our security situation."

"You mean, lack of!" Regina stage-whispered. Next to her, Bob snorted agreement.

Instead of ignoring their comments as he usually did, Marshall chose to respond. Unlike the rest of us, he displayed no embarrassment addressing Regina by her female-body-part name. In fact, he smiled every time.

"Exactly, Regina. Thank you. I'm sure none of us is comfortable with the situation, especially since Letty's experiencing continued harassment. Since we don't want any repetition of violence, we need to take a look at what can be done internally to promote security."

"What do you mean 'internally'?" Hannah asked.

"He means without having to beg for money from corporate," Regina said.

"Mmm… pretty much." Marshall admitted. "Let's face it. There *are* things we can do on our own that will help.

119

Meanwhile, I will continue lobbying for a better security system, something with a panic button and a hookup to the police. Any suggestions are welcome, but, remember, these things can be very pricey. At any rate, this afternoon I'm looking for solutions that we can implement today, without having to beg corporate, as Regina so astutely pointed out."

Having maneuvered his nemesis into the role of ally rather than the negative pain-in-the-butt she really was, Marshall tossed her a wink. From the look on her face, I wouldn't be surprised if she sued him for sexual discrimination. Or chopped him up into itty-bitty pieces and threw him into the Chippewa River. No sense of humor, that woman.

While I pondered Regina's potential for mutilation, Marshall flipped the pages on the tripod. A schematic of the staff parking lot was drawn out in black magic marker. Most of the diagrammed slots indicating staff parking ran along the back fence facing the clinic entrance, leaving the majority of parking spaces open for clients. About a half-dozen squares, however, were clustered around various light posts with the nearest two situated one row back, directly opposite the front doors. My name, in red marker, was centered in the square nearest the clinic's main entrance; Marshall's, in the adjacent. I could feel the burn coming off Regina from four chairs away.

"On what basis were the parking assignments made?" Bob's pompous tone broke through the silence.

"On the basis of safety, of course. What else?" Marshall fake-smiled. "And I want to thank everyone in advance for their cooperation. In fact, I was hoping that perhaps our resident expert in feminist psychology might be persuaded to give a presentation on self-defense strategies at our next staff meeting. Regina?"

Regina's face was a study in conflict. She wanted to raise a stink about the parking assignments but couldn't without sounding ridiculous and petty. Meeting Marshall's "innocent" eyes, she offered a Mona Lisa smile and a faint nod. Bob

120

harrumphed and started to object, but Regina placed a hand on his sleeve, silencing him. They'd been out-maneuvered; they would withdraw with dignity.

The meeting ended soon after. Regina and Bob led the charge for the door, while I hung back, feeling awkward. I wanted to thank Marshall but didn't want to fuel the rumor mills by having a private discussion. After being his designated driver and now getting what some would see as preferential treatment, I knew that there would be speculation—most joking, but some not—on whether I'd slept my way to a parking spot. I'd like to think most of my co-workers would know that I wasn't *that* cheap, but some people liked to think the worst. Sad to say, I worried less about the insult to my virtue than about the presumed, bargain-basement value assigned for it.

Luckily, Lisa stayed behind to gather the poster board and other materials. She'd not only serve as a chaperone, but would spread the exchange around the office like butter on hot toast.

"Marshall," I said. "I appreciate your new safety policy, but as soon as this thing with Wayne is settled, I would expect to have the parking spaces reassigned. After all, I don't have seniority or anything."

I became conscious of my lips, possibly because Marshall was staring at them. They were dry. A perverse urge to lick them almost drove me to distraction. Would he think it was a come-on? Would Lisa? Was there a way of demonstrating the innocence of dry lips without looking infinitely stupid?

Yes, yes, and not a chance.

Marshall's smile crinkled his eyes. "Of course. This is just a temporary measure."

Lisa, nose-deep in our conversation, dropped the set of markers, sending them skittering across the floor. "Damn."

"OK, then." I said, easing toward the door. I could feel cracks fissuring across my lips. "But thanks, though."

"My pleasure," he said and winked at me, alligator lips and all.

CHAPTER NINTEEN

Tuesday officially started when I pulled into the highly coveted, close-to-the-front-door parking space. It was the last nice thing to happen all day.

Lisa greeted me with a stack of mail and another magazine subscription as soon as I walked in the door. This one featured a parody of an all-grown-up Heidi, breasts mimicking the mighty Alps she frolicked across, being chased by a herd of wild "goats." A half-dozen men with fake horns and swatches of goat hair leaped after her in (apparently) full-rut. A second glance made me realize it wasn't horns plastered to their foreheads. Eww. Swearing off cashmere for life, I dropped it in the trash.

Before I could check my schedule, the phone rang. Standing next to Lisa's desk while she rescheduled the caller, I flipped through the real mail. Most was junk— circulars for continuing education training and an interoffice memo that I'd already read. I almost tossed them on top of the porn mag, until one near the bottom caught my attention. The return address read: Department of Regulation and Licensing.

I'd already paid the yearly fee for license renewal a few months ago. Hoping there hadn't been an oversight, I slit the envelope and read the enclosed notice.

My heart pumped wildly, sweat beading on my forehead.

"Letty?" Lisa's worried voice pierced the drumming in my ears. I looked at her, blankly. Her concern had driven her to her feet; she clutched my arm. "Letty, are you all right?"

"I need to see Marshall."

"I'll see what's available." She sat down at the computer to check his calendar, but I was already heading down the hall to his office.

He jumped when I banged through the door. "What's wrong?"

Fighting tears, I handed him the letter. He scanned it quickly, then sat back, looking strained.

"Can he do this?" My voice rasped like sandpaper.

Marshall shrugged. "He already has. Look, Letty... We know this is bogus, and so will the department as soon as they dig a little deeper."

"Dig a little *deeper*? What does that mean?"

"It means they're going to need access to your client file on Wayne, or whatever he called himself at the time. You'll have to send in your response to these allegations of sexual misconduct. Plus, they'll need to get the police report on the break-in incident. But that's all in your favor. He was obviously seeing you under false pretenses and there were only two sessions. Not to mention, we have the picture I took of the rat."

"We can't prove that Wayne had anything to do with the rat," I pointed out.

"No, but we can prove that a number of mysterious incidents have occurred since he busted in and threatened you. It shows a pattern of harassment, even if it's coincidental."

"Mary Kate is a witness, too."

Marshall looked confused. "To what?"

"She sat in the last time I met with Carrie. She can testify that I told Carrie about Wayne's allegations."

"Unfortunately, she can't, even if it concerns Wayne. We have no right to breach Carrie's confidentiality. Unless she agrees to waive it, that is. Would she be willing?"

"I don't even know where Carrie is. But at least Mary Kate can testify to what she heard when Wayne was holding me at knife-point! She can say that he never once mentioned any sexual contact, because there *wasn't* any. It was all about Carrie, and how Wayne thought—"

"Whoa, whoa, whoa!" Marshall held a hand up and abruptly sat forward. "She heard *what?*"

Oh, yeah.

I'd neglected to mention Mary Kate's eavesdropping behavior. It took a few minutes to explain how Mary Kate had snuck back to Regina's office to satisfy her curiosity—or prepare my eulogy, whichever came first. By the time I'd finished, Marshall had his head buried in his hands, groaning.

"That's bad, huh?" As an attempt at levity, it failed.

"Why haven't I heard about this until now?"

"Well, I had a few things on my mind, Marshall." Defensive *and* sarcastic—not attractive.

Marshall gave an exasperated sigh. "Letty—"

"Wait!" My turn to raise a STOP hand. "I'm sorry. You're right. I should have told you, and I should have addressed it in more detail with Mary Kate. I just ... I guess with everything going on, I dropped the ball."

He squinched his eyes, pinching the bridge of his nose. "I can't say that I blame you. We just need to figure out where to go from here."

We sat in silence for a few minutes. I wasn't sure what exactly needed to be figured out, but I was willing to turn the problem over to him. My mind was on overload from Alpine pornography and Wayne's latest sneak attack.

"OK, here's what I'm going to do," Marshall eventually said. "I'm going to reassign Mary Kate to Regina. If anyone can teach her about boundaries, it's Regina.

"And, for you—I think we need to increase your supervision for the duration of Wayne's acting out. What do you think?" His eyes smiled into mine.

Talk about boundaries. I couldn't meet regularly to discuss my clients' treatment progress with a guy I was having naughty lumberjack fantasies about. Damn that flannel jacket. Ever decisive, I broached the issue.

"Umm…"

"I know you enjoy working with Mary Kate, but—"

"No, it's not that. I mean, I do enjoy working with Mary Kate, but I understand. Her internship's almost over anyway. I'm not sure I'd assign her to Regina, but that's up to you."

"Then what's bothering you?"

I gave myself a mini-pep talk. I was a professional. I was a therapist, experienced in dealing with tense and embarrassing subjects. I was a *grown-up*, for pity's sake. Took a deep breath…

"I think it would be better if I met with someone else. Someone… not you."

A flash of something—irritation? Hurt?—crossed his face, but too quickly for me to identify. I braced for an argument.

A knock at the door interrupted, and Lisa poked her head in. My mind skittered back to the day after Wayne's attack when Marshall and I had shared that intense is-he-going-to-kiss-me? moment and only Lisa's entrance had stopped us from answering that question. Remembering, and not wanting to know if Marshall was also, I kept my eyes glued to Lisa.

"Letty, your first appointment is here."

"I'll just be a moment."

Lisa grinned as she shut the door. When I turned back to Marshall, his expression had softened, leading me to believe that he'd had his own déjà vu moment.

"Maybe it *would* be good for you to meet with someone 'not me.'" He crooked an eyebrow. "But it would need to be someone with a bit more experience than Carol or Hannah."

"Not Regina." That got a smile. An evil one. "You're already assigning Mary Kate to her; we don't want Regina overburdened! She's cranky enough as it is."

126

"That's true." He rocked back in his chair, steepling his hands before his face. He still smiled.

"I suppose," he drawled, "we'll have to assign Mary Kate to Hannah. They should do well together. And that will free up Regina for you."

"Oh goody," I said. All he did was laugh.

I spent the next fifty minutes trying to concentrate on Hillary, a married homemaker certain her husband was cheating on her but who couldn't decide whether to hire a private detective and a divorce attorney or even things up by having a fling with her son's band instructor. I'd met her husband and secretly rooted for the PI/attorney combo, but I didn't think Hill was ready for a showdown. Plus, she really had the hots for her band boy toy.

Unfortunately, her sense of helplessness was contagious. My thoughts kept circling back to Wayne's latest ploy. Once again, he'd managed to strike at the heart of my life. My own sobriety came about when my work was threatened. I'd never, *ever* had a complaint filed, and the fact that it was entirely baseless didn't lesson my shame. In fact, it made it harder to accept.

I made it through the rest of the day, but I wasn't proud of the work I did. Mostly I nodded and said "uh-huh" a lot, while clients shared their innermost concerns. Nobody noticed my inattention, which was also discouraging.

I needed a meeting.

As soon as I said good-bye to the last client, I took off for the HP & Me club. Twenty minutes later, crossing the parking lot, I found myself scanning the shadows, alert for a menacing presence.

Relief washed over me as soon as I entered the doors. My shoulders dropped at least an inch, as shoulder and neck muscles unclenched. Felt good; felt like home.

Taking note of the regulars and waving at a few friends, I crossed to the coffee counter, plucked my mug from the wall and poured a cup. The meeting didn't start for another fifteen minutes, so I joined the group clustered under the TV. I plopped down on the couch, joined moments later by Paul. To avoid talking, I tuned into the ongoing argument about whether or not the contestant on *Wheel of Fortune* was stupid to buy a vowel. Recovery folk are frugal with vowels, so the general consensus was yes.

A few minutes before start time, people started making their way to the meeting room. I hung back. I was pretty sure I knew the word for the "Before & After" clue and a bonus prize hung in the balance. The contestant had that I-bit-tin foil-with-my-filling look that didn't bode well for her.

"Hello, sweetheart."

Hot coffee scorched my hand, slopping into my lap. Wayne stood next to the couch, smiling down at me. I leapt to my feet.

"What are you doing here?" Fear contracted my voice into a thin, squeaky whisper. Paul, seated on the couch, looked simultaneously scared and fascinated.

"Well, you know after our little misunderstanding, I realized I needed help. I've been sober four days now. Aren't you proud of me?"

I'd seen him in many moods—shy and polite during our two phony therapy sessions, drunk and raging, and, of course, threatening. This playfully flirtatious approach was incomprehensible, until I realized it wasn't for me. He was performing for Paul and the few stragglers in the lobby, his audience.

"It wasn't a 'misunderstanding.' It was assault." From the corner of my eye, I saw Paul frown. "And since your harassment has progressed to a fraudulent complaint to the licensing board, my lawyers have advised me to have no contact with you." Sounded good anyway.

His eyes narrowed, not at all pleased with my assertiveness. He liked fear better. He fed on it.

"Then I guess you'll have to leave," he said.

"I'm not leaving. *You* are. I'm getting a restraining order against you. I've been documenting your harassment, and, don't forget, there are witnesses. Anyway, I've been coming here since..." My voice trailed off. I didn't want to get into details with this asshole. Besides, he was smiling again.

"I *can't* leave," he said in a sing-song. He leaned into my face. His breath stunk. "My sponsor wants me doing ninety meetings in ninety days. Plus—thanks to you!—I've been court-ordered to attend AA. I need *help*. Remember?"

"Nobody doubts that. Which will make getting a restraining order even easier."

"Sure, why not? You go to the court commissioner and explain how you need to come to AA, too. 'Cause you're a *drunk*. I think it's a great idea to make that part of public record. Then I can add *that* to my complaint. That'll make real good reading for the licensing board."

My heart pounded so hard my ribs ached. "I'm *not* going to tell you where Carrie is. You might as well—"

"Carrie? I don't give a shit about Carrie. You want to know where she is?"

"You're saying you know?"

He scoffed. "Carrie's not important anymore. That's settled."

"Then why are you *doing* this?"

He smiled again, spreading his arms wide. "Because I need help!"

Separated by inches, our eyes locked. I felt like I was staring down a cobra. *If I blinked...*

Behind me, a slight form moved and suddenly Paul was at my side. "Letty?" his voice quavered. Wayne broke eye contact to glare at the intrusion. "The meeting's started. Sh...shouldn't you...?"

Wayne laughed in Paul's earnest face. "My, my. You do get around, don't you, sweetheart? You might want to get this one some vitamins." He poked Paul in the chest. Hard. Paul paled but stood his ground.

A chair scraped back. One of the regulars stood. Harry was at least seventy, a grizzled and flabby retired truck driver, but, unlike Paul, he had dealt with a few bullies in his day. And had fun doing it.

Wayne raised his hands in mock surrender, laughing again. "No worries, old-timer. Just a little lovers' spat. I got to get in to my meeting anyway. Don't want to upset the judge, do I?" As he turned to leave, he blew me a kiss. Made my flesh crawl.

I sank to the couch as Wayne sauntered into the meeting. Paul sat next to me, rubbing his sore chest with one hand and awkwardly patting my shoulder with the other. Harry stomped over.

"You okay?" Harry growled. Harry lived in fear of being thought soft, and except with newcomers, worked hard at being an ass. He was outspoken, nasty, and sexist. It was all fake. I reached up and held his gnarled hand.

"Thank you."

He grunted, squeezed once, gently, then tossed my hand loose and stalked back to his chair.

I turned to Paul. "Thank you, too." My smile raised a blush and a stutter.

"I ... I ... didn't ... I mean, okay." He rubbed his sore spot hard enough to raise a blister.

"Look, I really appreciate what you did. But... um... I'm going to get out of here now."

"I know. I should go, too." He eyed the closed meeting room door. "But I'm not going to let him push me around. He doesn't scare me."

Right.

"Just be careful, Paul. He's not a nice guy."

CHAPTER TWENTY

There were things I should have asked. I realized that later as I cuddled with Siggy on the couch. Ever since I'd gotten home, I'd been replaying the scene over and over again—something I caution my clients against, but unable, as usual, to take my own advice. Like scab-picking, I poked and scratched at Wayne's intrusion into the club. AA was more than just a place to learn how to stay sober—it was both my sanctuary and my deepest secret. Heaven and hell. The violation was total.

He knew I'd never pursue a restraining order if there was a chance my alcoholism might be outed. Yet I couldn't risk my sobriety by avoiding meetings. I couldn't get rid of him and couldn't stay away from him, either.

And what did Wayne mean when he'd said Carrie was "not important anymore?" Did that mean he had found her? Was she okay? Carrie hadn't told me where she was going, but she *had* told me that her mother knew. A woman tough enough to scare Wayne? The thought filled me with awe. I'd have to check Carrie's file to see if her mother had been listed as an emergency contact. On the other hand, did I have an ethical right to contact her even if she was? As Marshall had pointed out, Wayne's right to confidentiality was nullified, at least as the investigation went, but Carrie's hadn't been. I batted the issue back and forth and decided to bounce the conflict off Regina when we met for supervision.

Something else bothered me, but it danced just out of reach, a mental vapor that evaporated on contact. It wasn't until I woke the next morning that it solidified.

Four days. Wayne said he'd been sober four days, which would be Friday night. The night I was Marshall's designated driver. The night Robert picked up a newbie to sponsor.

Even though I'd left an urgent message, I wasn't sure if Robert would return my call. As the day passed, I became more certain that he wouldn't, and was pleasantly surprised when his number popped up on my cell's Caller ID. Pleasant didn't last.

"What?" he said in greeting.

I took a deep breath, mentally deleting sarcasm from my repertoire, and gritted my teeth. "Thanks for getting back to me. Listen, I was wondering… You mentioned that you agreed to sponsor a new guy?"

I paused, but he declined to fill in the blank. He was still there, though; I could hear his breath puffing against the receiver.

"What's his name?" I'd planned to use more finesse, but puffy breathing annoyed the hell out of me.

"Oh, now you want to know? I thought you didn't give a shit about my sponsoring somebody?"

True. I didn't. But this wasn't the time to point that out. "I just need to know if it's a guy named Wayne. Big guy, dirty blond hair cut short."

"No, his name is Randy. And I don't have time for your—"

"No, it's not," I interrupted.

"What the hell do you know? You've never even met the guy!"

"No, I mean that Wayne called himself 'Randy' before he attacked me. I think you're sponsoring the guy who's been stalking me!"

The silence lasted long enough to get my hopes up. Silly me.

"What do you want from me? The guy says his name is Randy. If it's not, maybe he's trying to keep a low profile while all this stuff with you gets straightened out."

"*Straightened out?* Are you kidding me?"

"There's two sides to every story, Letty. You know that. If even half of what you're accusing him of is true, he still needs a sponsor. Randy's been court-ordered to AA and he's getting an alcohol and drug assessment, so maybe he's trying to turn himself around."

"His name isn't Randy! You obviously don't understand what he's been doing to me. He even stuck a dead rat in my car."

"Well, why don't I understand? Huh? Isn't that the point of all this? You kept me in the dark for weeks, and now you expect me to fix your problems for you?"

"The *point* is that you are sponsoring a violent, abusive woman-hater who's been attacking a ... a fellow AA member, a friend of yours."

"*Former* friend. What can I tell you, Letty? Women can make a guy crazy." And then the bastard hung up.

I looked forward to my Wednesday night meeting, the one place Wayne couldn't infiltrate unless he came in drag or had a sex change. Actually, if he did crash the party, most of the women would happily use his penis as a piñata. Another perk about women's meetings is that you can always find a man-hater when you need one. Since the meetings in April were at Rhonda's house, the service was built in. Plus, I had plenty of friends willing to jump on the bashing-wagon now that I'd broken up with Robert.

Unfortunately, Sue and Charlie soon forced us back on track, redirecting the focus to issues of sobriety. When my turn came around, I started with some of the concerns that had been raised when Sue and I spoke.

"One of the things that prolonged my drinking was the illusion of control that I clung to. I just couldn't admit that alcohol had control of me instead of vice versa. Like, being possessed by an evil spirit. Pun intended," I added.

"When Sue and I talked this week, I realized that my whole family does this and always has. And not just about alcohol." Around the room, women nodded, smiling softly, feeling their way through my words to their own truths. "We did it when my dad died. There's this whole *myth* about what really happened, and nobody speaks of it to this day. I don't even know if my brother and sister remember what really happened or if they've started believing the lie. I know Ma has. She's still claims the cops killed him.

"She's spent her whole life hating and blaming the cops for my dad's death, and teaching us to do the same. But they didn't do it. *He* did. He choked to death on his own vomit. The jailers found him, but they couldn't revive him.

"All these years later, and we still don't talk about it. I feel strange even now, here, with you all. Nobody is allowed—or ever was—to admit Dad died from booze. That he was an alcoholic.

"That's why they all ignore my getting sober. Sloppy drunk, falling-down drunk, is perfectly acceptable, but call myself an alcoholic? No way. They change the subject, won't even look at me when I try to tell them what it means to me. It's, like, this family legacy of secrets. Never admit you're scared. Never look at how crazy your life is. Never be... *weak*.

"That's what I've been doing with this harassment thing— pretending I'm not scared or that I'm in control of it. Now he's taken over my AA club. This meeting is the only place I can come without wondering if he's going to pop out at me like Freddy Krueger."

Suddenly exhausted, I passed to the next woman, which happened to be Charlie. After the traditional AA introduction, she said, "A family legacy of secrets? That's the alcoholic way, that's for sure! But it's good that you're looking at it. You might want to check out some ACOA meetings."

Trinnie, our newbie, looked confused.

"Adult Children of Alcoholics," Charlie explained.

"I'd have to go to the club," I objected. "I can't take that chance."

"I have an idea for that," Rhonda cut in. "I'll bring it up after the meeting."

The women continued, each taking her turn talking about life, sobriety, day-to-day hassles. As I listened, a sense of calm settled over me. It was this feeling of belonging to a group of people who, no matter how different we were, understood the worst about me and accepted it. That's what I couldn't stand losing, couldn't survive without.

Rhonda, my newly appointed guardian angel, had decided that wasn't going to happen.

"No man is going to keep you from anything. It'll just take a little extra planning, that's all." Her emphasis on "man" turned it into an obscenity. Given her animosity to the male gender, I wouldn't have been surprised to hear something about "Guida the Enforcer" and a "little accident."

"If we know when you plan to attend a meeting, one of us will just go with you. Bullies don't like witnesses, and the key is that you will never be alone. Simple."

It was simple, but my instinctive response was to decline. Sue, anticipating my reaction, chimed in.

"Rhonda's right. You've been thinking about this too narrowly. You don't have to do this alone and you're not going to isolate yourself. It's not too much trouble. You're not imposing. It doesn't mean you're weak."

She nailed it. I took a deep breath. As much as I hated having my friends rearrange their lives around my schedule, I gave in. Together, we figured out my meetings schedule for the week ahead—a process both humiliating and gratifying—before I took off for home.

CHAPTER TWENTY-ONE

When I got to the office Thursday morning, Lisa greeted me with a copy of *Big Boobed Babes* and the news that Mary Kate had met with Marshall to discuss her transfer to Hannah and was currently locked in her office crying. I tossed *Boobs* in the trash.

"She's upset?"

Lisa's eyebrows gave a "my, aren't you clever" twitch. "I'm guessing separation issues. Hannah will have to work with her on that." After years of typing our reports and transcribing our meetings, Lisa's grasp of psych theory rivaled anyone's.

"Maybe I should go talk to her."

"Uh-huh," Lisa mumbled on her way to the file room. Message delivered, she'd already moved on to the next task. As long as Mary Kate didn't interfere with Lisa's schedule, she could stay in her office until next Christmas.

I sighed and set off. As I passed Marshall's office, I peeked in. He was on the phone and gave me a little wave. I pointed down the hall at Mary Kate's closed door and mouthed "thanks a lot!" He shrugged, waggling his eyebrows at me. Not helpful, but it scored high on the cuteness scale.

I trudged on.

It took fifteen minutes to get Mary Kate to unlock her door, which was fourteen and a half minutes past ridiculous. If I'd had an axe, I'd have used it.

I felt a little more sympathy, however, when she finally let me in. Her eyes were red and swollen, her nose a puffy lump of misery. You'd think a mental health clinic would spring for a better quality tissue; ours were more effective as nose exfoliaters than as an absorbent for the liquidy stuff currently streaming down Mary Kate's face.

"Oh, Mary Kate," I said, shaking my head gently. "You have got yourself all worked up, haven't you?"

"I know I'm being stupid," she said. At least that's what I thought she said. It was a bit difficult to interpret since her sobs convulsed in those hiccup-gasps that my Grandma used to call the "huff-n-puffs."

I sat down in the client chair. Her space was much more sparsely furnished, given that it was a temporary office shared by the two or three interns who rotated through the clinic for their practicum each semester. The bookshelf held a half-dozen dusty psychology texts with USED labels slapped on the spines. A calendar, thumbtacked above the scratched desk, displayed the office hours of each intern. I realized that Mary Kate showed up at the office far more often than her ten hours of clinical practicum dictated.

Something else I'd missed.

"I'm sorry," she said, touching my arm and regaining my attention.

"Nothing to be sorry for, Mary Kate. I'm the one who should apologize. I didn't realize you would take this so hard. I just wish I'd been the one to let you know."

"I know I'm being silly, but I just don't want to start over with someone else. I've got finals coming up, and there's only a few weeks left of the internship anyway. Pretty soon I'm going to have to say good-bye to all my clients and that's hard enough.

Couldn't we just leave it that you'll be my supervisor? I promise I won't be a bother. We could even cut back on meeting every week, if that helps."

"With all the stress of finals and beginning the termination process with your clients, that's exactly what you can't do." Mary Kate winced at my use of the clinical phrase: termination. It *did* sound more like a Mafia expression than the professional lingo for ending a therapeutic relationship. "As you can see from your own reaction, this can be an emotionally charged experience. Separations bring up a lot of feelings for us as well as for our clients. Even for those who are ready—and I believe you are—it can stir up a lot of issues." Okay, I lied a little about thinking Mary Kate was ready, but Hannah was an excellent clinician and I'd give her the background.

"I've always hated endings," Mary Kate's chair squeaked as she leaned back. She kept her eyes on the carpet. "I was a Navy brat and we were always leaving friends when we moved to the next base. And I really don't want to screw up this internship. I've tried a lot of different things in my life—jobs, I mean—and I finally know what I want to be when I grow up." She smiled wanly.

Given her age, I knew she'd come to counseling the long way around. She'd previously admitted to changing her major five times. Mary Kate reminded me of the lost souls who used to wander around Europe trying to "find themselves." I could relate. I'd done my own kind of wandering.

Meanwhile, she sat looking up at me with big, drippy eyes. I felt like I was kicking a puppy. A sick, sad, lonely, orphaned, blind puppy. With fleas. We talked for another twenty minutes while I tried to convince her to see some of the advantages in the change. Among other things, she would get the benefit of a different professional perspective, a counselor-supervisor with a different set of skills, and she wouldn't have to worry about crazed, knife-wielding ex-clients crashing through the door during their meetings. While she never did seem fully convinced, she eventually resigned herself to its inevitability. At least she stopped crying, which was good enough for now. Besides, I had clients waiting.

When I got home that night, the phone was ringing. Not thinking, I snatched it up before checking the Caller I.D. I regretted my impulsivity even before hearing the strange male voice on the other end.

"Letty? Hi! Wow, I didn't think you'd answer. Cool!"

"Paul?"

"Yeah. Listen, I didn't see you tonight so I wanted to let you know that the coast is clear. You know? Like, if you wanted to come to a meeting. You don't have to worry—it's cool."

The disconnect between my ability to understand why I was talking to Paul, who as I far as I knew shouldn't even have my number, and his secret agent lingo made me hesitate a long moment.

"Hello?" Paul ventured.

"I went to a meeting last night. How did you get my number?"

"You did? Where at? Did you go to the one at the Methodist church? I thought that was on Thursdays."

"It is on Thursdays. I went to my women's group. We meet at each other's houses."

"Aw, that sounds cool. I wish the guys did that."

Actually, they did, but no one would tell Paul. I interrupted him as he started a rambling monologue about the meeting he'd just attended. "Paul? How did you get my number?"

Although I hadn't yet arranged for an unlisted number, Paul shouldn't have been able to look it up for the simple reason that he shouldn't know my last name. And even though he had driven me home one time, I'd made sure to have him drop me a few blocks over. If someone at the club was giving out my number, I wanted to know.

"Oh, I asked around. It wasn't easy, either." His voice projected pride in his sleuthing. "I didn't want you to stay away from the club just because of that guy. He's such a jerk. So I figured I'd come check it out and let you know it was all clear."

"You mean you went to the club even though you might run into Wayne?" I was kind of impressed. Still creeped out, but impressed.

"Yeah, well, I got here early and waited across the street to see if he went in. What did you say his name is?"

"Wayne, but he's calling himself Randy. Just... be careful, Paul. And you don't have to keep watch for me." Or call me. Ever. "The girls and I have come up with a plan so I can still make meetings and not have to worry about Wayne."

"Yeah, I have an idea, too. I just got a few things to check out first. But, listen, the other reason why I called? I was wondering if you maybe wanted to get something to eat sometime? Or coffee? With me?"

I should've seen it coming.

"Gee, thanks, Paul. But we're not supposed to date in the first year. No major changes, remember? And you've only been sober a couple weeks."

"Thirty-one days. You went out with Robert, didn't you?"

"And look how that turned out," I said. "I really need to focus on the program, and so do you. Things are just too crazy right now."

"Oh. Okay. I understand. Well, I'll see you at the club anyway. Right?"

"Sure. Hey, Paul, where did—"

"Well, okay then. I better call it a night. I'll see you soon. Be careful!"

"Paul?" I said to air. He'd hung up before I could continue my push for how he'd gotten my number. Whether that was calculated on his part or just another example of his social ineptitude, I couldn't tell. Didn't matter though; I'd corner him

140

face-to-face and get the answer I wanted. I resigned myself to getting an unlisted number the next day.

Several clients canceled on Friday, leaving me with a lot of down time. I pretended to file. What I really needed to do was call the phone company. Not to mention documenting everything that had been going on in order to make a police report. Every time I sat at my desk, however, my mind skittered away. I played lots of mind-numbing computer solitaire while subconsciously listening for footsteps of crazy men coming for me. *Man.* Eventually, I forced myself to document all of the recent nastiness.

First, I worked out the time line of his harassment. Although technically Wayne didn't attack me until March 11th, I included the dates of the two sessions we'd had under his false name.

February 19 and March 4 – phony counseling sessions
March 11 – Wayne, drunk, attacks in office
March 14 – Flowers delivered
March 15 – confrontation/threatens in work parking lot
March 20 and 21 – tires flattened
March 21 – followed to AA parking lot
March 24 – clown calls
March 28 – panties delivered and utilities tampered with
March 29 – rat in glove box
April 1 – fraudulent letter of complaint to state licensing board
Various phone call hang ups—undocumented
Porno mags arrived at the clinic sometime near the end of March

Depressing. Very, very depressing. And frightening when seen in its entirety. Since I was already immersed in the overwhelming evidence of my helplessness, I decided to address the licensing complaint. The time line came in handy, although I would have to delete the reference to AA before Marshall reviewed it and before sending it off to the state licensing board.

If I wasn't careful, I would prove my innocence of sexual impropriety while simultaneously outing myself as an alcoholic. The licensing board likes to keep tabs on little stuff like that, and I hadn't exactly updated them on my "condition."

Another problem that became blaringly apparent was the lack of any real evidence. Other than the sessions under a false name and the initial attack, the rest was just assumptions or my word against his. Not only that, but my avoidance of reporting the other events to the police looked suspicious.

Enough. Time for an AA meeting.

By the time Rhonda pulled up next to my little Focus, I was a bundle of raw nerves. Not only would I be facing Wayne, but I would be seeing Robert for the first time since breaking up.

Rhonda, on the other hand, was in her element. She stuck to me like dog poop in shoe tread and was about as offensive. She entered the club glaring at each man in turn, while I smiled meekly and sent little apology shrugs in her wake. There wasn't a man in the club who wasn't painfully aware of Rhonda's hater stance, and they fled before us.

As I expected, Robert and Wayne were there, but not surprisingly, neither made any attempt to approach. They stood in a huddle talking with Chad and a few others by the coffee bar. Robert cast a few carefully casual glances my way, but mostly kept his back turned. Wayne's expression was a slap-worthy smirk, but he, too, kept his distance. I caught Chad's eye once, relieved to see him smile and wink.

Already exhausted by the time we filed into the meeting, I passed when my turn came to talk. Though I tuned out during Robert's talk, I had to grit my teeth to keep from bursting out when Wayne spoke. He pretended to direct his words to the various other members, but with the sensitivity of a hunted rabbit, I sensed his attention was for me and me alone. He spoke with smarmy, false sincerity about changing his ways, about his love for his woman that would help him stay straight, and about how grateful he was that he could count on all his new friends to help him through his troubles.

After the meeting Rhonda needed to talk to a friend of hers for a minute, so by the time we got out to the lobby area, it was a man-free zone. Rhonda, a canister of *Slap My Ass And Call Me Sally* pepper spray clutched and eagerly ready for use on anyone with a penis, walked me to my car. Nevertheless, I strongly suspected she was disappointed when no one tried to mug us.

I thanked her, waiting until she started her own car, figuring she had at least as many enemies as I. Adventure over, we drove our separate ways.

Minutes later, I parked outside my apartment complex and made my way to the front. As I made my way up walked along the sidewalk, I envied Rhonda's pepper spray and decided to ask where she'd got it. And was it legal?

The back of my neck prickled as soon as I entered the lobby area. The light bulb at the top of the stairs had gone out, leaving the upper landing just outside my apartment in shadows. Adrenaline flipped the ON switch for my heart, racing blood through my body. *Fight or flight?*

I stood next to the main door wondering if I should call the police or rouse one of my neighbors. I'd feel stupid if it was just typical landlord miserliness, but I'd seen too many serial killer movies to discount my gut fear. I decided to climb halfway up the stairs, which would give me a sightline down the second floor hallway and still leave a safe exit if Wayne stood drooling in the shadows, clutching a chain saw. Fighting a nearly overwhelming need to pee, I moved forward, alternating between a stealthy crouch and the pee-pee dance.

The hallway was clear, but an object splotched with garish red dangled from the doorknob of my apartment. My mind registered it as blood, but a closer inspection showed a gift bag decorated in bright red Japanese anemones. A present?

I poked at the bag.

Some tissue shifted and a cloth doll with black button eyes peered up at me. Her face, round and sweet, peeped out from under a bonnet fashioned from an antique lace hankie. One arm rose out of the froth of tissue, waving.

I smiled. It really *was* a present. I reached to free her from the garish wrapping when my fingers closed around smooth metal. I gasped at a sharp pain. The bag dropped, spilling the contents to the floor.

Blood dripped from my ring finger, dotting the carpet and forming uneven blotches on the tissue paper. A fillet knife had been driven deep into her back, slicing through the rose-patterned dress, skewering a scrap of white paper to her tummy.

I wouldn't cry—part of me believed the bastard would somehow know, and I refused to give him that—but I couldn't stop the broken whimpers that slipped past gritted teeth. I nudged the doll over with my toe, kicking the tissue around, looking for more booby-traps. Apparently the bag had disclosed all its secrets—just the doll and the knife.

And the square of paper.

CHAPTER TWENTY-TWO

S ince it wasn't an emergency, it took the police an hour and a half to show up. While I waited, I bandaged my finger and took a picture of the knife and doll *in situ*. Not wanting my neighbors to trip over—or even see—the pile, I brought it all in to the kitchen table. I debated about 2.5 seconds before pulling the knife out and reading the note.

> *Being your flaue what fhould I doe but tend,*
> *Vpon the houres and times of your defire?*
> *I haue no precious time at al to fpend;*
> *Nor feruices to doe til you require.*

Whoa. I stopped after the first four lines. After a few moments of studying the scrawling calligraphy, I figured out that, yes, it really was English. Once I deciphered out that the letter "F" was an "S" and that "U" often meant "V," it made a wee bit more sense. I started over again.

> *"Being your slave, what should I do but tend*
> *Upon the hours and times of your desire?*
> *I have no precious time at all to spend*
> *Nor services to do 'til you require.*
> *Nor dare I chide the world-without-end hour*
> *Whilst I, my sovereign, watch the clock for you,*

Nor think the bitterness of absence sour
When you have bid your servant once adieu.
Nor dare I question with my jealous thought
Where you may be, or your affairs suppose,
But, like a sad slave, stay and think of nought
Save where you are how happy you make those.
So true a fool is love that in your will,
Though you do anything, he thinks no ill.

I copied it. I also took a few moments to delete all references on my time line to AA and just left "club." Let 'em think it was a health club. In a way, it was.

There wasn't a whole lot the police could do when they showed up, but I hadn't expected a whole CSI crew anyway. It was a different pair than had been by before; one older and fairly fit, the other a young, pre-obese rookie. They took the knife and sonnet to hold in case there were further developments but warned me that Chippewa Falls just didn't have the forensic resources to work up every case. Small town, small budget. However, if a "serious incident" occurred, it would help build the case. My finger throbbed in silent protest.

"Have you considered a restraining order?" Sgt. Durrant, the older cop, asked.

"I've considered it, but…" I shrugged helplessly.

"I know. There's not much a piece of paper can do, but it does give us a heads up when we respond to things like this." He held up the paper bag holding the knife. "For some creeps, an R.O. really is a deterrent."

"And sometimes it pisses the guy off even more," the slightly pudgy cop added. His partner gave him a dirty look. "I wasn't sure if I had enough for a restraining order, and the fact of the matter is"—I took a deep breath—"I'm in AA. I can't have that made public knowledge. It would really hurt me in my job." I swallowed with a suddenly dry throat. When I met the older cop's eyes, they were crinkled in a sun-weathered smile that made my stomach uncoil.

"I'm a friend of Bill W. myself," Sgt. Durrant said. Bill W., along with Dr. Bob, is a founder of AA; a reference to either is short-hand for a fellow Twelve Step member. "You don't have to mention it when you get the R.O."

"I know, but Wayne said that *he* would. I don't want to take that chance of him sending another letter to the state board. I just can't."

"I tell you what: we'll go talk to him. Sometimes that's enough, too."

Meanwhile, Pudgy was trying to decipher the poem, a confused look on his face. "Is this a code?"

"No, it's just an old-style font, I think." I explained about the F's and U's.

"Is that on purpose?" he asked. "You know, like, F U?" His partner rolled his eyes and sighed.

"I... uh... didn't think about it that way. I suppose it could. I think it's more likely from the Renaissance period or something."

"Well, I don't get it. It don't make sense," Pudgy said.

Changing the subject, I held up the doll. "Are you taking this?"

"We probably couldn't get fingerprints off that even if we tried. We have the picture," he held up a copy I'd handed over. "I think this is enough. Unless you want us to?"

"No, I'll keep her." I was secretly pleased. Both the doll and I had suffered similar brutalities under Wayne's hands. I felt a curious—and embarrassing—affinity to her.

Before leaving, Durrant agreed to call me after he'd talked to Wayne. I spent the night on the couch, clutching the doll since Siggy, sensing my anxiety, kept his distance. When I woke in the morning, stiff-necked, the doll was damp from my tears and Siggy lay curled on my belly.

I lay there fretting about the police talking to Wayne. The smart-me knew it was way past due, but my childhood indoctrination of secrecy kept my stomach churning. Instead of feeling better about involving the police, I regretted the decision. Completely illogical, of course.

Sighing, I rolled off the couch, nearly squishing Siggy, and trudged to the desk. The scanned copy of the FU-sonnet lay waiting. Jagged, black blotches defined where the knife had pierced the original, marring the clean, white spaces, top and bottom. A quick read-through of the text made my head hurt. I needed coffee.

Reading it outloud helped, too. While the exact meaning remained fuzzy, themes began to emerge. Slavery, jealousy, bitterness, humiliation—all combined to deny the overt message of devotion.

I couldn't imagine Wayne writing it, but maybe that was snobbish of me. Even if someone else did write it, which seemed more likely, the choice of the particular sonnet meant something for Wayne. Maybe it symbolized his "love" for Carrie. An abuser often accuses his victim of willfully inciting his anger— hence "deserving" it— portraying himself as powerless to prevent the ensuing violence. *"Why are you so demanding?" "Why do you question everything I do?" "Why do you make me hit you?"* The sonnet seemed to echo the very questions that are screamed in a woman's face right before the fist connects.

I could see Wayne's twisted mind believing that watching a clock, monitoring his woman's movements and interactions, proved his devotion. But I continued to struggle with the notion that he would express himself in iambic pentameter. And yet, in our two therapy sessions together, I had thought him a sensitive, hurting introvert.

The *knife* sure fit. The blade alone was six inches long and thin as a razor blade. Wayne seemed like the type of outdoorsy guy who would gut his own fish. And like it.

The viciousness inflicted on the doll fit, too. I picked her up. The sweetness of her face contrasted sharply with the image of the blade slicing through her from back to belly. I'd been ripped apart, too. A stand-in for someone else, target of an undeserved anger, helpless against the striking fist.

Suddenly determined, I rose and began digging through my junk drawer, searching for needle and thread. Not much for sewing, I dug out white, black, and a strange neon-orange thread that I must have bought when I was drunk. Not satisfied, I went to my bedroom dresser, rooting around the bottom section of my jewelry case where I threw the extra buttons that came with new sweaters. Lots of buttons and several lone, one-of-a-pair earrings, but no thread.

The buttons gave me another idea. I rummaged through the back of my closet, unearthing the heavily embroidered sweater that my brother Neil had given me four Christmases ago. I was pretty sure he had stolen it, and I'd never felt comfortable wearing it. Covered in elaborate, swirly, pink roses, I figured I could scavenge enough thread.

Sitting cross-legged on the couch, trying not to stab myself with the sharp needle, I made two vows. First, no one would *ever* know that I had so identified with a child's toy that I was driven to repair the damage she'd suffered. I absolutely refused to consider what that meant about my own feelings of vulnerability and victimization.

And, second, that I'd named her Anna.

As I stitched, I brooded over the sonnet. The more I considered Wayne's warped perception of love, the more worried for Carrie I became. Wayne had said she was no longer important. It didn't take a master's degree to understand that stabbing Anna in the back, skewering the sonnet to her chest, probably *didn't* demonstrate Wayne's acceptance of the end of their relationship.

Coming to a decision, I called the office and discovered Mary Kate manning the front desk for Saturday's clients. I had her check Carrie's file for the emergency contact. As I suspected, Carrie had listed her mother's name and number. It took some effort to fend off Mary Kate's curiosity, but I managed.

Feeling clever, I remembered to dial *67 to prevent my number from coming up on Carrie's mom's Caller ID. If I got her voice mail, I planned to hang up. My heart started pounding as a woman's husky, smoker's voice said, "Hello?"

"Mrs. Torgenson?"

"Maybe. Who's this?"

"My name is Violet Whittaker. I've worked with your daughter Carrie in counseling. She listed you as her emergency contact. Some things have happened recently that make me concerned regarding her physical safety. I understand that you can't tell me her whereabouts, but do you know if she's okay?"

She snorted. "Her 'whereabouts' ain't a secret no more. As for if she's okay, I'd say 'yes,' but prob'ly not for long."

I let that sink in a minute. "She's back with Wayne?"

"She is. He's *sorry* this time. Buncha bullshit, if you ask me. I never raised her to take crap from anyone, so don't go and blame me. What makes you think she's in trouble?"

"Wayne's been causing trouble for me," I said. "At first, he was after me to find out where Carrie was, which I didn't know anyway. But now it seems more ... personal."

"Yeah, I saw the TV news. Now that he's got Carrie back, he's gonna concentrate on making you pay for running her off in the first place. By the way, you did good there. I wouldn't be talkin' to you if I wasn't happy about her cuttin' loose from him."

"Well, if she wants to, please have her call me at the clinic."

"Sure, but don't hold your breath. He's got her reined in tight all over again. Probably take another six years before she has enough. If she lives that long."

A click told me she'd hung up, but I'd learned what I needed to know. Carrie was no longer important to Wayne because he had her back under his thumb. I figured his continued harassment served two purposes—revenge toward me for daring to help Carrie and a message to her about what would happen to others if she turned to anyone else in the future.

The next call came in around noon. It was Durrant letting me know that they had met with Wayne at his house.

"Was he angry?" I asked. Stupid question, but it translated to: is he going to flip out over this, too?

"He tried to play it off, but, yeah, I'd say so. Of course, he claimed that it was all a big misunderstanding, but they all do that. Nothing new there. Tell you what, though. For what it's worth, my gut tells me he'll back off a bit. For a while, anyway. Now, you can't take that as a guarantee or anything, but he seems like he's got just enough instinct for self-preservation to know that he'd be stupid to keep it up. He must've thought he had your hands tied pretty well over the AA thing—in fact, he brought it up—so he was real surprised that you'd taken this to the next level."

"What should I do next?"

"You got my card. If anything else happens, call me directly and we'll see what we can do next. And, hey, maybe I'll stop in for a meeting or two. It's been a while for me; it couldn't hurt."

I smiled. "I, for one, would love to see you there. I'll save you a seat." And I'd love to see Wayne's face if Durrant walked in one night.

I spent the rest of the weekend doing laundry and feeling sorry for Carrie. I couldn't imagine what had led her back to Wayne after the long, difficult struggle to escape. I hoped she would contact me. Even if I couldn't work with her myself, I'd have liked to recommend someone else. Maybe even Regina, although I wasn't sure if my motivation was to enlist her expertise or to sic Wayne on *her* narrow butt. Mostly, I felt

151

CHAPTER TWENTY-THREE

I f I wanted proof that Wayne had my home phone number, I got it Sunday night. Carrie called around 10:30. *Pissed.*

"Why are you doing this?" She skipped a greeting, not waiting for an answer. "You have no right to bother my mother! And I can't believe you called the *police* on Wayne after everything he's been through. He was your client! Aren't you supposed to keep his privacy or something?"

"He saw me under a fake name so he could keep tabs on *you*, Carrie. I only involved the police as a last resort. I'm sorry if you're upset that I called your mother. I was concerned for your safety and you listed her as your emergency contact person."

"My safety is *my* business. I want you to stop harassing Wayne. He's got enough to deal with and he doesn't need you spreading lies about him, or following him, or messing with his truck."

"*What?* Carrie, you know better. I'm not harassing Wayne; *he's* harassing *me*! He's furious that I helped you. He wants to keep you—"

"No!" she interrupted. "He's changed. He's sober now. He promised to never get mad at me like that again."

"He didn't just get 'mad,' Carrie. He hurt you, and he'll do it again. I'm really glad that he's sober and that's a good first step, but he needs therapy. So do you. If you want, I can—"

"I don't want *anything* from you, except to leave us alone. Don't call my mother, don't call me, and stay away from Wayne. And if you touch his truck again, I'll call the cops on you myself."

Why did everyone hang up on me?

After the weekend, I figured Monday would only get worse, but it started out smoothly. My clients arrived on time, no sleazy magazines were delivered, and there was a delightful hint of spring softening the air.

I actually started relaxing until Hannah caught me between afternoon sessions. "Letty? Got a minute?"

She didn't look troubled, but then Hannah was one of those innately serene people who smile gently at life and adversity. Even her name was well-balanced. Naturally blond and clear-skinned, she was pretty enough to not wear makeup and had the kind of metabolism that let her eat donuts everyday. Not that she would. She was a nature freak, seeming to subsist on nuts and berries and fiber-y muffins that hurt my teeth to chew. If I didn't like her so much I would hate her.

"I understand Mary Kate is having a little trouble transferring to me?"

"She sure is. I've been meaning to talk to you."

"We set up three meetings last week, two of which she rescheduled, but she blew off the third. I've left messages; she doesn't call back. I'm tempted to pose as an AVON lady and ring her doorbell, but that seems a bit extreme."

I grimaced. "I'm sorry, Hannah. We talked about her resistance and I really thought she was on board with the change. She's coming up on finals and is under a lot of stress, but I think most of it has to do with family history. Navy brat and all that. You might want to keep an eye on her when she has to start the termination process with her own clients."

"Can't very well do that if she won't even meet with me. I hate to go through Marshall; it's such a fuss, and I don't want to cause her any trouble. Maybe you could try meeting with her again. She might just need more closure."

Blech. But Hannah was right. Mary Kate displayed textbook passive-resistance and it wouldn't do her—or her internship—any good if she didn't get back on track. On my next trip up to the front, I asked Lisa to set up another meeting with Mary Kate.

Mary Kate must have jumped at the chance, because she came in from home in order to see me after sessions. At first she claimed her massive workload and school stress prevented her from following through with Hannah. We shoveled through those excuses fairly quickly, however, circling back to her distress at transferring. Although it wasn't the best move legally, I finally told her about Wayne's complaint. As she started to express her indignation, I held up a hand.

"We can't talk about this! Anything you or I say now might become part of the investigation. In fact, you may end up being called in as a witness to what happened in my office that day. The only reason why I'm telling you now is so that you understand why I *have* to step aside as your supervisor. Not only is it inappropriate for me to mentor you while I'm under investigation, but there is a substantial conflict of interest. This is the last time we can talk about this. Do you understand?"

Eyes wide, she made a tick-a-lock gesture over her mouth, throwing the "key" over her shoulder.

"So you'll make an appointment with Hannah and *keep* it?" I pushed.

"I will. I'll do it right now. I'm just so relieved that it wasn't anything I did that made you want to transfer me."

"No. Definitely not. I've enjoyed working with you very much."

After another five minutes of reassurances, Mary Kate trotted up to the front to have Lisa fit her into Hannah's schedule. I clunked my head on the desk and tried to channel acetaminophen psychically. Had to give up and root around in my purse for the real stuff. Mary Kate could be exhausting.

Before leaving the office, I forced myself to follow my own advice, reluctantly asking Lisa to set me up for supervision with Regina. While I was at it, I also had her schedule me in with Marshall. He needed to review my written response to Wayne's complaint and be updated on the recent events. Lisa hummed "Yo ho ho and a bottle of rum" under her breath as she scanned his calendar.

I ignored her. If I didn't hurry I'd be late for the AA meeting. Sue was my designated escort, and patience was a vastly overrated virtue in her book. Nonexistent, actually. I risked a speeding ticket, getting there with two minutes to spare.

"You're late," Sue said.

"I am not. You're early."

"How are you holding up?" she asked.

"Had the police over Friday night. Somebody stabbed a doll and left it on my doorstep."

"But you called the police? About time," she said.

"Actually, one of the cops was really nice. He's in recovery, too, or was. I don't think he comes anymore. Anyway, he and his partner went and talked to Wayne."

"Nice-schmice. The important thing is: Is he cute?" Sue asked as we went through the big double doors of the club.

"Judge for yourself. He's sitting right there." I smiled and waved.

Durrant, in jeans and T-shirt, grinned back. He sat at a table with Harry, big hand wrapped around a Styrofoam cup of coffee, looking entirely at home. Which, I supposed, he was. A famous poet once said that "Home is where, when you have to go there, they have to take you in." Summed up AA pretty well.

Sue and I joined them, and I felt a wave of comfort wash over me. Apparently my aversion to police was limited to the abstract. Big, sturdy, stand-between-me-and-a-lunatic cops were just peachy.

156

"Any new contact?" Durrant asked.

"None at all. It's great."

He nodded. "Hopefully, he got the message."

That was all that was said, although I noticed Sue look at his butt appreciatively as we headed into the meeting. She made a point of sitting next to him, too. Cheered her up immensely.

When I got into work the next morning, I stopped as usual at the front desk to check my schedule. Marshall had changed our meeting to the hour I normally blocked out for lunch.

"Was I supposed to brown bag it today?" I asked Lisa.

"No way. He had me make a reservation at Oscars." She waggled her eyebrows.

"Really?" Nerves closed my throat.

"You don't sound pleased."

Lisa, ever alert for dirt, picked up on my anxiety. I needed to toss her a bone. "I don't know. Eating lunch with the boss is always weird. What do you order? What if I get food stuck in my teeth? Or burp? I hate that."

"I guess you'll have to suffer through it. Do you want to take the you-know-what back to your office to get in the mood?" She patted the bottom drawer of her desk where the pirate porno resided in isolated glory.

"You really need to get rid of that thing," I warned.

"I'll die first."

By lunchtime, word had gotten around that Marshall was taking me to lunch. Even though he'd made a point of telling Lisa to pencil in lunch dates with alternating employees at the first of every month, the rumor mill churned. I hadn't felt so awkward since freshman year when Jimmy Podenka tried to kiss me in the back seat of my dad's old Buick. With my dad driving.

As Marshall and I crossed the parking lot, I felt my co-workers' eyes crawling over us like sleepy flies. I climbed into his car certain that, if I looked, I'd be able to count a half-dozen, newly made, smushed nose prints on the clinic windows. I pictured lots of ducking and giggling going on inside. Marshall played the whole thing off.

He had chosen the restaurant well. The atmosphere of Oscars was designed along the Baby Bear-scale of dining—not too loud and not too quiet, not too slow and not too fast. It accommodated the professional working crowd, getting you served and fed in under an hour without making you feel rushed.

After navigating the dining area and the menu, I settled down some. Having successfully avoided spinach, expensive dishes, and red sauce, I hoped I could manage the soup-and-sandwich special without making a fool of myself. That remained to be seen, however. The soup worried me a little.

While waiting for our food, I gave Marshall a copy of my time line and the FU-sonnet, explaining about the doll. I hoped he wouldn't ask about the "club" and mentally prepared a cover story, but he focused on the sonnet. As he read, I watched his face. He had gorgeous, feathery eye lashes. His eyes lifted, catching me practically drooling, and he smiled, slow and warm.

I nearly dumped my water glass over, then made a big show of scanning the restaurant, looking for the waitress. The wench must have been hiding in the back, because she was clearly unavailable for providing distractions. No tip for her.

"Any idea why Wayne is sending you Shakespearean love sonnets? I have to say, that doesn't really fit my picture of him."

I had a choice of pretending that I knew the sonnet was Shakespearean or throwing myself on the mercy of a better-educated peer. My natural inclinations would've had me lie, but I just didn't think I could pull it off.

"Not a lot of people read Shakespeare these days," Marshall said. "I majored in English for my undergrad."

"English? Not a lot of call for that in the mental health field."

"You'd be surprised how edifying Shakespeare is regarding human nature. But, actually, my girlfriend at the time was an English major. She decided we would be teachers. I—mistakenly—thought it would be an easy program, and was more interested in her *other* attributes."

"Shame on you," I said.

"Hey, I was twenty. What can I say? Anyway, I recognize this. I couldn't tell you what number it is, but I'm fairly sure it's from the Fair Youth half, which is another strange choice. Shakespeare's sonnets are roughly divided into two sections: those addressed to a young man, presumably handsome, and either a patron, a lover, or his son—depending on which expert you talk to—and then the Dark Lady sonnets. The Dark Lady's identity is also a mystery, but the sonnets seem to indicate she was promiscuous and fickle. There may have been some sort of love-triangle among her, Shakespeare, and the Youth.

"As I said, this one would have been addressed to the Youth, not the Dark Lady," his long-lashed eyes gazed at my own dark hair. "On the other hand, it *is* about rejection and rivalry, and its tone is primarily bitter, sarcastic. That *would* fit. The thing that really worries me is that it's also about losing the ability to think rationally."

"Not good," I agreed. "But there hasn't been any further trouble since the police talked to him."

Marshall nodded thoughtfully, still eying the sonnet. With a sigh, he set it aside and picked up the response I'd written refuting Wayne's complaint. "Hopefully there won't be anymore run-ins with him. I would say the danger would be greatest if he gets drunk.

"The good news," he continued, "is that with the two police reports and this rebuttal, I don't think there will be any problem dismissing the case."

The arrival of our food covered my sigh of relief. After that news, the soup was hardly any threat at all. Unfortunately, in addition to chicken wild rice, I got a taste of my own medicine when Marshall checked on whether I'd met with Regina for supervision. Hopefully I could dissemble better than Mary Kate had.

"We're meeting Thursday," I said, avoiding his eyes.

"Thursday? Couldn't you fit in anything sooner?"

"Well, she's carrying a full caseload and she's going away for the weekend." I winced. I'd made a tactical mistake.

"Oh, that's right. Wait a minute…" Marshall's face scrunched. "Regina's gone Thursday and Friday. She's using vacation days for a long weekend."

"Right," I said, concentrating on my soup.

He leaned back and spread his hands wide, gesturing me to go on.

"Well, she had a lot going on, so we're meeting Thursday." I cleared my throat. "Next week. When she's all nice and relaxed after her vacation."

"Not gonna happen. Regina doesn't do 'nice and relaxed,' but edgy seems to work for her. She's good at what she does, and she could be very helpful to you in your situation. Moreover, I don't want you going so long without supervision. Besides," he continued, "you don't want to work with someone after their vacation. They're all depressed, nothing to look forward to, and lots of work piled up that they're behind on. Get with her before she heads out, when she's still got something to look forward to. When we get back, see what she's got open for *this* week."

"You mean what's left of this week—today or tomorrow."

"So be it," he declared.

"So be it? Isn't that a little Pharaoh-esque? 'So let it be written; so let it be done!'" I thumped my chest.

He laughed. "Have you always been a smart-ass?"

"Always. Ever since I can remember."

"I've always thought of smart alecks as conflict magicians. Instead of making an elephant disappear into thin air, they use jokes to make the problem disappear." Although a slight smile

160

played on his lips, he'd turned serious, voice softening. I avoided his searching eyes, focusing instead on the waitress as she approached and plopped down the check.

"Abracadabra," I said.

CHAPTER TWENTY-FOUR

It was time to return to normal. I needed it. I function best in a rut, head down, chugging along the familiar groove of my life. Yet despite the apparent Wayne-lessness of my existence, I continued to be jittery and on edge. When Mary Kate walked up behind me in the file room, I nearly pulled the shelving unit over on top of me. Scared her, too. Apparently she wasn't prepared for co-workers literally climbing the walls. This was a mental health clinic, after all.

Regina fit me in for a supervision meeting first thing Wednesday morning. Unfortunately, Regina had no sense of humor, knew it, and didn't care. We grated on each other.

The first thing we did was review the time line I'd worked up, discussing each of the attacks chronologically. Then, she threw a supervisory curve ball.

"How are your feelings about being victimized affecting your work?"

I gritted my teeth. I usually avoided her name, but today I took a grim pleasure in bearing down on the syllables. "Well, I don't really see myself as a 'victim,' Regina."

Raising bushy, I-am-okay-with-my-body eyebrows, she said, "What does that word, 'victim,' say to you?"

"This isn't therapy, Regina. I'm more than willing to discuss how the recent events have been playing out in my work, but I don't want to get into word games." Nothing irritates a therapist more than being analyzed. That's why most of us went into the field to begin with.

She did the silent, do-you-hear-yourself? Therapist thing. Big deal. I liked silence. Bring it on.

After several minutes, she cleared her throat, shifting in her seat. I smiled inwardly at my petty victory and tossed her a bone. Anyway, I didn't want her telling Marshall I wasn't cooperating; she seemed like the type to snitch.

"The biggest issue has been distraction," I conceded. "There are sessions where I'm not focused on my clients. Instead, I'm worrying about the complaint he made."

She bludgeoned that topic to death, wrapping up with the ethics complaint. "I understand from Marshall that it's likely to be a non-issue," Regina observed. "Aside from reassigning Mary Kate, have there been any other repercussions from it?"

"No. Like what?"

"This is your first complaint?" she asked. Without waiting for my nod, she continued, "They could have done an internal review of your clients. That's a huge pain in the ass. Maybe even suspended you during the process. They could have asked you to hire your own lawyer. By the way, have you contacted one?"

"No, I figured I would wait to see what happens after my rebuttal is received. Do you think I should?"

"At this point, no. It wouldn't have hurt, though, to have an attorney go over the initial complaint. Too late now."

She picked the time line up, studied it, and frowned.

"What?" I asked.

"I don't know. This seems off somehow."

"What do you mean?"

"I'm sorry," she said, not sounding sorry at all. "I'm not trying to be obscure, but I can't quite put my finger on it. He certainly has been very active, hasn't he? Hardly a day's gone by that he hasn't pulled some kind of crap."

"Not lately though," I pointed out. "Not since the police talked to him. Do you think he's stopped?"

Regina continued to frown. "I wish I could say yes. The truth is, only he could tell you. He might. He might not. He could go for months without contacting you—especially if he finds a new target for his anger and, unfortunately for her, Carrie might be that target—or he might resume today. Since his motivation seems to be revenge, perhaps with Carrie back under his thumb, it will have burned itself out.

"I've known some stalkers to continue their behaviors for years. This one certainly seems creative and persistent. He's all over the board with the types of attacks he's using. On the other hand, he might have just enough self-preservation to back off now that you've involved the cops. Time will tell.

"My question for you," she continued, "is how are you going to handle living with the uncertainty? In my experience, that sensation of always waiting for the other shoe to drop is one of the most draining aspects of the ordeal."

"It is. I hate it. I find myself hoping that Durrant has scared Wayne off, but I'm nervous as hell. Jumpy."

"Are you sleeping well? Eating well?"

I smiled as Regina segued into a depression checklist. We finished up about ten minutes later, after convincing her I wasn't clinically depressed, suicidal, or homicidal, and we went our separate ways.

As I passed Marshall in the hall, he asked, "So, how'd it go?"

"Just peachy, thanks."

"Learn anything?"

"Yeah. This could go on forever. Or not."

He laughed and ducked into his office. Coward. As I headed toward my own, I had to admit that my gruffness was mostly a sham. Marshall was right. Regina *was* good at what she did. She definitely knew her stuff. We wouldn't ever be best buddies, but she had good insights into how my situation might interfere with my work and, for that, I was grateful. I wondered, idly, what had bothered her so much when she'd looked at the time line.

The illusion of peace shattered the next morning when, for the first time ever, Lisa interrupted me in a session. Closing the door behind me, I joined her in the hall.

"It's Edna Torgensen," she said. "Carrie's mother. She's on line three, and she's *way* hysterical."

"I still have twenty minutes left with Judith," I said, pointing to my office door. "Will you see if she wants to reschedule or how she wants to work it out? Tell her I'm very sorry."

"Not a problem. Regina's office is open; you can take it in there."

The first two minutes of the call was a torrent of squealing *oh my god's*, punctuated by gasps and wild sobbing. I tried stemming the flow but ultimately let her wind down on her own. The whole time my mind whirled, conjuring up violent images of Carrie, hurt or dead, and Wayne smirking at his conquest.

Edna finally regained control, and I asked, "Is it Carrie? What's happened?"

"No. I mean, yes, the bastard beat her bad, put her in the ER yesterday, but that's not it. It's him."

"Him?" My gut dropped and, instinctively, I stood, ready to run but stalled by the lack of information. "What? Is he coming here? What's going on?"

"No. Oh my god, no! He ain't going anywhere. He's *dead*."

"Dead? What? Are you sure?"

At that, she burst into a toxic fusion of horror and revulsion that disguised itself in hysterical laughter. I waited.

"Dead. Very, very dead. Head-blown-clear-off kind o' dead. I came over here this morning to see Carrie and found him layin' there in the drive. Somebody unloaded a lot of shot into that boy, that's for sure. He was just layin' there, on his back, blood and guts all over."

"Have you called the police?"

"Yeah, they're coming."

"Who could have...?" I swallowed the question, afraid to hear that Carrie was responsible.

"I don't know. I found him, so I s'pose the cops are going to think it was me, but it wasn't. Not that I ain't happy he's dead but... Anyway, I didn't do it. And Carrie didn't do it either!"

"You said he beat her up again? Is she in the hospital?"

"She was. I took her to the ER yesterday. He's been at her face this time, and I think he broke her nose. I couldn't stay 'cause I had to get back to work, but I told Carrie to call me when she needed a ride. She never did. After my shift, I tried calling her cell phone, and a nurse finally answered. Carrie must have left it there. They said she never even saw the doctor."

"Is she in danger from the injuries?"

"I don't think so. She'll be in some pain for a good while, but it won't kill her. I think she took off from him again. None of her clothes was took, either, and I'm about out of my mind not knowing where she is."

"She took off again."

"I think so. At first, I just thought she went back to the asshole and figured I'd give her a piece of my mind since she didn't seem to have enough brains on her own. That's what I came over here for. But she's not here. Just him."

If she had killed him, she'd be hiding for an entirely different reason, but Edna didn't seem to be considering that, and my own intuition told me that Carrie wasn't violent. At least, not in the manner Edna had described Wayne dying.

"If it wasn't Carrie, who. . . did it?" I skittered away from the M-word.

"I don't know. Anybody with any sense hated his guts, but not many would cross him. He's low-down mean and likes pushing people around, especially when he's drinkin'. I never

166

understood why Carrie took up with him. She coulda had her pick of men."

"Well, he won't bother her now."

"She'll probably pick up with someone just as bad or worse. You probably seen that before, in your line of work and all."

Silence stretched between us. I hated the thought, but odds were that she was right. At least she had calmed down and had her wits about her.

"I don't think she'll contact me. But if she does—"

"No, I don't expect that either. I just figured you should know. I mean, before the cops get here. I'm going to have to tell them about your troubles with him."

It hadn't occurred to me. Of course they would want to talk to me. I'd be a suspect. I pressed the phone against my ear, questions roiling in my mind, but one rose above the others.

"Why did you call? To warn me?"

"Look—if you did it, I don't blame you. In fact, I'm grateful. But if you didn't, you deserve a warning. I still thank you for trying with Carrie. And it was real brave for you to take his crap. Anyway, let me know if you hear from her." Sirens wailed in the background, growing louder.

Abruptly, she said good-bye and hung up. I stayed sitting, holding the phone so tight my knuckles hurt, and tried not to let fear drive me into doing something stupid. My mouth watered and I felt itchy in a way that only a drink could satisfy. Would the police really believe I had something to do with this?

CHAPTER TWENTY-FIVE

Would, could, and did.

A detective waited for me as I walked my four o'clock client up to the front desk. Tall and lanky, he wore a navy blue suit jacket that didn't reach his wrists and black slacks that looked as though they belonged to a separate suit. He appeared on the brink of retirement, deep-set brown eyes nearly lost in saggy folds of skin and the first impression suggested a lazy, easy-going temperament. If you didn't bother to look deeper, you'd miss the intelligence lurking in the depths of those sad, hound-dog eyes. This wasn't a lie-on-the-porch-and-wag-your-tail kind of cop. This was a bloodhound, and he was on the scent.

Lisa sounded nervous as she said, "Letty, Detective Blodgett wanted to catch a minute with you." Thankfully, she phrased it in such a way as to avoid sounding like he planned to slap the handcuffs on me as soon as I got in reach. I fervently hoped she was right.

"Sure," I smiled stiffly. Motioning him to follow, I tried projecting an aura of innocence as we walked back to my office. Difficult to do with just my backside to work with. The more I concentrated on not looking guilty, the guiltier my ass felt.

"I only have about ten minutes before my next client," I said as we sat. "But I'll be happy to set up a time to meet with you, if you think it's necessary." I was proud of that line. Made me look open and cooperative while setting boundaries. Good for me.

"That's very nice of you. Of course, I haven't said why I'm here yet…"

Blodgett left the statement hanging. The questions—why hadn't I asked what he was doing here? Why was I being so helpful?—only hinted at in the very slight rise in tone at the end, but filling that half-second tilt with all the suspicion a homicide detective could produce. Although he sat motionless, I could've sworn his nostrils flared, scenting fear. Meanwhile, his eyes tracked over my face, analyzing expressions, body language, posture. I was sitting in front of a human lie detector.

"I assumed you're here about Wayne—" I fumbled, not remembering Wayne's last name, and left it at that.

"About Wayne?" he repeated, willing to let me blunder on.

"I received a call this morning telling me he was dead. Murdered. Since he's been harassing me, I figured I would eventually be contacted by the police. I hadn't expected it to be so soon, however."

"Received a call from who?"

I shrugged. The smart-ass in me wanted to correct his grammar, but my better sense kicked in. I didn't want to get Edna in trouble so I avoided answering, at least for now. "I don't know who killed Wayne, but it wasn't me."

He tipped his head, giving me a that's-what-they-all-say look. "Tell you what— I must have just about used up that ten minutes. How about you stop by the station when you finish up this evening? What time might that be?"

I cleared my throat. "My last client is at six tonight. I should be done by seven or so. Will that work?"

"Works great," he smiled politely, handing me his card. "See you then."

I didn't bother to walk him up front, choosing instead to ponder over his abrupt departure. No way was he satisfied that easily. However, if his original intention had been to observe my reaction to Wayne's murder, then that had already been frustrated by Edna's warning. My guess was he'd decided he'd get more by interviewing me on his turf, without time constraints.

I got to the station by twenty after seven and had decided to go with all-out honesty. Why not try something new? I brought copies of Wayne's file, although I had no faith in any of the data being accurate. His right to confidentiality had been abrogated with his complaint, at least in the legal sense. Information about Carrie was a stickier situation, though. Blodgett would have to get a warrant for that one. I didn't imagine he would be too thrilled about that, but he couldn't really blame me for it either.

I hoped.

Blodgett left me cooling my heels in the lobby for over a half-hour. I didn't know if it was a power play or not, but wouldn't put it past him. When he finally showed up, the detective looked saggier and even more exhausted than when I'd seen him just two hours earlier.

He led me into the type of interview room that TV had taught me to expect. A heavy, metal table covered in coffee rings and scratches squatted in the middle of a room that had been slimed with queasy-green paint. A bright yellow, plastic wastebasket—more appropriate for a child's bathroom, but not likely to cause injury if used as a weapon—had been placed just inside the door. The only relief from the jangle of colors was the smoky mirror hanging across one side wall and several aging memos thumb-tacked to the other.

I declined Blodgett's drink offer, expecting him to take the seat across from me. Instead, he apologized and stepped out of the room. My eyes moved to the mirror. Gave a little wave. Leaning back in my seat—not easy because the hard edges cut into my shoulders—I practiced deep breathing relaxation techniques. He'd either give up or I'd get a nap. I was good either way.

Blodgett must have gotten the point because he only left me stewing for an additional fifteen minutes. By now, my stomach was rumbling and a headache crept up the back of my neck. He came in carrying a notepad and paper.

Since we moved at his ask-one-question, write-the-answer-down pace, it was slow going. We slogged through all my contact info, and he let me rattle on about my professional background. Polite, easy, ice-breaker conversation. If somebody had served those little, mini-hot dogs—which I was hungry enough to snarf down—it could have been a cocktail party. Or with slightly better furniture and no snacks, therapy.

Eventually, he asked the question I'd been expecting.

"Would you tell me everything about your relationship with Wayne Bristol?"

A nice, broad, open-ended question. I especially liked the *everything* touch. But it was what I came in to do, so I pulled out the clinical file and yet another copy of the time line and sonnet. At this rate, I should get them published and earn royalties on them.

Passing them over, I started with "Randy's" two sessions and the shock I'd felt when he pushed into my office brandishing the buck knife like a demented samurai warrior. Blodgett let me talk at my own pace, but I saw him scrawl two question marks next to the part where I talked about the knife. I figured he had read the police report of the incident and knew that the knife had never been found. After covering the attack at the office, I pulled out the time line and angled it between us, keeping my eyes on it rather than on Blodgett. By the time I finished relating every detail I could remember, including my AA involvement and the run-ins I had with Wayne there, I was sweating like a pig and trying not to throw up from nerves. I eyed the yellow plastic wastebasket, just in case.

And almost used it when Blodgett asked, "Where you were Wednesday evening?"

I managed to tell him about my Wednesday group and gave him Sue's number. "But I don't have any alibi after about 8:30 or so. I went home to bed."

His next question had me eyeing the basket a third time, black dots dancing in front of my eyes. "Do you own or have access to a shot gun, Ms. Whittaker?"

"No. I don't. Am I a suspect?" My voice shook on the last word.

"Why, no." His eyebrows raised languidly as if expressing surprise were just a mite too tiring. "Not unless you count that everyone who had a run-in with Bristol is a suspect; at least, until the evidence starts coming in, leading to the real killer. And it will. Besides, if I did consider you a suspect at this time, I would've read you your rights." His smile wasn't reassuring, probably wasn't meant to be. "If you had to *guess* what happened, what would you say?"

"I really don't have any idea. He was a bully. He was abusive. I imagine he pissed off a lot of people. I can tell you this— it wasn't me, and I don't think it was Carrie. Or her mother," I added.

Blodgett tapped the pen against his teeth. "Why don't you think it was Carrie? She's missing."

"As far as I know, she doesn't have any history of violence, except as a target. And yeah, I know, the whole burning-bed thing," I waved off the suggestion forming on his lips, "but I don't see it with Carrie. She's a runner. She ran before and she ran this time. She blames herself," (and me, I thought, but didn't say) "not Wayne."

He nodded politely, but I knew I hadn't convinced him. And could I really say what another person might be capable of? What had Carrie felt after trading in her freedom for a broken promise topped with a broken nose? She'd been frightened enough to leave the hospital before being treated. Had she settled her problem with a shotgun?

Blodgett drew my attention back. "Tell me a little more about the knife Bristol attacked you with. What do you remember about it?"

I sat for a moment, thinking. "It was big."

"Nothing that stands out about it?" he persisted.

"No. Not that I recall. It was just a big buck knife. Like hunters use to...um...gut deer." Ghastly image, that.

"And to your knowledge, it was never found?"

"Not that I know of, and I'm sure I would have heard. If it had been found by someone at the clinic, that is. What's the big deal about the knife anyway? I thought Wayne was shot."

"Oh, he was. Who else would have any information on Bristol?" His pen stood poised over the legal pad. He hadn't answered my question, and obviously didn't intend to.

"Um..." Robert would kill me, but as Wayne's sponsor he might have information that could be helpful. On the other hand, he was about as insightful as dirt and the second "A" wasn't Anonymous for a whim. I'd like to think it wasn't spite that made me give Blodgett Robert's contact information.

CHAPTER TWENTY-SIX

I was right. He was pissed.

Robert didn't even wait to talk at the club, but came into the clinic. Lisa left him cooling his heels in the lobby until my client, the last for the day, finished up.

By the time I got up to the front, word had spread, and we had an audience. Both Marshall and Mary Kate loitered around Lisa's desk; Mary Kate, with an armful of files, at least pretended to be working. Marshall simply leaned against the wall eyeing the lobby, shirt sleeves rolled up, a corporate bad boy.

Robert stood with his arms crossed and lips so tight that if he kissed me I'd get a paper-cut. Which he didn't seem inclined to do.

After sending my client off for the weekend, I had Robert follow me back to my office. As I passed by, Marshall's right eye twitched in a wink. I hoped Robert missed it, but his scowl deepened significantly.

"Who was that?" was the first thing out of his mouth, proving he had.

"My boss. We're all a little jumpy about angry men showing up unannounced. Why are you here, Robert?" *Now* I pretended.

"Don't be coy. How dare you give my name to the police? I would think a *therapist*"—he practically spit the word—"would have some concept of anonymity."

174

Heat flushed up from my body, singeing my face, leaving my hands cold and clammy. I hated that he might be right. Still...

"You were Wayne's sponsor. I thought you would want to help find his murderer. Besides, what are you so worried about? Your precious reputation won't be tarnished this far from home and you were, like, what? A hundred and fifty miles away, in another state?"

His eyes went from angry to skittish, darting away like a bumblebee on meth, red blotches breaking out across his face and throat. "It's none of your business where I was. That's not the point."

"So you *were* in town, huh? How come?"

Something thumped against the wall in Regina's office next door.

"I said that's not the point! You had no business dragging my name into this mess."

He was so obviously lying that I considered pushing the issue. *What had he been doing in town on a Wednesday night? And with whom?* But I couldn't figure out how to do it without sounding either jealous or nosy. Anyway, I was sick of arguing.

"Look, the police wanted to talk to someone who might know what was going on with Wayne in the last few days. I really thought you would be the best resource for that. It had nothing to do with our... history." It was worth the bullshit just to shut him up.

He snorted, shaking his head. "Yeah, whatever. You're lucky I don't plan on bringing this up at the club. Remember, 'principles before personalities.'"

As he quoted the AA slogan at me, it was all I could do not to smack his face. He didn't want to help solve the murder of his so-called AA buddy, but he could spout off about putting principles ahead of petty grievances to me. What an ass.

I had to put up with his sanctimonious crap for another five minutes before he finally let me maneuver him up to the front. Mary Kate had disappeared, although I suspected I could find her hunkered down in Regina's office with her ear pressed against the thin wall. The thump while Robert and I argued had been a tad obvious. We'd have to talk.

Marshall was nowhere to be seen, so after I packed Robert off, I went looking for the boss. He was kicked back in his chair, feet propped on the desk when I cracked open his office door. He smiled as I walked in and took the chair across the desk from him.

"You weren't camped out in Regina's office banging on the wall, were you?" I asked.

His brows drew together. "Is this a trick question?"

"Never mind. It's something I'll have to talk to Mary Kate about."

"Oh. Mary Kate. Do I even want to know?"

"I could be wrong, but she seems to have set up a listening post in Regina's office."

Marshall pinched the bridge of his nose and sighed. "She seems to be a little fuzzy on the concept of confidentiality. Why don't I have Hannah take a run at it this time? It's her turn."

"Sounds good." I heaved myself up. "I'm takin' off."

"You are?" He looked as if he wanted to say more, but I kept moving.

Regina's office was empty when I went by, and Mary Kate was nowhere to be found. Lisa told me she'd left. I decided to go with Marshall's plan: let Hannah deal with it.

Minutes later, as I climbed into my car, I debated whether I should go to a meeting or not. On the plus side, I wouldn't have to worry about running into Wayne, but I really didn't want to deal with Robert any more tonight, and I seriously didn't want to see Sandra, whom I suspected was the reason for Robert's midweek visit. He never drove in to see *me* in the middle of the week, but then I didn't have sexercise equipment either.

Sighing, I shoved the key in the ignition. Inexplicably, I shivered, muscles taut as a sense of foreboding swept over me. I held very still, scanning the parking lot, unable to locate the danger that my gut told me existed. Dread curdled my stomach as I raised my eyes to the rearview mirror, certain Wayne would be staring at me from the back seat—an urban legend killer-zombie.

The mirror was twisted—cranked up, tilted sideways.

The same angle as on the day of the rat. My eyes skittered to the glove box. I reached for it, then pulled my hand back, flesh crawling as though a swarm of ants writhed under the skin. I looked toward the clinic, willing Marshall to come out. He ignored the ESP-instant message, so I stared at the glove box for a few more minutes, sweating and shaking.

It *looked* like a regular, nonsurprise-holding glove box.

Pulling Blodgett's card from my pocket, I reached for my cell phone, flipped it open. I punched in his number, starting over twice as my shaking fingers fumbled the tiny number pads. Punched SEND and waited. I don't know how long I sat there before realizing nothing was happening. I pulled the phone away from my ear—dead.

No more stalling. I'd call Blodgett later. Taking a deep breath, I leaned over, popped the latch. The door dropped open with a little clunk, displaying not a rat, but a white, oblong object banded with a strip of bright red. The package sat quiescently in the gap, resting on my map of Minnesota. I stared at it dully. Another present—this one done up in white writing paper and tied with a bow.

My heart, already beating in the high aerobic-range, kicked up another notch as I analyzed the situation. Even if Wayne had planted the package before his murder, he couldn't have tampered with the mirror. Unless he really *was* a zombie. Which meant the mirror was coincidental or . . . there was yet another player involved in this game of terror. My stomach cramped, and I bent forward so quickly my head banged off the steering wheel.

How could that be? And *who?* Carrie? I eyed the oblong package warily. Had she left me a message, something to explain why she had killed Wayne? It didn't look like a mere note. The paper wrapped something bulky, I could tell.

Or was it somebody else? Some unknown factor? I felt exposed and raw sitting in the parking lot. For all I knew, someone was watching me right now.

Outside my car, the world went on as if nothing was happening. People drove down the street thinking about what to make for supper, whether they could juggle the checkbook to pay the mortgage, whether the Big Mac they ate for lunch would show up on their ass just in time for Cousin Darlene's wedding. And maybe someone sat in a car or stared at me from an office window, watching, seeing the fear and helplessness play out on my face. Watching me realize that I was still caught in the trap—had never really been free—still caught, writhing, heart thumping, kicking helplessly at the enemy I couldn't see.

CHAPTER TWENTY-SEVEN

Without benefit of alcohol, I drove home in a blackout. It took three attempts to angle my car into the parking space outside my apartment, and when I'd finally shut the car off I was still shaking. Opening the glove box, I used a pen to wiggle the package into my briefcase. I pretended I was being careful for evidentiary purposes, but I just couldn't stand touching it.

When I finally made it to the cool, dim recesses of my home, I dropped the briefcase on the floor, shoving it sideways with my foot. Scared the crap out of Siggy, who took off for the bedroom and hid under the bed. Exactly where I wanted to be. I pondered making him scoot over. We could live together, he and I, happy among the dust woofies, coming out only to use the bathroom and watch "American Idol." It could work.

Sighing, I dumped the contents on my coffee table, the paper-wrapped parcel landing with a muffled thud. Then, I called Blodgett, getting his voice mail. Left a rambling, barely coherent message and hung up.

That was enough decisiveness for the moment. Time for a break. I made use of the bathroom, then detoured into the bedroom to see if Siggy wanted to cuddle. He declined.

Running out of stalling maneuvers, I trudged back to the living room and stared dully at the package for several moments, projecting hatred on it, working up my courage. Courage stayed AWOL, so, settling for resignation, I pulled the red ribbon. A very familiar looking buck knife—except for the newly applied, dried blood—tumbled out. Wayne's knife. I knew it instantly.

My spine tingled, raising the hair on the back of my neck at the sight of it. Details that I hadn't remembered when talking with Blodgett emerged. End to end, the whole knife was at least nine inches long, the shiny tip arching gracefully toward my throat. The wooden hand grip curved the opposite way in a faint S-curve. Muddy-brown blood caked the joinery where blade met grip, smudging the patina on the wood grain and dulling the blade's polished surface.

Whose blood?

Stuck my head between my knees and contemplated leaving it there forever. The view of my own crotch got old pretty quick, especially since it had been so recent since the last curl-up. I rallied, sitting up. Shuddering, I remembered Blodgett's questions about the missing knife. Was this what he was after? But Carrie's mom had said Wayne had been shot, and Blodgett later confirmed it.

I reached for my phone and dialed Edna Torgensen. Abruptly, I slammed the receiver back to the cradle, jabbing my finger in the process. I'd forgotten to dial *67. More importantly, the police obviously weren't disclosing the fact that a knife had been involved, if indeed it had. Did I really want to start floating around the idea that I had inside information on Wayne's murder?

I needed to slow down, think this through very carefully.

Hands shaking, I picked up the paper. Another sonnet— the thin, slanting calligraphy looking like a colony of aberrant spiders had trailed black ink across it.

Unable to concentrate, my attention skittered back to the knife. Had Carrie left it? Did she murder Wayne and plant the knife to implicate me? But if Wayne *had* been shot wouldn't she (or whomever) have left the *shotgun*? And where did she get the knife? When he ran from my office, had Wayne been able to evade the cops long enough to fling it somewhere, then gone back to retrieve it later? It was possible, I supposed, but hardly likely.

Or was someone else involved? Someone ready to pick up where Wayne had left off. Was he acting on Wayne's behalf or his own? One fact stood out, undeniable and chilling: it was someone I knew. Someone close to me with access to both my home and my car. Someone, maybe, whom I trusted.

Back to the sonnet. I did the F and U decoding thing again.

> *My love is as a fever, longing still*
> *For that which longer nurseth the disease,*
> *Feeding on that which doth preserve the ill,*
> *Th' uncertain sickly appetite to please:*
> *My reason the Physician to my love,*
> *Angry that his prescriptions are not kept*
> *Hath left me, and I desperate now approve,*
> *Desire is death, which physic did except.*
> *Past cure I am, now Reason is past care,*
> *And frantic-mad with ever-more unrest,*
> *My thoughts and my discourse as madmen's are,*
> *At random from the truth vainly expressed.*
> *For I have sworn thee faire, and thought thee bright,*
> *Who are as black as hell, as dark as night.*

Yeesh.

Unfortunately, the clearer it became, the freakier it seemed. I didn't understand every line, but once again themes emerged. Love—a crazy, diseased lust feeding on itself, repellant to its captive—had driven the writer insane. Abandoned by reason, he raged with fever, enslaved to the demonic mistress he both lusted for and despised.

Other phrases, "desire is death," "my thoughts and discourse are as madmen's," and "black as hell, dark as night" needed no explanation.

Shakespeare was one scary dude.

I could feel the mastery of the language he wielded like a weapon, but in my present situation, could only recoil from the harsh brutality of the poetry. Why anyone, Marshall included, would have made a study of these ravings was beyond me.

Why *would* Marshall...?

Questions stirred the acid in my stomach, making me retch. I ran to the bathroom. Here, my past came in handy, having taught me how to slide across wide expanses of tile when unexpectedly puking. Even still, I barely made it to the toilet in time. Must be rusty.

But I could make up for that.

The trick to doing things you know you'll regret is to do them fast. I made it to The Bear Cub in less than ten minutes. More than enough time to have reconsidered, but I couldn't concentrate with the radio blasting. I turned it up twice. Cubs hadn't changed. Its décor fell on the cheap side of typical Northern Wisconsin rustic. A mounted deer head, dusty Christmas lights twining through his antlers, hung lopsided over the cash register. A few feet over curled a stuffed muskie, its spike-toothed mouth gaping in protest at the wayward steel dart dangling just behind its gills. Bets had been placed as to when the dart would fall, but it'd been seven years since Moby Muskie had been harpooned, and the dart hung tough. A shame. I had money on that bet.

I passed by my usual stool—a mental contortion attempted in order to maintain the pretense that I wasn't really here, wasn't doing what I was obviously doing—and took a seat at the end of the bar. I also ignored the various "look what the cat dragged in" comments from the regulars. None of my so-called friends had bothered to call after I'd gotten sober, so I didn't even spare a blink in their direction. I wasn't here for them anyway.

Jerry ambled down the bar, automatically snagging a frosted stein from the cooler and aiming it under the tap. I shook my head at him.

"Just a diet pop, Jerry," I said. My hands shook, leaving a sweaty smear on the polished counter.

He made a face but complied, plunking it down in front of me and snatching up my two bucks. He moved off to the register and then leaned against the back bar, watching me. Ignoring him, I stared at the corner TV programmed to ESPN.

The pop tasted like a laxative. I shoved it aside, and caught Jerry eyeballing me again.

"Gimme a beer, Jerry." *In for a penny.* "And a shot." *In for a pound.* I didn't even have to specify; he poured the Leinenkugel into an iced mug, Jack Daniels riding shotgun.

It didn't take long. It felt like forever. Spit pooled in my mouth during the wait, excited about coming attractions, ready for action. Jerry set the mug down, the shot glass next to it. I reached, but he didn't let go of either.

"You sure?" he said, forcing eye contact.

I'd never liked Jerry. He insisted he was six foot, when he was at least an inch shorter than my five-seven; I hated people who played with facts. I couldn't stand the pencil-thin mustache he sported under his sharp nose. If you can't grow a real one, don't bother.

And I really, *really* didn't need him adding to the chorus of anticipatory remorse that hummed in my head.

"I ordered it, didn't I?"

Shrugging off my snottiness, he released his hold but kept staring. I didn't want to betray the aching need that pulsed through my very cells, twisting my gut and mind into a fever of craving. I didn't want to betray the riot of desire incited by the scent of hops.

And then it didn't matter.

The whiskey was fire, the beer smooth ice. My eyes closed in relief as every cell in my body said, "ahh!" Muscles I didn't know were taut instantly relaxed. Shame hovered, ready to settle in, but like any good alcoholic, I drank past that. When I opened my eyes, Jerry was at the other end of the bar, wiping glasses.

I kept drinking. Jerry, his face a careful blank, kept pouring. At some point, Angie, an old "friend," ambled over and struck up a conversation. Tried to, that is.

"So, where ya been?"

Before my world had caved in, we were best friends. We talked almost daily, usually at Cubs, but if not there, then on the phone. She'd known details about my love life, feuds at work, my family history—all of it. And I knew hers. It was Angie whom I'd called the night I was trying to decide if I should give AA a try or just hop in the tub and slice my wrists. She brought a case of Heineken over, and I made it through the night. I also made it to AA—hungover and alone—but not until the next day.

I'd called her three times in those shaky first weeks, getting her voice mail each time. She never called back.

"You got that fifty you owe me?" I asked.

"Geez! What crawled up your butt and died? I was just trying to say hi."

"You said it." I turned away.

"Listen, I meant to call you, but you know how it goes. I just figured we'd catch up when you got back."

"Got *back*?" Incredulous, I faced her. "Angie, I wasn't on vacation! I was getting sober."

"Yeah, well, here you are. So, what's the big deal?"

Only the arrival of a fresh drink kept me from smacking her. I swallowed a cocktail of beer and anger, and Angie drifted away, miffed. After that, only Jerry entered my sphere, exchanging beer for cash and keeping his "significant eye contact" to himself.

Drunk hit hard and fast, a not unexpected sucker-punch dealt from the bottle, by-passing tipsy and going straight to blasted. Things got blurry.

CHAPTER TWENTY-EIGHT

I woke up somewhere. Somewhere *else*.

A searing beam of sunlight sliced the fragile barrier of my eyelids, stabbing my brain mercilessly. The parts of my body that weren't throbbing felt as hollow and dry as a scraped-out gourd. Very slowly, I looked around.

I laid in somebody's bed, legs twisted and trapped in a blue and green comforter, a tarnished, hungover Goldilocks. A generic, masculine room—neat, clean, and spare. It told nothing of its owner.

Crap.

At least I was still dressed, although my day-old clothes smelled of musk and stale cigarette smoke. Bile roiled in my stomach, rising in a thin, burning crest. I closed my eyes, swallowed, determined not to cherry-top this latest experience by barfing in the somebody's bed.

After a few minutes, I felt safe enough to crawl out of bed and venture out the door. I found myself on a loft landing looking down into a familiar, rustic living area.

Marshall's.

The cabin was quiet with no evidence of its owner, except for a rumpled blanket and a pillow that bore witness I'd slept alone. Gratitude made my head pound.

The rich smell of dark roast drew me into the small kitchen, where I shakily poured a mug. A quick plunder of the cabinets failed to unearth any aspirin or its chemical cousins, so I took off at a dead shuffle, aiming for the bathroom.

A Pavlov-reflex at the sight of the toilet almost made me throw up, but I knew if I did, my head would split open, leaking brain-yolk all over Marshall's shiny ceramic tile. The thought of "brain-yolk" made me puke anyway.

I squirted toothpaste on my finger and rubbed it around my mouth. After spitting, I leaned over the sink and guzzled about a quart of water straight from the tap. I'd probably throw that up, too, but I felt better.

Back in the living room, I dropped on the couch, pulling the quilt over my legs. I caught the scent of Marshall's cologne, spicy and crisp, and the terror I'd felt yesterday reading the sonnet swelled up inside me.

Could Marshall be the one sending the sonnets?

He'd freely admitted that he'd studied English literature in college, specifically Shakespeare. Would he have been that open if he was the one sending me mutilated dolls and twisted sixteenth-century poetry? But what about the knife? Since the police never found it, it made sense that Marshall, first down the hall after the police gave chase, could have found and pocketed Wayne's knife. I shivered, sweating and chilled at the same time.

Realizing I had an opportunity that might not come along again, I forced myself off the couch. Marshall's décor was certainly rustic, but I didn't see any rifles—at least not out in the open.

Before starting my search, I peeked out the window. Marshall's car was missing; I only hoped I would hear it when he returned. Not surprisingly, the coat closet held coats, boots, and an assortment of fishing poles leaning against the back corner. A little more unexpected, and decidedly more disturbing, was the axe that balanced between two nails driven into the side wall.

But no rifles. Maybe Marshall was one of the few men in Northern Wisconsin who didn't own firearms. If so, then he couldn't have killed Wayne.

A thought occurred, and after another peek outside, I headed back upstairs to the bedroom. Found the gun cabinet. My heart dropped into my stomach, acid eating away at it. The closet itself was surprisingly deep. It had to be. Marshall's business suits, dress shirts and slacks and a line of shoes ran on either side, but the main purpose of the closet—or, indeed, of the entire cabin—seemed to be to enshrine the massive gun safe pushed against the back wall.

Nearly as tall as me and over three feet wide, it looked like it could hold an arsenal of weapons. Pretty fancy, too. A shiny black exterior contrasted with the gold etchings of manufacturer's name and a wildlife scene depicting a stately buck. Dead-center in the door was a gold-plated, five-spoke wheel handle that you had to spin to unlock the dang thing. It was a monster of a gun safe.

Locked, too. No way a jumbo paperclip was getting into this thing. Besides, having no clue what Wayne had been shot with, I didn't know what to look for. A door slammed. Taking a deep breath, I left the bedroom.

Marshall stood in the kitchen, pouring himself a cup of coffee. He turned at my entrance and smiled warmly, eyes crinkling.

"Well, look who's up," he said. He gestured toward the small kitchen table covered with plastic grocery bags. "I wasn't sure if you could manage food, but I didn't have anything decent anyway, so I ran to the store."

"You didn't have to bother," I said. Nausea made the thought of food repugnant.

Still shaking and not able to meet his smiling eyes, I sat at the table. For the first time, I tried to dredge up the details of how I ended up ensconced in Marshall's bed to begin with. My head hurt. It refused to provide information about the previous night. I wanted to know, but didn't want to ask. Didn't, in fact, want to admit even to myself that I'd had a blackout. Shame poured in, flooding my soul, making me tremble. I covered my eyes, not wanting Marshall to see me cry. Luckily, he was moving back and forth putting the food away, whistling quietly.

He plunked a bottle of Excedrin next to my elbow and reached over to tousle my hair. That hurt.

"You're gonna live," he said, apparently thinking the physical aspect of my hangover caused my distress. I didn't enlighten him.

Instead I worked at pulling myself together, fumbling weakly with the cap. *Friggin' child proof. . .* He took it away, popping the top with ease. But I forgave him when he handed over two pills and a glass of orange juice.

"You were pretty wasted last night, huh?" He joined me at the table, opening a pastry box. My nose had a schizophrenic episode, simultaneously loving and hating the sugary smell of coffee cake. My stomach was clearer, rolling ominously.

"I guess so," I answered weakly. "Uh, thanks for picking me up." I could assume that much since my car had been nowhere in sight when I looked outside.

I must have guessed correctly, because he nodded and mumbled "you're welcome" through a full mouth. Swallowing, he said, "Almost didn't happen though. Next time you call, stay on the phone long enough to tell me where you're at."

I just didn't have enough functioning brain cells to pull off the bluff. "What do you mean?"

"Don't remember, huh? I'm not surprised, as blasted as you were. You called me about one saying something about Wayne—that's how I knew it was you—and saying "why?" Couldn't really catch that part. Anyway, I tried to get you to tell me where you were 'cause you were in *no* condition to be on the roads, but you mumbled that I should do something anatomically impossible to myself—I'm paraphrasing here—and dropped the phone. Luckily, somebody passing by picked it up and told me you were at The Bear Club."

"Cub," I muttered.

"Whatever. Anyway, by the time I show up, you were all happy and surprised to see me. So that worked out well. And you very nicely refrained from throwing up in my car."

"Did you bring the ice cream bucket?" An unexpected smile bubbled up at the memory.

"Forgot it. And I didn't have to lose my keys either. You came willingly." His smile was decidedly more erotic, and I flushed, making my head throb in triple-time.

"So what happened, Letty?" He turned serious on me. Serious and gentle. *Could I trust it?* Could I trust *him?*

"It just. . . got to be too much. It kind of caved in, all at once. But I'm okay now. This won't affect my work."

"No, of course not. I didn't think it would. I expect that's what set Wayne off."

"What did?"

"You're a fighter. You don't give up. That can be an insult to a certain type of man," he leaned back in his chair. His smile stretched like warm, sweet taffy. "To others, it's a challenge."

"A challenge?" I swallowed. "So, is all this character analysis part of your supervisory duties?"

"Oh, no. I came up with this on my free-time. Just trying to be helpful."

"Uh-huh. Okay, then. As long as you're being so helpful, how about getting me to my car?"

He sighed regretfully. "I suppose. You sure you don't want breakfast?" he said, and then laughed at my expression. Maybe he *was* evil enough to be a killer.

A half-hour later, Marshall dropped me off outside Cubs, where my car, abandoned and forlorn, had waited out the night. Nothing had been disturbed. Of course, if Marshall *was* the Shakespeare stalker, he'd be crazy to vandalize my car when he'd be the prime suspect. On the other hand, my Shakespeare stalker *was* crazy, so that meant Marshall could be the killer. *So I could clearly* not *choose the wine in front of me. . .*

I was having *Princess Bride* flashbacks.

After making sure my car started, he waved, and we drove off in opposite directions.

When I got home, I found Blodgett's business card sticking out of my door frame. On the back, he'd written "Call me" with his cell phone number. I'd forgotten that I'd called Blodgett before unwrapping the knife. The *murder* weapon. The weapon Blodgett had questioned me about, that I'd denied knowledge of, that was now covered in what I could only assume was Wayne's blood. With Blodgett's bloodhound instincts, he'd probably scented the incriminating evidence through the door. Would he believe me if I told him the real killer had left it as a little present? In my glove box? Wisconsin didn't have the death penalty, but I had no illusions about my ability to survive prison. My heart thudded dully. Ma was right. Cops could get you killed.

Locking the door behind me, I stood staring at the knife and sonnet lying in plain view on my coffee table. If I turned the knife over to the cops, as I very much wanted to do, I'd catapult myself to the top of Blodgett's suspect list. If I wasn't already in the lead position to begin with.

With so much going on, I didn't know what to panic over first, but I was pretty sure panic was a reasonable response. It came easily. Unfortunately, hyperventilating and running in dithery circles did very little in the nature of problem-solving. The bloody knife still gleamed evilly at me from the kitchen table, the cops suspected me in my stalker's murder while I suspected my hunky boss of that same murder, and I'd apparently acquired a second, more schizoid stalker who carried attention seeking to a homicidal level. Plus, I was going to have to confess my relapse to Sue and that might be the scariest issue yet.

I reverted to the Serenity Prayer.

What could I change? I couldn't change what the police thought, and I couldn't figure out whether Marshall was involved or not. At least not yet. I couldn't change the fact that somebody was sending me psychotic presents.

The knife. It was the only thing I had any influence over. I almost curled up in the fetal position at my next thought: *I had to get rid of it.* I didn't want to destroy it or lose it irretrievably; it was still evidence in a murder, even if Wayne was the victim. But right now it would only implicate *me*, which was probably what the real killer hoped for. A search warrant would likely cover my apartment and office. Probably my car, too. I needed to hide the knife somewhere that I would have access to, if needed. Somewhere that wouldn't involve or implicate anyone else. And somewhere that Blodgett wouldn't look.

Or *couldn't* look.

CHAPTER TWENTY-NINE

I made it to the office just before closing. Mary Kate manned the desk, as she often did on Saturdays. She lit up when I came in.

"What's new, Gazoo?" she greeted me. No, really. She did.

"Oh, nothing much. I just had some reports to finish up." I edged my way toward my office.

"Really? On a Saturday? You don't usually come in. And, no offense, but you don't look so hot."

"I think I'm coming down with the flu. So I wanted to finish up these reports in case I get sick. Sicker, I mean. Next week."

I gave her credit; she honestly tried to follow the convoluted crap I'd just rattled off. Her face scrunched in an origami of confusion from the effort. The hangover had obviously weakened my lying powers. Or maybe sobriety had.

Locking myself in my office, I dug a copy of the sonnet and the buck knife out of my purse. I pulled a sheaf of intake forms from my desk. What I was doing was probably against some licensing regulation. I hesitated. Then with a snort, I realized that was the very *least* of my worries and got busy doctoring up a false client file.

I blanked at the very first question: name. The trick was coming up with one that I'd remember later after, hopefully, things cleared up. A possibility floated up from the fog. Larry

Harmon, aka "Bozo the Clown." One of the names Wayne had used to sabotage my client schedule. Seemed fitting; I'd always been terrified of clowns.

I plunked a red circle sticker indicating inactive on the tab next to *Harmon, Lawrence* and shoved the knife in. I'd left one copy of the sonnet at home, so I added the other to the file. Blodgett would get the original.

Except for a soft murmur of voices coming from Carol's office, the clinic was quiet. I couldn't tell if Mary Kate was still up front, but only a few minutes remained until Carol's session was over and the clinic closed for the day. I'd have to chance it.

Luckily, the front was empty. My heart trip-hammered erratically as I tiptoed across the reception area to the dark file room. The lights had been turned off in preparation of closing, and I assumed Mary Kate was using the bathroom adjoining the lobby area.

Flipping the light on, I hurried over to the "H" section. Instead of cabinets, the files were arranged on shelves stretching the perimeter of the small room. A toilet flushed next door, and I nearly plastered the ceiling with my armful of camouflage files. A *leetle* jumpy. And if it was Mary Kate in the potty, I only had moments before she returned to run the front desk.

Grabbing the *Harmon* file, I shoved it between Harland, Lois and Harstaad, Kenneth, two people I'd never heard of, but whose deepest secrets now bracketed my own. I heard the bathroom door swish open at the same time as the remaining stack of legitimate client records slithered from my shaking hands.

Mary Kate, co-dependent senses tuned to subliminal frequencies, stuck a helpful face around the corner.

"Whoa! Need some help?"

"No, no. I've got it." Too late, though. She was already on her knees in the middle of the paper heap, sorting names and making piles. I lowered myself to the floor, struggling to look normal. My hands shook like castanets, stale, booze-scented

194

sweat patches ringed my pits and streaked the back of my shirt as I worked hard to keep from throwing up in Mary Kate's lap. "Normal" was a stretch.

Lucky for me, shaking, sweating, pale, and disoriented fit with my earlier story of illness and Mary Kate chattered on about the efficacy of chicken soup versus tea with honey. I tried to disconnect from the food talk. After I gagged ominously a couple times, she took the hint and changed the subject. Even better, she sent me home, promising to assemble the scattered records into their appropriate jackets.

Weak and done in, I let her push me out the door.

At least at home I could puke and shake in private. Throughout the afternoon, panic competed against remorse for the honor of being named Most Over-Powering Emotion. For the most part, they ran neck-and-neck, making me both fear for my life and hate it.

I'd gotten drunk again. Shame and bile undulated in slow, feverish waves through my body every time a memory of the night before rose to the surface. And recall it, I did. The parts I hadn't blacked out, that is. In an orgy of self-disgust, I examined my failure, moment by moment, picking mercilessly at each instance of weakness, exposing them to the harsh light of the day after.

All this insight made me want to get drunk.

Well, hell. That wasn't working. I sighed, rolled off the couch, and headed for the shower. At least I could clean up the outside self. Afterward, I wrapped up in the ugliest, most comfortable garment I owned—my old bathrobe—thus satisfying both needs of punishment and comfort.

I was a mess.

I had to call Sue, but I decided to wait until she was at the Saturday night meeting. I'd leave a message, face her tomorrow.

Besides, there were other issues—life or death issues—that were even more pressing. If indeed some crazy freak had me in his sights, I'd jeopardized more than just my sobriety, precious though that was. Drunk, I'd left myself completely vulnerable. The fact remained that I didn't know who had been standing in Wayne's shadow, didn't know who had used Wayne's harassment as a decoy for his own sly invasion. I wasn't even sure how to differentiate between the two.

I could avoid it no longer. I had to face the question that had catapulted me to the bar last night. It—and booze—would kill me if I didn't.

Was *Marshall* that crazy freak?

It was true that he had rifles at his cabin, but so did nearly everyone in northern Wisconsin. Hunting was as common as cheese and beer, and if a person wasn't an avid hunter, he was guaranteed to know someone who was. Or, not to be sexist, "she." Screw fashion. Come November, there would be plenty of women perched on a couple of jerry-rigged planks nailed to the branches of an oak, wearing blaze orange and eau de la deer pee. My own dad had taken me out a time or two, but after hiking three miles through dense bracken in the crisp air, I ate all the candy and fell asleep in the tree-stand. Shortly followed by falling *out* of the stand. Not an endearing father-daughter moment.

The study of Shakespearean sonnets, on the other hand, was not a particularly regional pastime. Which is not to say that Wisconsinites are a bunch of backwoods hicks; as a whole, however, we gravitated more toward Thoreau and the pond experiment. Not only had Marshall admitted that he'd studied English literature in college, but he was familiar enough to recognize the sonnets in an unusual context.

Would he have brought that to my attention if he really was guilty, though? Or was his admission a covert message, a code, that he expected me to pick up on? The electricity between us fairly crackled at times, but hadn't he initiated it? Though I tried, I couldn't recall any flirtatiousness prior to Wayne's attack. Perhaps the incident triggered something? If so, was it as simple as a white knight complex—not unusual for males in the mental health field—or as sinister as an opportunist preying on a victim's vulnerabilities? Did he feel protective of me, or possessive?

I didn't know.

The white rectangle of Blodgett's business card caught my attention again. I could put off calling Sue, but the detective was another matter. He'd be wondering about my hysterical message, and it would look strange if I waited too much longer. Plus, if I *was* a suspect, it wouldn't help to appear uncooperative or evasive. Fighting against that common sense rationale, every fiber of my alcoholic nature screamed to run, hide, ignore, deny.

Drink.

Maybe I'd call Sue first after all.

CHAPTER THIRTY

She picked me up and hauled me to a meeting. I couldn't stand the thought of running into Robert so we went to an Open Speaker meeting two towns over. At least I didn't have to share tonight, but five minutes after the speaker stepped down I realized I hadn't heard a word he'd said. It was probably inspirational, uplifting even, but I spaced the whole thing, instead pondering if I was about to be arrested for Wayne's murder and whether prison orange would make my skin look sallow.

Sue's attitude surprised me. Given her usual orneriness, I'd been prepared for wrath on a biblical scale. Instead, she maintained a sympathetic matter-of-factness that left me alternating between relief and bouts of spasmodic flinching if she moved too abruptly. I didn't altogether trust her nice side.

Afterward, she took me out for coffee and pie. I ended up confessing everything except where I'd hidden the knife. The telling of it made me queasy and I pushed my plate away. Apparently, nothing short of murder—her own, that is—could turn Sue off of her pie. It was a raspberry cream cheese, so I kind of understood. She did slow down and acquire a pensive look, however.

"There can't ever be an excuse for relapsing, but damn," she said, "you sure push the limits, girl."

"I've always been an overachiever," I said.

"So, what you're telling me is that you're a murder suspect, somebody even crazier than Wayne is stalking you, and you think it might be your boss with the cute butt."

I buried my face in my hands. "And I think I'm being framed. And I'm a drunk."

"That, too," Sue said. "But I don't get the knife part. First, it's there; then, it's missing. The cops can't find it and nobody else seems to have, either. Then after Wayne gets *shot*, they're asking about his *knife*? What the hell is going on? Put your head up and think."

Reluctantly, I complied. "It's crazy. Carrie's mom was really clear about finding Wayne shot." I swallowed against the image that rose to mind when I recalled Edna's description. Waving a quivery hand around my ear, I said, "She specifically talked about... his head." I gagged. Sue pulled my pie over to her side.

I pulled it back. It was lemon meringue, after all. The nausea would pass.

"So, if he's shot, why ask about the knife? And what's the knife doing showing up on your doorstep?"

"The *bloody* knife," I whispered. "What? Did whoever shoot him...?" I made "Psycho" stabbing motions at my pie.

Sue grimaced, finally pushing her plate away. It was scraped clean enough to serve to the next customer, but the symbolism of repugnance was still there. Pointless, but there.

"Okay, well, how did he get the knife? The police couldn't even find it."

I'd been thinking about this. "Either Wayne had it on him when he was killed and the shooter took and used it after Wayne died, or it was someone who was in position to pick it up after the initial attack at the clinic, before the police could."

"Marshall," Sue pointed out the obvious.

I shrugged, not wanting to voice the thought. I pulled the pie closer, twining my fork through the yellow and white goo. Sue sighed.

"So, are you looking for a stalker or a killer, or is that the same person?"

Good question.

"It would be an awfully big coincidence to have a killer trying to frame me *and* a stalker trying to. . . well, stalk me."

"It all depends on the knife," Sue said. "If the knife was involved in Wayne's murder, then the killer and stalker would *have* to be the same person. The sonnet and the knife were part of a package deal, so to speak. But if the knife has no connection to Wayne's death, then, I suppose, it's possible that there are two separate people involved. After all, the blood could be anyone's, and we don't know for sure that Wayne was stabbed."

"Then where did the blood come from?" I asked. "And why was Blodgett focusing on the knife? He spent as much time on that as on the gun. Why would it show up all bloody and wrapped up in some psycho poetry about death and desire if it wasn't connected?"

We sat mulling over the many questions for a bit.

"I wonder if Pete would know about the knife," she finally said.

"Pete?" My mind blanked. Pete who?

"Pete Durrant," she said, vamping a little, fluffing her hair. "He's taking me out tomorrow night. I'll see what I can find out."

"Sue, I doubt he's going to spill any police secrets over the Sunday meatloaf special. He's a cop, after all."

"We're going out for prime rib. And, anyway, I'll wear my sexy underwear." She batted her eyes and waggled her hips a la Mae West. Sue as a scheming seductress? The images that developed were not welcome. And I seriously doubted that Mae's hips would've made squeaky fart sounds on the cheap pleather seat.

"You've only known him a few days. Isn't sexy lingerie a bit premature?"

200

"Yeah, but it sets the tone." She winked.

"In that case, you better shave your legs, too."

Every little bit helps.

Sunday's are supposed to be peaceful. I slept in, waking nose-to-whiskers with a dead mouse. Shrieking, I flung the pillow one direction and scrambled wildly off the bed in the other. Landed with a bone-crunching thud on my butt and looked up to see Siggy peering over the edge of the bed at my lunacy. His ears twitched as he tried to fathom my reaction to a perfectly *nice* little gift.

"Is that yours?" I asked, pointing to the rodent.

He walked over, picked it up in his mouth and made for the kitchen.

I bounded down the hall after him, squealing various versions of "Eww!" and trying to convince him to drop it. He finally complied, giving me a disgusted look as if to say, "Make up your mind, woman." I used a file folder and a broom to scoop the limp little body up, tossing it in the garbage. Then, even though it wasn't nearly full, I grabbed the bag, tied it off and took it outside to the dumpster. Threw the broom in, too, for good measure. Bleh!

Siggy was miffed with me all day, staring with squinty, green eyes while I poked in drawers and in closet corners looking for mouse droppings. I never found any. Avoiding places where Siggy would have access, I set a couple of traps anyway. I'd filled my quota for rodent encounters for the year. Maybe the decade.

After the poop hunt, I stripped the bed and hauled the mound of sheets, pillow cases, and blankets to the laundromat. The last time I'd been here had been the day after I'd chaperoned Marshall at his birthday party and the weekend my utilities had been tampered with. Distracted, I overshot the laundromat entrance and had to make a sharp right in order to swing back around the block. Almost got rear-ended by a big, blue Buick, which had been riding my tail.

If I was going to have a shot at figuring out the sonnet stalker, I was going to have to reanalyze everything that had happened and decipher *which* behavior was caused by *which* asshole.

So many assholes in the world.

Obviously the sonnets had originated with the stalker and not Wayne. My earlier skepticism that Wayne would express himself in Shakespearian works was correct. He was more of a "Beans, beans, the musical fruit" kind of guy.

The first sonnet, impaled to the cloth doll with the fillet knife, had appeared on a Friday, just over a week ago. The second sonnet popped out of my glove box two days ago, also on a Friday.

A coincidence? Was there something significant about Fridays? It was too soon to tell, but I'd have to keep that in mind. I wondered if there was anything else I'd mistakenly attributed to Wayne.

With a start, I remembered the bouquet. At the time, the card's message had seemed quaint, adoring. I grabbed my AA book, rifling through the pages. Scraps of paper with phone numbers and other miscellaneous notes fluttered to the floor, the floralist's card among them.

"To my 'forward Violet'—Thou hast all the all of me."

So much for romantic. Now, it felt creepy as hell. More importantly, though, it matched the language of the sonnets. I was going to have to get a book on Shakespeare, preferably one with commentary. I certainly wasn't going to Marshall for an interpretation.

Just then the dryer buzzer went off, hurling me out of my reverie, scaring the crap out of me. I got several strange looks from other patrons. Apparently, a wild-eyed woman shrieking at the appliances unnerved them. Wimps.

I called in sick on Monday. Being alone with my thoughts about sent me crazy, but I couldn't deal with seeing Marshall.

I didn't hear from Sue until later that night. When she heard I hadn't gone in to work, she nagged about "isolating"—an AA term for withdrawing from the world and a warning sign for potential relapse.

"Sue, it's not isolating. It's protecting my ass!"

"Your ass is up for grabs anyway, unless you figure out what's going on. That won't happen if you're cowering on the couch waiting for it to all just go away."

I moved from the couch to the rocking chair—*how did she know?*—and changed the subject. "Did you learn anything from Durrant?"

"Not much," she admitted. "He's divorced and has four adult kids. At least I won't have to deal with the ex. And he's—"

"About Wayne's murder," I said through gritted teeth.

"I was getting to that. And it's still not much, because it's not like I could ask him straight out about the knife. But I did ask if he thought this Blodgett was a good detective. He was, like, 'Why?' And, so I go, 'Because the jerk is going on and on about the knife Wayne was wavin' in Letty's face a *month* ago instead of worrying about who shot the asshole.'"

"What did he say?"

"He got a funny look on his face, kind of constipated, you know? And he wouldn't look at me. But he did say that Blodgett was a good cop. And I finally got him to say there was no doubt that a shotgun was the cause of death."

"He looked funny, though?" I persisted.

"Yeah, like there was more that he wanted to say, but couldn't. Crazy as it sounds, I think the knife was involved somehow, even if he *was* killed with a shotgun blast. There's something weird going on about that knife."

"I know."

CHAPTER THIRTY-ONE

M y first client wasn't scheduled until ten o'clock, so I had just enough time to run to the bookstore. There was a ton of books on Shakespeare—various plays, theories on his true identity, and, of course, sonnets. I got caught up in the mystery of Shakespeare. I hadn't known that his very identity was a subject of controversy. Apparently, no one even knew for sure if Shakespeare was really the actor/playwright from Stratford-on-Avon or if some notable had taken the name as a pseudonym.

I finally refocused, picking a collection of sonnets that should have been subtitled "Shakespeare For Dummies," and speed-walked to the checkout. I'd never in my life gotten out of a bookstore with only one book, but I had time constraints and stalker issues.

As soon as I walked through the clinic doors, my mind latched relentlessly on two subjects: the knife and Marshall. Before starting sessions, I slipped into the file room to peek at the Harmon file. Resisting the urge to pull it out, I ran my fingers between it and its neighbor, feeling for knife lumps. A line of sweat beaded my upper lip. I didn't just dream it. It was there.

An innate ability to deny harsh reality came in handy; focusing on my clients as they rotated in and out of my office was a blessed relief, but it only lasted as long as each session. As soon as the client crossed into the lobby, my brain circled back on itself, picking at the identity of the Shakespeare stalker like an infected scab. I avoided Marshall, skirting the reception area if I heard his voice and scooting past his open office door with head down, face buried in reports.

For the rest of the week, my mood fell into the same pattern: distracted, skittish, and isolated. Marshall's eyes followed me, questioning. Lisa asked three times if I was feeling all right, and Mary Kate brought me homemade chicken noodle soup.

In between sessions and at night locked in my apartment, I read sonnets 'til my eyes blurred. After a while, I found myself understanding the cadence of the language, making sense of the music of the words. Deep in the middle of the sonnets, I found the "forward Violet" sonnet, although it wasn't capitalized in the original. It was one of the lighter sonnets, thankfully, speaking as though the flowers had stolen color and fragrance from the writer's loved one to adorn themselves. I also noted that the flowers in my bouquet were taken from the sonnet as well. Violets, baby's breath, marjoram and the three roses— pink, white, and red—were all specified.

At work, I couldn't stop myself from visiting the file room several times a day, inventing reasons, slipping in when the front was empty, volunteering to file. It was as if I'd found a new addiction, just as dangerous, substituting checking on the knife for alcohol. I vowed to stay away, but the tension fed on the ever-present fear until I felt like I'd explode or go crazy. More importantly, I knew the sheer physical relief—the sudden loosening of neck and back muscles, unclenching of stomach muscles, smoothing out of forehead—just from checking on the knife was completely illogical. The killer was still out there, after all.

I knew it was stupid. I knew it was risky. Like any good addict, I did it anyway. Maybe because, somehow, the knife was the connection. Touching it, making sure it was in reach, keeping it under *my* control, let me believe that I could uncover its secrets.

On Wednesday, Mary Kate and Hannah dragged me out to lunch. Mary Kate's going-away party was scheduled for Friday, a fact I'd known but hadn't really paid attention to. Tradition required the supervising therapist take her intern out for lunch during his or her final week. Hannah had graciously invited me along as well, even though Mary Kate's transfer to her care continued to be difficult. Hannah was good that way.

Mary Kate chose Olive Garden, which suited everyone. She ordered first, asking for the mushroom stuffed ravioli, which sounded heavenly. Hannah went with the chicken scampi; I ordered soup and salad.

"Oh, wait!" Mary Kate stopped the server. "I've changed my mind. I'll have the scampi, too."

Hannah smiled slightly. She reached over, lightly resting her hand on Mary Kate's. "I just wanted to tell you what a pleasure it's been working with you, Mary Kate. You have such energy and passion for helping people that I've felt re-energized in my own work. That's one reason why I like working with interns. I'm sure Letty agrees." Hannah turned to include me, and I smiled in agreement. It had certainly been interesting, that's for sure. Mary Kate slipped her hand from under Hannah's, unrolling her silverware from the cloth napkin, spreading the latter in her lap.

"I wish I could stay forever," Mary Kate said. "I can't believe the semester is almost over."

"Are you ready for finals?" I asked.

Mary Kate shrugged. "I guess. Do you think Marshall is going to hire someone to cover the Saturday front desk? Like, part-time?"

"I doubt it," Hannah said. "More than likely we'll just make do until we get another intern in."

"So, Mary Kate, have you been wrapping up with your clients?" I purposely avoided the word "termination." "How's that been going?"

She faced me with a wistful look on her puppy-dog face. "Not too bad, really. I think the toughest one was my teenager. Remember her? I think she'll be okay, though. She's got a good relationship with the school counselor who referred her, and they're looking at colleges for next year. She's excited."

"Moving on to the next phase of life can be exciting," I said.

"I know, I know. But I've been so happy at the clinic. It's so hard getting this close"—she pinched her fingertips together—"to your dream and being told to go away."

Hannah said, "Well, finishing your schooling will bring you even closer to your goals. And then you can come back, if not to our clinic, then to another."

Our dishes arrived, diverting our attention. We fussed with handing around the bread sticks and dug in, abandoning conversation in favor of eating. After a while, I couldn't help noticing Mary Kate picking at her scampi, shifting the noodles around with her fork. Although most interns took the end of their rotation with equanimity, others struggled. Mary Kate's passion fueled both her empathy for the people she helped and depression at the thought of leaving them. At least she seemed to be trying with Hannah now.

"Mary Kate, what're the plan for the interns' going away party?" Hannah asked.

The right question. Mary Kate immediately sparkled, sitting up straight, filling her skin again.

The intern parties, low-budget and low-key, were usually held after hours in the clinic conference room, the arrangements dumped on Lisa. This year, Mary Kate had commandeered the social-planner duties. As long as she stayed in budget and didn't make a mess, Lisa wouldn't interfere. Nobody else cared.

Mary Kate chattered on happily, discussing the merits of regular cake versus ice cream cake and whether anyone would want to go out drinking afterward. I half-expected her to have purchased her own gift, but apparently Lisa had managed to hold onto the reins for that task.

By the time we made it back to the clinic, Mary Kate was her usual bouncy self and I returned to obsessing about knives and sexy bosses who might be killers. The usual.

Instead of TGIF, Friday turned into OMG-IF. I got back from lunch to find Robert, of all people, waiting for me in the lobby, suffering under Lisa's baleful stare. She'd heard we'd broken up and, like any good woman friend, assumed it was his fault. Plus, she didn't like real estate agents or guys who got manicures.

After we said hello, I stood looking at him. Waiting.

"Uh, listen Letty, I was wondering if I could talk to you?"

My eyebrows raised involuntarily. "You mean more than this?" I asked, twirling my finger to include our already-talking position in the lobby.

He flushed, lips thinning slightly. He'd never liked or understood my sense of humor. Maybe I should hook him up with Regina.

"Look, I'd really like to talk to you. Please."

The "please" got me. Since I had back-to-back clients and didn't know how long the interns' party would take, we agreed that he'd phone me later that evening.

Later, as I walked a client up to the front, Marshall materialized at my side.

"Letty, do you have a moment?"

"Um, I'm taking Judith up to reschedule."

"Oh, I'm sure Judith knows her way. Do you mind?" He smiled warmly into my client's eyes and grasped my elbow. "I'm pulling a boss's prerogative."

His charm was palpable, his grip unshakable. Judith laughed and tossed a wave over her shoulder as she headed for the front. I followed Marshall in to his office, taking a seat. He shut the door.

"Changing your open door policy?" I said lightly.

He took his seat behind his desk. Steepling his hands in front of his face, he gazed at me over the tips. "I thought you might like a moment in private to look at this." He slid an envelope with the Wisconsin state seal in the return address corner across the desk.

I opened it. Wayne's complaint had been determined to be unfounded. I let out a sigh of relief at the first good news I'd had in ages. Marshall grinned from across the desk.

"I take it the review board showed some sense?" he asked.

"Was there any doubt?" I laughed.

"Not of *your* actions," he said quietly.

I blushed, knowing he referred to more than the board's decision. My recent avoidance stood in stark contrast to our earlier rapport, but I couldn't discount my suspicions. Something would have to give pretty soon, though. Professionally, I couldn't continue dodging him. I told myself "professionally" was all that mattered.

"Going to be at the party tonight?" he asked after several long moments of awkward silence.

"I wouldn't miss it for the world." I cleared my throat.

"I'm glad Mary Kate's not carting us off to the roller rink this time." He smiled again, laugh lines crinkling. I avoided his eyes, standing and moving to the door.

"I'd better get my next client."

"I guess I'll see you later, then," he said, his voice thick with disappointment.

CHAPTER THIRTY-TWO

The intern party sucked.

Sarah, our sorority girl intern who squinted and tossed her hair a lot, went to ridiculous lengths to avoid mingling with Mary Kate—at one point, knocking over a pickle tray to place the food table between them. Much of her time was spent rolling her eyes at her co-intern, making me wonder if she and Mary Kate had had "office-mate" issues. Occasionally, interns set up a competitive atmosphere a la "The Apprentice," although the real-life version had zero entertainment value.

Or it could have been the aura of depression seeping like sewer water from Mary Kate. Although normally Mary Kate would have adored the attention, on this occasion she alternated between weepy gratitude and weepy wistfulness. I felt like calling the local radio station and requesting "It's My Party (And I'll Cry If I Want To)."

Hannah stuck by Mary Kate's side trying to encourage her, which couldn't have been easy since Mary Kate wouldn't acknowledge her. Regina and boring Bob stopped in long enough for Regina to corner me and suggest another supervision meeting. I lied and promised I would. After scanning the room with jaded eye, she and her entourage of one left. Marshall worked the room as best he could, moving from colleague to colleague, smiling and bestowing the boss's benediction on the crowd. I coordinated my movements with his, keeping the length of the room between us and avoiding eye contact.

The ice cream cake melted.

After an hour I was ready to fake an epileptic seizure to get out of the room, but, less dramatically, Robert called. I would've gone out in the hall to talk, but there were still counseling sessions going on, so I stood in the corner, finger stuffed in my ear to block the room noise. We kept it brief, deciding to meet at Chandlers, a favorite of Robert's, in forty-five minutes.

If all I got out of the lousy relationship with Robert was an excuse to leave this party, it was worth it.

I went over to give Mary Kate a good-bye hug, but she clung to me, all forlorn.

"Are you leaving? I wanted to talk to you. *Please?*" The abused puppy was back.

"Um, well, I have to be somewhere in a few minutes"—her eyes welled up with tears—"but, yeah, sure."

Her smile split wide enough to show back molars. "But not here," she said. "In private."

We went to my office, where Mary Kate scooched down in her usual seat.

"Just like old times, huh?" I said.

Mary Kate smiled wistfully. "I wish. These last few weeks have been so hard. Finals and saying good-bye and all that."

"I know," I said. "Changes are difficult, but once you get through finals it should lighten up, right? Have you thought about taking some time off?"

"Yeah, it's funny you should say that. I have been thinking about whether or not to continue with school. I was thinking that maybe—"

"Whoa! I didn't mean quitting school. I meant, like, a vacation. Some down-time. Quitting school is such a big decision. I thought you wanted to counsel? Are you sure?"

"I don't know. Everything is just getting so hard, you know? I thought maybe I could take a break, maybe work here for a while. Like I could do phones and stuff while I decide."

"I don't even think we're hiring, Mary Kate. You'd have to talk to Marshall about that. I just..." My voice trailed off. I had a natural therapist's reluctance to giving advice, but as a friend I hated keeping quiet on such a huge issue. "I just hope you really think this through before making a decision. I know you'd make a good therapist and you seemed so passionate about the field. Why don't you get through finals and take that vacation? Then you can see how you feel."

"I guess." She didn't look convinced.

"All right, then, let's get you back to your party." I stood, and she reluctantly followed suit. She shadowed me back to the conference room looking more dejected than ever.

A chorus of "Here she is!" greeted us. When Lisa gathered up the two interns for opening the presents, Mary Kate perked up a tiny bit. I waited until she was ripping into the bright orange tissue paper before sneaking out. Just as I made my move for the door, Marshall caught my eye.

He stood just behind Mary Kate and Sarah, watching me. I hesitated. For half a heartbeat, we stared at each other, eyes searching. I shivered. Mentally shaking myself, I slipped out the door.

Chandlers, known for its surf-n-turf special, was crowded as usual. Robert was already seated at a discreet table near the stone fireplace when I got there. As I crossed the room, I wished I'd had a chance to go home and change, but it would have made me late. Robert stood as I approached, smiling in a way that reminded me why I'd fallen for him in the first place. The firelight danced in his hair, turning his honey-blond a deeper gold. He held the back of the chair for me as I sat.

As we made small talk and looked the menu over, it dawned on me that he was shoveling charm down my throat

213

with both hands. He was attentive: asking about my day, complimenting me on my blouse. He was solicitous: asking what I might order, the temperature—too hot? Too cold?— near the fire. He was interested: asking whether the licensing complaint, which he referred to as "that witch hunt"—a phrase he'd never uttered when we were dating, had been resolved. When he asked how Sue was doing I decided he'd either smoked his lunch or wanted something from me.

If I was a person of stellar ethics, I would have cut the meal short knowing I had no intention of doing any favors for my ex. But technically, having just relapsed, I'd only been sober for a few days and was still a work in progress. Or maybe I'd have felt more generous if he'd been straightforward instead of being such a smarmy butt kisser.

As matters stood I had no compunction about ordering, and enjoying, a thick, juicy slab of prime rib. And, besides, it was nice, really nice, to sit quietly in pleasant surroundings and not wonder if the man across from me got his jollies from dark Renaissance verse and doll mutilation. Robert was far too self-absorbed to be obsessed with anyone who didn't look back at him in the mirror. At least, I hoped.

About midway through the meal, Robert cleared his throat nervously. I felt the table jounce and knew if I peeked underneath I'd see Robert's leg jiggling nervously. The bullshit cometh. . .

He cleared his throat again, looking to the side, avoiding eye contact. "So, that's some pretty weird shit with Randy, huh?" He glanced back, checking my reaction.

I finished chewing, swallowed. "You mean *Wayne*, don't you? And even if I hated him, 'weird' is an quite understatement. Horrible, maybe."

"Have the police been talking to you?" He feigned interest in chasing a green bean around his plate.

"Of course. I'm probably the main suspect." With a start, I realized I'd forgotten to call Blodgett back. So much for appearing cooperative.

"That's crazy," his voice strangely emphatic. "Obviously Rand—uh, Wayne—had a lot of problems. Anybody could have done it. I think they're just taking the easy way out, focusing on the first people they come across." A frown crossed his face as he probably recalled just *how* he came to the attention of the police in the first place. But he let it slide.

"I don't believe that. After all, it makes sense that they need to check me out." I paused, watching his face tighten as I declined the "us versus them" alliance he proposed. "I didn't do it, of course, but how can they know that?"

"It's too bad you don't have an alibi, huh?" His eyes skittered away again, a line of sweat glistening on his upper lip. Ah.

"I guess." I stayed noncommittal, interested to see how he would continue.

"Listen, Letty. Just because we've had our differences doesn't mean I won't be there for you. If there's anything, I can do...?"

He finally made eye contact, gazing with "significance" across the debris of our meal. What a crock. He'd left me dangling when I went to him for help with Wayne. It was obviously not my lack of alibi that had him sweating, and on top of that, the jerk apparently wanted *me* to proposition *him* into vouching for each other.

"Nope. Can't think of anything," I chirped. "But thanks."

More throat noises. "It's just so stupid, you know? I can't believe the cops are stupid enough to think you would actually kill someone."

"Maybe they don't. Maybe they have someone else they're considering. Like you said, 'anybody could have done it.'" I stared at him, a slight smile on my face. Evil of me, I know.

He reached for his water glass, nearly tipping it over. "Have you heard anything about that? I mean, there must be a bunch of people mad at Wayne. He wasn't a nice guy, you know."

Well, no shit. Suddenly, I was sick of the whole charade. "Robert, what's this all about? Why did you ask me here? And don't give me any bullshit about enjoying my company or burying the hatchet or whatever else you might come up with. You're obviously afraid the police consider you a suspect. Why?"

His lips thinned, but for the first time, he looked me straight in the eyes. "Because they heard you and I were dating."

"So, that means, what? That you were avenging my honor or something?" I snorted. "Would it help if I told them that's not your style?"

His eyes narrowed into flinty slits. "I'm not some Cro-Magnon, who can't control himself. And it's not like you came to me for help. You shut me out, so don't blame me for not being there."

The theme song from *Rocky* tinkled from his hip. He glanced at the Caller ID and mumbled, "I need to get this. I'll be right back." He stood and strode off to the front lobby.

"Rocky?" I snorted to his retreating back. "Puh-lease."

The server walked up and motioned to the half-empty plates. "Did you want me to wrap any of this?"

"No, there's nothing worth saving."

"Oh," he said, eyes wide. "One of *those* dates? Would dessert help?"

I smiled for the first time. "It might, but I don't want to get bogged down here. If he's not back in the next few minutes, I'm out of here."

"Good for you, hon. Don't take any you-know-what from any of them." With a wink, he moved off to another table. I'd make sure he got a big tip even if I had to leave it myself.

Robert showed up minutes later, apologizing. Not for his earlier boorishness, of course, but for the minor indiscretion of the phone call. What a boob.

By unspoken agreement, we let the discussion die. The walk up to the lobby was awkward enough, so I ditched into the bathroom to avoid continuing the farce into the parking lot. We said our good-byes quickly, and I hurried through the door with the triangle-shaped brass woman affixed to it.

After using the facilities, washing my hands twice, and counting one-Mississippi three hundred times, I decided it was safe to go. The relief I felt upon noticing Robert's truck gone, however, was short-lived.

As I crossed the lot, I could see something the color of mottled blood on my windshield. I stopped, heart thudding. Screwing up my courage and uncapping my very own, handy-dandy "Slap My Ass And Call Me Sally" pepper spray, I moved forward.

A dead rose. Several petals littered the hood, leaving the flower nearly denuded, canting listlessly to the side. The stem had been thrust behind the wiper, thorns glinting sickly yellow in the lot's sodium lighting. I shivered.

He'd been here.

CHAPTER THIRTY-THREE

I waited until the next night to go to a meeting. The bad news was the first person I saw at the club was Sandra. I'd either have to face her or forgo a cup of badly needed coffee. She stood at the coffee bar—a fruit bowl in a sleeveless top that looked and clung to her fat chest like an orange peel. She'd had her highlights touched up, too, adding a lemony glow.

The good news was that I was in the mood for a fight.

"Wow, Letty, no offense, but you look like something the cat puked up. You weren't out drinking again, were you?"

Having been up all night brooding on the subject of dead flora, I probably did look like a hacked-up hairball. But the reference to my relapse was a low blow. Knowing she was all dolled up for Robert, I plastered a fake smile on my face and said, "Of course not. I had a lovely dinner at Chandlers. I just *love* their prime rib."

"Chandlers?" Sandra's eyes narrowed at the mention of Robert's favorite restaurant.

Ignoring her, I grabbed my mug from its peg, pouring myself some surprisingly fresh coffee.

"What time were you there?" she persisted.

The people around the counter quieted, the better to enjoy the unfolding drama.

"I'm sorry. Did you say something?" I smiled sleepily as though the cause of my late night was a certain blond real estate agent rather than a Shakespearian psychopath with a flower fetish.

"What *time* were you at Chandlers?" At least I think that's what she said. Her teeth were gritted hard enough to splinter into tiny shards.

"About 7:30 or so. Why?" I asked, all Shirley Temple-innocent.

"Oh, no reason," she lied. Then unable to stop herself, she blurted, "I guess you must have seen Robert there, too."

I let my eyebrows rise as if surprised at her naiveté. "Well, sure," I said with a laugh. "It would have been hard not to. He was sitting across from me."

Several sucked-in "Ooh's!" whistled through the air, heightening both my pleasure and Sandra's rage.

And then Robert, proving he'd been born under a particularly *un*lucky star, chose that moment to walk in to the club. He looked nice and relaxed for approximately 1.5 nanoseconds, which is how long it took his brain to process the information that his ex was standing next to his slut, and they were both pissed. Pure guy hell.

For a brief, satisfying moment, it looked like he was going to turn and run. Paul, one of the spectators, laughed out loud. Sandra got to Robert first, crossing the room like an orange puma with the scent of meat teasing her nostrils. I smiled at Robert's startled face and waggled my fingers "hi!"

"Did you enjoy your dinner last night, Robert?" Sandra snarled. "Huh? While I sat at home waiting for you? Did you have a good time?" She punctuated every fifth or sixth word by poking him in the chest with long, tangerine-tipped claws. Looked painful.

Robert looked over at me desperately. I shrugged, hands wide as though "*Gosh, was I not supposed to have mentioned that to Sandra?*"

Sandra stabbed again. This time, his forehead, leaving a red, half-moon dent. "Look at me when I'm talking to you! What?

I'm not good enough to take out to dinner, but you'll take Miss Priss? She must not be putting out yet, 'cause you sure were panting for it when you finally showed up at my door. Was she sitting right there when I called? Is that *all* I am to you?"

So that's who'd called during dinner. I shook my head in disgust. Strangely, my anger at Sandra faded away.

Just then, she looked over at me and must have decided I looked too complacent. Or, worse, maybe she saw pity. "Oh, and by the way? Where do you think he's been every Wednesday and Sunday night while you sat at home with your legs crossed like an ice princess? Don't fall off that high horse or you'll ram the stick up your ass."

With that wild flurry of mixed metaphors, she slammed out of the club.

Robert's face took on an alarming, red-and-white toile pattern. Again, he looked my way. But not for help.

I squinted "bring it on," pointing outside, having just enough class to not want an Act II screaming match in the lobby. I regretted beating him through the door, though, because that meant he got to slam it. Normally I'd be freaking out over a confrontation of this nature, but all the fear and frustrated anger of the last few weeks had finally found a target. He'd been cheating on me the *whole* time?

Unfortunately, we never got farther than the sidewalk leading to the parking lot. Before we could get into it, the sound of a racing engine made us turn around. Sandra's Accord jounced wildly over the three speed bumps. Her hands clenched the wheel and her eyes, glittering weirdly, met mine. For a moment, I thought she might add a couple of human speed bumps to the lot, but she settled for whipping us the bird before squealing out of the lot.

"Are you happy now?" Robert spit the words at me.

"Yes. Yes, I am. See?" I laughed, just to prove it. Sounded more than a little maniacal, but he was too pissed to notice.

"Listen, you little bitch, I've got half a mind—"

"Somehow I always knew you only had half a mind."

"—to smack the crap out of you. *What* did you say?"

I rolled my eyes. This was too easy. "Robert, you are a narcissistic asshole and definitely not worth my time." I flicked a hand as if waving away our past. "If you were only half the man I thought you were I might feel bad about breaking up, but now? I'm just glad I only wasted a few months on you."

He grabbed my upper arm, and I forced myself not to show fear.

"Hey!"

Paul had followed us. His face showed the fear I'd schooled mine to hide. "Let go of her!" His voice trembled, but he pushed at Robert's hand, trying to peel his fingers off my bicep. Robert released me, slapping Paul's hand away.

"Get off me, you little asswipe! This is none of your business."

But Paul was caught up in an emotion stronger than his fear. "You are such a j-jerk. I can't believe you treat her this way. You should be treating her like a princess, but instead you cheat on her with that skank! *I would worship her.*"

Robert grabbed Paul by the front of the shirt, lifting the slight man off his feet.

"Robert! Stop it!" I pushed between them. "*Stop it!*"

Robert threw Paul down to the ground, flinging him into the grass, not the concrete sidewalk. Paul's face scrunched up, as tears, snot, and a trickle of blood where Robert's hand had clipped his bottom lip, trickled down his face. Robert looked stunned, wiping his hand across his own face as though to scrub it clean.

"Ah, shit," he said, running his hand through his blond mop. He reached a hand down to Paul, offering to pull him up. Paul kicked at it.

"Get away!"

"Shit," Robert said again. "I'm sorry, Letty." Then he turned and walked away, heading for his car.

I stood on the sidewalk feeling like a tsunami had just washed over me, leaving debris and dead bodies in its wake. Paul pulled his knees up to his chest, burying his face in the crook of his arm.

I knelt, touching his hand. It was cold and shaking. "Paul?"

A muffled "go away" warned me off.

"Okay, I'll leave, but I want to say thank you. Paul, I—"

"Go away!" he howled.

"Okay. Okay, Paul. I'm leaving." I walked backward, not wanting to leave him, knowing that staying would only make his humiliation worse. I got in my car and sat, trying to think. Then I pulled my cell phone out, scrolled through my contact list, found Chad's number and called. I could only hope that he'd get here before Paul took off for the nearest bar to deaden his shame.

As I sat slouched in my car, watching the sobbing, huddled mess from afar, a horrible suspicion rose and bloomed.

Worship me?

Chad showed up a few minutes later, his calm demeanor a welcome presence. He walked over to the side of my car and leaned in the window, keeping a steady eye on Paul.

"Thanks, Chad. I didn't know who else to call."

"No thanks needed, Letty. You did right." He glanced at me with a worried frown. "You said Robert and Paul got into it?"

Raising his head, Paul noticed us staring. He slowly got to his feet, wiping his face with his t-shirt.

"Actually, Sandra and I got into it, and then Sandra and Robert. Then me and Robert, and *then* Robert and Paul."

"Busy day at the club, huh?"

"You could say that."

Chad pointed at the red welts left on my arm. "Robert?"

Robert's actions still stunned me. I'd never seen that side of him, didn't ever imagine him capable of violence. Maybe I'd

222

been blind, ignoring the signs. Inexplicably embarrassed and unable to speak, I just nodded.

Eyes red and swollen, a smear of snot trailing across his cheek, Paul walked up. He kept his eyes averted, refusing to look at me. Chad reached out, cuffing him on the shoulder in that strange man-code that translated to "I'm here for you, brother."

"I'm not. . ." I cleared my throat, started again. "I don't know what would have happened if Paul hadn't come out. I can't believe Robert would have. . ." My voice deserted me again.

"Listen, I don't know what's going on with Robert," Chad said. "I know he's freaked out about Randy's murder and the police questioning him. But that doesn't excuse this."

"Wayne," I said automatically. "But what's the big deal? They can't seriously believe he killed Wayne, can they?"

Paul listened avidly, Robert's woes perking him up.

"I guess he didn't mention the wrangle he and Wayne got into at the restaurant, huh?"

"They fought?"

"Wayne showed up drunk—not the best move for a meeting with your sponsor. Robert refused to talk to him, which is natural"—I nodded agreement—"and Wayne got pissy. Sounds like there was some pushing and shoving, and a whole lot more cussing. The restaurant manager threatened to call the police, and Wayne took off.

"Anyway, he was killed later that night, so it looks bad. Plus, I know breaking up with you is weighing heavy. Not that it wasn't the right thing for him to do."

"He didn't break up with *me*. I broke up with *him*." It shouldn't matter who broke up with whom. Even if it did.

Chad smiled. "Even worse. For him, I mean." Turning to Paul, he said, "Anyway, I guess we can thank you for stepping in. How about we go get some coffee?"

I pulled out, heading for home. Chad could handle the rest.

CHAPTER THIRTY-FOUR

I woke up to one of those rare Wisconsin freebies—a warm, spring morning. The air smelled fresh and green, the kind of scent laundry detergent manufacturers try to conjure up out of a bunch of chemicals. I cracked some windows and watched Siggy poke his nose at the screen. I wished I could enjoy it as much as he obviously did.

For me, the morning alternated between anger at Robert and worry for Paul, worry for Robert and suspicion of Paul, and, finally, a generalized disgust and suspicion toward the male species altogether. That about covered everything.

I got the time line out. The flowers could have come from Paul. He'd have had to find out where I worked, but he'd proved capable of that. Maybe he sent them to make me feel better, after learning about Wayne's attack. The enclosed card *"Thou hast all the all of me"* certainly fit with the idolization Paul revealed last night. Or was I overreacting? Was it just a crush?

Paul's social skills rated just higher than a house plant's. He was a nerd's nerd, a born victim. He had to realize how the guys avoided him, how he was the butt of so many jokes when they couldn't. Most of the jerks didn't even wait until his back was turned to treat him like crap. How long could a man take that kind of treatment without retaliating?

He was so hungry for acceptance that he licked up the crumbs of civility dropped by chance from those around him.

The only thing I'd ever done for him was to not be overly mean, and he'd been attached to me like a wood tick ever since. I didn't know anything about him, other than how long he'd been sober, and I even dated *that* in terms of how long he'd been around to annoy me.

Could he have sent the sonnets? I could imagine him reading Shakespeare. Burying himself in the dusty pages of old books, shutting out the present day where he was picked on, maybe feeling pride at understanding and appreciating a literary icon, while those around him watched *Jon and Kate* reruns. Too much pride? Did it morph into superiority, contempt?

I didn't know.

There were times I'd felt uncomfortable with Paul, but mainly that involved the type of social embarrassment that came from geek-adoration. Although, there *had* been that time in the AA parking lot when I'd been so frightened, but the fear had emanated from Wayne's presence, not Paul's. Hadn't it?

The phone call, too. I'd never discovered how he'd gotten my phone number; it indicated a resourcefulness that I hadn't expected. Slyness, even. And enough disregard for a person's privacy to go ahead and call despite AA's doctrines about anonymity.

Had Paul been the one messing with Wayne's truck? Carrie hadn't been very specific, but I could imagine Paul keying the side of Wayne's vehicle or something similar. Something that didn't involve direct confrontation, of course. Some type of slap-and-dash retaliation that only required secrecy and a sharp instrument. Was that what Paul had meant when he'd assured me he had an idea?

I tried to recall what I knew about Paul, but he was a blank. I'd always imagined him as some kind of computer techie, but that was probably just stereotyping. Thanks to anonymity and complete disinterest, I didn't even know his last name or where he lived.

And Robert? Had I ever really known him? On the one hand—charming, attractive, athletic. Cheating, self-centered, and a bully, on the flip. I felt stupid. Of course, I'd only dated the guy a few months. It could've been worse.

The police apparently weren't taken in by his good-guy charm. What had they seen that I hadn't? Perhaps I'd spent an inordinate amount of time admiring Robert's butt.

Although on the surface Robert seemed confident, his difficulty with relationships was obvious and predated our dating. He preferred to keep people at a distance, requiring little investment on his part. The two that he'd taken a risk on—myself and Wayne—had blown up in his face within days of each other. Did that trigger the violence?

I supposed it was conceivable that he'd killed Wayne.

I grabbed the time line again. The first sonnet, the doll "present," arrived literally on my door step the Friday after I broke up with Robert. In fact, all of the sonnets arrived on a Friday, although the last was early morning, a time when Robert was supposedly at work. Or so he said.

He'd certainly been able to adjust his work schedule around his booty calls with skanky Sandra.

As with Paul, there were few people I could ask. I'd never met any of Robert's friends or family. I had his home and office numbers in Minnesota, but I'd never been to either.

I could, however, ask Chad. He'd been willing to help last night and was the best resource for both men that I could think of. The only resource, as far as that went.

The phone rang interrupting my plotting. Sue's number popped up.

"Hel—"

"Letty!" Sue's voice boomed through the receiver. I could hear a car engine and assumed she was driving.

"Sue? Are you okay?"

"Listen! I'm on my way to Robert's. You're not going to believe this, but Sandra just busted into the club saying Robert is dead!"

"*What?*"

"Yeah, I know! She said he was *shot*. Sound familiar? Anyway, Pete was there, right? At the club, I mean, not Robert's. We were going to brunch and—"

"Sue!"

"Oh. Right. Okay, so Pete took off to secure the scene or whatever, and I'm heading over, too. He doesn't know that part yet. It's a surprise."

"I'm sure it will be," I said.

"Are you coming?"

"Already on my way."

I made the half-hour trip to Robert's rental in eighteen minutes. Durrant must have called it in en route because the road was clogged with police cars and curious neighbors. Parking a block away, I raced up the sidewalk, searching for Sue, whom I wanted to find, and Durrant, whom I didn't.

The house was a small ranch, typically rented by college kids for the school year. It had been deserted back in January; the students bailing out of college and rental lease simultaneously. They'd left a dozen holes in the walls, trashed the floor, and for some obscure reason, re-hung the kitchen cabinets in the living room. During the extensive remodeling, Robert had taken to using it as a base when he came up on weekends and planned to lease it out again come fall.

I'd only been over a couple of times and, in my panic, had forgotten that the detached garage and driveway were located at the rear of the house. Two police officers were stringing yellow crime scene tape around a wide perimeter while several others worked at keeping the looky-loos away. And probably ex-girlfriends, too.

They hadn't figured on deranged, former schoolteachers, however.

A row of overgrown lilac bushes separated Robert's from the house next door. An oak stood in the back of the neighboring property, branches hanging over the rental's back yard. A dilapidated treehouse, really only a bunch of warped two-by-sixes crisscrossing each other, balanced precariously in the spring-bare branches.

Said deranged, former schoolteacher perched like a vulture, peering into the rental's backyard. Oh shit. Bad image, the vulture and all.

I scurried down the line of lilacs hissing, "Sue!"

She shushed me with a finger to her lips, pointing at a row of boards nailed to the back of the tree trunk. This was supposed to be a ladder. Right. Taking a deep breath and sending a brief 911 to a god I'd always avoided, but who suddenly seemed handy, I climbed.

Each rickety board had been nailed with enough metal to build a space ship, although only a bare minimum of nails had actually made it *through* the wood to the trunk beyond. Seemed like an important detail to have been overlooked. The majority of nails had only kept the desired course (straight) part way and then folded over on themselves from inexpertly wielded hammers clutched in chubby, boy hands. The remaining nail stubs were then re-pounded, burrowing the shank into the boards sideways and askew, so that several dozen rusting and completely superfluous nail bits decorated the rungs.

About midway up, the board I clung to creaked ominously; I nearly wet my pants. I was suddenly convinced that I was either going to fall on my head, thus becoming a quadriplegic, completely at the mercy of the Shakespeare stalker a la "Rear Window," or one of the cops would see us and shoot us out of our perch.

I also realized I was just high enough to see over the lilac barrier. Somebody in a white space alien suit and booties was videotaping the scene. Three others likewise bootied but still in street clothes, stood in a half-circle about twenty yards from a recumbent figure on the patchy grass. I thought I recognized Durrant's back. Thankfully, the group was facing away from our tree. I scrambled up beside Sue.

"Are you crazy?" I whispered.

"Pete knows I'm here. Every few minutes he glares and waves at me to go away. I've got permission from the Sterlings though." She hitched a thumb at the house behind us. "I taught their kids."

"Can't they arrest us or something?"

"I don't see how. We're not interfering with the scene or getting in their way. We don't even have cameras. The most they can do is sneer.

"Can you see anything?" she asked.

I'd been avoiding looking at poor Robert, but I did now. At first, because of the milling investigators, I could only see legs. Grey slacks speckled with what I hoped, but didn't believe, was mud. All I could think of was how badly he would hate lying on the dirty ground like that. Then a cop moved.

"Unh…" we both said. Recoiling, I almost took a header out of the tree. Robert lay on his back, arms splayed out like his body had been flung forcefully back and down. As indeed it had. His face…

I gulped and shut my eyes. Dizzy. Right when I could have used it most, the adrenaline ebbed away, leaving me weak and shaky, a tinny aftertaste sliming my mouth. This, every part of this, was a terrible mistake. I turned to climb down, but Sue grabbed my arm.

"Do you see that?" she asked in a voice that had shrunk to a brittle whisper.

"I can't look. I don't want to see any more."

"I know. Just…I don't know…just look at his chest. Not the rest. Is that blood?"

"Sue, there's blood all over!" I gestured wildly at the body, accidentally forgetting my pledge not to look, almost plunging headlong out of the tree for the third time in as many minutes.

She was right. There, centered on his favorite blue, button-down shirt was a heavier saturation of blood, not the splattered spray pattern of the head wound. A pooled concentration the size of my fist, just over the heart.

"You think he was stabbed?" I asked. I wrapped my arms around the trunk as much for solace as for security. The raspy bark scratched my forearms.

"It would fit. If they were looking for a knife in Wayne's murder, maybe this explains why."

"So, somebody shoots him—Robert, I mean, and Wayne, too, for that matter—and then, what? Stabs him, too? *Why?* And why would anyone shoot Robert? He was an ass, but this is crazy!"

"Those are real good questions, miss." A voice spoke from the bushes, and I felt an entirely unexpected kinship with Moses. But not in a good way.

CHAPTER THIRTY-FIVE

Tree climbing *down* is markedly more harrowing than tree climbing *up*, especially with Blodgett waiting impatiently below. If I fell, I planned to land on Blodgett, thus ending both our problems.

Fortunately—or, unfortunately, if Blodgett succeeded in throwing me in a dark cell for the rest of my life—I made it to the ground without mishap. Sue was still three-quarters of the way up, stuck and grumbling. I ignored her.

Blodgett wore a dirt-brown suit, as wrinkled as a basset, that matched his eyes. His expression hovered between somber and blank. Not a lot of range. He ran his gaze up and down my body without the slightest bit of seductive energy. Looking for blood or defense wounds, more likely.

"Hello, Detective," I said. "What can I do for you?"

"You can stop playing Tarzan, for starters," he said.

A voice from above grunted, "Me Jane." Blodgett ignored her.

"I know," I glanced upward. "It wasn't my idea. I'm sorry. And I'm *really* sorry about Robert. I can't believe he's dead. It doesn't make sense." At best, I sounded fake as hell; at worst, heartless. The situation was so surreal that I hadn't yet accepted the fact of Robert's death—much less his murder—despite having seen his body with my own eyes.

"Gee, for a minute there, I thought you were confessing."

231

Halfway up the tree, the branches rustled, assorted swear words drifted down like dead leaves.

"Of course not," I said. "I didn't kill him—or Wayne, either. But I want to help you catch whoever did."

"Good." Blodgett was a keep-it-simple kind of guy. "We found his driver's license in his wallet, but the nature of the wound makes it impossible to use it as an I.D." Then, he asked, "Would you be willing to identify him?"

"You mean *now*?" My voice sounded like it came from very far away.

He had his notepad in his hand, ready to go. "Not just yet. Why don't you tell me what you know?" Another big, open-ended question—he liked them.

"I saw Robert last night at the club." I swallowed. "The AA club. Um, a little after six or so. We argued." I looked Blodgett straight in the eyes, hoping the admission wasn't going to cause him to whip out the handcuffs. "Or, rather, I was arguing with Sandra, the sleaze he was cheating on me with while we were dating. And, yes, I know what that looks like, but if I was going to kill all the guys that couldn't keep it in their pants, there'd be a whole lot more dead guys lying around Chippewa Falls and surrounding counties. A couple in Minnesota, too.

"Anyway," I continued, "he left the club before I did." I stuttered to a stop, realizing too late that I was about to provide Blodgett with another sacrificial lamb. Or with the Shakespeare stalker, if my suspicion du jour were true. Sue provided a distraction by dropping the last few feet and falling on her butt. Blodgett reached a hand down and hauled her up.

"You were saying?" On the scent, not deterred by crazy women falling out of the sky.

"Well, he left before I did. And I haven't seen him since, until..." I pointed over the lilac bushes.

"So, this Sandra? Is this the same Sandra that found Mr. Preston this morning?"

"Yes. Yes, it was." I perked up. A silver lining. Maybe he'd arrest Sandra instead of me. Blodgett nodded as he wrote. "Actually, she was mad at Robert, too, because he took me out to Chandlers Friday night."

Blodgett just looked at me. "I thought you just said you were broke up?"

Oh. Well, that might look bad. Behind Blodgett's back, Sue rolled her eyes at my blunder. Her snort, however, could be heard from any direction. Without taking his eyes off me, Blodgett turned to speak over his shoulder. "How about you wait in the front yard, Ms. Reed." It wasn't a question.

"We did break up, but he came to my office Friday afternoon, asking to talk to me. We decided on Chandlers. Anyway, he wanted to... Well, he seemed to be worried about his alibi for Wayne's murder. I don't know why." I studied Blodgett's eyes while I said that, watching for a sign that Robert had reason to worry. Blodgett gave nothing away. "He seemed to think we could alibi each other, but, of course, that wouldn't work since we'd already given statements."

"Was he stupid, or did he just think we were?" Blodgett asked.

"Neither. I think he was just scared. His reputation is really, really important to him. He owns a real estate agency in Minnesota and is very active in the community. That's why he comes up here on weekends for his AA meetings. He didn't want to run the risk of running into anyone who might find out he was an alcoholic.

"From something he'd said earlier, I took it that he was in town that night, but if the police think he was trying to avenge me or something. . ." I shrugged. "Let's just say that wouldn't have been in character for him.

"Anyway," I continued, "the dinner was a waste of time. We parted amicably, and I thought it would help us get along, at least while we were at the club. Except then, the next night,

Sandra started in on me and clued me in on Robert's extracurricular activities."

"This 'argument' you and Prescott had. It was in public?"

"More or less. Sandra made a scene inside the club, but Robert and I stepped outside. We were right on the sidewalk, though. Anybody could see us by looking out the window. In fact, someone did."

"What? Who?"

"Well, another member, Paul, came out when we were arguing. He kind of intervened when Robert grabbed me, and Robert pushed him down."

"So Prescott grabs you, and then some other guy jumps in? What's this Paul-guy's last name?"

"I don't know—anonymity and all—but you can ask at the club. Somebody might know," I said doubtfully. Aside from Chad, I couldn't imagine who might, but the police could ask. Despite my misgivings, I felt strangely protective. *My* nerd.

Or… my crazed, psychotic stalker-killer, which put it in a slightly different perspective.

Blodgett folded his notebook.

"Um…" I said.

Blodgett opened his notebook.

"This might not be connected, but I'm still getting weird messages from an anonymous…" I paused, searching for the right word. Stalker? Psycho? Freak? "…person. Even after Wayne was killed, so it's obviously not him."

"Obviously," Blodgett said, deadpan. "What kind of messages?"

"Another sonnet," I said, while chanting *don't think about the knife . . . don't think about the knife* in my head, just in case Blodgett could read minds. "I got the first one a little over two weeks ago, pinned to a cloth doll with a knife through its back. At the time, I thought it was another one of Wayne's stunts, although the sonnet did seem a bit of a reach."

"A knife?" He stiffened, eyes sharp.

"A fillet knife. You guys have it. I mean, Officer Durrant took the report and the knife.

"The second sonnet came after Wayne had been murdered." *Don't think about the knife . . . don't think about the knife... don't think about the knife . . .*

"And you don't think it could it have been Mr. Preston?"

My mind blanked for a minute. *Preston?* "Oh. You mean, Robert. I guess I'll find out."

"I guess you will. When you do, you call me right away." He handed me another card.

"Detective?" A uniformed policewoman stood at the side of the Sterlings' house. Sandra, looking pale and wan, huddled next to her. They must have picked her up at the club and brought her here to interview. I almost felt sorry for her.

Then she went and ruined my magnanimous moment by sneering at me, making me hope her prison cellmate would be especially attracted to buff biceps. For all I knew, *she* could be the killer. She had the heart—or lack of—for it.

Blodgett turned, giving them a just-a-sec finger. Eyeing Sandra, I was tempted to gesture with a slightly different digit.

"You'll be available if we have more questions, won't you?"

"Is that like saying 'Don't leave town?'" I laughed.

He didn't.

I cleared my throat, pretending the laugh had been an allergic reaction to lilac bushes or blond hussies. Either/or.

We left it at that.

CHAPTER THIRTY-SIX

I had the feeling that if Sandra and Paul hadn't been equally plausible suspects for Robert's murder, I'd have ended up in jail. Finally found a use for those two.

On the ride home, I kept waiting to fall apart, but I didn't. The beginnings of a migraine crept up my neck, but I couldn't seem to wrap my mind around the need for grief.

Guilt, yes. Lots of guilt. I couldn't believe I'd been searching for reasons to prove Robert had murdered Wayne, even as he lay dead in the dirt a few miles away.

Worse, if it weren't for me, Robert would still be alive.

My apartment felt dreary and empty, all the fresh promise of spring sucked away. I flopped on the couch, burying my face in the cushion. Maybe I would suffocate. Instead, I sneezed.

Images of Robert's savaged body kept sneaking past barriers, which I expected and was prepared for. But wondering why I wasn't crying disturbed me almost as much as the memory. Was I heartless? Even if I hadn't been in love with Robert, I'd certainly been close to it. At the very least, I'd been deeply "in like" and willing, eager, for a deeper relationship. If only he hadn't been such a self-centered jerk.

Maybe I was in shock.

I thought back to when we'd first met, he'd been so charming and persistent. I could almost feel the jealous eyes cutting in our direction whenever he made his way to my side or sat next to me at meetings. I'd felt so lost and emptied just then, hollowed out of everything I'd valued about myself, and he'd seemed strong and sure. His arrogance, which I'd interpreted as confidence, had been as alluring as his cologne. And now he was dead, horribly dead, and I felt nothing. Maybe *I* was the disturbed one.

But I hadn't killed him. I just hadn't loved him.

I sneezed again. Dust and car hair interfered with self-destruction, so I rolled on my back and waited for Siggy to curl up on my stomach. And waited.

I sat up. "Siggy?"

The apartment felt. . . empty? I stood, looking in his usual kitty haunts. Nothing. I assured myself there was no need for worry. He was sure to be curled up on my bed, snoozing. The bedroom was dark and quiet. The curtain rustled just as I walked in. I smiled with relief.

"Are you still in here?" I pulled the curtain back, revealing an empty void where the screen should have been. A soft breeze tickled my face.

I finally cried. Cried all night. For Robert, for Siggy, for myself. Roaming the neighborhood, I walked blisters on my feet, juggling pepper spray, a flashlight, and an opened can of smelly, gourmet cat food. I walked until my legs ached. Finally, long after the rest of the world made peace with their day, I dragged myself back up the stairs, falling onto the couch.

The phone rang, pulling me out of a slumber that seemed closer to a swirling black hole than a period of rest. I'd fallen asleep after all. I grabbed for the phone, irrationally hoping that it was news about Siggy.

"H'lo?" The primitive instinct designed to mask the deep vulnerability of sleep made me try for one of those alert, "of-course-I'm-wide-awake!" tones. It never worked.

"Sorry to wake you, Letty, but we have a problem here." A briskly efficient voice told me.

"Um…" I rubbed puffy eyes.

"Letty, wake up. This is serious. Someone broke into the clinic. I've got to cancel all the clients, and this place is absolutely trashed. Can you come in and help us get things in order? We might have to call a temp service, because I just don't see—"

"*Lisa?*"

"Good morning, sunshine. Have you caught up yet?"

"No."

"I bought donuts."

"I'm coming." I banged the phone down. There'd better be sprinkles.

Makeup couldn't unpuff my eyes. I threw some clothes on, ran a brush through snarly hair and, forty minutes later, pulled in the clinic lot where yet another police car sat parked. I was tired of police and their cars. Then it occurred to me that perhaps the break-in might not be a coincidence. But what could Shakespeare want from the clinic? We didn't prescribe medication; notices stating that hung both inside and out to prevent this very thing. And what did Lisa mean by needing to hire temp services?

When I walked through the front doors, I saw right away that yes, indeed, we needed extra help. Heart thudding, I suddenly realized what Shakespeare had been after. Grief was going to have to wait, because this asshole wouldn't.

Manila files and paper covered every flat surface of the front office and the lobby, cascading in a white and tan fountain from its primary source: the file room. Drawers had been ripped out of desks and cabinets, their contents upturned and scattered, adding to the chaos. It looked like an office supply store had puked all over the clinic.

Lisa stood by the shell of her desk next to the pudgy cop, who'd taken my report the night of the knife-and-sonnet incident. A box of pastry sat in isolated splendor on her desk, but I'd lost all appetite. I waded through a pool of papers, skidding as they slithered under my feet.

"What happened?"

Lisa raised an eye brow at my disheveled appearance. "I could ask the same of you." Turning back to the officer, she said, "Letty Whittaker, one of our counselors."

"Yeah, we've met," he said.

I squinted at his name tag since I couldn't very well call him Officer Pudgy.

"Hello again, Officer…um…Putzke." Well, that wasn't any better.

"Ma'am," Putzke said.

Lisa rolled her eyes as Putzke folded his notebook and stuck it in his back pocket. Her system had been fouled beyond recognition and she was in… a… *mood.*

"Like I was saying, the guy got in through the back window," Putzke said, pointing down the hall. "Third office on the left. You need to make a list of all the damage and anything that's missing. If you stop by tomorrow sometime, we should be able to get you a copy of the report for your insurance."

"But are you going to *do* anything?"

He stayed patient. "Somebody will be over to test for prints, but it's gonna make a heck of a mess. I wouldn't count on anything. Between the staff and all your clients, there's got to be a million prints and no way to separate the vandal's from the ones that are legitimate. But we'll check around and see if other businesses have reported any problems like this. Maybe it was teenagers or something unrelated to the…uh… mental stuff here."

"Officer, could I have a minute?" I interrupted before he could twirl his finger next to his ear in the universal "cuckoo" sign. Lisa looked ready to bite.

We slithered to the door, stepping outside.

"You might want to check with Detective Blodgett," I said. "This might be connected to the guy that's been stalking me or with the two murders."

"You think so?"

"I don't know. It's just worth checking, is all I'm saying. It seems strange that all these things could be happening without a common denominator. And, *no*," the denial tumbled out, "I am *not* that common denominator."

"I wouldn't have said that, ma'am." Which was probably true, because I doubted the words "common denominator" were an active part of his vocabulary. "But it's more likely that one of your clients"—a raised eyebrow indicated I should replace "client" with "wacko"—"got a little upset and decided to break in for some payback."

He leaned back through the door and needlessly reminded Lisa to leave the mess untouched until the crime scene tech, or whomever, showed up.

Back in the office, I found Lisa wandering from office to office checking the damage. Hannah and Bob were already in, each of them in their own offices, with equally disgusted looks on their faces, although on Hannah, it was a new expression and for Bob, it was standard. I expected my office to have received the brunt of the damage, but to my surprise the vandal had been even-handed.

"Marshall's on his way in," Lisa said. "Regina's on vacation, and Carol's in the Cities shopping with her daughter-in-law. She said to just shut the door to her office and pretend the mess isn't there; that's what she did when her kids were teenagers. I'm trying to get a hold of some of our part-timers, but most are working.

"I don't know," Lisa continued, throwing her hands up in the air. "I just have no idea where to start. Has anyone discovered anything stolen? We need to make a list."

"Whoa!" Hearing Marshall's opinion of the mess from down the hall, we went out en masse to turn the problem over to the boss.

He stood stock-still in the center of the office, which was probably wise since he was precariously balanced on a lumpy pile of documents. His hands were on his hips, chin raised as he surveyed the damage. I fake-coughed a laugh into my fist at the adventurer-in-the-new-world image he unknowingly portrayed. Lisa must have had the same thought because she made a beeline for the bottom drawer in her desk, apparently having forgotten that all that was left were five gaping metal cavities.

"Damn," she muttered.

"Don't worry. Whatever it is that's missing, we'll find it when we start to go through all this." Marshall meant to be comforting, but Lisa just looked crankier.

"I told you to get rid of that thing," I told her. Maybe a little too smugly.

"I'm not worried. After all, it's *your* name on the address label."

"Damn," I muttered.

Marshall clapped his hands together, rubbing them briskly. "Okay, here's the plan." He sounded like a camp leader, but we were all grateful for direction. "Lisa, you start calling clients and reschedule them for next week. Don't mention the break-in. We don't want people freaking out over somebody rustling through their confidential files."

"What if the media gets hold of the story?"

"We'll cross that bridge if we get to it. Don't lie to anyone, but don't go into details either. I'm going to call corporate and fill them in. They might be able to spare some of the hospital staff so we don't have to worry about bringing in anyone new. At the very least, they'll have to approve the expenditure if we get some temps.

"The rest of you," he spoke to us all but looked directly at me, "I suggest you start gathering files. Try to set up a system.

Maybe divide the rooms up amongst yourselves." He waved a hand aimlessly over the mounds.

"Office Poopsie told us to wait until they get someone over here to fingerprint," Lisa informed her boss.

"Okay, but we can at least work up a plan of action while we wait."

"I'll take the file room," I said. "If I get that cleared, we'll have the space to re-organize the files in their proper place." And I'd be able to hunt for the *Harmon* file and its lethal contents. *How had the stalker known?*

As soon as Marshall disappeared into his office, Bob started bellyaching. "So, does he expect *us* to put all this together?" He glanced from me to Hannah, pointedly ignoring Lisa, whose natural province he assumed included filing already. A legend in his own mind, Bob felt above all this. He tried stomping around to illustrate his masculinity and ended up shooting his legs out from underneath himself, landing smack on his pompous and overly wide ass.

Cheered us girls right up.

CHAPTER THIRTY-SEVEN

Stingy, paranoid corporate decided that they "really preferred that the matter be handled in-house," which meant no temps. Bob claimed he'd injured his back when he fell on his butt, spending the rest of Monday morning moaning and wincing whenever anybody looked in his direction. He skipped out just before lunch, claiming to have made a chiropractic appointment, leaving us even more shorthanded. The toad was probably sitting at Denny's scarfing up lunch and admiring his own cleverness.

Most of the other counselors were part-timers, working at other jobs. Some were able to pitch in, but most could only spare a few hours here and there. Marshall finally resorted to calling each of the interns we'd just said good-bye to. Not surprisingly, Mary Kate was thrilled to drop everything and come in. Marshall made her promise to finish her finals, forbidding her from lending a hand until after her last test Wednesday afternoon. She vowed to show up as soon as she was done and indicated she could work through the night. Probably by candlelight.

Another officer showed up about twenty minutes later, took one look at the drifts of paper, and decided she'd limit the fingerprinting to the window where the intruder broke in.

"And maybe the desk drawers," she added, "but it'd make a god-awful mess if I try all these papers. It'll ruin the documents, too."

She got busy, and I scurried to the file room, heart thudding, suddenly imagining the knife magically materializing to implicate me. It hadn't, but unfortunately, neither had the *Harmon* file or the Marshall-the-pirate porn magazine, for that matter.

The task of gathering and matching the appropriate records with their matching file jacket was incredibly daunting. The intruder had cleared the shelves entirely; stacks of files pitched to the floor, others presumably grabbed by the armful, hurled from one end of the clinic to the other. Our offices had received similar treatment, with the added bonus of personal items smashed or otherwise destroyed. Even the impoverished interns' room had been ransacked, the spines of the old textbooks broken, pages ripped in chunks and cast about like educational confetti.

I set to work, although it was difficult to concentrate between cold sweats and bouts of shaking that verged on seizures whenever I thought about Shakespeare finding the *Harmon* file and using the knife on poor Robert, because that would effectively rule Paul out and rule *in* Marshall.

Very little progress was made until Lisa got over her shock, reasserted her inner office-dominatrix, and began slinging orders around like a whip. She arranged a simple system of alphabetized piles and decreed that we'd tackle sorting each pile later in the week.

Good enough. I was in no shape for complications anyway.

Blodgett showed up that afternoon, banging on the locked front door as if we should have been expecting him. Maybe I was. He looked fresher than usual, but a closer examination told me he was just on high alert, probably running on reserve energy. Drab brown eyes scanned the mess, picking their way across each section of the chaos, touching on each of my co-workers briefly, but with a frightening intensity, before landing on me. I waggled my fingers at him.

He didn't return-waggle.

Repressing a sigh, I motioned him back, picking my way down the littered hallway while he shuffled behind. In my office, I picked my chair up from the floor and let him deal with his own seat, which he did by the expedient method of tilting the client chair, letting everything slide to the floor.

"Why do you think this might be connected to the murders?" No greeting, no small talk, no lead up to the question. Just "wham-bam, answer the question, ma'am."

"It seems like too much of a coincidence. Nobody else has been having problems with clients, at least that I've heard. I guess you should check with Marshall."

"I will. Anything you're leaving out?"

Like the Amazing Disappearing/Reappearing (and currently missing) Murder Weapon? "My cat is missing."

"Uh-huh." He didn't seem ready to put out a kitty version of BOLO. His deceptively languid gaze roved over me, watching not only my face, but my hands and feet, too. While we can train ourselves to offer blank features, jittery feet and clenched hands often give us away. I deliberately relaxed, breathing deep and concentrating on thoughts of warm, yellow sunshine and happy laughter, soft, placid muscles and innocence. It was a nice rest.

He didn't buy it but couldn't prove anything. Yet.

Grunting, Blodgett heaved himself up. At the door, he went the opposite direction, walking down the hall, peering in each office. Without a word, he continued to the emergency exit, which Wayne had bolted through running from the police. Blodgett opened it, scrutinizing the back alley from the doorway. Shutting the door, he checked the lock, then walked back to Regina's office, where the intruder had presumably broken in. Sooty, grimy-looking fingerprint powder covered the sill and desk top, the tech having finished long ago. Careful not to lean against it, Blodgett peered out the window.

"You'll want to have them vacuum real good first to clean that up," he mentioned. "Then use 'Scrubby Bubbles' or whatever that stuff is called."

"I'll tell them. What are you looking for?" I pointed at the window.

He shrugged, walking away. He paused at Marshall's office. It, too, had been trashed. Marshall had tossed his jacket over the back of his chair and stood cradling a stack of books, searching for a flat surface on which to deposit them. He turned as if sensing the detective, a polite smile on his face. He nodded for Blodgett to enter, and for a moment, as his eyes brushed over me, his smile warmed. Blodgett's hypervigilant gaze took in the tableau, eyes traveling back and forth between my boss and me, but made no comment.

I blushed, making matters worse.

As Blodgett shut the door behind him, I booked it for the front. Lisa was muttering to herself, trying to realign one of the desk drawers into the groove that would allow it to slide in and out.

"Did you find your magazine yet?" I asked.

The drawer fell, nearly severing her toes, and she kicked it viciously. Coming eye to eye, she said, "No. But I will."

I had no doubt.

Still wondering what Blodgett had been looking for, I walked out to the parking lot to look at the window the intruder had used. Most of the clinic windows were easily visible from the lot, except for Regina's. A scraggily, overgrown bush obscured two-thirds of the window, making it the best choice if someone wanted access. I tried picturing Marshall crawling through the opening, but I got distracted by the image of his cute butt hanging half-in, half-out of the window. And why would he have bothered getting in that way when he had keys to the clinic.

On second thought, I realized that fact couldn't exonerate Marshall since, besides Lisa, he was the *only* one who had keys. If it was either one of them—and I honestly couldn't see Lisa wreaking the kind of havoc that had been inflicted on her precious filing system—he or she would have had to break in or risk pointing an accusatory finger directly at himself. Or herself, I supposed.

Ultimately, I had no one to blame, but myself. Somebody had to have noticed my compulsive trips to the file room. Somebody close by had been watching, aware of my distress and the reason for it, knowing my obsession was connected to Wayne's murder. More specifically, to the horrific package sent to me.

He liked to show off, this Shakespeare-stalker did. And, like Siggy proudly dropping his dead mouse on my pillow, he liked to bequeath his trophies to *me*. If he'd just wanted attention, he could have sent his souvenirs to the media or even to the police.

So why me? Continuing to mull this over, I returned to the file room, no longer expecting to find the knife. Whoever the stalker was wouldn't want to take the chance that I'd turn it in to the police, which was by far the smartest thing I could have done. And, conversely, the stupidest thing I hadn't.

At the end of the day, I crawled in my car, slinging my purse on the passenger seat. I'd found two blank forms that may have been part of those I'd used as filler in the *Harmon* file. I could think of no other reason for them to have been part of the mound of paper. But so far no file folder, no sonnet, and, certainly, no bloody knife.

Too tired to be afraid, I leaned over and popped the glove box. Empty. I went home and walked the neighborhood.

Over the next couple of days, order—and Lisa—slowly prevailed. Dress was casual and, aside from my own, moods lifted into almost a holiday spirit. Lisa's radio became a source of hilarity as a "poltergeist" kept turning her classic rock station to wailing country western.

Trying to rein in the compulsive behavior that had betrayed the knife's hiding place, I only allowed myself to check the glove box twice a day—morning and night. Not that I had anything more to hide, but I'd be damned if I'd play puppet for him again. I varied my routine as much as possible, taking different routes to work, and carrying my pepper spray just *hoping* someone would give me an excuse. Even the thought that I was turning into Rhonda didn't sway me.

None of which mattered, since Shakespeare was probably signing my paychecks every week. It was the principle of the thing, I guess.

CHAPTER THIRTY-EIGHT

As I made a pot of coffee early Wednesday morning, I heard a muffled thump against the front door. A sliding rustle followed.

"Hello?" Grabbing my can of pepper spray, I put an eye to the peephole. Nothing. But the thump thumped again, then meowed.

I flung the door open and was greeted by the pungent odor of cat crap and my slinky kitty. Scooping him up, we serenaded each other with a mishmash of cooing and purring. I kicked the door shut and hurried to set out fresh food and water.

Siggy sniffed and deigned to take a few delicate nibbles, humoring me. Wherever he'd been for the last few days, he'd had food. I sat on the floor, grinning. With an unexpected tinkle, he jumped in my lap, rubbing his chin against mine. Kitty kisses. More strange tinkling sounds mixed with his rumbling purrs.

"What is that, Sig? Whatcha got there?"

Somewhere on his travels, he'd acquired some bling. I scratched under his chin and he rolled to his side. In an orgy of feel-good, he wrapped his paws around my hand, biting my finger lightly. Meanwhile, I unhooked the collar with my free hand.

Except it wasn't a collar. Silver links with dangling crescent moons and chunky stars, it looked more like a woman's bracelet. My stomach rolled.

"Where did you get this, big guy?"

I fingered the charms. All but one were silver; the exception—neither a moon nor a star—was some kind of gold flower.

Uneasiness brought me to my feet. I strode from window to window, checking the locks. I was going to be late for work, and I didn't give a . . .

Which reminded me. Grabbing a paper towel and can of rug cleaning foam, I ventured into the hall to deal with the downside of cat ownership.

Finishing, I gathered the supplies in one hand, gingerly holding the icky wad of paper toweling in the other. My mind was busy trying to figure out how to manage the lock—teeth? feet?—while my eyes processed a different message.

There's a paper stuck to the door.

Shit.

Back inside, I unfolded the paper to the now familiar fourteen lines of scrawl.

Let those who are in favour with their stars
Of public honour and proud titles boast,
Whilst I, whom fortune of such triumph bars
Unlook'd for joy in that I honour most.
Great princes' favourites their fair leaves spread
But as the marigold at the sun's eye,
And in themselves their pride lies buried,
For at a frown they in their glory did.
The painful warrior famoused for fight,
After a thousand victories once foiled,
Is from the book of honour razed quite,
And all the rest forgot for which he toiled:

Then happy I, that love and am beloved,
Where I may not remove nor be removed.

They served the search warrants later that afternoon. After letting them in, my landlord called me at work. By the time I made it up to the front desk, an officer was standing there, holding an official looking document, asking for me. The warrant covered my apartment, my office and related common areas of the clinic, and my car. They were looking for "knives which may cause trauma or injury consistent with injuries observed on the victim(s)." Also included in the warrant were "firearms; magazines for firearms; DNA samples including but not limited to blood droplets, blood splatters, and blood smears; clothing which bears blood or bloodstains and other biological fluids." There was more legal blah-blah-blah, but I skipped it. The black spots dancing in front of my eyes made reading difficult.

I handed over my keys and sat on a chair with my head between my knees, a recent affectation of mine. Lisa directed the officer to my office, which had just begun to get reassembled. At least I didn't have to be embarrassed in front of my clients. Marshall sat next to me, a sign of respect and solidarity that would have meant much more if I could be sure he wasn't Shakespeare.

Mary Kate showed up halfway through the exercise, looking haggard and disheveled from finals week. The unfolding drama sparked her up immensely, though, and she ran giddily from window to door to my office, giving verbal updates on everything the police did, touched, or looked at, as well as her interpretations of what they may or may not have been thinking. Most annoying.

Marshall continued to sit beside me, at one point reaching over and taking my hand. He generated warmth, the slight calluses of his palm giving tactile proof of masculine strength

251

and comfort. I let it be, just for a moment, allowing the illusion of compassion to carry me through the next few minutes. What could it hurt?

However, Lisa and Mary Kate converging on us with her-and-her expressions of alertness for our joined hands gave me a good excuse for pulling away. I stood up as the two officers assigned to search my car entered the clinic. They were finished, looking every bit as frustrated as I felt, which pleased my inner brat.

After a brief conference with the officer searching my office, they split up—one to the miniature staff lunch room, the other to the file room. My stomach clenched. If the knife were found, it would happen now.

But it wasn't. I finally accepted that the knife had indeed been the motive for the break-in, and worse, had been used to kill Robert. They didn't find the sonnet, either and, of course, didn't know enough to be looking for the *Harmon* file. So far, I was in the clear.

An hour and a half later, the cop who had originally served me the warrant approached. He had my car keys and a pile of forms to sign—receipts—which I did without bothering to read through them. This gave Lisa fits, but by now I had a migraine and decided jail would be kind of peaceful in comparison. Safer, too.

"Are they still going through my place?" I gathered enough energy to ask.

"They just finished up, ma'am. A receipt for all properties removed will be left with your landlord."

"Was Detective Blodgett there?" For some reason, I cared more about his presence than whether they were carting away my set of steak knives. Probably because I knew the only blood they'd find on the utensils would be bovine. But more importantly, and not just because he had the power to toss me in jail, I didn't want Blodgett to think I was a murderer. Freud would say it was a father-figure thing, but my head hurt too much for self-analysis. Freud could kiss my butt, and I'm sure he'd have had something to say about that phrase, too.

Meanwhile, the cop either didn't care or wasn't listening, because he gathered up the forms and left.

It was only 2:30, but I turned to Marshall. "I'm going home. I need to see what they did."

"Do you want me to drive you?" His eyes, so darkly mysterious, hinted at nothing but compassion. I didn't trust it. I couldn't.

"No. I can manage." Marshall looked as though he wanted to argue. Not wanting to raise his suspicions, I added, truthfully, "I just need to be alone."

He nodded in understanding. Just behind him, Mary Kate shifted from foot to foot like a toddler doing the pee-pee dance. I could tell she was dying to commiserate with me, eager for a blow-by-blow of the intrusion. I couldn't deal with it.

"Bye, Mary Kate. I'll see you tomorrow."

"Bye-bye. I'll call you tonight!"

My phone would be off the hook. Rather than argue, I grimaced a smile, and left.

My car felt violated, my apartment more so. Siggy was hiding and not even an open can of tuna fish could cajole him out from under the bed. Wide, "this wasn't what I signed up for" kitty eyes stared at me from the darkest, dust-woofiest corner. I eyed the dark, cozy space wistfully, but forced myself back into the living room. Evidence of government-sanctioned intruders was everywhere. Even objects not included in the search had been moved, disarranged, giving my home an unsettling sense of being slightly off-kilter. It felt like a stage set of my apartment, familiar but wrong and disorienting. I scanned the receipts that my landlord had left on the coffee table.

The bastards had taken Anna. And my stainless steel Ginsu knives.

Just before I'd gotten sober, I'd found myself at a point of despair so intense that I literally could not continue life as I was then living it. The pain of being me reached a pinnacle, a Mount Everest of misery, and I just didn't have enough resources to get back from the precipice in one piece. Life was unendurable. My choice was to kill myself—and I took comfort in plotting various methods for that, considerately choosing those that would cause the least amount of clean up for whomever found me—or change. I didn't know how that would work, but I knew of AA, of course. I figured "what the hell, I could always kill myself later."

I was at that point again.

Back anything up into a corner and it'll turn savage. Knowing it faces certain death, it turns to face it. It might die in the fight, but chunks of its attacker will go, too—a better than nothing proposition. Shakespeare blowing my head off and cutting me up into itty-bitty pieces was suddenly more tolerable than living like this. Therefore, I no longer had to be afraid of facing the stalker, of tracking him down. Not only that, but prison came in a distant third in the fear ranking.

So I needed a plan. Marshall recognized that I had pulled back from the emotional attraction tugging between us, but he hopefully assumed it was a reaction to recent events. If I was going to be in a position to investigate, I'd have to send out some wily, feminine signals that I was back in the game.

That was doable.

CHAPTER THIRTY-NINE

Casual dress and a warm, end-of-April break in the weather helped with my femme fatale mission. I let my hair hang free, pulling on a tight denim skirt with a light, equally tight, V-necked coral-colored sweater. Just to seal the deal, I splashed a little come-find-me Chanel down the V. Not exactly "office harlot," but a far cry from my usual conservative attire.

Bob liked it.

Marshall had insisted on a doctor's excuse, and Bob either ran out of bribe money or had a relatively honest doctor because he was back spreading sunshine Thursday morning. The rest of us had gotten our own offices back into shape and were concentrating on the mammoth task of sorting the alphabetized stacks of paperwork in the lobby and file room. I had staked a claim on the latter, although I no longer expected to find the knife.

Aside from my sweater, there was no reason for Bob to visit the file room every twenty minutes, but Lisa started timing his appearances, and that was the average. Odds were cast on his visit per minute ratio, bets laid, and Carol won a six-dollar pot at the end of the day. Helped make up for her Mall of America trip.

Thankfully, given my goal, Marshall's reaction was just as potent, at least to my eyes. And Lisa's. And Carol's. Mary Kate just looked puzzled by the whole thing. Bob was too busy looking at my chest.

Marshall's eyes, on the other hand, traveled. Equal opportunity orbs, were Marshall's eyes. He came in later than usual, wearing snug, faded jeans and a Led Zeppelin T-shirt, smelling fresh and woodsy. He was even a little scruffy in that highly lickable kind of way. At the sight of him, efficient Lisa dropped an armful of files that she'd just sorted and didn't even cuss. It was that worth it.

As I stood in the doorway laughing at the spectacle, his attention pinpointed on me like a heat-seeking missile. Eyebrows raised, he slowly did the head-toe-head scan, then swallowed and looked away. I felt a little drooly myself.

Trying to restore an appearance of nonchalance, Marshall asked Lisa if he had any messages. Unfortunately, he'd already asked that and stood holding four pink message slips in his hand. Lisa reached over and tapped them gently.

Without another word, he took off down the hall, manfully ignoring the chorus of giggles in his wake. He was made of sterner stuff than Bob, however. He lasted thirty minutes before he ventured back.

I needed to wear this sweater more often.

About 11:30, Lisa took off for the office supply store, leaving Mary Kate alone in the front office. The others were either puttering around in their individual offices or taking a break in the kitchenette. Bob had just brought a file to me (he seemed to be bringing them one at a time) and reluctantly departed from my chest. Marshall must have figured the coast was clear.

I jumped a little when I caught sight of him in the door. I hadn't heard him come up, didn't know how long he'd been standing there, watching. His slow, sexy smile crinkled his eyes attractively, though, and I couldn't discern whether my nervousness was due to my suspicions or because I wanted to leap on him like a wild cat on spring meat. My plan threatened to overtake me in ways I hadn't entirely foreseen.

"Do you have plans for lunch?" he asked.

"Um," I said, ever the sophisticate.

The crinkles deepened. "How about The Old Mill at 12:30?"

"I'll meet you there."

He retired to his office, leaving me shaking and Mary Kate wide-eyed. Plan A was now in motion.

And then it wasn't.

When Lisa pried the details out of Mary Kate—which, upon Lisa's return from the store, she accomplished by saying "Hi, what's new?"—the word that lunch was at The Old Mill spread as quickly as Lisa could navigate the hallways. She made reservations for eight. Nonsmoking.

Mary Kate and Lisa made a game out of keeping Marshall and me apart. They each plunked down on either side of him, smiling gleefully, giving him no choice but to concede defeat and smile back. The party atmosphere continued, though, heightened by the opportunity to prank the boss. He couldn't very well complain.

The intrusion suited my purposes, too. I needed time to collect my thoughts and remind myself that neither crinkly eyes nor round, firm buttocks were an adequate character reference in a murder investigation. After all, cute buttocks had gotten me in trouble before.

Motion, in the form of a frenetically waving arm, grabbed my attention. Across the restaurant, Paul sat all by himself, an open book propped at his elbow. Even though the last time I'd seen him had been an exercise in humiliation, he beamed at me like he'd just opened a Christmas present. Must be the sweater.

I waved—slightly—and he came bounding over like a puppy let off his leash. Next to me, Mary Kate gaped at the sight of yet another suitor. I couldn't blame her. I felt like

Scarlett O'Hara juggling beaus at the barbecue. Flushing, I made stilted introductions, hoping nobody noticed that I left off his last name or that I refrained from labeling him a friend. Or an acquaintance. Or anything else that might indicate any sort of connection whatsoever. Paul didn't notice either.

Scared to death that he would say something about AA, I stood and tried to shoo him back to his own table. It almost worked until Paul zeroed in on Mary Kate, who was still staring.

"Oh, hey! Don't I know you? You're in Schneider's class, right? Did you get that paper turned in?"

Mary Kate flushed and nodded. For a second, I considered matchmaking. Then I remembered about procreation and was suddenly remotivated to get Paul back to his green salad and iced tea. I managed to get him resettled just as our order came.

I did make sure to say good-bye before leaving, trying to ignore his sad eyes. I'd have to make it up by sitting next to him at a meeting.

Back at the office, things settled into a routine. Bob gave up on my sweater, closing himself in his office, presumably to teleconference with some clients. Either the light on the console unit was broke or "teleconference" meant taking a nap in Bob-speak.

Marshall picked up some of the slack by joining the troops sorting records in the front office. Such a helpful guy. Lisa's eyes twinkled, but she wasn't foolish enough to refuse the help. We had a full roster of clients scheduled for next week and a mountain of files left to reorganize. Fun time was over.

Marshall worked steadily for an hour and a half before taking a break. He returned from the lunch room carrying two cups of coffee, bringing me one. Cream and two sugars, just the way I liked it.

The file room, about the size of a large walk-in closet, already felt cramped with the rows of shelving covering each wall and the stacks and stacks of files waiting to be replaced. Marshall's presence made it even more confining. Made my heart thud erratically, too. Whether killer or lover, I was certainly getting an aerobic workout.

"How are you holding up?" he asked. "Have you heard from the police since yesterday?"

"Not really. I guess now that they checked me out, they know there isn't anything to find." Mary Kate walked in with an armful of recompiled records. "Now that everything is over, I feel like I can move on."

Mary Kate stood holding the files, a blank look on her face, searching for a place to set them down.

"Here, I've got those." Marshall took the pile, setting them on top of a two-foot high stack. She looked like she wanted to hang around, but the boss's nod of dismissal sent her from the room.

Turning back to me, he said, "*Is* everything over?"

"Of course, it's not. I don't mean to sound naïve. But I don't have to worry about Wayne anymore, the licensing board cleared me, and the police are focusing on finding the killer rather than on me. I'm ready for good news."

"I don't blame you. You've had a long haul. I really—"

"Marshall, telephone!" Lisa interrupted. "It's corporate."

Sighing, he turned to go. Looking over his shoulder, he tipped me a wink. "Duty calls."

He walked back to his office and Lisa stuck her head around the corner. Waving her hand in front of her face, she said, "Whew! It's steamy in here."

"Don't be silly. He's just concerned and checking up on me."

"Checking you out, you mean. But enough about that, looky here." She waved a glossy magazine so fast the colors blurred. Despite that, I knew what it was.

"Where did you find it?"

"Buried under mounds of stupid paper. Want another peek?"

I almost caved in, but held strong. I needed to keep focused; lusting over dangly pirate parts wouldn't help. Interesting, but not helpful.

Lisa laughed out loud. "Don't want to be disappointed by the real thing, huh?"

Pulling my shoe off, I chucked it at her head. She was too quick, dancing over to her desk, stuffing her cherished treasure back in its bottom drawer.

"Are you sure it'll be safe there?" I asked.

"Why? You planning on taking it home tonight, or you got a back-up plan?" She waggled her hips in a bump-and-grind, and I reached for my other shoe.

Strangely, given Robert's murder and my efforts to seduce a possible stone-cold killer, it was a fun day.

Which is why finding the next sonnet wasn't as upsetting as I would've imagined.

CHAPTER FORTY

Sometime in the night, a plastic baggie filled with brown mystery goo had been shoved under the driver's side windshield wiper of my Focus. A folded sheet of paper promised more psychotic verbiage, but since no knife materialized, I called Blodgett before touching anything else.

Well, okay. I searched the car, the glove box, the trunk, and the surrounding areas for the murder weapon, but I did *not* touch the baggie. It was gross.

Besides, I was wearing a cute, 1950s-style sundress with a full skirt. The blue floral made my usually flat grey eyes hint blue. Or so I'd been told. I'd paid a ridiculous amount for the shoes, but the matching shade and ankle-strap bows were too perfect. Going for broke, I'd wrestled my hair into a French twist, which was sure to give me a headache by noon. Hopefully, I wouldn't end up smelling like the contents of the baggie.

Apparently there were matters of higher priority than poop-on-a-windshield; I was told not to expect Blodgett for about an hour. I translated that to mean "sometime before nightfall" and suggested he meet me at the clinic.

The poop traveled well.

When I got to work, I left it *in situ*—if anyone wanted to steal it off my hood, they were welcome to it—and walked inside. Everyone was already hard at it, and for the first time, progress was noticeable. Even Bob looked busy. In his case, it was a burst that only lasted forty minutes, but it added to the general feeling of accomplishment.

In contrast, Mary Kate looked stressed. Dark circles marred the pale skin under her eyes, and angry, red half-moons ringed her fingertips where she'd gnawed the nails to the quick. Understandable given all the extra hours she'd been putting in during finals' week. I felt bad, though, because I knew she was also stewing about her career direction, and I hadn't been very sympathetic. Technically, I'd been replaced as her internship mentor precisely *because* I couldn't give her the attention she needed. But I still felt guilty.

I promised myself I'd give her a pep talk later today. With Mary Kate, a little attention went a long way.

Blodgett showed up at the clinic around 10:00. It was a half-hour later than he'd said, but a whole lot earlier than I'd expected. His normally hangdog expression brightened noticeably at the sight of my sundress snapping crisply in the breeze. A particularly wayward gust almost shifted me from "Breakfast At Tiffany's" Audrey to Marilyn over the subway grate. At the sight of the vile baggie, however, he sobered up.

"All the other stuff you got, and *this* is one you decide to call me about?" Strictly speaking, it was a question, but it didn't have that little lilt at the end that questions usually have. In fact, Blodgett's voice was distinctly lacking in lilt this morning. Poop in a baggie will do that.

Snapping on a pair of latex gloves, he pulled the wiper blade up. With pinchy-fingers and an "ick" face, he carefully tugged the baggie's seal open, and picked the paper out. A noxious whiff confirmed our suspicions of the brown mess; we groaned in stereo. It was nice to bond.

Instead of unfolding it on my car—an act of kindness I wouldn't forget—Blodgett knelt on the blacktop, using a twig to hold the paper from blowing away. Of course, it was another sonnet. That was the first thing I noticed. Knowing Blodgett wouldn't let me handle the original, I got a pad of paper out of my car and copied it out by hand.

> *The expense of spirit in a waste of shame*
> *Is lust in action: and till action, lust*
> *Is perjured, murderous, bloody, full of blame,*
> *Savage, extreme, rude, cruel, not to trust;*
> *Enjoyed no sooner but despised straight;*
> *Past reason hunted; and no sooner had,*
> *Past reason hated, as a swallowed bait,*
> *On purpose laid to make the taker mad.*
> *Mad in pursuit and in possession so:*
> *Had, having, and in quest to have extreme;*
> *A bliss in proof, and proved, a very woe;*
> *Before, a joy proposed; behind a dream.*
> *All this the world well knows; yet none knows well*
> *To shun the heaven that leads me to this hell.*

The second thing I noticed was the reddish-brown smudges staining the paper. It didn't look like poop.

"Is that...?"

"Yeah," Blodgett said. "That's blood. I'll have to test it to confirm, but, yeah. And see here?" He pointed at one of the smudges, darker than the rest, more defined.

"What is that?" I asked.

"I could be wrong, but I think that's an imprint of a knife. Hopefully, *the* knife. I think the killer's doin' a little Show-and-Tell. We'll see." He pulled a paper bag out of his jacket pocket, slid the sonnet in, and carried both bags over to his car. Shaking his head in disgust, he popped the trunk, stowing the stinky baggie in the back. The paper bag got the primo spot next to Blodgett on the passenger seat. Leaving the door ajar, he sat drumming his fingers on the steering wheel, lost in thought.

"Do you believe me?" I blurted, yanking him out of his reverie. I wanted to pull the words back as soon as they cleared my lips.

Watching his carefully expressionless face, I decided he was going to leave me hanging.

"I don't believe anybody," he finally said. Then turning away and starting the car, he continued, "But you don't look like the type to take a crap in a baggie."

I teared up, smiling a wobbly "thanks" when he glanced back.

"Don't do that. I'm still going to test your DNA, see if it matches." He slammed the car door. I stepped back to keep my toes from getting run over as he roared away.

I pulled a Bob, hiding out in my office, mulling over the copy of the latest literary offering. Or "psycho-babble," as I called it. I didn't have my book on Shakespeare, so I Googled the first line. About twenty thousand hits popped up for "Sonnet 129." Apparently, this was one of Shakespeare's more famous sonnets, probably because it was as wacky as a fly swatter. Professionally speaking. The perception of sexual desire, its effect on the writer, and the murderous rage it induced frightened the crap out of me. It described a person driven insane by his desire, writhing and twisting from the poisonous "bait" presumably laid by the object of his desires. Purposefully trapped, left in "hell."

Not a lot of warm, snuggly feelings about love for this guy, that's for sure. This person would kill again. That, also, was certain.

The black eye dots came out to dance again, and just to spice things up I started to hyperventilate. New twist on old panic. Needing a distraction, I called Mary Kate in to my office to see what was going on with her. She was the next best thing to a client, and her happiness at the invitation was balm on my psyche.

264

"So, you know Paul Grisko?" she asked, after settling herself in her usual spot.

"Kind of. You two had a class together, huh?"

"Yeah. Ethics. What a bore."

I smiled, shaking my head. That explained her lackadaisical attitude about confidentiality. "Mary Kate—"

"I know, I know. But Schneider talks really, really slow and it puts me to sleep. Anyway, it was a pretty easy class for me, since I've been working here. I got a lot of questions from the others about what it's like in the real world." Mary Kate's fingers twitched quote signs over her last words. I could imagine the cache that working in a mental health clinic garnered for her among her classmates. With her basketful of insecurities, I guessed that Mary Kate had pumped up the prestige of her position, too. "I was able to tell them about HPPA and client rights and documentation and all that. I even brought in one of our Mental Status checklists."

Something was tickling my brain. I frowned. "You did?"

"Don't worry. It was a blank."

So was my mind. I let it be, knowing it would come to me if I didn't chase it, like love, presumably.

"Have you thought more about your career path?" I asked. "You've seemed kind of distracted lately."

Her fingers went to her mouth. "Not really. I've got a lot going on. I'm just going to wait and see."

I nodded helpfully, but since Mary Kate didn't seem inclined to expand, I couldn't push her. She wasn't a client. She wasn't my responsibility. "Well, if there's anything I can do…" I inched forward on my chair, secretly relieved, ready to get back to the filing.

"Well, there is one thing," she said. I sat back. "You know how Hannah had to turn in my progress report to my adviser? I'm not really happy with her review."

"Actually, since you spent the majority of your internship under my supervision, I did most of the review. Hannah only added to it. Is there something in particular that concerned you?" I'd filled it out as fairly as I could, listing her strengths as well as the issues that needed continued attention.

"No, your part was great! I know I need to work on boundaries. I think you really nailed it. I just don't feel like I really connected with Hannah. Maybe she resented that."

I didn't think Hannah was that sensitive, but Mary Kate was right in that they didn't connect. "Would you like me to speak to her?" Reluctance made my face squinch up.

"No. Never mind. It's something I need to work out myself. I just really appreciate being able to talk to you about it. It helps."

We said some awkward good-bye things, which really didn't make sense because we still had several hours of filing to do. Maybe she was as distracted as I was. That brain tickle still bugged me.

As I buried myself in the file room, I tried going over what Mary Kate and I had been talking about when the tickle commenced tickling. Ethics. Her teacher. Paul. Client rights.

Oh.

CHAPTER FORTY-ONE

I stuck my head around the corner. Mary Kate was back at work, moving quicker. More cheerfully. Maybe our talk had helped.

"What is Paul going to school for?" I asked.

Mary Kate jumped a little, as if coming out of a daydream. "Social work, I think. Why?"

"Oh, just curious. I can't quite picture him as a social worker, I guess."

Or as a murderer, but the possibility raised itself again. Paul knew about client rights, records protocols, and confidentiality issues. Although it was a long shot, he could have reasoned the same way I had about where to hide the knife. Ransacking the entire clinic indicated that Shakespeare *hadn't* been privy to my many trips to the file room.

Paul had certainly been threatened and publicly humiliated by both Wayne and Robert. They'd died right after.

The way they had died didn't rule Paul out, either. Scrawny and timid, the only hope he had of overpowering a bully like Wayne or a semi-athlete like Robert would be from a distance. A shotgun would work nicely. And the stab through the heart was both cowardly and an indication of personal rage.

Paul was back on the list.

I needed to know more about Paul: where he lived and worked, his hobbies, his habits. Maybe I'd wear my coral sweater to the next meeting. It wouldn't take much.

But that didn't mean Marshall was off the hook, either. And I hadn't worn my cleavage-dipping, repressed Donna Reed outfit for nothing. I needed to get back to the cabin where I could search for the knife and check out his Shakespeare collection.

About 3:00, I heard Marshall out in the front area. I wandered out and, by unspoken agreement, we all took a break. With another half-day of effort, we could probably get the rest of the records pulled together. Whatever was left could be caught up during regular work hours.

I volunteered to come in the next day, Saturday, as did Mary Kate and Hannah. The three of us entered into negotiations regarding organic coffee cake versus donuts. Donuts won, although it was hardly fair since Mary Kate automatically voted with me. Not that I protested.

Taking advantage of the festive mood, I suggested we all head out after work to the Northern Lights, a local bar-and-grill. Much loud, joy noises erupted.

Marshall looked at me quizzically, but I simply smiled at the group, letting Lisa sort out the details. She was so happy, she spent the rest of the afternoon humming pirate songs.

Not everyone made it to the bar. Bob claimed his wife wanted him home, Carol had to pick up her kids, and Regina didn't bother to explain. Marshall was right—her vacation hadn't done a thing for her attitude.

We convoyed over to the Lights. As everyone clamored in to the bar, I hung back, timing it so that Marshall and I reached the doorstep at the same time. He grasped the handle, but instead of entering, he stood starting down at me.

My heart thudded, draining the moisture from my mouth. Be careful what you ask for...

"Do you think this is such a good idea?" he asked. His dark eyes were impossible to read in the shadows. *What did he know?*

I had to clear my throat twice before asking what he meant.

"Well, you may not have the search warrant issue hanging over your head, but I imagine the police are still… attentive, shall we say?"

I was a Northern girl, so I couldn't bat my eyes without making it look like I had a facial tic, but I licked my lips, smiling softly.

"I hadn't planned on drinking. Maybe I should be 'designated driver' again?" I offered.

His breathing slowed, eyes narrowing as they flicked over the afternoon shadows dappling my sundress. My heart was banging so hard I was afraid my boobs might bounce. After a lengthy pause, he said, "That could work." Then he pulled the door open, letting me pass before him. "Maybe we can get you to let your hair down," he murmured.

Shiver.

The evening slid into a weird holding pattern. I tried joining in the conversations around me, especially since the outing was my idea in the first place, but my mind kept clicking around a hamster-wheel of worries. I did manage to get the bartender to dress up my nonalcoholic drink so I wouldn't be hassled by the "just one won't hurt" crowd. He gave an understanding wink, and I spent the rest of the night trying not to stab myself in the nose with the toothpick-speared fruit wedges floating as camouflage in my ginger ale.

Marshall didn't sit next to me, choosing instead a spot off to the side where he could watch me. My skin would tingle, and I'd turn to find his gaze on me, hot and languid. I kept watch on his drink so I could signal the bartender to refresh it as soon as the booze sank below the ice cubes, but after only two bourbons, he asked the bartender for a Coke.

Not only were my alcoholic sensibilities taken aback by his restraint, but this was not the plan at all. I needed him blitzed.

Preferably passed-out, dead-drunk, so-I-can-ransack-your-cabin blitzed.

Most of our group took off for home before midnight, although, as before, a few die-hard stragglers remained. Marshall caught my eye and winked, tipping his head to the exit in a "meet me outside" signal. Although he hadn't drunk enough for my purposes, he wasn't as subtle as he might have thought; Lisa's eyes glittered in delight at the intercepted message. Marshall said his good-byes, telling everyone to drive safe, and thanking us all for the amazing amount of work we'd put in that week.

"If I'm going to help finish up tomorrow, I better take off, too," I said at the end of his little speech.

"I'll walk you out," said Marshall, ever the gentleman. Lisa snickered quietly but let us play the scene out without heckling. Unexpectedly tactful for her—a kindness I knew I'd pay for later.

Outside, despite the supposed advent of spring, the air had a zing that mirrored my nerves. I hugged myself, wishing sexy 1950s vixens wore parkas and snow boots. And chastity belts.

"I think we're both okay to drive," Marshall's voice broke into my shivering. "It'll be less obvious if you follow me. That is, if I didn't get my signals crossed?" He tucked his hands into his pants pockets for warmth and stood facing me, his back taking the brunt of the wind, providing a harbor. His tentative, questioning expression made it clear that I could pull back if I chose.

I didn't choose.

Clouds covered whatever sliver of moon there might have been, and the high-beams from our two vehicles swept the clearing like synchronized blades of light. Our headlights clicked off, leaving a mass of twining black shadows, the image of the house disappearing into the inky swirl like the negative of a mirage.

If Marshall hadn't been there to lead the blind, I'd never have made it the fifty or so yards to the porch without falling on my face. Silently, he took me by the hand, escorting me across the dark expanse. Dependent and alone with him in the widespread farm country drove home the fact that I was acting like every dumb ingénue in any slasher movie ever made.

There appeared to be a subtle difference between "not wanting to go on anymore" and holding hands with a potential psychotic murderer moments before he hacked me to death and tossed my body parts into the shrubs for the bears to devour. I was no longer so sanguine about my own death.

This would have been a handy insight to have back at Northern Lights.

It took forever to cross the yard. Frost soaked through my inappropriate high-heeled pumps. Hobbled by my unsuitable shoes and ridiculously swirly skirt, I was defenseless—a detail that had slipped through Quality Control in the seduce-the-killer planning stages. If he attacked now, it would serve me right.

I kept waiting for the blow to fall, for his hand to drop mine, only to wrap around my throat. Tears pricked my eyes. So helpless. So stupid.

CHAPTER FORTY-TWO

Instead, Marshall led me through the night, continuing to grip my hand gently in his even after we were safely inside. Mine were chilled—from nerves as much as the night air—and with a wash of relief that was nearly erotic in its intensity, I suddenly felt absurd. And a little tingly.

Adding to that, Marshall's thumb rubbed against my palm, sensual and inviting, setting an electrical frisson slicing through my body.

As we stood blinking like libidinous moles in the sudden light of the cabin's foyer, he took both my hands, cupping them with his own, raising them to his mouth, breathing soft, warm air over them. More tinglies. Shutting my eyes, I shivered. As though coming awake from a deep slumber, my rational self sent up a Hail Mary-pass, inserting the image of the bloody hunting knife, effectively dissolving the pirate fantasies that yo-ho-ho'd in my head. Or in parts more southerly.

More shivering—different motivations. I gently pulled my hands free, stepping back, gaining some nonhand-holding breathing room and made a big production of looking around the room. Yep. The cabin. Just as I remembered it. And not a single bloody hunting knife to be seen.

"Something to drink?" Marshall asked, grinning.

"Maybe just some coffee."

"Sounds good. I've got a bit of a headache," he said as he walked into the kitchen.

Since he wasn't drunk, I had to revert to Plan B. Unfortunately, I was entirely without such a fine thing as a Plan B—another Quality Control issue—so while Marshall puttered in the kitchen, I retired to the "thinking place" to see if I could figure something out. If I couldn't, the bathroom had a window, although I'd probably break my neck in the stygian darkness trying to find my car.

Cover down, I sat on the stool, giving a fierce lecture to my vacillating girl-parts and sorting through the various issues. First of all, I was alone in the woods in an enchanted cabin with my boss who A) at the very least, was infatuated with me and with whom a relationship would complicate both my work situation and my sobriety or B) was a Shakespeare-In-Lust, psycho-killer stalker. Secondly, I had to figure out how to render my boss/beau/bad guy unconscious so I could scour the enchanted cabin for the grisly murder weapon.

I don't think this is what my AA gurus meant when they told me not to make any major changes in the first year of sobriety.

I nearly opted for the window, but then I noticed the medicine chest. Actually, I noticed the medicine chest when I was trying to shimmy myself up to the windowsill. My foot slipped off the sweating porcelain tank, and I almost fell in the sink.

"Everything okay in there?" Marshall called.

"Doing good."

Nestled inside the medicine chest was a nice assortment of generic acetaminophen products, including one that promised a good night's rest. I've tried those sleep aids; they knock you on your butt. Thankfully, enough time had passed from Marshall's two measly drinks that I didn't have to worry about sending him on the "Big Sleep," if I doped him up. I had enough on my plate without that. Snagging two capsules, I strolled out to the main room.

Marshall lounged on the chocolate-colored leather couch. In his beige button-down shirt, he looked like a smooth and creamy truffle, just waiting to be unwrapped. Or just possibly one of those goopy surprise candies that look like an eyeball when you oh-so-unsuspectingly bite into them. I wondered briefly if this was how schizophrenia developed.

Sade's "Kiss of Life" played softly in the background, emphasizing the sensual turn the evening had taken. I joined Marshall on the couch, spreading my skirt like Scarlett at the picnic, leaving enough space between us to park a bus.

"Here you go," I said in a fake chirpy voice. I dropped the two pills into his cupped palm. Hopefully, he wouldn't notice where I'd scratched "PM" off on the little devils.

"What's this?"

"You said you had a headache. I'm just returning the favor. You saved me from a killer hangover the last time I was here."

He grinned, popped them both in his mouth with a swallow of coffee. I squelched a premature sigh of relief. There was a lot that could still go wrong before Marshall felt the effects.

I debated my next move. I could leave—although that might be awkward—wait an hour, and then sneak back in. Marshall left his doors unlocked, so that wouldn't be a problem, but I didn't want to risk him grabbing a beer before tucking in for the night.

Of course, if he did, he would be less likely to wake up while I was digging through his desk drawers. Or ever. That would be the down side.

It would be just my luck to prove my innocence in two murders during the commission of the third. Plus, Lisa would kill me if we had to break in a new boss, and I'd never find out if Marshall was pirate-worthy.

So I stayed.

The stereo clicked over to a new CD and another of my favorite artists, Ray LaMontagne, came on. Liquid sound. Marshall added a log to the fire. Sparks flew, snapping like a feral animal, as the fire bit into the dry wood. A burst of heat fanned over my bare skin, making me conscious of the chill everywhere else.

Marshall came back, sliding my skirt over, sitting close. His eyes, dipping to my cleavage, did that sexy crinkle thing I liked, warming me even more than the fire.

"I haven't mentioned how much I liked your dress, have I?" he murmured staring at the swell of my breasts. *Thank you, Miraclebra.*

"That's not my dress," I pointed out.

"That's why I didn't mention it at work. I didn't want to risk a sexual harassment suit."

I stiffened slightly, and he leaned back, opening the space. "I talked with Detective Blodgett," he said, changing the subject. "But I haven't had a chance to see how *you* are, or to tell you how sorry I am that your friend was murdered. Have there been other developments?"

Even if he hadn't seen Blodgett, Marshall had to have known the detective had met with me at the clinic earlier. The dancing firelight was playing tricks with my eyes, making Marhall's difficult to read. The uncertainty made me answer more abruptly than I should have.

"Another crazy sonnet." I meant to go on, but my throat closed up when Marshall stretched his arm across the back of the couch, his expression troubled. By turning my head slightly, I could brush my lips against the warmth of his wrist. Not that I wanted to.

"Crazy?" he asked.

I cleared my throat, gaze flitting nervously to the bookshelves lined with English literature. Flitted *away* from the large hand that rested just over my left shoulder. I forced myself to look at him when I answered. "I'd say so. Yes."

He nodded thoughtfully. "Context can influence our perspective, of course. Which sonnet was it? Another of Shakespeare's?"

"One twenty-nine. The one that goes, 'The expense of spirit in a waste of shame is lust in action.' And then it goes on to talk about sex as murderous and bloody and leading to insanity or hell, whichever comes first, I guess."

"Not sex, per se, but sexual *desire*. I know the one you mean." His fingers absently reached out to toy with a strand of hair that had escaped my twist. I shivered.

Goosebumps rose, making me want to wrap my arms around myself. "Regardless of context," I heard myself say, "you must agree that the images are beyond horrible. There's such a profound hatred of women—"

"Not 'women,'" Marshall interrupted. "*Woman*. The Dark Lady, to be specific, although there's some debate as to whether she was the subject of that sonnet at all. Shakespeare never specified, though it seems likely. No other sonnet in the Fair Youth series comes close to the level of rancor shown in this one.

"But what I meant by 'context,' before I so rudely interrupted you," he smiled, "had to do with the Western viewpoint of sexuality and with the traditionally repressive nature of sexual morality. That is as long as you don't count the Bible's own 'Song of Songs,' which is pretty hot stuff. But, at any rate, I didn't mean to imply that your situation was skewing your perspective. Just the opposite, in fact. I believe that your experience gives you a deeper insight into … this person." His fingers dropped to my neck, stroking my skin lightly.

"You do?" A whisper.

"Oh, yes. There's a connection between you. He's after you. He wants you. I understand that."

Marshall's eyes, deep, black pools where gold reflections of fire danced like pagan spirits, pulled me in. He leaned forward, just slightly, just enough to signal his desire, eyes never releasing mine. I didn't think I moved, but I must have. Maybe I leaned. Still, it surprised me when our lips met. Met, moving and sliding and shaping one to the other, testing the surface before deepening. Warm and soft and silky, it felt like I was melting.

He moaned, slipping his arm behind my back, down my waist, levering my hips forward so I slid against the length of him, under and alongside the length of his lean body. I wasn't sure of much, but this I knew: he was pirate-worthy.

The CD switched again. The between-tracks silence dropped into the room, exaggerating the slight night-sounds of labored breathing, the fire's snap, the shush of rustling clothes, the rasp of his axe-calloused hand as it slid along my thigh. The music kicked in—Portishead's "All Mine"—a smooth counterpoint to the pulsing beat of our hearts. The hauntingly eerie noir tones filtered through my consciousness, moving us deeper into the night. Gasping, I pulled back and away, levering up.

"What is that?" I asked, though I loved the band and was completely familiar with their work. Familiar enough to know that the song—disturbing in its chilling sensuality—could have been chosen as the anthem for the next Stalkers Association of America convention.

"It's...um...I thought you liked this band." Marshall spoke slow and carefully, as if trying to calm a jumper on a ledge. Or possibly he was just having difficulty shifting gears from lust to loony. Alternatively, perhaps someone had drugged him with over-the-counter sleep aids. Eenie meanie minie mo.

"How do you know what bands I like?" In contrast, my voice sounded shrill and accusatory, the panic reined in only by confusion and leftover horniness.

Marshall straightened up, running a hand over his face, yawning. "I don't know. Maybe we talked about it?"

"Marshall, we never talked about music. I don't remember telling anybody..." I trailed off.

"What?"

277

"Lisa and I talked about our favorite bands. A couple of ks ago."

"Well, there you go. She must have mentioned it."

"Why would Lisa tell you what bands I like? That makes no sense. Maybe you heard us?"

"Maybe. Look, I don't know. I just wanted you to feel comfortable. I didn't mean to upset you." He unsuccessfully squelched another yawn.

"Right. I'm sorry. I'm just on edge these days. You know."

"Don't apologize. I understand completely. It's my fault for pushing too soon."

Taking that as my cue, I stood, simultaneously smoothing my skirt and trying to stuff wispy tendrils back into the French knot in an effort to ignore that we'd been making out like hormonally charged teenagers at the drive-in. Marshall looked dazed and befuddled. He'd pass out as soon as I left, or so I hoped. If he locked his door or turned into an insomniac despite the drugs I'd slipped him, I'd give up. For the night anyway.

CHAPTER FORTY-THREE

It wasn't a stormy night, but it was still pretty damn dark. Chilly, too. I'd let Marshall walk me to the door, turning on his porch lights so I could make my way to the car without mishap. I'd hoped he would be too woozy to remember to turn them off, but no such luck. They clicked off as soon as my headlights pointed toward the road.

I let the car roll forward until a stand of bushes and scrub trees blocked the view from the cabin. After smoking a gotta-stay-calm cigarette, I fished in my glove box, momentarily freaking out when my hand closed on something soft and fuzzy—my slightly shredded "emergency" tampon, not a dead rodent as I first imagined. I finally found a mini-flashlight. Slightly more powerful than a firefly's butt, it was capable of shedding just enough light to match key to keyhole on a dark night. Not so good, however, for willful trespassing in the enchanted forest. Come Monday, Quality Control would be pink-slipped.

As expected, the cheap thing died halfway to the cabin. Banging it viciously against an oak tree did nothing to convince it to return to life. Crying didn't create miraculous illumination either, but after a few minutes, my eyes adjusted to the night, letting me stumble between the dark roadway and the slightly-darker-than dark edges of grass. I cursed my shoes all over again.

It took so long to reach the cabin that Marshall could have cycled through all five sleep stages twice and gotten up for a middle-of-the-night snack to boot. Even though navigating the driveway had taken a lot longer than I'd anticipated, I took some time to rest on the porch steps. I just wanted to go home. Nerves and unrequited hormones had used up all my energy reserves. Got my butt wet on the frosty wood.

Teeth chattering, I stood and tiptoed to the nearest window. Marshall had left a nightlight on in the kitchen, comforting but only slightly brighter than my now defunct mini-flashlight.

It would've been smart to do some kind of reconnaissance around the cabin, maybe peeking in the windows and verifying Marshall's exact whereabouts, but I no longer gave a crap. I decided if Marshall woke up and caught me, I'd jump him. It remained to be seen whether that would end as a booty call or a beat down.

Chanting "please be locked, please be locked," I turned the knob. Of course, it opened. The fire had died down to embers, leaving warmth and orange, glowing ashes. It was quiet.

I debated calling a soft "halloo" to add verisimilitude to my "I come in peace" story, but fell back on the jump-Marshall-first, explain-later plan. I could always make up a cover story mid-straddle. As if he'd notice.

The first thing I did was tiptoe up the stairs to listen at Marshall's door. Soft, not-quite-snores drifted rhythmically through the partially opened door. I eased it shut. Then down to the kitchen, where I began pawing through the junk drawer. Luckily, I found one of those skinny pen-lights that all the real cat burglars on TV use. Moving to Marshall's desk, I clamped the pen-light between my teeth like a Bond girl, pulling out the top drawer. Two drawers down, my jaws ached, and I realized cat burglars must have crappy dental health. A person could break a tooth doing this stuff.

But no buck knife.

I slid over to the bookshelves. As remembered, the shelves held a scattering of English lit, a wider assortment of Clancy and Grisham novels, and some old psych texts. I pulled a few out, checking to make sure the knife hadn't been thrust behind them. Since I already knew that Marshall had studied Shakespeare, I only briefly examined his copies, making sure the sonnets that had been sent to me weren't in some way singled out. On the other hand, if I found a term paper analyzing Sonnets 57, 147, 35, and 129, specifically, I'd stuff a pillow over Marshall's sleeping face. Or, at the very least, I'd turn the paper over to Blodgett, although that lacked the keen resonance of pillow justice.

Every few minutes, I eased over to the foot of the stairs, listening. Finding nothing more dangerous than a sticky note, I shifted to the closet. As before, it held only closet stuff. Even the axe was gone.

Further exploration of the cabin uncovered a small laundry area. A load of jeans, slightly damp and musty smelling, had been left too long in the washer. I resisted running them through the wash cycle again. I couldn't help noting that one minute I wanted to asphyxiate and the next domesticate the same man. Worrisome dichotomy.

After sliding and shifting every object and peering under and into every orifice on the main level of the cabin, I was reasonably certain the buck knife wasn't there. Marshall's bedroom, specifically the gun cabinet, was all that remained.

My legs were shaking uncontrollably before I even made it to the stair landing. I took a couple of deep breaths, trying to calm down, but almost hyperventilated myself. Just as I forced my knees to unlock and climb the next riser, Marshall coughed. I almost wet myself. Then he coughed again.

Time to go.

By the time I'd made it back through the hellish darkness and gained the safety of my car, I'd convinced myself that the gun cabinet would, of course, be the first place searched by law enforcement and so presumably the *last* place a killer would hide a murder weapon. Alcoholics, even those in recovery, can work up excuses and rationalizations faster than almost anybody. Except politicians. They still got us beat.

I'd search Marshall's office at the clinic tomorrow.

Neither Hannah nor I had remembered to get the keys; we ended up having to call Lisa in to open up. She was not amused. When she finally showed up, her hair, flat on one side and snarled into a froth on the other, told the same story as the bright orange pajama pants emblazoned with red "kissy" lips. As if we didn't get the point, she clutched a large, gas station-logoed cup of coffee like she intended to mainline the brew. Hannah stood a prudent five feet away, eyeing her warily.

I gave the sleep-deprived diva much therapeutic space, expecting her to bolt as soon as the locks snapped open. She surprised me by following us into the front office and plopping down at her desk. Hannah raised an eyebrow and continued toward her own office.

Lisa waited until Hannah's door shut before turning to me with an evil grin and a drawn out, "Well?"

"That's a deep subject," I said.

She frowned in confusion, a state Lisa did not tolerate with grace. "*What?*"

"Wells? They're deep. Get it?"

"If you make my head hurt worse than it already does, I will peel the skin off your body with my staple remover." She brandished the metal pincers menacingly, clicking them like malevolent castanets. They looked like they could do some damage. "Tell me everything, babe. I want the dirt."

"I don't know what you're talking about"—the blush spreading over my face gave away the lie—"and even if I did, I don't do 'dirt.'"

"Well, I do. Okay, just tell me this…" Reaching into her drawer, she pulled out the magazine and held it up, pointing a shapely, manicured nail at the Marshall look-alike. "Huh? *Huh?*"

The flare from first- to third-degree blush almost ignited my eyebrows. Lisa laughed so uproariously, it drew Hannah back to the front. I tried grabbing the sleazy magazine, but Lisa fended me off with the staple remover.

"What's going on?" Hannah asked.

Lisa tossed her the magazine. Hannah's naturally placid features broke into a slight grin. "Oh, my," she said.

"No, no, no. That's not the best part. Check out the dude up in the little basket thing."

"It's a crow's nest," I said. I don't know why.

Holding the magazine at arm's length, Hannah shifted it back and forth, trying to focus on the Marshall-pirate without putting her reading glasses on. "*Oh, my!*" She got it.

"Is that…? Do you think…?"

I snatched the magazine away. "No, of course not. It's just some guy who bears a slight…" I broke off, eyeing the naked buccaneer. *Could it be?*

Lisa leaned over my shoulder. "I don't care who you are, that ain't 'slight.'"

Hannah leaned over the other. "Maybe he needed money in college or something. Because, look!" She pointed at a spot on the pirate's neck. "Doesn't Marshall have a mole right there?"

"That's just a water spot," I said. "Probably from Lisa drooling over it."

"I never drool. That's a mole! I need a magnifying glass." Lisa started to rummage through her desk drawer. While she was distracted, I grabbed my car keys, sprinting for the door.

"Hey!" Lisa protested. Ignoring her, I made for my car, tossed the magazine in the trunk, slammed it shut. Damn thing had *my* name on it anyway.

When I got back inside, Lisa sat slumped in her chair, a thwarted frown pursing her lips. "I'll get it back."

Unimpressed, I leaned a hip against her desk. "How? You gonna tell Marshall I took back the porn magazine that you think *he* posed for?" Her eyes narrowed to slits, darting back and forth as she mentally scanned her choices.

She didn't have any. Yet. Sniffing, she stood, smoothing down the wrinkles in her pajama top. "Well, have fun working all day, ladies. I'm going back to bed."

"Leave the keys unless you want us to call you back to lock up."

She didn't bother with an answer. Instead, she dropped the keys on her desk, little pinky extended to show royal disdain. Then she sashayed out the door, letting quiet descend on the clinic.

Almost too quiet. I looked around. "Isn't Mary Kate supposed to be here?"

CHAPTER FORTY-FOUR

"Don't ask me. Maybe she overslept," Hannah said.

"Mary Kate? I've never known her to be late. Besides, she's bringing the donuts." This was a very important point.

"She must be exhausted with finals and helping out here. She was looking pretty tired last night, but all I got was a glare when I suggested she sleep in this morning. Anyway, let's get started. We can get a lot of this cleared away if we hustle."

I agreed, but my mind wasn't on filing. I was obsessed with getting into Marshall's office undetected. Humming a John Denver tune, Hannah disappeared into the file room to track down those files we'd need for Monday's clients.

"Oh, I forgot. I have a phone call to make. Shouldn't take long." My voice sounded phony to me, but Hannah was deep into sunshine and mountains and re-establishing order to her world. She didn't care what I did.

Trying not to jingle the keys, I slipped down the hall and into Marshall's office. Not wanting Hannah to spy a band of light under the door, I left the overhead off. Of course, she'd have to turn off all the lights and lie on the carpet to see under the door, but I was more than a little freaked out. Besides, there was enough sun seeping through the blinds for what I needed to do.

The file cabinet was locked, but the desk wasn't. I started there. It contained the usual administrator's office crap—

nothing surprising. No vodka flasks or baggies of white powder or pornography. Unfortunately for me, also no file cabinet keys and nary a sign of the knife. The bottom right drawer was one of those deep ones, probably another file cabinet, and unlike the other drawers, locked. I wished that I could have stolen Marshall's keys when I searched his place, but I'd been sure he'd have a duplicate set of the tiny, easy-to-lose cabinet keys somewhere close by.

Not knowing how to pick locks—they don't teach such useful skills in grad school—I was nevertheless determined to get in, one way or another. It made sense that if the knife was here, it would be locked up, so the cabinets were especially tantalizing. While I pondered the problem, I rifled through the book shelves, neither expecting nor finding anything suspicious.

Other than the locked cabinets, there was really no other hiding place. I sat in Marshall's chair, trying to get a feel for his space. Yanked open the top right drawer, stuffed with pens, pencils, and other miscellaneous supplies, and rummaged through it a second time even though I'd been meticulous the first search.

Nothing.

I checked my watch. I'd already used up twelve minutes, and even easygoing Hannah would start to question my continued absence. The office felt hot and stuffy, sweat beading my upper lip in a most annoying way.

With a burst of inspiration, I picked up the potted plant that Marshall had tipped over when Lisa had walked in on our "awkward" moment. Nothing but dust and a milky-white water stain.

Time to admit defeat.

Standing, I wiped sweaty hands on my jeans. A flash of silver caught my eye. Not the keys, but a small container of paperclips next to the phone console. I rattled it back and forth. Aha!

One silver mini-key and one bronze ditto.

I started on the big cabinet, which was full of boring paperwork that I neither understood nor cared about. I slid a hand under and behind the rows of hanging files, looking for the telltale gap that a solid object stuck in the middle of a file would make.

I repeated the routine in the desk drawer. This drawer held personnel records and I had to fight the urge to peek. My good angel was winning until I spied Mary Kate's name.

After all, I *had* promised Mary Kate that I would look into the matter of her progress report, and it *would* be kind of awkward to bring it up to Hannah. I wouldn't want Hannah to think I didn't trust her judgment. That would be rude. And Marshall might not let me check Hannah's section anyway. And I did promise.

I tweaked the file out. The progress report was right on top, so I was hardly trespassing at all. Skipping over the sections I'd filled in, I focused on Hannah's pristine handwriting. I read it through once.

Then a second time.

Mary Kate must have misunderstood. Hannah had written a very even-handed evaluation. She did note that they'd had difficulty bonding, pointing out the unusual circumstances of the transfer. She praised Mary Kate's willingness and dedication, gave her high marks for her ability to empathize with her clients. It was a good evaluation.

Forgetting that I was only going to peek at the progress report, I paged absently through the rest of the file. Mary Kate had never gotten along with Hannah, but I'd just assumed it was because of the abrupt transition. I pulled out her resume—a stunning list of career stops and starts. I smiled at the wide variety of enthusiasms that had led Mary Kate to explore culinary arts, accounting, day care administration, and horticulture before settling on counseling. I flipped the page. Her education history reflected the same scatter-gun approach. Botany, psychiatric nursing, literature, geology.

Wait. *Literature?* I paged through until I came to her college transcripts—three separate schools, which didn't help. I found it on the second transcript. She'd come within three credits of graduating with a bachelor's degree in Renaissance literature. Three credits shy, and then she'd switched to psychology, basically starting all over.

Mary Kate?

I shoved the papers back in the file, leaping to my feet. Clutching it tightly, I ran to the front office. Hannah sat at Lisa's desk separating the files we'd need tomorrow. She looked up in startled surprise at my hurry.

"What…?"

"Where's Mary Kate?" My voice sounded thin and squished, coming via breathless lungs.

"She's not here yet. Are you okay?"

I stood clutching the file to my chest, trying to sort through the crazy idea that bounced around my brain like a bunny on crack. I'd never considered Mary Kate. I'd never seriously considered a woman.

I sank into a chair, ignoring Hannah's worried noises, focusing inward, looking for a hole in the theory. Looking for the mistake. A wave of dizziness swept over me. Hannah squawked louder, and I dimly sensed her kneeling next to me, rubbing my back. When the word "ambulance" penetrated, I roused myself.

"No! I don't need an ambulance."

"What on earth is going on? Do you want me to call someone?"

"No. No, that's okay. I'm just…" No way to explain. I could barely even wrap my own mind around the possibility that Mary Kate might be the one responsible for the sonnets, the doll, the… killings.

My heart thudded erratically. The killings. The killing of two men who—for good or bad—showed interest in me. The two men who captured my attention, who made the sonnet-giver "question with jealous thought where [I] may be, or [my] affairs suppose."

And what about the *third* man?

CHAPTER FORTY-FIVE

Once I cleared town, I pushed my little Focus up to eighty, figuring if a cop tried to pull me over, I'd let him chase me clear to the cabin. A cop would also come in handy if I slammed into a wayward deer, making hamburger out of both of us. I ached for a cigarette.

I considered calling Blodgett but was too scared to let go of the steering wheel; besides, what could I say? Mary Kate studied literature from the same era that the stalker's sonnets derived from? So did Marshall. And, logically speaking, Paul had the more compelling motive for murder than either Mary Kate or Marshall.

But my gut knew it was Mary Kate, knew it with a certainty that I'd never had with either of the two men. Her whimsical devotion concealed deeper passions; her difficulty with letting go, a rage-filled fear of abandonment.

I sucked as a supervisor.

Tires churned a dust cloud going up Marshall's dirt road, gravel pinging off the tree trunks. Marshall's Saab, the only vehicle in the clearing besides my own, sat parked in the same spot as when I'd left last night. I got out and stood next to my car, listening. The engine ticked loudly, but otherwise silence blanketed the property. Too quiet?

The crank of the hinge as I shut the door exploded into the hushed clearing like a shot.

I made for the cabin and was halfway to the door before remembering the killer's habit of ambushing his prey from behind bushes and shrubs. *Her* prey. Might as well get in the habit of saying that. I darted from side to side in an approximation of evasive moves that I'd seen on TV. If Marshall wasn't in trouble and happened to look out his window, he'd probably assume I was psychotic.

Nobody shot at me. I made it to the porch feeling like an imbecile and checked the doorknob. Unlocked, as always. Feeling like a storybook character, I poked my head around the corner, calling out a neighborly "yoo-hoo!"

The cabin was dusky and quiet. The same eerie silence as the clearing—ominous, watchful, not at all peaceful. Goldilocks must have had balls of steel, because I could barely force myself across the threshold. Marshall was obviously not in the kitchen or living room, and a quick scan of the laundry room didn't uncover anybody either. Or any *body*. I shuddered, hating my imagination, and checked the washer and dryer, just in case. Same musty jeans, but nothing scarier.

Heart pounding, I moved back to the living room, heading for the loft stairs. When my knees gave out, I decided crawling was eminently sensible and not the least bit undignified. Marshall's bedroom door stood open, the sun pouring in with a cheerful vigor that mocked the realities of danger and death. His room was orderly, bed made, clothes hung up. It certainly didn't look like any kind of struggle had occurred.

Feeling foolish and more than a little relieved, I went back downstairs. I still hadn't found Marshall, but maybe he was out chopping wood or fishing or doing some other manly, woodsy activity. I decided to try the bell again.

I saw the blood as soon as I stepped outside.

About five yards to the left of the path, a section of the grass had a chaotic, churned look. Droplets and ragged smears of blood splattered the fresh, green blades. In my headlong, scurry-dash evasive maneuvers, I'd rushed right passed the signs, only spying them from the higher vantage point of the porch.

Pulling my cell phone out, I dialed Blodgett's number with surprisingly steady hands. Only two reception bars showed, the call immediately switching to voice mail. I told Blodgett my suspicions, gave directions, hung up.

I was a northern girl. I'd gone deer hunting with my dad. Kind of. I knew how to follow the blood track. I took off down the ATV trail, walking on the center strip of foliage between the two parallel ruts of dirt. Ominous dots and random smears of crimson sprouted like sinister blossoms. After a short distance, I realized I couldn't create a more perfect shooting target unless I drew target circles on my chest and yodeled.

I scurried off-trail, pushing through the scrub trees and bracken, ignoring the branches stabbing my arms and legs. I'd made a god-awful lot of noise, so I stood silent, listening. Only the leaves, oblivious to the human drama below, rustled in the light breeze. The birds stayed mum; small mammals, hidden.

It was the larger ones I was worried about.

The problem with being off the path was that I couldn't see the blood trail any more. It looked like the bleeder was heading straight down the ATV path, but I'd miss the signs if he veered off. Moreover, the thick undergrowth made it next to impossible to move with any stealth.

I hoped that all this was unnecessary, that Mary Kate had taken off, but could I be sure? The tinny flavor of fear coating my mouth argued against that hope. I kept going. Someone was hurt and that someone was surely Marshall.

Swallowing past the pounding heart currently relocated to my throat, I moved back to the ATV path. Prepared to dive back into the brush, I crept forward as fast as my spotty vision and shaking limbs could carry me. The bloody smears grew fainter and farther apart. I scurried along, hoping the

292

diminishing marks meant that the wound wasn't too bad rather than that he was bleeding out.

It took forever and a day before I finally came to the edge of another clearing. A tall oak had been felled, the branches scavenged for firewood and cleared away. The stump, sheared nearly flat except for a taller segment that had been ripped away from the falling tree, resembled a throne for a kingly wood elf. A golden carpet of shavings and wood chips littered the forest floor, making it all too easy to spot the gory splash of fresh blood.

I didn't faint. Almost, but I didn't. If I had, I wouldn't have heard the slight panting coming from behind the five-foot-high wall of stacked logs at the very edge of the clearing.

"Marshall?" I called. Tried to, that is. The only sound that escaped my dry mouth was a cross between a moan and a hiss. I cleared my throat, and the panting stopped.

"Marshall?" This time my voice traveled far enough that it made me nervous.

I took it as a good sign when nobody popped out and shot me. I crept forward, twigs snapping under foot, the sharp aroma of cut wood filling my nose. A decades-absent yearning for my daddy flooded my soul, forcing me to choke down a sob. Holding my breath, I peeked around the pile. Marshall lay curled on his back, head propped against the side of the stacked logs, legs braced to keep his body angled upright. One hand clamped tight over his lower right abdomen, his blood tie-dyeing his formerly white t-shirt. The other hand clutched an axe.

Our eyes met, but he didn't seem to recognize me. His lips, white and thinned with pain, trembled; his body shook. I took a step forward, stopped when he raised the axe. It wobbled, the effort making him pant harder. I sank to my knees. We didn't have time for this. *He* didn't have time.

"Marshall," I whispered. "It's okay. It's me, Letty. I'm not going to hurt you."

Something flickered behind his eyes. He lowered the axe slightly.

"We've got to get you out of here, bud. We've got to get help."

He whispered something I didn't catch and lowered the axe to the ground. I pulled my cell phone out, flipped it open—no bars.

"I've got to stop the bleeding, Marshall." I pulled my T-shirt over my head, shivering as the breeze cooled the sweat on my body. Wadding it up, I crawled to his side, praying he didn't bury the axe in my head.

When he didn't, I moved his hand, placing the shirt against his wound, and applied pressure. Now that I got a good look, I could see that he'd been pegged by a bunch of buckshot, ragged holes speckled his abdomen like a grisly version of connect-the-dots. Shock and prolonged exposure added to the danger. "Look, bud, this is all the first aid I know. We have to get you back to the clearing."

He mumbled again. This time I got it.

"She's out there? Are you sure? I just came from the cabin; she could have shot me anytime if she was still here." Nevertheless, skin tingling, I scanned the clearing—including the sky—as if Mary Kate might be perched like a sniper in a tree top. Or a vulture, to keep the image true. Hell, for all I knew, she could have had military training along with geology and cake baking. She was certainly eclectic.

"Outta shells," Marshall whispered. "Back . . . more."

"She's gone for more ammo?" Great, now I was talking like a commando.

He nodded weakly, eyelids fluttering against his cheek like papers caught in a draft. Red splotches where he'd wiped his face glistened against pale, clammy skin; his long, black eyelashes, a series of stark commas.

I had to get help.

CHAPTER FORTY-SIX

"I've got to get back to where my phone has signal." No response. "*Marshall*, do you hear me?"

"...hear you." He opened his eyes, stretched a smile and licked his lips—a dry, raspy exercise. His gaze dropped to my bra. "See you, too."

"You gotta be kidding me." Although I *was* wearing a particularly cute bra—orange with pink trim, reminded me of sherbet. Not that it mattered, of course. "I can't believe you're trying to flirt now."

". . . last chance." He reached out, clasped my wrist. His grip was ice-cold but surprisingly forceful, fingers digging into my skin. "...knife!"

The blood drained from my head. "She has the knife?" I repeated dully. Of course, she did. *All the better to stab you in the heart, my dear.*

Eyes closed again, he nodded and let go my wrist.

"I'll hurry," I said.

I took off running as fast as my donut-eating, caffeine-fueled body would allow. I prayed that Marshall was wrong, that Mary Kate had fled when her ambush had failed and didn't plan to come back. She'd be crazy to stick around.

Oh, wait...

Something crashed wildly through the branches, and I tripped over a root and fell, nearly gouging my eye out on a

295

spiny branch. A freaked-out squirrel leaped in panicked frenzy from limb to limb. I could relate. Jumping to my feet as though the loamy ground was made of rubber, I took off again, checking the bars on my phone every few feet. The reception flirted with me, once going up as high as two bars. As soon as I stopped to attempt a call, they winked out again, not even returning when I held the phone straight up at arm's length, turning like a human antenna.

By the time I made the clearing, sweat slicked my body like a glaze, sherbet-bra heaving as my lungs struggled for air. Bent over, gasping like a landed fish, I peered blearily at the face of my cell phone. Three bars. Good deal.

At first, 9-1-1 thought I was a pervert, but when I finally caught my breath enough to sputter out "shooting!" we all got on the same page.

I didn't know Marshall's address, so I gave the operator his name and a series of country directions, involving instructions like "Take Highway 29 east past the big red barn with the llamas and turn north on the corner where the old gas station that closed down used to be."

As I talked, I spied a tool shed tucked a few feet into the woods about fifty yards from where I sprawled. A dingy brown, on-the-To-Do-list paint job and a scraggly hedge of wild grasses and scrub trees nearly camouflaged the structure, explaining how I'd missed it.

The operator wanted me to stay on the line, but I was afraid of running down my batteries. Besides, I had an idea.

I pulled on one side of the double doors, making the hinges squeal like a stepped-on rat, and stood blinking helplessly as my eyes coped with the abrupt change from sunlight to darkness. Heart thumping, I imagined my pupils struggling to adjust, willing them to expand quicker. If Mary Kate lurked in the shadows clutching her knife, I'd certainly cooperated in my own demise. At least I couldn't hear any maniacal giggles coming from inside. According to every scary movie I'd ever watched, that was a good sign.

My pupils finally did their job, and I stepped inside. A wooden shelf ran along one wall cluttered with tools, garden utensils, some crumpled beer cans and other manly doodads. The usual shed things.

Cobwebs coated the ceiling, stretching across the two-by-four rafters like eco-friendly insulation. Probably not very effective though. They wafted gently in the breeze, undulating like a cloud. Thoughts of spiders dropping from the heavens onto my bare head and even barer shoulders made my skin twitch. I started sweating again. A sherbet-bra was clearly not an effective spider barrier.

I couldn't leave Marshall bleeding on the woodchips, though, so I forced myself deeper inside. Besides, my entire back was probably covered with deer ticks anyway, what difference would a few spiders make? That happy thought made my knees buckle. I grabbed the shelf for support, taking a deep breath.

The whole place reeked of gasoline. Spying a huge, tarp-covered lump in the center of the dirt floor, I let out a yelp, then promptly slapped a hand over my mouth hard enough to cut my lip. I could never have been an Indian scout.

I yanked the tarp off, uncovering the ATV. It was beautiful. Unfortunately, no keys rested in the ignition and, for a second, my heart seized, certain that Marshall had the keys buried deep in his pocket or secreted somewhere in the house. I didn't have time to rummage through his junk drawer.

But, no. Like any good northwoods, Wisconsin boy, he'd driven a nail into the shed wall for the sole purpose of dangling the key ring from it. I snatched them down, stuck them in the ignition, and whirled to swing the doors open.

A figure stood in the door, the sun back lighting her into a shadow woman. Now *she'd* have made a good Indian scout.

CHAPTER FORTY-SEVEN

W here is your *shirt?*" She sounded like my mother. I glanced down at my nearly naked torso in the same stupefied bewilderment as when I'd been forced to explain to my real mother why Toby Zuckerman was hiding under my bed. Didn't have a shirt then, either.

"Hey, Mary Kate. How are you doing?"

Not the most inspired response, I admit, but I was a little distracted. It didn't matter. She was entirely fixated on my lack of attire.

"Did you spill something on it? Aren't you cold?" She took a few steps into the shed, her features materializing as she moved away from the light. Her face—flaccid and empty and haggard—had aged. She held the buck knife in her right hand, angling herself between me and the door.

"No. I gave it to Marshall to stop the bleeding." My throat made a sticky clacking sound as I tried to swallow.

Mary Kate's face remained scary-blank. "Oh," she said. Just that. Her eyes moved, traveling around the shed, searching and skittish.

My own eyes flitted after, trying to catch up, trying to identify what she was looking for before she found it. Trying to find something to defend myself with. My stomach roiled with acid at the sight of all the objects—screwdrivers, chisels, garden claws, hammers—that Mary Kate could use to kill me dead. The Spanish Inquisition would have *loved* this place.

A wad of gray fabric caught my attention.

"Oh, look!" I said in the world's most unnatural "surprised" voice. "Is that a shirt?" Pretending I didn't believe Mary Kate was about to plunge the buck knife into my heart, I took two shaky steps over to the work bench.

She shifted nervously, bringing the knife up. Keeping my movements broad and open, I reached over, picked the rag up. I stepped back carefully, away from the arsenal of wannabe weapons that I both coveted and feared, and moved closer to the ATV.

Still holding the wad of cloth at arm's length, I shook it out, demonstrating its harmlessness. It was an old, ratty T-shirt covered in blotchy oil streaks and gooey brown spots. A dead spider, legs curled in brittle arcs, fell out of the folds.

"Eww," Mary Kate said.

Grimacing, I pulled the shirt over my head. Unfortunately, it wasn't much of an improvement in the modesty department since a large, jagged hole exposed one scoop of boob. I twitched the fabric sideways.

"Oh, there you go," Mary Kate said. "That's better." For the first time, an emotion—relief—showed on her face.

"Yeah," I lied.

Now that I'd addressed her shirt concern and demonstrated trustworthiness by not flinging a trowel at her head, I took a chance.

"Mary Kate, I'm worried for you. If something. . . um, *bad*. . . happens to Marshall, you might get in trouble."

Discretion seemed wise. Thus, the word choices of "bad" and "trouble" in lieu of "fatal" or "sent to prison or straight to hell, whichever comes first." Semantics 101.

She sighed and rubbed her forehead, her face leaching of emotion again. "It didn't work out right, but I think it will be okay pretty soon."

My stomach clenched. Her idea of a good outcome didn't bode well for our boss. I debated telling her that the cops were coming, but she still gripped the knife and still blocked the door, and she *might* just wonder who called the police in the first place.

"Mary Kate, why do you want to hurt Marshall? He's been a good friend to you. And besides, it might be kind of hard for him to hire you back if you . . . you know. . . kill him." Lame, so lame. I winced at my ineptitude, but Mary Kate reacted with a slight glimmer of emotion.

She frowned, just a little. "Yeah, I know. That part sucks. I liked working at the clinic."

"Mary Kate, don't do this. It's not right. You need to let me go help Marshall."

I didn't think I'd moved, but in my mind I was preparing to step forward and Mary Kate sensed it. She raised the knife, pointing it toward me. The edge caught a stray bit of light from the outside, making a tiny beam dance along the blade like a malicious sprite. Mesmerized, I couldn't look away. I couldn't breathe. Couldn't think.

"You were so sad," Mary Kate said in a raspy whisper. I dragged my eyes away from the knife to meet hers. "The week he pulled us apart. I didn't understand at first; I thought it was you. I thought you didn't want me anymore, but then you shared your secret with me. You let me in. That's when I knew that you felt the same way I did." She smiled then, but it was ghastly—a caricature of her former self, a rictus of pain frozen in a death mask.

I couldn't answer. She waited for my response, and when the silence dragged on, she nodded, turning away to stare blankly at the cobwebs tethered to the walls. "I did it for you, you know. I understood. Every time I looked at you, I could feel you drawing me to you, giving me all your pain and fears to hold for you. Like a present." Her eyes flicked sideways at me, then away again. "It made an ache inside, like frostbite in my heart. You know? I mean, how long could that go on? He was killing you and that was killing me. I couldn't let that happen. I even tried to warn him to back off. So I finally did what you always tell me to do. I set boundaries." Another eye flick and a sly *proud-of-me?* smile.

"I never wanted you to kill," I made myself say. "Not Wayne, not Robert, and not Marshall."

The smile slid off her face as she turned back to me. "Don't. Just *don't*. You can't take it back now. Not after everything I did for you. I knew it was you, right from the start, when you asked for me to be assigned to you. *You* picked *me*." She pointed the knife at my chest. Her hand shook, making the tiny mote of light jig wildly down the knife's edge. "And at lunch? I saw how you looked at me when I switched my order. I don't even like scampi, but I wanted you to know what it felt like to be pushed away. But of course, I couldn't really do that. I was just teasing. It meant so much, you know? That you picked me. And then to just push me aside?"

"You were *assigned* to me," I said. Rage swelled, filling my head, pushing reason to the far corners. "Marshall picks out the supervisors for the interns. I didn't even know you. And if I *had*—"

"Don't—"

"*If I had*—"

"Don't say it!"

"*I wouldn't have asked for you! I would have refused to work with you. I would ha*—"

Howling, she flung herself at me, so ravaged with pain she didn't even remember the knife clutched in her hand. I was ready, leaping sideways to the work bench, grabbing the first thing in reach. I struck, aiming for her head and missing, hitting her in the shoulder with a torque wrench. Swung again and hit her in the ear. Now she had a reason to howl.

And she did, too.

She also remembered the knife, which was unfortunate. The romantic in her obviously had a thing for hearts and she stabbed at the center of my nasty, ratty T-shirt. So much for true love. Dancing back, I flung the wrench at her face, smacking her in the mouth with it. A fountain of blood gushed out and she fell to her knees, clunking up against a rusty, red can. A guttural sound, a hybrid of moan and growl, erupted from her split lips. Blood sprayed in an arcing mist as she screamed, splattering her shirt front, dripping down the gas can to the concrete below.

She rose to her feet, swaying a bit, but hanging tough. Through all this, she'd managed to keep the knife and retain her position in front of the door. I grabbed a chisel and skittered sideways, putting the ATV between us. We stood in an impasse, each breathing heavy and watching the other through narrowed eyes. The bottom half of her face looked like a gory Halloween mask.

In the distance, I heard sirens.

CHAPTER FORTY-EIGHT

I saw the awareness as she registered the sirens, too. Her head tilted slightly as if trying to make sense of the sound, then her eyes found mine. A look of disbelief spread over her bloody face, eyes widening in shock.

"You called the cops?" she asked, as incredulous as if I'd cheated at checkers.

She flailed both hands in a tantrum, spitting blood, and grunting, "nnhh, nnhh, nnhh!" The knife whistled thinly through the dusty air. Wild-eyed, she started backing toward the door, and I felt a surge of hope.

Until she stumbled over the gas can again. I knew what she would do even as the idea formed in her head. She had the gas can overturned and the liquid glugging out, washing the blood from her chin, before I could scream "No!" The shed filled with gas fumes, thick and choking. She stood there, dripping, eyes staring out at me from under a gasoline haze.

"Now what?" I whispered. "You don't smoke. You don't have a lighter."

"No," she said. "But you did."

And she pulled out my lighter.

Her hands shook so wildly that the lighter didn't catch right off. Not even the second time. Not waiting for her to work out the kinks, I leaped onto the ATV, twisted the key, the engine roaring to life like a trapped beast. Slamming it into gear, it

303

lurched forward, crashing into Mary Kate and flinging her up on the hood, a disproportionately large hood ornament. I aimed for the double door and got half of it—the closed half—and took out part of the wall as well.

We plowed through, boards cracking and spinning out into the clearing like pinwheels. Scared the crap out of the cops milling around the yard looking for a simple, little shooting incident. Mary Kate flipped off the front of the ATV, rolling through the weeds.

She still grasped the lighter, though, and third time's a charm. A sickening whoosh exploded in front of me, and I ducked away from the searing flash and heat. She shrieked an all-too-human wail, stretching her arms out to me, hands reaching for me even as the flames bit into her. No matter what Mary Kate intended—to hold or be held—the flames had her now, and they bent her backward, buckling her over. Trying to escape, she stumbled, flinging herself in senseless frenzy.

Mary Kate couldn't escape her pyre, and I couldn't help her. One of the officers responded with amazing presence of mind, covering Mary Kate's thrashing body with his jacket while another ran for the squad. A third popped up with a First Aid kit the size of a textbook. It was a nice thought, but I didn't think a gauze pad and an antiseptic wipe was going to be enough. The second cop barreled through with a blanket, flinging it over Mary Kate and the first guy, and pig-piled on them both. The screams muffled, so they were either suffocating the flames or Mary Kate. She probably didn't care which.

I sat, a numb and passive bystander on the ATV, watching. The ambulance wailed like a lost soul up the dirt road, slinging rocks. It skidded to a stop, EMTs jumping out like an exploding clown car. Mary Kate was still screaming under the blanket, and the cops were still patting at the smoldering cloth, their professionally trained faces unable to contain their horror even as their hands coped with the crisis.

Almost forgot about Marshall.

Stumbling off the ATV, I made my way over to a cop. He was just standing there, uselessly holding the kit in one hand, his other clamped over his mouth. It didn't help. When they pulled the blanket off Mary Kate, he leaned over crisply at the waist and threw up on his nicely polished shoes. She was still alive, however, although whether that would prove a blessing or a curse would likely remain in doubt for some time.

Marshall, though. I grabbed the cop by his arm, shaking it back and forth. He yanked it back, intent on vomiting in peace.

"Stop puking. My boss is bleeding to death out there."

He spit and gagged. *"What?"* I had his attention. He remained bent over, but at least he was focusing on my knees. I leaned over, eye-to-eye, just to make sure.

"My boss is gut-shot." I pointed at Mary Kate—a mistake since he gagged again. "She shot him, and he's out in the woods bleeding to death. He needs help."

He recovered remarkably fast, probably relieved to deal with a normal GSW instead of the charred and blistered heap that the EMTs frantically worked over.

"Out there?" he asked, pointing toward the trail.

"Yeah."

He commandeered the ATV. I sat on the grass. I sat on the grass and prayed to a god I wasn't even sure existed. Just in case.

The ambulance with Mary Kate roared off soon after the second one had pulled up. Several more police cars skidded up behind the second ambulance, cops from nearby counties piling out and scattering with choreographed purpose.

From the few glimpses I managed, Marshall was still alive but unconscious, his skin grayed out, lips blue. They tended to him quickly but less frantically, loading him and taking off.

Somebody had taken up a position next to and over me, his presence a shadow-image flickering in and out of my consciousness. When Marshall's ambulance finally spun off down the road, I tried to stand. Made it to my knees and got stuck. A hand reached down, hovering next to my face. I grabbed it, let it pull me to my feet.

Blodgett. He wore old jeans—the kind called dungarees, which had never attempted to be fashionable—and a local high school sweatshirt in only slightly better condition than the oil rag I wore. His eyes, though, were kind. Tired and penetrating, but kind.

"About time," I said, not really knowing what I meant.

CHAPTER FORTY-NINE

I didn't drink, but it was only because Sue and the Wednesday night women stapled themselves to my ass. I don't even know how long they kept watch. With no appetite and endless insomnia, I lost all sense of time. Days ran into nights, a blurry cycle devoid of purpose or meaning. What little energy I spent was used to keep it that way. I didn't want to make sense of it. Insight would kill me.

Despite my best efforts at self-induced oblivion, Blodgett kept me tethered to reality. He stopped in regularly to see if I'd remembered anything new. I tried insisting on a search warrant to keep him out, but Sue and the girls kept letting him in.

He came to update me on Mary Kate's recovery and the case's progression. I didn't want to know. I didn't want to know about the public defender that had been assigned or the court dates that kept being postponed. I *certainly* didn't want to know about her IV drips or the coma they induced or the start of the skin grafts.

But Blodgett kept up a steady barrage of updates, determined to keep me abreast of the developments, slowly helping me regain a sense of perspective, a reduction of Mary Kate to person-status. Disturbed and obsessed and dangerous— yes, all that. But not a monster, not a Glen Close-jump-back-out-of-the-bathtub freak of nature. Not immortal.

I need to know that.

As I lie through the long days and longer nights waiting for them to announce a trial date, a cloak of dread wraps around me, weighting my arms and legs and heart. I never want to see Mary Kate again. I never want *her* to see *me*. I can't understand what invisible, arbitrary, and completely imaginary signal she created that drew her to me in the first place. Draws her still.

Both creator and captive of her own obsession, she remains convinced of my love for her, of her destiny with me. She sends letters and cards, first from the hospital and later from the jail infirmary. I finally got a restraining order, but it was about as effective as waving the peace sign at a rabid pitbull. She convinced one of the jailers—a sworn member of one of the most cynical, hardened professions on earth—to call me from his cell phone with the message that her latest surgery had gone well. I wasn't to worry, he said.

Because of the surgeries and medications, they're waiting on a psyc-eval, but Blodgett tells me that it's doubtful she'll stand trial anytime soon. I don't know if that's good or bad.

If I were at all interested in my surroundings, I'd have to admit that Regina, of all people, has been wonderful. She started picking me up and dragging me to the women's shelter where she volunteers. The first thing she did was give me a tour of the facility, showing me the security devises and safety protocols. I hate it.

I hate being shown the exterior video camera system, the keypad alarm consoles, the motion-activated lights. I hate hearing about the drills they run in case one of the abusers show up or the precautions they take to keep the safe house a secret. It doesn't make me feel safer, knowing there are ways to protect myself from bad people. It doesn't make me feel better knowing I haven't been the only person harmed by someone I trusted.

I come home from these little field trips with blinding headaches, my scalp and skin stretched so tight and thin from the swelling of rage that I fear it will split open, cracking like an egg.

But Regina keeps coming, and I keep going. She makes me sit in Group at the shelter, too. When I tried to hide behind my therapist mask, she forbade me from commenting on anyone else's story; I can only share my own experience or listen quietly. I spent the first three Groups with arms crossed and mouth shut, reciting Mother Goose rhymes in my head to keep the other women's words from penetrating.

Strangely, it never occurred to me to get up and leave or even to refuse to go in the first place. The last time I exercised my own will had been sending the puking cop into the woods after Marshall.

While that effort saved Marshall's life, it hasn't saved our friendship. I visited him, once, in the hospital. When I apologized for essentially leading a killer to his doorstep, he offered forgiveness for another peek at my bra. But he grew silent when he learned that I'd searched his home and office. When I admitted to dosing him with sleep aids, the sparkle in his eyes dulled and he turned his face to the wall. After a long while, I left.

The next day I discovered that he put me on the No Visitor list. Within hours of being discharged, he left for his brother's house in Wyoming. To recuperate, he told Regina. To hide, I told her. But who could blame him?

His taking off has had the benefit of rousing me from my stupor. I listened at the next Group and started paying attention to the sun's course across the sky. Sue dragged me outside one day. It was hot. The sun felt good. It was summer. I'd almost missed it.

I finally felt strong enough to read the last sonnet. The one Mary Kate left in my glove box while I'd been tending Marshall in the woods. Blodgett has the original, of course, but Regina convinced him to leave me a copy. I think he's scared of her, too.

But it's my choice. My decision—to read or not to read.

No more be grieved at that which thou has done:
Roses have thorns, and silver fountains mud:
Clouds and eclipses stain both the moon and sun,
And loathsome canker lives in sweetest bud.
All men make faults, and even I in this,
Authorizing thy trespass with compare,
Myself corrupting, salving thy amiss,
Excusing thy sins more than thy sins are;
For to thy sensual fault I bring in sense,
Thy adverse party is thy advocate,
And 'gainst myself a lawful plea commence:
Such civil war is in my love and hate,
That I an accessory needs must be,
To that sweet thief which sourly robs from me.

Shakespeare, thou are one freaky dude.

Thank you for reading THE ENEMY WE KNOW. I hope you enjoyed it! Please check my website http://www.donnawhiteglaser.com/ for more Letty Whittaker 12 Step Mysteries coming soon.

CONNECT WITH ME:

Twitter: http://twitter.com/readdonnaglaser
Facebook: http://facebook.com/donnawhiteglaser.com
donnawglaser@gmail.com

ACKNOWLEDGMENTS

As a writer, I'm supposed to be able to write beautiful words, but when it comes to this section I get all thumb-tied. Needless to say—although I appear to be saying it anyway—without these people, I'd have given up on this dream long ago.

To my first readers, Ma and Neecie and Katie. You laughed in all the right places and held me up through all the bad. I love you ladies.

To the most talented group of writers anywhere! My critique writers' group, past and present: Helen Block, Marjorie Doering, Gail Francis, Darren Kirby, Marla Madison, April Solberg, and Bob Stokes. (We miss you, Bob!) You slashed the whip when I grew weary, sliced and diced when my metaphors got too goofy, and kept my BIC-FOK. (That's not swearing, Pastor Craig. I promise.) Best of all, you made me a better writer.

To Kristin Lindstrom: thanks for believing.

To Sisters In Crime and the Guppies: to these groups, I owe a debt too big to be repaid, except, perhaps, by emulating your generosity. I hope every new writer discovers the riches of SinC.

To Rob Walker: you were the first professional writer I'd ever approached with questions about the industry. You treated me as an equal instead of the naïve wannabe I was so certain I was. Thank you for the advice and encouragement.

To Joe Konrath: I've never actually met you, but you had a hand in this process nonetheless. You've made indie publishing, not only respectable, but advisable. Bless you for A Newbies Guide to Publishing. http://jakonrath.blogspot.com/

To the most important people in my world: Joe, Levi and Leah. I'm sorry for all the times we had a 'fend for yourself' supper night or had three inch dust woofies rolling across the kitchen floor like misbegotten tumbleweeds. Thank you for hanging in there.

But I'm still not dusting

.

Suggested Study Guide Questions

After Wayne's attack on Letty, she shares her experience with her Wednesday AA women's group. She becomes even more confused when the group's advice is divided between telling her to get a restraining order or not to get one. How would you have advised Letty?

Despite working in the mental health field, Letty is afraid of revealing her alcoholism to her work circle. Do you feel she has a basis for concealing it? Why?

How does Letty's childhood play into the decisions she makes as an adult about Wayne's harassment?

How did the use of Shakespearian sonnets add or subtract from your reading experience?

Siggy appears to act as an emotional barometer for Letty. What is your experience with animals' abilities to "read" their humans?

Letty's fears about the truth of her alcoholism coming to light keep her trying to balance between a work life and personal life. As a character, does that struggle make her more relatable or less? Discuss.

Sue, Letty's AA sponsor, is an abrasive character. Why then do you suppose Letty chose her as an AA mentor?

The series is based on AA's 12 Step program. How did you see the First Step—We admitted we were powerless over alcohol and our lives had become unmanageable.—play into this novel's them.